Advance Praise for
Problems of Translation

"An **insanely amusing** adventure that has a deep love of language at its belly-shaking core."
—**Gary Shteyngart**, author of *Little Failure*
and *A Super Sad True Love Story*

"The greatest comedians by the slightest of gestures . . . can send an audience falling off their seats in laughter. There are moments in Problems of Translation, where even a 'The' at the beginning of a sentence would have me laughing out loud. For I knew something wild, uproarious and totally unexpected was about to happen next. In this **comic masterpiece**, an **adventure**, a **mystery story of intrigue, betrayal and total absurdity**, we take a wild ride with Charles Abel Baker (Charlie) through the underside of the literary world into the underside of multiple other worlds as he stumbles and careens into all kinds of trouble in an obsessive pursuit of his Dream.
"In addition to everything else the book is laced with so much interesting information about literature, history, countries and languages that you find yourself learning things almost by osmosis. And then there are those wonderful, occasional sex scenes—hot as they are ridiculous—that for me at least are **a total turn on**."
—**Robert Roth**, author of *Health Proxy*
and co-creator of *And Then*

D1518137

"Jim Story's name says it all: he was meant to be a writer. I've never met an author more dedicated to his craft. **I hope everyone reads this book!**"

—**Hannah Tinti**, author of *The Good Thief* and *Animal Crackers*, and co-founder and editor-in-chief of *One Story*

"One of the most enjoyable books . . . in recent memory . . . practically every paragraph **twinkles with humor** . . . . [A] **remarkable protagonist**, who's a little innocent, a little haunted, but never flags . . . . [T]winkles with not only humor but sexuality. . . . [E]rudite from start to finish, . . . **ingeniously plotted**, every sentence finely chiseled, touches of the surreal . . . . **Marvelous touches of true poignancy** that don't, however, delay the progress of the story toward its delectable conclusion. It's **pretty much perfectly done.**"

—**Ron Story** (no relation), Emeritus Professor, University of Massachusetts at Amherst, and author of *Jonathan Edwards and the Gospel of Love*

"Tired of novels dealing with existential angst, nihilistic dread or the undead? Jim Story's Problems of Translation is the perfect antidote, as **refreshing, amusing and captivating as that first glass of chilled Chablis** along about four o'clock in the afternoon. It tells of the adventures and misadventures of Charlie Abel Baker, member of a writers' group in Manhattan, who sets out on **a globe-trotting escapade tied up with literary ambitions, jealousies and skullduggery**—sort of a literary Around the World in 80 Days. Except it takes Charlie about

365 days. Problems of Translation is **a witty entertainment guaranteed to give you sweet dreams**."

—**Jonathan Woods**, author of *Bad Juju & Other Tales of Madness and Mayhem*, and the forthcoming *Kiss the Devil Good Night*

"Problems of Translation is **an engaging, entertaining novel** about **a most unlikely middle-aged hero**. His original idea for a series of translations is appropriated by a tweedy old-line editor whose thuggery is hidden deep inside his suave manner. **A fascinating look at the issues of translation, publishing, and an unglamorous middle-age**."

—**Edith Grossman**, author of *Why Translation Matters*, and award-winning translator of Cervantes' *Don Quixote* as well as works by Gabriel Garcia Marquez, Mario Vargas Llosa, and others

"This aptly named author serves up not just one story, but a series of adventures as entertaining as they are unlikely. Jim Story is a skillful writer with an engaging style, a turbulent imagination, a seemingly inexhaustible fund of cultural and literary lore, and a passion—indeed, as he calls it, a 'reverence'—for language. 'Charlie' keeps us with him for **a lively and sometimes disastrous romp, with nice undertones of a personal journey**."

—**Hilary Orbach**, author of *Transgressions and Other Stories*

PROBLEMS OF
TRANSLATION

To Jim,
With gratitude. Enjoy!
I'm sure "Aaron" is as great as
everyone says + look forward
to reading it. All best,
Jim

PROBLEMS OF
TRANSLATION

or

Charlie's Comic, Terrifying, Romantic,
Loopy, Round-the-World Journey in
Search of Linguistic Happiness

A NOVEL

BY

JIM STORY

BLUE MILE BOOKS

For Jill

"When I use a word," said Humpty Dumpty, "it means just what I choose it to mean—neither more nor less."

"The question is," said Alice, "whether you can make words mean so many different things."

"The question is," said Humpty Dumpty, "which is to be master—that's all."

Lewis Carroll, Through the Looking Glass

In a Bucharest hotel lobby:

    The lift is being fixed for the next day.

    During that time we regret that you will be unbearable.

In a Bangkok dry cleaners:

    Drop your trousers here for best results.

In a Hong Kong dentist's advertisement:

    Teeth extracted by the latest Methodists.

Lost, is it, buried? One more missing piece?
But nothing's lost. Or else: all is translation
And every bit of us is lost in it . . . .

James Merrill, Lost in Translation

CONTENTS

PROLOGUE:
ALL THIS FROM EATING SUSHI?

"BY GOD, I'M going to do it!"

Charles Abel Baker, Charlie to his friends, sat at a corner table of a midtown Japanese restaurant, daring himself to launch an adventure.

"Do what?" asked Trish Truex, sitting to his immediate left, near the window.

It didn't matter that it was raining. It didn't matter that the summer was gone. It didn't matter that he was living alone on Social Security and a modest pension. Here he was at Suehiro's, surrounded by friends, chewing his lower lip and looking to commit himself.

"Do what?" asked the fellow across the table from him, Jake Cash, small, wiry, a musician who worked as a headhunter.

The eight people at the table were not friends whose bond was a shared past, but comrades sharing a common present: a yen to write. Eight souls with only a handful of published short stories among them, and a novel—each was convinced—simmering fruitfully on the back burner. They gathered here each time their workshop had completed on the second and fourth Thursday of every month. It was a leaderless group, but Jonathan Belknap, who sat nearest the window, was *primus inter pares*, by virtue of the fact that they met in a conference room of his midtown public relations firm. It was a rare evening when two of the eight didn't feel as if his or her only child had just been put through a paper-shredder. But then they would reassemble their egos and repair to Suehiro's with the others, nursing their wounds over drinks and late-night supper.

"Do what?" Jonathan asked, flourishing his chopsticks to seize a morsel of caramelized clam.

Charles fitted his own chopsticks carefully into his hand and stabbed at the wasabi. "My translation project."

Xavier Krill, a lawyer, now retired, downed a swig of Glenfiddich single malt. "What are you translating?"

Charles took a sip of water.

"Not me. Most of my adult life I've had this hankering to see a short story translated successively into ten different languages, then back into English, to find out how different it would be from the version one started with."

"Hah!" said Buffy St. Olaf between mouthfuls of chicken *yakitori* washed down with Sapporo. "Like telephone, you mean?" Buffy had raven hair and lustrous white skin, and was head of her own small cosmetics firm. She and Jake were the only members of the group under forty.

"Exactly. Like the old children's party game. What happens when so many people have fondled a story in all those different languages? Does the end product bear any resemblance to the original?"

Cash was chewing thoughtfully on some sort of salad studded with pieces of marinated eel. "How will that help your writing?"

"Hey, I just want to do it. Back when I was an academic—"

"Oh, no!" protested Cash. "Here we go again!"

"No, no, Jake. This is just . . . . You see, my ex-wife, an

anthropologist, introduced me to a concept called the Sapir-Whorf hypothesis: *language structures thought.*"

"Profound, my boy," said Jonathan, crunching an edamame. "Deeply moving."

"How the nature of one's language shapes one's view of the world. I myself did some translating while working on my dissertation, and, well, whenever I translated Russian to English or English to Russian, I marveled at how different the 'sense' of each was," Charles continued. He made a gesture with his arms as if embracing a small cloud. "Some things translate okay, and some don't. By the way, do you know about the origins of the expression 'okay?' It's an interesting story. Back in slave-trading days . . ."

"Charlie!" shot back Cash. "Does this story have an end? I feel the need to relieve my bladder."

Charles, formerly an Assistant Professor of Russian history at a university in New York and the only academic in the bunch, sometimes thought Jake resented his past. Though at other times, Jake seemed an equal-opportunity attack dog.

"Well, to be brief, that's when I started thinking about what might happen when a short story went through *many* different languages before being shoe-horned back into its mother tongue."

"Who'll do the translating?" asked Becky. A small dark woman who taught English as a Second Language at a public school in the Bronx, she put check marks beside passages she found enjoyable in the writing group's stories, just as she did with her students.

"Damned if I know," said Charles. "But my first step is to take it to a publisher because there's gotta be a book in it somewhere, don't you think? And maybe—" He hesitated.

"Maybe they'll ask me to fly to different parts of the world to supervise. Wouldn't that be great?"

Krill belched, covered his face with a napkin, and blushed.

After a pause, Charles tiptoed into the silence that followed, "I mean, they claim to be hurting these days, publishers. But there's a book in there. Somewhere. Don't you think?"

Jonathan sniffed and looked away a moment. "Speaking for myself, Charlie, I'm not sure I do. But it's your project, my man! Take your best shot!"

PART ONE

1
TAKE THAT, CHARLIE!

CHARLES STOOD OUTSIDE an etched glass door on the twenty-eighth floor of the Fifth Avenue address, lips twitching. He was not timid, but neither was he comfortable in the role of pitchman. The whole idea of talking to a well-known editor he found intimidating. That he had a scheduled meeting here at all he owed to that previous spring's enrollment in a New School writer's conference where Derek Wainscot was speaking. Hastening down the aisle at the panel's conclusion, Charles had yelled to the editor—a desperate bark, which he was embarrassed about as soon as he uttered it—just as Wainscot was about to disappear backstage. Wainscot had stopped in his tracks. Pivoting, smiling unconvincingly, he approached the lip of the stage, hunkered down uncomfortably, and cupped his ear to hear what Charles had to say. Although the man's entire body language betrayed an eagerness to be off, to backpedal though the curtains and vamoose, Charles had managed to wangle a card out of him and a hasty, dismissive "call me when you have something to show me."

A week after the last meeting with the writer's group, Charles had made the call. Now, standing at the door, he exhaled sharply. He hoped he looked presentable in his off-the-rack charcoal suit. Ribbons of gray threaded their way through his fading blonde hair; a small paunch overhung his black belt. A weight-lifter's past, long abandoned, showed through in the broad shoulders, while the neatly trimmed beard, reserved manner, and dark-framed glasses suggested a scholar, a mold he'd once tried, with limited success, to fit into. He was no longer happy with that image but had no idea what to put in its place, nor how to achieve it if he did. There were moments in his past when he'd shown considerably more self-confidence, but then he'd usually been drunk. He'd abandoned the drink long after the weightlifting.

He took a deep breath, turned the knob and entered the office.

A few minutes later he found himself seated in a large conference room, quite possibly the largest he'd ever seen. The receptionist, trim and neat in a steel-gray blouse and dark skirt, had led him down a long corridor, made one turn to the right, and asked him to wait, assuring him that Mr. Wainscot would be with him shortly.

Charles looked at the paintings on the wall. Large and correctly spaced, they looked tastefully modern. Geometries of broad lines and bold colors, two of them in a style that was popular in the sixties. The others betrayed an older parentage, overlaid with swoops and smatters of idiosyncratic shape and color, owing a lot, he supposed, to Arshile Gorky.

"Do forgive me," Derek Wainscot said, bursting in a moment later. "No, no, don't get up." He extended his hand. "I was detained on a transatlantic call."

Sitting, he folded his bony hands in front of him and smiled. "But now I'm all yours. How may I help you?"

Charles willed himself to feel comfortable. Wainscot was all angles and planes, the very image of Ichabod Crane from childhood texts. His nose was beaked, his forehead went on forever, and the hair was sparse and brown. The eyeglasses hanging around his neck on a black lanyard made him look even more scholarly than Charles. It was rumored that he translated poems from some Eastern European language. That was hopeful, wasn't it? Someone who was not only an editor at a major publishing house but a translator?

This should go well, he assured himself. He cleared his throat and began.

Wainscot corralled one of the yellow tablets spaced at neat intervals around the table, plucked a fountain pen from the vest of his three-piece Armani pin-stripe, and rapidly jotted notes. After a few minutes, when Charles started to run dry, he placed the pen on the table and sighed. He slipped on the glasses to scrutinize his notes, riffling through them as if weighing the gravity of their message, then splayed his long fingers flat on the polished mahogany surface.

"Mr. Baker," he said, and paused, as if considering an alternate form of address.

"I want you to know how much I truly appreciate your coming down today. You have outlined a most unusual, a most *interesting* idea. Let's think for a moment. Did you have in mind a particular short story to begin its labyrinthine voyage through the languages of the world?"

"Ah, well. That's an important question, of course. Could be something by Deborah Eisenberg or Tobias Wolff? Reaching back, Katherine Anne Porter comes to mind. One could go farther back, of course, to Faulkner or Steinbeck. Hemingway might be too simple and Carver too much of a challenge, in terms of . . . . Well, I'd guess it's important that it's not too short nor too long, you know what I mean? And, I don't know. Alice Munro may be the best around right now, but she's Canadian and I was pretty much thinking American, though from the standpoint of an English-language starting point—"

Wainscot held up his hand like a traffic cop. "So many choices, clearly. But tell me. It never crossed your mind to suggest a story of your own?"

Of course it had. Charles was thrilled and surprised that Wainscot had broached the subject, since he'd felt too timid to raise it himself.

"Yes, but I'm not exactly a household name among the literati, which might be a disadvantage in terms of generating publicity for whatever book might result . . . ."

"Or perhaps not a disadvantage when you consider cost—" Wainscot stopped himself, waved his large hands in the air dramatically. Chuckling, he placed them palms down on the table where they'd been before.

"Look at us!" he exclaimed. "How we do go on! It's so appealing, isn't it? To sit and speculate about such things? To dream? To dream bravely in the face of the most implacable economic logic?

"But, Mr. Baker. I'm sure you're aware of the state of the economy now and how it's affected publishers, among others? Fresh and tempting as your idea is, much as it sends me off on my own voyages of imagination, I regret I'm going to have to decline. I'm sure others have told you this before. It's just too expensive a proposition, balanced against such minimal expectations of gain. There would be little chance, probably one might say, *no* chance, of this project's ever having a profitable outcome. And that's what we have to be concerned about ultimately, is it not? We do not publish books for free. We sell them, alas."

He looked off into the distance. Or perhaps at one of the

paintings. "Ah, so many regrets in a short lifetime! The roads not taken."

His gaze returned to Charles. He stretched out a hand. "I do apologize," he said. "And I thank you. It was nice to dream awhile. You've given me a real affective boost this morning."

Charles rose as the editor rose, shaking his hand distractedly. It was over so quickly. His eyes scanned the room, longing desperately to establish some kind of bond with this man—a translator, after all! a publisher!—even as his dream lay gasping in the sand.

"Hey!" he asked jauntily, "Who did the Frank Stella look-alikes on your wall?'

Wainscot's smile fled; he stuffed his hands in his suit coat pocket. "That would be Frank Stella. A family friend. A fellow Phillips-Exeter man."

"Ah!" Charles said, turning crimson. A nervous squeak of laughter. "And I suppose those are real Arshile Gorkys?" A wink-wink tone to his voice.

"They are indeed," said the editor. "Have a good day, Mr. Baker. Stay as long as you like. I'm sure you can find your way out."

Charles stood there a moment after Wainscot's exit, feeling like the last dregs in a cup of day-old coffee. Then he gathered his notebook to his bosom and sought the nearest elevator.

•

Alone in his office, Wainscot sat for a long moment, drumming his fingers on his desk. Finally, he pushed a button on his telephone console.

"Beverly," he said. "Would you see if Jocelyn Lynne Barley is available for lunch?"

2

A RESOLVE IS A RESOLVE
IS A RESOLVE

DEAR BEN, DEAR Boyd, Dear Jenny, Dear Luther, Dear Dino, Dear Linda, Dear . . . . The names tumbled through his mind like brightly colored marbles, clicking softly as they swarmed and rearranged themselves.

Charles blinked and shuddered awake, stretched out on his couch, one arm draped over the side and a book on the rug where it had slipped from his hand. His laptop sat on the coffee table in front of him, still open, asleep now but still cooling. A tattered address book, a pen, envelopes, and several sheets of notepaper lay nearby. A stack of letters had been pushed off to one corner.

The afternoon had been spent writing emails to almost everyone he knew, telling them about the trip he was planning. Partly because he was excited, partly because he was anxious, partly because he was lonely. He hadn't left yet, and he was already lonely.

For those whose email he'd never captured, he'd dug out an old address book and scanned its pages, stabbing each chosen target with his finger and writing letters for posting later. He knew that some were probably to people who'd moved, died, or changed their names through marriage. He knew most of his emails and letters would generate no response, that only one or two might result in a note or a phone call. It didn't matter.

None to his ex-wife, of course, and certainly none to his former colleagues at the university.

He tapped a key of the laptop and it sprang to life, still open on his inbox. So far, one response, from Marisol Lapinsky. He smiled. Of course. Before he could read past her first sentence, the phone rang, and it was she.

"What's up?" she said. "You okay?"

"I'm fine, Marcy," he said, and added, a bit defensively, "Why wouldn't I be?"

Marisol was his friend, his buddy. No matter that he saw her only once or twice a year. (She lived a mere twenty blocks away.) They had traveled down similar roads in the past, vibrated on the same wavelength. She was a fellow historian, in fact, a Russianist like himself, though, unlike Charles, she still taught.

"So you're fine," Marisol repeated. "Glad to hear it. And it's neat about your trip. But there's something else going on I'm not so sure about. A tone."

"Hey, I'm excited! I've never done something like this. You've been to lots of places, including dozens of trips to Russia. Me, to Moscow and St. Petersburg only once, in 1974. Brezhnev's bad-ass years."

She was quiet a moment. "Okay, I get that. But still. I found an edge of . . . something in your email. Desperation maybe? How many people did you write to?"

"Dozens, I guess. Just pulled out the old address book and started firing away."

"Uh huh. Have you also made out your Last Will and

Testament? You sounded as if this trip were a departure into the void. You *are* planning to come back, aren't you, Charlie?"

"You channeling Dr. Freud today?"

"I'm channeling whomever I need to channel to find out if my old chum is of sound mind and body. Okay? I'm just concerned, is all."

"Well, don't worry! I'm just a little nervous, I guess. This is a big dream. For me, a big, BIG dream. And nervous-making: I don't even have all my destinations nailed down yet. You know, the itinerary? I'm winging it."

"That's partly what I mean, Charlie. You're not usually a 'winging it' kind of guy. Not the last twenty years. Now, back in the day . . . ."

"Yes! I'm resurrecting something! The New Me is the Old Me Revisited!" His voice sounded hollow, even to himself.

"It sounds exciting, Charlie, I'll grant you. And I hate to bring up anything so mundane as money—but you got the dough, bro? Flitting about the globe costs money. I didn't think you were exactly rolling in it."

"I have a little savings, and I figure, if I'm careful, I can manage."

"With nothing left when you get back? For a rainy day, say? It does rain in this universe, you know, Charlie."

"Of course. But . . . well, there's always a risk, isn't there? My feeling is, I'll be all right. Day by day, I'll figure it out. I'll be fine."

"Okay, so tell me, how did you get interested in this language into language into language stuff? I mean, translating something from Russian is enough for me. But successively into ten tongues? From *Angliskii* to begin with, then back into *Angliskii* at the end? What's the payoff? You got a thesis, Charlie? An axe to grind? You got some skin in this game?"

Damn, she could be irritating, he thought. She'd once wanted to be a courtroom lawyer, and it showed. "I'm not trying to prove anything exactly. It's just, you know, no one has ever done it! I just wanted to see what the end result would be. I guess it's like starting out with a bucket of white paint and adding drops of other colors. Seeing the colors change. First red, then magenta, then orange, then—I don't know—chartreuse, maybe. Then pouring the whole mixture back into another bucket of white and seeing what the results would be."

"I wouldn't want to paint my living room with it."

He sighed. "I don't know. Maybe that's not a good analogy, but . . . I've always loved language, you know. That's why I write. You know I love words, how they collide and collude, how they color and interpenetrate. But it's not just words per se I love, it's language itself—the whole idea of it."

"Hmmm. You sound like Rozanov."

"Hah! Yes! The greatest writer in the Russian language that no one has ever read." A nervous chuckle. "Is it possible to be great if no one reads you? Y'know, the old tree in the forest thing?"

Marisol, a mother of two teenaged boys, did not answer. *Words to occupy the air*, she thought, *a fence thrown up against his fears*. After a minute, she spoke into the silence.

"You still there?"

"I'm here, I'm here. I was just thinking . . . ." He picked up from the rug the book he'd been browsing earlier. "You know Sequoya, the great Cherokee who single-handedly invented the Cherokee written language? To help unify his people? I'm kind of obsessed with him recently—you remember that my father was part Cherokee?"

Charles had discovered this about his father only a few years earlier.

15

"I was considering writing a fictionalized biography of him, a novel. Mainly about his trek to Mexico to discover a lost Cherokee tribe. That's the part I'd have to make up. He was never seen again. What happened in Mexico? How did he die? There was no lost Cherokee tribe, in all probability. I suppose he was a bit mad at the end. One becomes obsessed, you know? And it leads you to . . . wherever. Anyway, that's another project I was thinking of instead of this one. This translation thing. But—*ta dah!*—the translation project wins out."

"Having second thoughts, Bucky?"

"Oh, Marcy." He laughed nervously. "Second thoughts, third thoughts, fourth thoughts. But I'm gonna do it, Marcy. I'm gonna do it."

3
LOUISA & PIG

ROBERTO'S WAS A dark, cozy Italian restaurant on East 54th, just off Madison. Although Derek Wainscot could afford a trendier cuisine, he loved the veal scaloppini with a side of grilled Portobello mushrooms, the Tuscan Chianti extra-virgin olive oil laced with minced garlic and served with generous portions of ciabatta, and the panna cotta he inhaled at the climax of every meal. But what he loved most was the perfect opportunity his quiet corner table provided for meals unobserved and unheard by anyone except the trustworthy waiter he had known for seventeen years and whose silence he paid for with scandalously generous tips. He sat at that table now, across from a man whose sporty attire and stubby body contrasted sharply with Wainscot's appearance.

If Wainscot was a giraffe in a Giorgio Armani suit, his companion was a badger in a Brooks Brothers knockoff. Those who knew his dinner guest well (and few did) might have chosen wolverine as a more appropriate likeness. A foot shorter than Wainscot and far more compact, he wore a conservative dark tie that managed to make him appear, despite his squat bulk, presentable. It was not that he couldn't afford to dress as showily as his host. He simply cared less about his appearance.

Despite the editor's sartorial elegance and his companion's lack of it, each attacked the bread and olive oil with equal gusto. Wainscot was on the cusp of signaling Eduardo for another round of bread—and perhaps some olives?—when he changed his mind and leaned back in his chair.

"Pig, how many years have I known you?"

Morton Cruickshank took no offense at Wainscot's nickname, which he'd picked up at Yale many years before. In time, it had even invaded the precincts of his profession. A good many of his fellow spooks knew him by the same moniker. So Cruikshank was unfazed. He'd been called worse in any number of languages. "I'd assume for the same number of years I've known you."

A chuckle from Wainscot. "Hah! Remember those Italian meals Mrs. Giordano served us back at Old Eli?"

"The best, Alcott, the best."

"Alcott" or "Louisa May" was how Wainscot had been known to a few familiars at Yale. As an undergraduate, he'd harbored serious literary ambitions, but his Skull and Crossbones brethren refused to christen him "Ernie" or "F. Scott," as he had begged, conferring instead not only a lesser moniker, but a feminine one at that. The name rankled, but stuck. Cruikshank's use of it now was not so much a put-down as a sign of longstanding intimacy.

Eduardo, ever the unobtrusive waiter, quietly went about distributing salads and entrees, whisking away plates, combing off crumbs. The scaloppini got served and consumed. The panna cotta was enthusiastically reviewed. Small talk continued until the espresso arrived. Then Wainscot dabbed at his mouth with a starched napkin.

"Pig, I asked you here to request a favor."

"I never doubted it, Louisa."

"There's a project I'm trying to get done. A very special one that I've asked Jocelyn Lynne Barley to sign onto. I spoke with her last week, and she's agreed. It involves translation of one of her short stories into a succession of different languages then back into English. More a scholarly than a commercial project, yet I think I can find a way to make it profitable. I'd write an introduction. The prestige factor would, I think, be considerable."

"I could probably help you out with the Chinese."

"Ah! I'd entirely forgotten your expertise in that language!"

"Oh, sure. Mandarin, Cantonese, Szechuan. Also Vietnamese and a little Urdu. I've done mostly documents, you understand, hardly literature, not a lot of symbolism and fancy metaphors, but—"

"What you picked up 'in the field,' correct?"

Cruikshank bristled. "Hey, not only in the field! That outfit I'm retired from runs a lot of upscale language-training programs." He was quiet a moment, thinking. "But, you're right, I learned mostly on the ground."

"No offense, Pig. But my problem is not in finding translators. I have those contacts. I've done a few translations myself, Rumanian poets mostly. Nichita Stănescu my specialty. Finding translators is hardly my problem."

"So what is?"

"Seems there's another gent, a very minor writer, no reputation to speak of—no creds at all, really—who's trying to accomplish the same thing with one of his own stories. I don't know what stage he's at right now, but it could become a major annoyance, should two manuscripts with the same *raison d'etre* be circulating at the same time. Know what I mean?"

"Pay him off?"

The editor rubbed his nose briskly and adjusted his

dark-framed glasses. "Perhaps not. He may be a bit clueless, and certainly minor, but he seems . . . obsessive. Determined, and therefore probably immune to pecuniary leveraging. No, that's not the direction I want to go."

"What, then?"

"I just don't want him to *succeed*, Pig. I'd like someone to keep tabs on him, first of all. See how he's doing. Give me an occasional heads up. I have the feeling he may be traveling around the world trying to accomplish his version of the project—which is, to say the least, outrageously silly. This is New York! I can do what he wants without roaming more than twenty blocks from my office. He thinks of it as an adventure, I suspect. He came to me with this idea, and I'm afraid I laughed at it."

He paused a moment. "Now. He'll not succeed, I think. If he gets very far, he'll surely shoot himself in the foot. But . . . just in case, I'd like someone to, in some way, shadow his meanderings and, if it seems that failure on his part requires any . . . push, so to speak, provide the circumstances by which such failure can be most expeditiously accomplished. You catch my drift? All hidden from me—and Ms. Barley, of course."

Cruikshank had withdrawn a small notebook from his breast pocket and was making notes.

Wainscot took a swallow of espresso and signaled Eduardo for another before returning the cup to its saucer. "Now, does that sound like something that a person with your résumé might reasonably be expected to accomplish?"

Cruikshank put his tablet down carefully on the table. "He came to you, did you say?"

"I did, Pig. I did. Do I hear a faint rumbling of moral scruples?"

"Well, you *are* doing him dirty, don't you think?"

"Your judgmental tone sounds a bit out of place, if I may

say so. You've been doing whole nations dirty for years. In fact, it's *all* you've done, isn't it?"

"Doesn't matter to me, Louisa. Not in the slightest. Just trying to get the lay of the land here. So. Let me get this straight. You want to pay me my very hefty fee, plus hotel bills, plane fare, and all the rest of it, to prevent something you're pretty damned sure won't happen in the first place?"

"It's insurance, Pig. I need to be certain."

"Won't the outfit you work for find that a little exorbitant?"

"Corporate won't know until I'm ready to reveal it. It's a project I'd prefer to keep under my hat until it's accomplished. Don't worry, Pig. You have some sense of my personal worth, I believe. I'll be spending my money, not theirs."

Cruikshank shrugged and tucked his notebook back in his jacket pocket. "It's your dime, Louisa. So how do we . . . ."

"Don't worry. I'll set up an account for you with Lloyds tomorrow. You can draw on it whenever you need."

"Not Lloyd's. Cayman Islands. *Banco Estafadores, SA.*"

"*Estafadores.* Got it. Just tell me which of your many names you'd like me to use."

PART TWO

4
BEGGING THE BEAR TO TALK

I T WAS LIKE clutching the mane of a wild horse. Charles grasped frantically at straps, arm rests, seat cushions— whatever he could find—as the taxi bounced, lurched and careened, spending more time in the air than on the pavement. He wasn't sure how much more his sixty-year-old body could take. He'd already met the ceiling twice and been tossed against the door handles on both sides. His driver—with frizzy red locks, budding facial hair, and a wide-eyed, fixed smile— looked like an Irish farm-boy. Was this really a taxi? Was this really Russia? Despite his misgivings, however, the young driver seemed not only to know the fastest route from *Sheremetyevo* Airport to downtown Moscow, but to have signed a blood oath to get there before anyone else. Fortunately, the cobblestone streets over which he pushed his hovercraft were clean and dry, snowdrifts visible only in scattered, unattended courtyards.

Charles barely recognized the multi-colored crazy-quilt of St. Vasili's onion domes as they plowed across Red Square scattering pedestrians and, in fact, saw very little else that was familiar from his visit some thirty-odd years before.

The cab jolted to a stop in front of the hotel, and Charles crawled out cautiously. He gave the *mal'chik* a few more rubles than he had planned on. "Protection money," he muttered under his breath, hoping the boy had no English.

His room on the eighth floor was practical, with double bed, wardrobe, and a small table that would serve nicely as a desk. Much comfier than his digs in the old days.

He decided to email Murmantsev immediately. He'd learned from the desk that the room was wired for Internet. *And probably everything else*, he muttered to himself, remembering Brezhnev's Russia.

He quickly wrote:

> Dear Professor Murmantsev,
>
> Here at last!
>
> I'm at the Mirsky on Moskovskyi Prospect, Room 846. I'd be delighted to meet at your convenience to hand over my story. Please send a message through cyber-space the moment you receive this, or whenever you are free from berating a student, turning a page, or munching a carrot.
>
> Moscow is beautiful, though colder than New York.
>
> Charles Abel Baker

Then he frowned and erased the line about the student and the carrot. What did he know about this guy's sense of humor?

As he was slipping off his shoes for a nap, the phone rang.

So soon? Certainly no problem with Internet over here!

"*Tak*, Russian history professor," came a woman's voice. "No trouble finding your hotel?"

My God! Svetlana?

•

They'd met, and flirted, on the plane, but he'd never really expected to see her again. A statuesque blonde in her early forties, she'd worn her turquoise Aeroflot cap like a tiara. She was royalty, he'd thought, an empress of the air! And what was he? A fit but slightly over the hill ex-history professor and small-time writer. With a smallish tummy, unless he sucked it in. She was Guinevere, and he certainly no Lancelot! Yet he was so smitten on the plane he'd had a hard time stumbling through his stiff-spined, half-remembered Russian (beginning with a trusted old sentence that described himself as having once been a Russian History professor).

Somehow she'd apparently found his shaky declensions charming. When she'd learned he was a writer, even more so. She, he'd discovered, had once studied world literature at a university in Siberia. Then become a stewardess. Though her English was heavily accented, it was miles ahead of his Russian. Charles wasn't even sure she'd understood why he was traveling to Russia, despite his attempts to explain. Nor did it matter, he figured, since he'd surely never see her again. He'd assumed she was only being polite when she'd asked which hotel . . . .

"What a surprise! No, my driver had no trouble getting me here. He just drove in a straight line all the way from the airport, ignoring streets, stoplights, and even other cars."

"Typical. Which way he took you?"

"Had my eyes closed most of the time. I did peek through my fingers at the Moscow River every once in a while."

She laughed. "The long way. But never mind. I was hoping you might like some company. You would like a visit?"

Although she couldn't see it, Charles's eyebrows had lifted off like a Saturn rocket. What was she proposing? Should he be flattered or wary? "A visit from you?"

"Who you are expecting? Maria Sharapova? Of course me!"

"Ah, well! I would, of course, love a visit from you! My goodness! I'm just so . . . surprised!"

"Silly man. You flirt with me on plane and now you act surprised. Shall I come over now?"

"Are you far away?"

She giggled. "Same hotel. Fifteen minutes?"

•

It was closer to twenty-five, but worth the wait. When he opened the door, she was leaning against the doorjamb, one hand behind her back, Veronica Lake in an old Humphrey Bogart film. Except that her blonde hair was swept up, and fixed in place by . . . was that a small paintbrush? Or a tool for applying cosmetics? Odd, in any case. She wore no uniform now, however, sporting a black mini-skirt and gold lamé blouse, with pearls at her throat. All she needed was a rose between her gleaming white teeth. He'd noticed she was tall, but never guessed how much was due to her long legs.

She reacted to his surprised expression. "I know, I know! Is very sixties. Your sixties, not ours. In our sixties, I was little girl. But I like retro. You know Screaming Mimi's in New York? I also have satin frock with taffeta petticoat, from fifties. Like musical 'Oklahoma!' You prefer?"

"Hey, no! Please! Don't change a thing! You look . . . wonderful." He stepped back.

"Your wardrobe certainly beats mine," he added, reaching for neutral small talk. "Right now, I have only a change of shirt, some underwear, and two pairs of socks. Oh, and a second tie."

"Then we must get you out of that suit as soon as possible. Hang it up in bathroom with steam. You agree?" She swept forth her hidden arm, revealing a bottle of *Stolichnaya*. "Shall I pour us a glass?"

She was inside the room but—unable to tear his eyes from her—he'd still not managed to close the door. He did so now, watching as she disappeared into the bathroom and returned with two water glasses.

"Svetlana, this is all very lovely, but . . . I'm afraid I don't drink. Anymore. I used to, but—"

"Is so?" she asked, placing the vodka and glasses on a bedside table with exaggerated care and seating herself primly on the bed. "In that case, we skip vodka altogether. I don't need warm-ups. Is more time to make love. You are agreeable?"

In New York, Charles lived alone and had not shared his apartment—or bed—with anyone for some time now.

"Uh, wow! Are you sure? This is so . . . unexpected!" The hum in his head that had begun when he'd first caught sight of her in the Aeroflot aisle had returned, only twice as loud.

"You do not wish? You are married perhaps?"

"*Nyet! Nyet!* Nothing like that! *Ya nye mogu* . . . I just . . . can't believe my luck!"

"Oh, please! I am lucky one! I study literature in school, but you know how many writers I have meet on my travels? *Nikovo.* I love history, but . . . how many historians you think I meet up in air? *Nikovo.* Now I meet both in one big, strong man. I also love buried treasure; why should I not want to get acquainted? Perhaps you do not find me attractive?"

He laughed softly, looked down a moment, then crossed the intervening distance and sank to the carpet in front of her. Okay. Fine. Through her eyes, he was happy to be historian, writer, strong man, and a piece of buried treasure waiting to be dug up after a thousand years spent below ground. He no longer felt old, only grateful. "Yes. I find you attractive," he said. His voice gathered force. "Honestly? You make my head spin."

"*Nyet,* my goodness! When young, maybe, I turn heads, but

am old lady in my forties now. Thank you for saying, however. You are not only professor, you are romantic! Is true? Or maybe just good writer?"

He took her hands, kissing first one, then the other. Her long legs were thrillingly close. "Thank you. As an American minister might intone to his congregation, 'For the bounty we are about to receive, we thank you.'"

She smiled. "Silly man."

•

He awoke with a little gasp two hours after they'd fallen asleep, for a minute unsure of his surroundings. Then, realizing someone slept beside him—*Svetlana* slept beside him!—he raised himself on one elbow to look at her. Her brow looked prominent from this angle, the deep-set eyes in such shadow he could not have said whether they were open or closed. He noticed tiny wisps of golden hair along the brow ridge that glistened in such moonlight as slipped past the window-curtains. High cheekbones whose undersides looked so soft he ached to reach out and stroke them, but stopped himself. Almond eyes, with a small Slavic cant to them. Though why did one imagine those traits as Slavic? Slavs were European. Those were Asian genes, Tatar, perhaps, or Scythian. Remember when Russian *literati* in the pre-revolutionary decade spoke of the Asiatic connection as something intrinsic? In his view, a kind of shared cultural delusion. Well, a *soupçon* of truth there perhaps. Some Russians with Tatar names, for example, a long ago heritage of Kublai Khan and the Mongol domination: Arakcheev, Bakhmet'ev, Berdiaev, Karamzin, Kochubei, Shakhmatov . . . .

He cut short his reverie, realizing he'd been whispering those names softly out loud. God forbid he should wake her! Returning his eyes to her face, he saw her lips pinch together.

Pain? Anguish? A bad dream? Does she have anxieties about our coupling, he wondered, just as I do? Does she doubt its reality, even as I, though lying in bed beside her warm body, doubt it? He watched her lips relax now and a smile break over her face. Those dimples once again.

Prone to analyze, he decided she was two people: one cloaked, mysterious, private, fraught, impenetrable; the other relaxed and . . . friendly, warmly open to the outside world. Two souls, perhaps?

Oh, stop it, Charlie! he shouted inside his head. *Romantic claptrap. She's beautiful, and you're smitten. That's all you really know.*

A moment later he squirreled back underneath the sheets and found the easy sleep that had eluded him for so long.

•

Jerking upright, he searched the other side of the bed. Hardly rumpled. A dream? He cranked his head round to see the bedside table. There stood the *Stolichnaya*. Unopened.

Quickly finding his pants, he examined his wallet. Money, credit cards, keys? All there. Laptop sleeping quietly on the table? There. Briefcase, containing the paper copy of his story, ready to be translated into its first foreign tongue? Also there. Then, his puzzled gaze furtively seeking wider views of he room, he spied a folded paper beneath the liquor bottle. Snatching it, he hastened to the window, drawing aside the curtain. Realizing he was without his glasses, he swore softly, reclaimed them, and returned to the window's light.

—4 a. m.

Dear Russian History Professor,

I leave to catch early flight.

Last night was *wonderful!* Are you sure you taught Russian history and not *seksualnost'* to your little female students?

I hope you did not think me too—is it "forward" Americans say? *Vperyod* does not work in Russian. Somewhere—is in Miss Jane Austen?—I am encountering word "smitten." If I have right word, this is what I am.

Here is phone number in Petersburg, where I have apartment. 278-40-34. I have answer machine. Otherwise get in touch through airline. Tell them you are my *kotik*, and hear them blush.

Goodbye for now, Charlie Baker. *Pozvonitye mnye, pazhalsta.* (If you have trouble reading my Cyrillic, that means "call me, please.")

I can still feel you inside me.

Svyeta

Charles, who could scarcely remember raising such a passionate response in any woman, let alone a beauty like Svetlana, turned and leaned back against the window frame. Jesus! How unreal! To have this gorgeous, passionate—and, doggone it, literate!—creature offer herself so . . . forthrightly!

He wandered back to the bed, crossed his arms behind his head and closed his eyes, recalling her little yelps, the way she tossed her head—

"Enough!" he said aloud. He was losing time. *Stay focused!*

Quickly he opened his notebook and sat down at the desk, anticipating a message from Professor Murmantsev. But when the screen brightened and he clicked on his email: nothing. It had been many hours since he'd sent his note.

He tugged on his briefs and opened his computer, searching

his contact list for the number of Moscow University. He asked the desk to connect him.

"*Alo?*"

"*Dobroye utro,*" said Charles. *Good morning.* Several heartbeats passed before he could remember what came next.

"*Izvaniteye mne, pazhalsta,* I wish to speak with Professor Murmantsev?"

The woman at the other end excused herself to find another party. A man's voice came on the line.

"Yes, hello," said Charles. "This is Charles Baker, a writer from America? I am supposed to be meeting Professor Murmantsev to discuss a translation project?"

"Ah, Professor Baker! *Da, da.* I was told. This is Professor Kovalev, a colleague. Professor Murmantsev wished to inform you he is sorry, but cannot do your project. Unexpected death in family summoned him to Obozersky. His father, I believe."

"Obozersky! Beyond the Arctic Circle? Near Arkhangelsk?"

"*Da, da.* He will be one month away, he said. Took leave of absence, so will not be able to help you."

"But, how am I . . . how can I . . . ?" Charles trailed off, his mind doing back flips.

"He wish for me to apologize abjectly. He is sorry. He cannot."

Charles sighed. "Of course. Forgive my impatience. Please tell him when you see him how sorry I am for his loss."

"Yes, of course. No problem."

Hanging up the phone, Charles sat down hard on the bed. *Shit!* His shoulders slumped. He remembered the bottle of *Stolichnaya* and stared at it a moment. Tempting, but no.

Besides Marcy, Charles had one other graduate school buddy with whom he'd remained in contact. Lytton Searles had left New York after graduate school, and had been teaching at Princeton his entire academic life. Their contact over the years had been cordial but limited to an occasional email. In fact, Charles was vaguely envious of Lytton's very respectable career. Lytton had traveled to the Soviet Union—and then, after its collapse, to Russia—for 45 years, burying himself in the archives in Moscow and St. Petersburg, conducting research for his dozen or so well-regarded books. Because Lytton knew so many of the top Russian scholars, it was to him that Charles had appealed for contacts who might be capable and willing to translate his short story. Lytton had responded with two names, both of whom he'd recommended most enthusiastically. And each of whom, in subsequent email correspondence, had agreed to his project.

"By God, that's why one has a back-up plan!" Charles muttered out loud in the empty hotel room. "Thank God Lytton found two scholars willing to take this on!" Searching his laptop, he found Nicolai Pnin's number. Oh, right. Not Moscow, but St. Petersburg. Well, so what? Wasn't that where Svetlana lived, anyway? Maybe he'd be able to see her while Pnin was translating his story? The flight took only an hour and a half. If he could survive another cab ride, he'd be there in no time.

He showered and dressed in front of the mirror on the back of the bathroom door. Then he called the desk and gave them Pnin's number.

5

MIKHAILOVSKY, GRIBOEDOV, BLOK, BYELI, IVANOV, MEREZHKOVSKY

THE PLACE PNIN had chosen for their luncheon was named—appropriately enough—*Kafe Literaturnoye*, in front of which Charles had been pacing and frowning for some moments now. While waiting, he'd been looking around and remembering. To lay the foundation for his city, Peter the Great had forced man and beast to drag huge stone blocks halfway across Russia, only to watch them sink out of sight in the slime and mud of a northern swamp. In Andrei Byeli's novel, *St. Petersburg*, the city itself ultimately disappears back into the swamp.

But when it was completed: Venice of the North! The whole of St. Petersburg crisscrossed by rivers, canals, tributaries, river-walks.

The café Pnin had selected lay just west of the Moyka River. Nearby were the Griboedov Canal, the Fontanka Canal. Besides the Neva River itself, which flowed from Lake Ladoga through St. Petersburg and on to the Gulf of Finland, there were the so-called Big Neva and Little Neva, not to mention the Little Nevka.

Charles stood breathing it all in. So much history within the reach of his vision! It jumped out at him from street signs and markers. Kazan Square, for example, taking its name from the Mongol khanate Ivan the Terrible had defeated in the sixteenth century. The Griboedov Canal, named after the man whose novel bequeathed to the world the concept of a "superfluous man." Mikhailovsky Street, called so after a nineteenth-century theoretician of peasant socialism. Why, one could walk from the sixteenth to the nineteenth century in four minutes! And all this paled beside the layered history of that monumental Rococo structure only a ten-minute walk from the café where he now stood. The Hermitage, once known as the Winter Palace, and home to the Romanov dynasty for 150 years. In whose courtyard troops had mowed down street demonstrators on Bloody Sunday in 1905. Home, as well, to the Provisional Government after the February Revolution of 1917, which surrendered it to an even more radical cast of characters in October.

Of course, nearby too was the storied apartment where—in the heady days before war and revolution—there gathered intellectuals and poets awaiting their days of greater fame: Vyacheslav Invanov, Andrei Byeli, Alexander Blok, Dimitri Merezhkovksy, Zinaida Gippius. In fact, that was where the Russian philosopher on whom Charles had written his dissertation had once . . . had once . . . .

Charles stopped, looking down at the cold pavement. Thoughts of his dissertation led to thoughts of his promotion, and thoughts of his promotion led to thoughts of his dismissal one year later. However bright the sun, his vision slowly dimmed, as if someone were shuttering, by slow degrees, Venetian blinds. He could hear his own heartbeat. Then he shook his head, shuddered, and the moment passed. Get a grip, he told himself. For God's sake, Baker, get a grip.

In the present moment again, he checked his watch. Pnin was thirty minutes late and counting. Should he call? He'd described himself as balding, late forties, black horn-rims. Big head on small shoulders. (Laughing when he'd said this.) Also gently rounded, he'd said. Wearing a charcoal business suit and flowered tie.

Something about that description stopped him. Had he met such a man at some time in the past? Well, never mind. Unlikely, and of no importance.

Charles stepped inside the restaurant, scanned the room. The café was bustling, customers everywhere, but no Pnin. He reached for his cell, stepped back outside, made the call.

"*Alo?*"

"Professor Pnin?"

"*Da.*"

"*Gospodin* Baker. We were supposed to meet at the *Kafe Literaturnoye* at 2?"

"Is correct? Oh, me-oh-my! Lunch! I proposed lunch! Yes, of course. I will be there in four shakes of a puppy dog's tail."

Charles returned the phone to his pocket and frowned. This was the man who had translated William Trevor?

Forty-five minutes later (*how many shakes of a puppy dog's tail was that?* Charles wondered), Nicolai Pnin appeared, breathless, coatless, hatless, bouncing and jovial, a large volume tucked under one short arm, the other dangling a black umbrella despite the brilliant sunshine. They soon found themselves seated at a corner table. Charles ordered borsch and herring, Pnin the *Amerikanskii* plate: grilled chicken on pita bread.

"So nice to meet you, *Gospodin* Baker! So how are you liking our *Sankt Peterburg?*"

"I'm very thrilled by it all, of course! Very different from when I was here in 1974. Yet much the same, in some ways. So much history! Each block reminds you of a famous figure or event."

"*Da, da*! Sorry we don't have better weather."

"I think it's lovely! What's that you're reading, by the way?"

"Is library book am returning. *Zolotoy Fond Literaturi*. You are acquainted?"

Something tugged at Charles's memory, just out of reach. "Heard of it."

"I kept it out too long; someone is asking. So, you are embarked on a big translation project, yes? This is of special interest?"

"Well, yes. I'm no translator, but I've been interested in the process for a long while. When I wrote my dissertation, my subject was a Russian philosopher, and while reading one of his books, I came across a paragraph I thought was profound— *genialnyi*, in fact! Brilliant! So I translated it as precisely as I could, but when I read it in English, it seemed very ho-hum."

Pnin, tearing at his chicken with aggressive vigor, kept his attention focused on Charles over the tops of thick glasses.

"I swam through dictionaries, checked case endings, aspects, scrambled to find what nuances I had missed, but could find no fault with my translation! Still, the intellectual charge it gave me in Russian continued to elude me in English! My first inkling of the impossibility of rendering certain thoughts successfully in another tongue!"

Nicolai's large head bobbed up and down like a child's toy on a spring. "All translators know this! Nabokov has passage where he talks about translating a few words of Pushkin—'perfect beginning to a perfect poem,' he calls it— into spectacularly dull English. Words that soar into words that squat. I can quote exactly: 'What is to be done with this bird you have shot down only to find that it is not a bird of paradise, but an escaped parrot, still screeching its idiotic message as it flaps on the ground?'"

"Hah! Perfect. 'A squawking parrot!' Or perhaps 'an *escaped* parrot,' which makes clear that something has gotten away!"

"Still," said the Russian, ripping off another bite of chicken and losing a well-fought battle to keep all of it in his mouth while he talked, "Nabokov believed it was nevertheless possible, given time, patience—and genius!—to translate perfectly."

Having finished his borsch, Charles stared momentarily into space. He signaled the waiter for another cup of *chai*. "As a translator, Nabokov has always been puzzling to me. While doing *Onegin*, he scolded other translators for their lack of faithfulness, yet what he came up with seemed so bereft of Pushkin's music!"

"You are not wrong, my friend! In fact, there's a passage in the book which hijacked my name . . . ."

Charles found himself staring at the volume Nicolai had brought with him, now resting on the table beside them, whose gold-leaf letters he could read on the spine. *Sovietskoy Zolotoy Fond Literatury*, vol. 18. What was it about that book? Then he forced himself back to what his future translator was saying.

"He talks in that novel about yearning to write a sentence where each word shares its neighbors' 'sheen, heat, shadow,' yet that is precisely where his translation of *Onegin* falls short. One word throbs, another slithers, another skids, but they don't add up to an ensemble."

Charles was pleased by Nicolai's choice of words. Perhaps he was a capable translator, after all? He took a sip of tea, then started in on the herring.

"So, you are a writer too, *Gospodin* Baker?"

"Please, call me Charlie."

"And you will do me the honor to call me, perhaps, Nicolai?"

"Delighted!"

"Good! So, my new-found friend, Charlie, does your own work slither or skid?" He grinned.

"Now I feel embarrassed. I'm nowhere near the writer Nabokov was."

"Who is? Yet in the kitchen of world literature are many cooks, is it not? Perhaps you are too modest."

They talked on and on. A companionable glow suffused Charles. This was all working out! They talked, in fact, for a good twenty minutes past that afternoon hour when the clank and tinkle of silverware had faded to nothingness, and shadows began to creep across white tablecloths. Then, feeling the time had at last arrived, he eased from his jacket pocket the copy of his story.

"We come to the point of my visit, Nicolai," he said, beaming. "I have the honor to present you—"

The portly Russian was already holding up his hand, striking that same, ghastly traffic-cop pose that Wainscot had confronted him with only a few weeks earlier.

"Charlie, my good friend. It is wonderful to meet you, but—*k sozhaleniyu*—unfortunately—I cannot translate your story."

Charles almost lowered his pages into the beet-stained bowl in front of him.

"Excuse me? You're saying you won't do it?"

"*Nyet*! I am saying un-*able*. At this moment. Such misfortune! Another project has intervened since we wrote. Demanded by head of department. I cannot refuse."

Charles stared at his newly minted Russian colleague with

disbelief. It was as if the captain of the Titanic had just pointed with alarm to a gigantic slab of ice dead ahead.

"I know I can't offer you much money, Nicolai, but—"

"Please, Charlie! Do not insult! Perhaps next year? No? You need sooner? I am sorry, my friend. Right now is impossible."

Charles felt like one of Peter's rocks, sinking into the swamp. He'd traveled 6,000 miles for this? And that other thing. How was it the man spoke such unassailable English one moment and at others dropped articles and bungled tenses like a *muzhik* from the countryside?

"Now, you must excuse," Nicolai said, rising from the table. "I go back. Thanks so much for meeting, and with delightful conversation. Please look up again when next in Petersburg. *Nyet*, allow me."

Tossing some rubles on the table, he vanished out the front door without looking back.

Charles stared for another minute at the sheaf of papers he clutched in front of him. Out of the corner of his eye he saw two waiters begin to smoke. *Kurit'*. Was that it? The Russian verb, to smoke? In New York City, they'd no longer be allowed. He straightened out the crimped pages and slipped them into the pocket of his overcoat.

6
DOSTOYEVKSY, TCHAIKOVSKY, MUSSORGSKY, BORODIN, NEVSKY

H E DID NOT return to his *gostinitsa*, the Hotel Moscow, but ambled along the Nevsky Prospect in a daze, past cathedrals, palaces, squares, statues of Catherine the Great among several lovers, across the Anichkov Bridge with its famous sculpture of rearing horses in whose testicles hid the image of the sculptor's wife's lover. These things he both noticed, and did not notice. Though the evening remained clear, a fog had enveloped him that he could find no will to pierce. As if immersed in Dostoyevky's "white nights" or the fantasy landscape of Gogol's "Overcoat."

Two hours had lapsed by the time he reached the Alexander Nevsky Monastery, across from his hotel. He did not return to his room, but dragged on, past cemeteries that had become the resting places of Tchaikovsky, Borodin, Mussorgsky, and Rimsky-Korsakov. To them he paid no heed, running his index finger along the fence as if strumming a harp. Somewhere among the moldering earth and decaying sepulchers was the tomb of an early hero, Dostoyevsky, but at this moment, he didn't care.

Should he go back to New York? Give up this stupid obsession? How could he have thought he'd pull it off, with such meager resources, such paltry contacts? Stymied on the very first leg of a ten-leg journey. He had bet the pot on a pair of deuces, and someone had turned over three kings.

Now, alone by the Neva, feeling rejected—feeling old — Charles screwed up his courage to phone Svetlana. He left a message on her machine and, after watching the waves lap the riverbank a few more times, returned to his hotel. Bereft and unhungry, he collapsed on his bed fully clothed and sank into sleep.

•

He dreamed first of Marisol, and then of Ignacio. Charles had grown up motherless in the Great Central Valley of California, after his father had moved the two of them from Oklahoma. As a young boy on the corporation farm where his father found work, he'd made friends with another boy without a mother. Ignacio was the closest friend Charles had ever had, would ever have. They palled around in school, became crossing guards together, helping smaller youngsters across Highway 33, which stretched along the west side of the San Joaquin Valley and directly through the town where their school was located. On weekends, back on the ranch, they'd gone hiking in the nearby foothills, gawked at badgers and jackrabbits, noted the trajectories of hawks through a sky so hot it could turn asphalt into taffy.

Sometimes, on Saturdays, Ignacio would bring his guitar to Charles's house, which by then was larger than the first one that had housed him and his father, owing to the fact that his father had worked his way up to become a foreman. Ignacio was an enthusiastic singer of country-and-western songs, and Charles would sing along. Sometimes they did passable duets. Though nobody else was around to listen.

After several years, Ignacio became a Catholic. He was already Catholic, of course, but overnight he became *really, really* Catholic. And Charles, at almost exactly the same moment, became *really, really* Protestant. Converted at a Southern Baptist revival meeting in the small town nearest the ranch, he cried and lamented and studied texts and quoted scripture, but when it came to being baptized —that solemn, serious, and seemingly irreversible commitment—he hesitated. After many days of thinking and fretting, he quit the church, quit religion, tucked his Bible in the deepest drawer he could find, and declared that henceforth he would refuse to accept *anything* on faith. His father, who'd had nothing to say when Charles announced his conversion, was equally mute when he changed his mind. As for Charles's friendship with Ignacio, it was as if their seemingly indissoluble bond had been severed by a meat cleaver.

Then Ignacio moved away. An aunt would pay his way to a private Catholic high school in San Jose, seventy or eighty miles off. It would help out the family, was the last thing his friend had told him. Charles suspected that his formerly bosom buddy was on his way to becoming a priest.

7

A LONG NIGHT'S JOURNEY
INTO DAYLIGHT

THE OLD-FASHIONED PHONE jangled rather than burped. The room's previous occupant had apparently adjusted its volume for maximum clamor. By the time Charles was awake, his nerves were already fried.

"Hello?"

"Char-lee?"

"Svetlana, is that you? Thank goodness! How are you? *Kak vuy?*"

"*Khorosho, spasibo.* But you are not so well, I think. Your voice on my answer machine sounded like you maybe lost your best friend."

An image from his recent dream flashed into his head.

"You are okay?" she asked.

"Not really. I'm in Petersburg now, where I came to find someone to translate my story, the second person to turn me down. My project is going down the tubes."

"'Down these tubes means finished?"

"*Da, konchil,* finished, over, kaput, kerflooey. I've failed, Svetlana. I might as well go back home."

A pause.

"If you need go home is one thing, but how can be you failed? *They* failed, these people, it sounds like. Not you."

"However you slice it, the jig is up."

Another pause.

"I don't know from these 'jigs' and 'tubes,' but Charlie, stay where you are. I will come over right away. I'm calling from *Kulikovo*. I am there in forty-five minutes. Okay? Don't do nothing."

He could hear his own heart beat. After a moment's silence, he heaved a heavy sigh. "Okay."

He had showered and pulled on his pants but not yet managed his shirt when the buzzer sounded.

"Oh, Charlie!"

She fell into his arms and squeezed him hard. After a moment, conjoined like runners in a three-legged race, they struggled to the bed and collapsed on its edge. He buried his face in her breasts, while she stroked his back.

"All will be right, Charlie, I promise! Now, tell me. What happened?"

He began, but faltered, staring instead at a worn place in the carpet.

"Charlie," she said, "don't talk right now. Lie back. Let me take care for you." She pushed him down. Gently.

When she began unzipping his trousers, he offered a token resistance.

"Is good for you," she insisted. "Don't move."

Charles's reluctance stemmed from doubting his capacity to respond.

Svetlana, it seemed, knew better. After she had brought him to soldierly attention with her mouth, she gathered up her skirt (she'd removed her panties in the taxi) and mounted him. Their coupling was near silent at first, save for the sough of indrawn breath and exhalations that grew increasingly ragged. Hovering above, her eyes probing his, her pelvis moving patiently, her face reflected some inscrutable junction between agony and joy.

"*Gospodi, Gospodi, Gospodi,*" she murmured, as if immersed in the ritual of an Orthodox church service—the tonsured priest swinging his censer, back and forth, back and forth, trailing clouds of heady smoke. When Charles's low moans joined her own incantations, she moved faster.

"O mine God!" she muttered finally. "I need this too, Charlie Baker! Oh, thank you, *kotik*! *Gospodi!* I love it! I LOVE IT!"

·

When they awoke from a brief nap, Svetlana was beside him, fingers interlaced with his, looking at a painting on the wall.

"Is terrible painting!" she said. "Colors is all wrong! They should post real art."

The print was typical hotel kitsch, blood-red flowers on a soggy blue background; he was not at all sure what about it exercised her so. He kissed her shoulder. "Thank you, *dusha*. That was wonderful. God, what a lover you are for me!" His tone grew regretful. "I only wish it changed something. I still don't know how to get my story translated."

She propped herself on one elbow, the better to see his face. "Tell me what happened."

He told her about Murmantsev and Pnin, not without rancor. When he'd finished, she said, "Charlie, what was plan for next leg?"

"Next leg? Well, my hope was to get it translated from Russian into Japanese."

"This is all set up?"

"Naw. I was trying to get in touch with someone in Tokyo, but no luck as yet."

"Could be Chinese instead?"

"Why not? I had them later on my list, but yes, it's possible."

"How much time you need for each translation?"

"Depends. I've allowed a month, but I figured some would go faster, some slower. And, of course, time for travel in between. But you get the idea. The whole trip was supposed to take about a year."

"A year! But, Charlie, you are in Russia three days! And you are throwing in the towels? This makes no sense! Is plenty of time!"

He laughed. "Well, sure. But I'm stumped, Svyeta! Who do I get to translate it now? The two people who agreed have both backed out!"

She sat up and placed her fingers on his lips, seeking to control his agitation. Then she lay back down again.

"I think perhaps to help you."

"*Dusha*, that's sweet, really sweet, but I think you perhaps don't get how carefully these translations need to be done. I need a professional."

She smiled, was thoughtful a moment, then nodded her head as if she'd come to a decision. She leaned close, whispered into his ear.

"Not me. *Moy otets*."

He drew himself up on one elbow and looked at her.

"Your father?"

8

MEANWHILE, BACK
AT THE RANCH

DEREK WAINSCOT WAS not in his office. Instead, he sat at the broad oak desk in his comfortable East Side apartment near the United Nations, scribbling words and x-ing them out, thumbing through pages of a tattered Rumanian dictionary, occasionally moistening the tip of his pencil (he always did first drafts by hand). He was at work on a new translation of Nichita Stănescu's poems for a start-up poetry press called *Pipsqueak*. And he did this work at home, not on company time. He glanced at the clock. Twenty past midnight. He would soon need to retire for the night.

Over the years, Wainscot had translated many individual Stănescu poems, which lay scattered about in various issues of *The New Yorker*, *The Atlantic Monthly*, *Poets Magazine* and a few others. But what he was working on now would be referred to as the "compleat" (he preferred the old English spelling) Stănescu. He drummed his fingers on the desk, scratched his ear, returned his gaze to the yellow pad in front of him. Unlike the duties he performed for Apollo Imprints, translating Stănescu was a labor of love. Derek smiled. Apollo was his baby. Yet Apollo was an offshoot of Random & O'Malley, which was now a division of the German publishing behemoth Riesige und Huger, itself a wholly owned subsidiary of Johnson & Pfizer Pharmaceuticals. J&P was also rumored to have a shadowy fiduciary connection to Halliburton. But these days—what else?—wasn't every company an offshoot of Halliburton somewhere down the line?

Though such speculation amused him, the fact was that Wainscot did not even need the job at R&O. Or anyplace else. His family—and he himself, as sole heir— had been wealthy so long it was almost impossible to determine when they weren't. Either they'd pulled up at the dock on the Mayflower and unloaded a couple of trunks of gold ducats, or they'd begun swindling their less savvy New Englanders from the moment they climbed down from the boat, for from the mid-seventeenth century on, they were funneling investments of others' capital into projects that lined their own pockets. Charter members of the New York Stock Exchange, the Wainscot family had somehow survived the panics and crashes of 1819, '37, '69, '73, '92, 1902, '16, '29, '87, and 2007, and all the various smaller skirmishes that had beleaguered the financial world, or else they had managed in each case to staunch their suppurating wounds and rebuild. Derek was rich enough to not even know how rich he was. He hoped his accountant kept good track.

He sighed and swept off his black horn rims, slipping an embroidered handkerchief from the pocket of his silk smoking jacket and polishing his lenses vigorously. He stood and paced the living room, scarcely noticing the Stellas, Rothkos and O'Keefes winking at each other from opposing walls of his living room. No Picassos. He hated Picasso.

He went to the window, allowed his eyes to linger a moment on the East River. Talk about translations. Why was he investing so much time and energy (not to mention money!) in the scheme that fellow Baker had brought to him? Well, the idea had intrigued him. The question for the R&O higher-ups would be, of course, as one of his cruder Economics profs at Yale had put it, "Would it feed the bulldog?" Could it possibly make money?

Derek thought maybe it could. Or sometimes he did. He was in no event imagining bestsellerdom; he was focused instead on a niche market. When he'd decided to call Jocelyn Lynne Barley and run with it, he'd resolved to keep the project under wraps until it had gained a little traction. What he intended to do was issue the whole volume of translations as a single book. It went without saying that he would ask Harold Bloom for a foreword, but the principal commentary would be supplied by him. So who was his target audience? Conceivably, every college and university in the country, every modern language program, every languages and literatures program. He could imagine it in French classes, in English classes, in so many others. The sales would be to the students, year after year. Not just in the States! Libraries and universities in all countries whose languages were represented in the volume's serial translations would be eager to have it. Wouldn't they? Online sales were another possibility; there could certainly be a digital version. Perhaps one could even promote a contest to guess how many words ended up the same from the first English version to the last.

And of course he'd been correct to turn that fellow down. A short story by Charles Baker would never be a big enough hook to generate sales. But a short story by Jocelyn Lynne Barley! Now there was an idea. So what if he had cribbed it from Baker?

He frowned. He'd never done anything so underhanded before, never even been tempted, but wouldn't this become a much better project in his hands? Besides, he was convinced that Baker—if he wasn't already bollixed, hoodwinked, stoppered, and blocked—would be going for a different set of languages. That's how he measured the man, that Baker would be pursuing the esoteric, Tagalog and Swahili and—who knows?—whatever was spoken by the Aborigines in the Australian Outback. Derek, on the other hand, was sure that the Romance languages—French, Italian, Spanish, and Rumanian—would generate larger sales. Plus Russian, German, maybe Turkish and Arabic. Oh, yes, Hebrew for the Israeli crowd. The book's value as a teaching tool, it seemed to him, was considerable. And what if he was wrong? What if it tanked? So what? He'd worked himself into a position over the years that gave him some latitude. One of the reasons he'd hired his friend Pig to keep tabs on Baker was so that nothing got back to the parent company until the project was completed, a success. Besides, he had plenty of high-profile authors, whose heavy sellers kept the company coffers in the black. He could afford an indulgence like this. Or so he hoped.

Derek had worked hard to gain the latitude he had now. Though he'd realized early on that he'd never be more than a mediocre writer, he was still drawn to the book trade. He saw his position as allowing him to touch something authentic and real once in a while, like *almost* being the person you had wanted to become. (Much like translating, when you came right down to it. A borrowed joy.) Plus the light! Reflected light, perhaps, but shining on you nonetheless.

In any event, he would never give up the position he'd had to fight so hard to achieve. His forbears, bless them, had learned to profit in the rough-and-tumble world of high finance, and though he played in a different ballpark, he was just as adept as they.

He yawned, gave up his pacing and collapsed into his desk chair. One a.m. Enough. Stănescu can wait, he thought. Time to sleep. That corporate time-and-motion study lackey (bless his Gilbrethian heart) was due in his office tomorrow at 9 a.m. He must be on his best game.

9
THE GRIZZLY BECOMES A TEDDY

G ENNADY PAVLOVICH NOVGORODTSEV—
SVETLANA'S father—was a prominent Russian
mathematician to whom the decades following the
collapse of the Soviet Union had been unkind. The vast
resources devoted to science had vaporized overnight, and
Akademgorodok, that thriving, vibrant, prestigious Siberian
"science city"—where Svetlana's father had spent almost his
entire adult life—had sunk into an economic twilight zone.

Svetlana, Charles learned, grew up there. Near the Siberian
city of Novosibirsk, the town had been carved out of dirt and
mud in the fifties at the behest of Nikita Khrushchev. Its design
team sported no fabulous foreign architects, such as those
Peter had lassoed to build St. Petersburg, so it never became a
city of great beauty or charm. What it shared with Peter's city,
however, was heroic scale and grand purpose. Plus one other
characteristic: it was built on a "sea." Never mind that it was
only a lake created by damming the Ob River; "the Ob Sea" was
what locals called it nonetheless.

Charles had read the articles; he knew about
Akademgorodok. All the while it was being built, scientists had
flocked to it like pigeons to a tourist scattering bread. Pressure,

yes, but also opportunity. With the sharp elbows of the state nudging it along, the Academy of Sciences appealed to its members' pioneering spirit—but also offered perks. Salaries and equipment undreamed of in stodgy old Moscow or gorgeous St. Petersburg! Laboratories fully equipped! Supplies! Instruments! Staff! Stuff!

Hence, to the shores of the Ob came not only scientists whose careers were in full bloom, but also the young, brilliant, brash, and ambitious. Particle physicists yearned to use the world's first particle accelerator with colliding beams. Cryogenicists lusted after rooms and equipment sturdy enough to measure the effects of extremely low temperatures. Organic chemists salivated over the opportunities they espied to tease out amino acids, synthesize polymers, untangle the strands of the recently discovered double helix—without the usual restrictions as to resources or size. And mathematicians—including Svetlana's father—came to untie knots in their string theories, stretch and compress topologies, differentiate their equations.

In fact, Gennady was an early arrival. Not yet 30, he'd already developed a name for himself. His young wife, Natalya, came with him from Moscow and, once woods were cleared and bungalows built, settled into a lavish cottage in the Golden Valley. Medals and citations, from mathematical societies at home and abroad, soon adorned his mantelpiece. He and Natalya decided to start a family. Enter Svetlana. When she was five, her mother died while attempting to birth a second child (who succumbed along with its mother), and Gennady had raised his daughter by himself.

So life for the two-member family ebbed and flowed. Prizes and accolades came and went, the work got easier or harder as waves of "correctness" and "control" washed over the Siberian city of science. But Gennady needed few resources for his work, and by and large, what he needed was at hand. With pencil, paper, chalk, and chalkboard, he worked alone. His society was other mathematicians; he corresponded with his fellows the world over. He discovered a gift for languages; in the evenings he read literature and wrote poetry.

At the beginning of the nineties, when the Soviet Union crumbled like a bad dream, Svetlana told Charles, the national budget for research—at one time almost three percent of the gross national product—simply evaporated. Now well into his sixties, Gennady watched as a few of his younger colleagues furiously wrote grant proposals, or accepted offers from abroad. He was declared eligible for a small state pension, with a few extra rubles thrown in for the titles he'd once held. He gave up his bungalow in the Golden Valley, with its wrap-around balcony and large picture windows looking out on the Siberian woodland—Svetlana's childhood home—and sought cheaper quarters, settling into a so-called *malogabaritnaya*, one of the smallest of the fifties-vintage apartments dubbed *krhushchevki*. Three hundred fifty square feet on Nikolai Street, where he burned candles whenever possible because electricity was expensive, looking on with sadness as many of his fellow scientists chopped and sold firewood, hawked used cars, and peddled vegetables in the local market. The younger ones joined computer software companies as programmers. Gennady, instead, used his astonishing gift for languages to find sporadic translating work from grant-seekers whose work depended on keeping abreast of the latest research reported in English, German, Italian, or French journals. He got by.

•

Svetlana was cooking *coq au vin* for Charles at her modest apartment in St. Petersburg's Vyborg district. They had transferred to her apartment from his hotel the moment she'd grasped the limitations of his budget.

"So, *dusha,* what you think? I have little bit vacation time. I propose we fly to Akademgorodok to visit my father while he translates your story. It will cost us nothing. I have privileges."

Charles popped a morsel of chicken into his mouth and wiped his lips.

"He agreed to do it?"

"He is careful, *moi otets.* He say he will make final decision after he reads. But *of course* he will do it! And meanwhile! We frolic in Akademgorodok while he works. Or Novosibirsk! They have jazz! You like jazz? I have two weeks away from airline. Is good?"

Charles looked down at his hands and then up again. From euphoria to despair to a vague hope. With a few dashes of ecstasy to cushion the switchbacks. He smiled.

"Is good."

10

URSINE HOPES

THE FLIGHT TO Novosibirsk took seven hours. Charles and Svetlana left early in the morning, but with the earth rotating in the opposite direction, the sky had already darkened by the time they arrived.

Charles's first realization, just off the aircraft, was that he could not understand a word spoken by anyone in Western Siberia.

"Is the accent," Svetlana assured him, as they huddled together for warmth in the taxi they'd decided to take to Akademgorodok. "I remember was hard when I first hear Muscovites speak."

An hour or so later, they stood outside an institutional-looking building as the cab driver slithered off through the fresh snow.

Svetlana smiled at Charles, who hoisted his valise in one hand and his laptop in the other.

"*Nu*, Dr. Charles. You are prepared to meet my father?"

They entered the stairwell and climbed one flight. Svetlana knocked. The door was opened immediately; in a rush, she was being hugged. All Charles could see was a pair of arms in a long-sleeved flannel shirt, and the dome of a slightly bald head.

When they at last broke apart and the apartment's occupant stepped back, Charles dropped his valise in astonishment. It landed with a clatter. Fortunately, the laptop, in his other hand, remained within his grasp.

"Professor Hazard!!?" he exclaimed.

The elderly man in front of him—slender and tall, with a broad forehead and a genial smile—extended his hand. Blue eyes danced behind gold wire-rimmed spectacles such as Trotsky had once worn.

"Gennady Novgorodtsev, at your service," he said in perfect, slightly accented English. "Very pleased to meet you, Dr. Baker. And, indeed, I know the gentleman to whom you refer. Columbia University, is it not?"

"Right! Right! John Hazard was a professor of international law and a specialist in the Soviet Union. You're the spitting image."

"I know. I met him here. He was conducting summer tours, I believe, with a very attractive young woman by the name of . . . Lapinsky, was it?"

"Marisol? Are you kidding? You know Marisol, as well?"

"I do indeed. While here, we met with some of my friends, and even they had difficulty in telling us apart. Is it Nabokov who always maintained that everyone has a double somewhere? A small world, as you Americans say. And how is Professor Hazard?"

"Dead."

"Ah! Sorry to hear that."

"Brain hemorrhage. Several years ago."

"A fine man. Spoke Russian fluently, though with a deep southern accent. And how is Ms. Lapinsky? Still living, I hope?"

"Svetlana, your father looks exactly—"

"I get it!" she said, beaming at the two of them. Then she

pinched her eyebrows together suspiciously. "So who is this Marisol Lapinsky?"

Ignoring her question, Charles looked around. One couch, one armchair, one small table with a starched doily and a copper candelabrum. Also, a straight-backed wooden chair and a small desk supporting an ancient computer and a darkened lamp. Above the desk, a small icon, painted on wood with a brass overlay, cast ghostly shadows in the meager light. On the wall opposite the desk hung another picture, a portrait of Gennady, executed in pen and ink, but somehow resembling an icon. *So beautifully rendered!* thought Charles. Through a doorway off to the right, a small room contained a single bed, and through a door on the left was a kitchen where a hot plate rested atop a wooden cabinet. The corner of a table was visible, but no oven. A single sixty-watt bulb in the living room ceiling provided the only light.

"In your honor, I have turned on the overhead, Dr. Charles. Later I shall resort to candles, however. Please! Take off your coats! You would like tea?"

A short while later, they had settled themselves, delicately beautiful china cups and saucers at rest in hands or laps (survivors, Charles assumed, from a time when a woman ran the household). Charles had taken the armchair; Gennady was at one end of the couch with his daughter beside him. The overhead light had been doused; a single white candle flickered in a candelabrum meant to hold three. In the dancing light, the face of Jesus in the icon, from deep within its raised brass penumbra, glowed mysteriously. His painted hands loomed out of their brass setting, beckoning. Charles struggled to read the message incised in the Bible one hand held open: *P[i]ditye ko mne . . . ." Ah!* he thought. *Come unto me all you who labor and are heavy-laden, and I shall give you rest.*

"Where are your medals, Papa?"

"In the closet, Svyetochka. In a box. They are safe."

"In Golden Valley, before," she said, turning to Charles, "we had great fireplace." She stretched out her arms. "Above it, hung all his medals and certificates. So many prizes, from so many countries, including Crayfish. You know Crayfish? Is like Nobel, only Nobel don't give math prizes. I play with them when I was little."

To say Charles was impressed would be an understatement. "You still do some mathematics, sir?"

In the chiaroscuro of the small room, Gennady looked composed, even serene. He sat erect, long legs tightly braided, light from the candle glinting off his spectacles. *This is so film noir!* thought Charles. Her father made him think of a tall, skinny Buddha.

"I amuse myself, in my spare moments, solving problems."

"What sorts of problems?" Charles asked. Feeling the need to be polite. He knew nothing about mathematics.

"Do cognitive algorithms mean much to you?"

"Afraid not."

"*A posteriori* error control?"

"Uhh—"

"Fourth-order degenerate parabolic equations?"

"Father!" scolded Svetlana. "You are making Charlie feel bad for himself."

Charles shrugged helplessly. "It's as if you're speaking a language I've never even heard."

Gennady looked at the candle-flame, and chuckled.

"Forgive me, Dr. Baker. Just a little fun. But it *is* like a foreign language, isn't it? A language without ethnic boundaries, with no geographical limitations, requiring no translation whatsoever."

"Math, you mean?"

"Not the words, of course. Descriptions need to be translated, like anything else. Words muddle things. But the symbols, the numerals, the equations! Such a purity to the syntax! Such universality! Here in Siberia you may think I am isolated, Dr. Baker, but in my mind I've been all over the world! Travel outside the country was limited for a long while. Though I did travel to Beijing. My point is there's no need for translation in the language of mathematics! But when you return to the real world . . . ."

The older man sighed and shrugged, fell silent.

"Are you a religious man, sir?" asked Charles, anxious not to let the silence linger.

"The icon, you mean? No. I revere them for their beauty; the depth of human reverence they reveal. The yearning that breathes through them. I once had books and books of icons. You remember, Svyetochka?"

She smiled at him, clearly with adoration. "*Ya pomniu*, Papa. We spent hours looking. What happened to your books?"

"Sold."

"Papa! You had to do this?" Charles could feel her distress.

He laid three fingers gently on her lips. "They are all in here." He tapped his forehead. "I do not need them anymore. Don't worry, Svyetochka. I am happy. I had one life, now I have another. A life that connects me more to the world of flesh and blood. And the quiet joys of reading. I am fine."

Charles watched all this in silence. It was like watching a play unfold. Then he said, "That picture, sir. The pen and ink sketch, in iconic style. It's very nice. Who did this?"

Svetlana spoke. "In English is called 'Portrait of Mathematician as Icon.' I am guilty one."

"*You* did this! It's beautiful. Svyeta, you never told me!"

"My daughter is a very talented artist, *Gospodin* Baker."

She shrugged. "Was," she said. "I don't do any more." She looked at her father and then away, into a corner.

"But why?" asked Charles.

When she did not answer, Gennady looked at Charles, cleared his throat, and smiled sadly. "Perhaps we should get on with it, Professor Baker. May I see your story, please?"

Charles swallowed. "Ah, sure."

He handed the manuscript to Gennady, who moved to the small table, switched on the lamp, and settled in to read. Svetlana and Charles exchanged glances but said nothing. Presently she rose, made more tea, and served the two of them, not wishing to interrupt her father by asking if he wanted a second cup.

After a third of the pages in the old man's hand had been meticulously turned over, he abruptly flipped them back.

"I have read enough. Of course I will translate your story for you, Dr. Baker. I will be honored."

Charles had not realized how tense he'd been until this moment. It was as if he'd broken the surface after swimming underwater across a deep lake. He inhaled sharply.

"So very, very appreciated, sir. I only budgeted $500 for the job, I'm afraid. I'm truly sorry it's not more."

"Not to worry. That will be fine."

"How long do you expect it to take?"

"Two weeks to a finished translation, I think. Acceptable?"

"Fantastic, sir." He was grinning broadly. He felt like singing.

"Please. Call me Gennady."

Svetlana managed to piece together a meal for them from leftovers she found in the kitchen, and two hours later the entire household was asleep in the quiet winter deep of Siberia, Charles and Svetlana on a pallet in the living room.

11

BELKNAP'S AGITA

JONATHAN BELKNAP STOOD, arms folded, in the kitchen of his East Side apartment, attempting with his tongue to dislodge an arugula stem that had set up residence between his molars. It was Sunday, and his wife, Abigail, had gone shopping, intent on taking advantage of a sale of something or other that was happening at Barney's. Christ, he'd made a mint in his successful public relations business, and Abigail still clipped coupons and scanned circulars in the newspaper for sales! Go figure. So, this noon, he'd snipped, sliced, and snapped a tasty salad for himself and was now busy rummaging through the cupboard for a can of soup to complete his lunch. But he was preoccupied.

What concerned him was his friend and fellow writer, Charlie Baker. Charlie was a decent man, a good writer, and he loved him dearly, but there was a frustrating aspect of Charlie's personality that seemed permanently irreversible: a kind of naïve, hopeless romanticism. Kept in check, it was not necessarily a bad quality for a writer, but it led, in Jonathan's opinion, to occasional passages of truly overblown prose. Purple—as metaphor—was never far from Jonathan's mind when he gave his critiques of Charlie's stuff. His most frequent suggestions were for cutting and pruning, toning down. And in matters of real life—in dealing with the quotidian world—Jonathan considered Charlie's condition a characterological defect.

But why was his old friend traipsing through his brain at the moment? He wasn't sure. Someone had raised Charlie's name at last night's writing group ("Too bad Charlie's not here"), and it had lingered in the back of his mind ever since. His friend was on a round-the-world jaunt to fulfill some cockamamie dream of mongrelizing one of his short stories by feeding it into the meat grinder of a dozen languages. Something like that. Hard enough to get published in English these days, why the hell would you want *that*?

Jonathan was anything but naïve. Only during the last twenty-five of his eighty-plus years had he worked in public relations at the Madison Avenue firm where he was a senior vice president and partner. Before that, he'd been a spook. He'd started in the OSS during the latter stages of the Second World War and slipped noiselessly into the newly named CIA afterwards. In his capacity as officer and operative, he'd been to more places on the globe than he wanted to remember, although most of his time had been spent in the Far East. In Japan during the post-war period, he'd infiltrated and monitored several groups whose political ideas and social advocacy had worried the honchos in the Beltway.

Next came Korea. The coldest Belknap had ever been was in that country. He'd been sent there for intelligence during the Korean War, but had been caught up in actual combat. Assigned to a MASH unit, masquerading as a high-ranking administrative officer, he would send back reports on the morale of American troops as well as the attitude of the average Korean in that northern part of the peninsula. When the troops had been forced to flee south, Jonathan had fled with them, rifle slung across his back. No, Belknap was not naïve. Korea was where he'd realized no one was reading his reports.

Out of concern for what he viewed as his friend's naïveté, Jonathan had revealed his CIA past to Charlie the evening of their last workshop before his departure. In the cloistered men's room of his PR firm, after everyone else from the writing group had departed, he'd given him a couple of phone numbers that he'd shared with no one else.

He chose a can of split pea soup from his kitchen cupboard and dumped its contents into a saucepan. So why was he bothered about Charlie now? After all, though there certainly were trouble spots in various places these days, and the threat of terrorism targeting Americans could erupt suddenly anywhere on the globe, was there anything in what Charlie was doing that suggested he might be exposed to danger? Hardly! Charlie would be hanging out with people whose principal skills were translating literature from one language to another. Mostly college profs, he'd imagine. Jonathan's rational appraisal of the situation could identify no strand that ought to provoke his wariness. Yet there it was, that nagging. Like the arugula that was still stuck between his teeth. And an all-too-familiar troupe of performing acrobats had set up camp in his belly.

Call it a hunch. In the Far East, he'd had to live by the seat of his pants time after time, so he'd grown to rely on his instincts. And . . . he still knew people. You left the agency, but if you'd been under cover, you never really left the agency. You had friends. At least among the Old Boys. Maybe it was not too early to alert his network. Just a precaution.

As he spooned the last dribble of soup into his mouth he heard Abigail's key in the front door. Stealthily, he deposited both bowl and spoon in the sink and retreated to his study before she could confront him with the results of her shopping spree, and her unending chatter could wrench his mind in another direction. Once the door was closed, he pulled open a drawer in his desk where he kept a secure phone. He hoped it was secure. These days, who could be sure? He dialed a number.

A male voice answered after four rings. "Yes?"

"Eduardo? Jonathan here. I've got something I'd like to talk over with you. Can we meet?"

12
URSINE DREAMS

CHARLES AND SVETLANA spent their days exploring Akademgorodok or venturing into the woodlands, which were at first blanketed with snow that later melted, forming runnels that dribbled down the hillsides, as Indian Summer settled on Western Siberia.

Sometimes they would rove quietly, absorbed by the bewitching natural beauty. But at other times, elated, they would gabble to each other in sentences that tumbled forth in broken Russian (Charles) or broken English (Svetlana), like the bubbling commotion of two rills running together. He told her about the ranch; his childhood chum, Ignacio; his loneliness. He told her about his cow. She told him about the gap in her own life after her mother died. Reluctantly at first, she told him about her childhood crush on her art teacher, who taught her to draw, to understand shadow, line and light. How they had pored over drawings of David and Delacroix, of Ingres, Kirchner and Schiele. And about how, later, he had taken advantage of her infatuation in ways she found inappropriate. How the experience had confused and pained her.

"We struggle. I resist. He become quiet and angry. One day is final straw. We are both painting, easels side by side. Suddenly, he look at my picture, grab my brush and—*whoosh! whoosh!*—make big, angry strokes all over my canvas. Portrait I am painting disappears, becomes something different, something ugly. 'Like so! Like so!' he shout. I know he punish me because I refuse to give him my body. I never paint again."

Later, she said, her husband, a gentle soul, had managed to ease her anger toward men, but her artwork remained a thing of the past.

Charles thought about this, but chose to keep quiet. Her revelation was so personal, he felt privileged, trusted, and began to tell her about his dismissal from the university, but halfway through, he stumbled and grew quiet. She put her arms around him.

At one point, she asked, "Did I hear correct that you at one time wrote *rasskaz* that made you famous for awhile—"

"Oh, not famous, darling. *Izvestnyi*, I suppose—notorious. And even that is an exaggeration. This particular short story was published in a respectable Midwestern literary magazine, and a few people read it—professors, I suppose—and they told their students and they told others and . . . well, for a while, I got letters. Some people were scandalized, others called it daring. But not really *that* famous. And it didn't last."

"No matter. What I am ask is, you said you call it, 'Doing Mama.' Is mean what I think it means?"

He laughed. "I'm afraid it does, love. Pure fantasy, of course. I never really knew my mother. Maybe that was why I wrote it? An effort to overcome that . . . lacuna? That hole in my life? It was sort of a dark story with a light touch. A spoof, if you will."

She hugged him once more.

Later, that same evening, as she began bringing his flesh to life under the blanket, he was beguiled by the whisper, "Little Charlie. Little Charlie misses his mama? Oh, my goodness!

What this? Little Charlie not so little anymore! Is Big Charlie now! I show how to make Big Charlie happy."

•

During the day Gennady was left alone in his apartment to work on the translation, but he also worked at night, after dinner. He would retire to his small bedroom with a candle and lie there, scribbling, consulting the dictionary that lay beside him on the floor. Charles and Svetlana would lie on their pallet, and night after night, rediscovered each other's bodies with a devotion that rivaled her father's concentration on the manuscript.

During one of their whispered, post-coital conversations, he told her of his failed marriage to the brilliant but willful Celeste. She confided, in the same *sotto voce* tones, information about her own marriage. Wed at twenty to a young hydroelectric engineer who worked on the local dam. For the first five years of their marriage, she told him, they'd slept on a mattress on the floor of the family bungalow, to avoid the sound of squeaky springs.

Much like now! thought Charles. *Does history move on, or circle back like a boomerang?*

"And then—four years ago—he is being killed in a fall from—how you say it—*stroitelnyi lesa . . . .*"

"Uh . . . not sure. Scaffolding?"

"*Tak*, if you say so. *On padyol* from scaffolding inside dam. That was when I go to work for airline. Oh, Charlie! After he die, I think I go crazy! I was so lonely. And need sex so bad, you know? *Oderzhimyi!* I was obsessed! Too many lovers. You know? But I get over it. Finally."

"Umm. People grieve in different ways. You loved him, right?"

She hugged him but said nothing.

•

Later, while they walked hand in hand along a deserted beach by the Ob Sea, he asked again.

"Of course I love Dmitri! He was not educated like Papa, but extremely nice, *priyatnyi. Tikhii chelovek.* Quiet man. But did I love him like Papa love Mama? I don't think so. Papa never even look at another woman after Mama died. He just take care of me. Perhaps that helped him lose his . . . *dolor.*"

A few days later, she asked would he like to see her old school in Akademgorodok? When they entered the building, most people, students and teachers alike, had left for the day. They did encounter one of her old teachers, a small woman with white hair and sloping shoulders, her face haunted and sad. The gloom disappeared momentarily when she spotted Svetlana. But after they'd chatted awhile, as she consulted her watch and said goodbye, they watched her gloom descend like a mask.

When the woman was clearly out of earshot, Svetlana hunched her shoulders a mite and whispered, "We think she was KGB then."

This surprised Charles, although he said nothing. *Wouldn't there have been comparatively little KGB in a place like Akademgorodok?* he asked himself. *And why is she whispering? There is no longer a KGB.* He wondered for a moment at the ineradicable nature of some fears.

A few minutes later, they entered a classroom where Svetlana had once studied chemistry. After she had closed the door and twisted its simple lock, she strolled to the front of the room, pivoted and leaned back against a deep brown desk, defaced by years of scratches and burn marks. She smiled at him in a way that made his heart race. Slowly, she inched up her skirt.

"I always dream to do it in a classroom, Charlie. Do you mind?"

His tongue was stuck to the roof his mouth. He cast a glance around to make sure no one was watching. He shook his head in amazement. What had he done to deserve such moments?

It was his fantasy, too, that they were fulfilling. They seesawed passionately against the edge of the desk, she grunting, he gasping, she with one long leg on the floor and the other up around his ears. His heart fibrillating wildly, teetering on the edge of explosion, Charles stared straight ahead at a formula on the blackboard that had escaped erasure: $Al_2(SO_4)_3$.

A few minutes later, as they recovered together on top of the desk, "Aluminate sulfate, I still remember," Svetlana whispered, in what he first thought was a term of endearment. "That formula." Then, in her most girl-reciting-to-the-teacher voice, "Formed by process, which called in English, is *flocculation*."

"Wonderful," he answered, heart beating normally at last. "And we have just flocculated magnificently, *dusha*. But how much longer do you imagine I can keep this up? I'm not a young man, darling. Do you have any idea how old I am?"

"Piffle," she said. "So you sleep an extra hour tomorrow morning."

•

Suddenly, it was over. Twenty-four days after he'd boarded the plane for Russia, the translation was complete. Travel plans had now been made for the next stage of Charles's journey. It was late December. Snow and cold had returned.

Svetlana, who'd read her father's translation, told Charles how happy he'd be with the result. His original creation was now two stories, she joked, an excellent story in English and a fantastic story in Russian. (Charles wondered if she actually thought Gennady had improved it, but he was reluctant to ask.)

"You do not want to read it yourself?" Gennady inquired as he handed Charles the CD and the hard copy in Russian. They were sitting once more in the candle-lit living room, drinking tea. "Your Russian is good enough if you use a dictionary and read slowly, yes?"

"*Da*," said Charles. "And, of course I'm curious. If it were just a question of achieving the best translation into Russian, I'd want to go over it and discuss it. Who knows? I might even be inspired to re-write some passages of the English version! But that wouldn't conform to the spirit of my idea. As far as my project is concerned, this story might as well have been written by someone else, Updike say, or Jocelyn Lynne Barley. I wouldn't change their stories, so I won't change mine. My task here is just to keep the hoop rolling, so to speak. My question now is *not* how beautifully the Russian version reads, as I'm sure it does, but how it will read once it's translated into . . . Chinese. And then the next, and the next."

"Hmmm. As you wish. You have contacted Lu Chi?"

Gennady had saved Charles's bacon in a second important respect, which was part of Svetlana's original plan when they lay on the hotel bed in St. Petersburg. At her request, Gennady had gotten in touch with Lu Chi, a particle physicist. Having become acquainted many years ago at a conference in Beijing, they'd enjoyed a long friendship, sustained mostly through an avid correspondence. His friend was a perfect choice, according to Gennady. He spoke and read Russian fluently and was also a devotee of literature, writing not only poetry but also a novel that had been published in China only recently. Once Charles and Lu Chi been put in touch by Svetlana's father, and the project described, a meeting with him had been warmly accommodated. They'd agreed to meet at Beijing University in early December, now only a week or so away.

"You will be traveling by rail this time?" asked Gennady.

"*Da da!* Frugality is the name of the game! Svyeta convinced me that the Trans-Siberian is not only cheaper but—since I have the time—more fun!"

•

The next afternoon, three figures clustered among the scattered groups on the railway platform at Novosibirsk, minutes before the scheduled departure. The train stood at attention in the station, panting in big, white, mechanical breaths. A copy of the Russian translation had been mailed to Charles's post office box in New York that morning. Gennady had been paid and Charles's ready cash replenished, a mixture of rubles and renminbis, the Chinese currency.

Stuffed into his bag was a sweater, lovingly knitted by Svetlana. At one point, Charles had silently asked himself: did he still want to persist in this journey, now that he'd met this remarkable woman? But his project pulled him on. After all, perhaps her sharing this crazy undertaking with him was part of what drove their passion? Besides, he worried about his age. A lot. How could their passion ever survive such a cold scrutiny? In any event, there was always email, wasn't there?

At ten minutes to the hour, Gennady smiled and angled his head toward the train. "You'd better board, my friend," he said. "The Trans-Siberian is the one thing in Russia that runs on time. Good luck with the rest of your journey. My regards to Lu Chi." He tipped his hat and walked discreetly to the end of the platform, so that Charles and Svetlana could say their good-byes.

"So, *dusha*," she said. He returned her hug and caught a tear on his glove as he stroked her face.

"I have pictures," she said. She touched her purse, which sheltered the digital camera she'd been using that morning to take photographs. Of them, and him, and her, and the three of them together. "I email them to you."

"Also," she added. "When is birthday?"

"My birthday?" he asked, already picking up his luggage and starting to lope, as he noticed the conductor beckoning emphatically. "July!" he yelled. "July 22nd."

"Good!" she shouted at him. "I find you. Goodbye, Charlie!"

He waved at her and vaulted onto the train, nearly dropping his valise and computer, just before the door closed with an air-boosted hiss. The big, lumbering engine lunged forward with its human cargo toward Lake Baikal, Mongolia, and Beijing.

13
A BIG KNIGHT MOVE TO BEIJING

THE FIRST PART of the journey lay through low-lying hills and meadowlands, a gentle roll and tilt to the landscape, such as Charles had experienced . . . where? Southern Indiana? He'd been there once, to a summer language program years ago, brushing up on his Russian. But on that occasion, everything was green, steamily hot. Here, the flowing hillsides were impossibly white. Other colors made cameo appearances: a farm, a copse, a pond. He remembered a line from Chekhov about a journey along the old post road that had preceded this railroad: "You'll be bored from the Urals to the Yenisei."

Surely not! he thought. His memory coughed up a few more words from the master: "A cold valley, crooked birches, fields, once in a while a lake, snow"—something, something—"on the barren, cheerless banks of the Ob tributaries."

Well, okay. Chekhov was an old crab, Charles decided. *I'm not bored*. There was a grandeur here. An epic quality. Miles and miles of nothing but snow and trees. Trees and snow. Snow and trees.

As hour followed hour, however, as time stretched and

distances widened, as the excitement of fresh discovery began to dissipate, he conceded that Chekhov had a point.

A full day elapsed before they reached the Yenisei, second of the three mighty rivers that lumbered through Siberia toward the Arctic. He knew from Gennady—as well as from the timetable tucked into his breast pocket—that to reach the shores of Lake Baikal, only half his journey, would take many more hours still. He remembered telling his classes that the sun never set on the Russian Empire at its broadest reach, before the sale of Alaska to the United States in 1867, and that even just before the Revolution of 1917, especially after the addition of Finland in the Russo-Finnish War, it was the longest contiguous land-mass empire the world had ever known.

He fell asleep, rousing when the train began its climb through the Sayan Mountains. Like a huge snake that thrived on snowy ground, it swept first one way, then the other, through the world's largest stand of birch and pine. The *taiga*. Beautiful, peaceful, utterly hypnotic. Hours would go by when Charles was unsure whether he was awake or asleep. It was like being slipped into a white envelope, and the black trees were large letters etched thereon.

Siberia. Lenin had been exiled here. And Stalin. Both had escaped. No escape for Dostoyevksy, of course, who'd been imprisoned here. He'd called his memoir of the experience *The House of the Dead*.

At intervals, he patted his possessions, fantasizing that handcuffs shackled him to his laptop. He was transporting a secret code! Then he grew embarrassed, searching the coach to see if others had witnessed his folly. *No, you fool!* he told himself. *They can't see inside your head!* Eventually, he returned his gaze to the countryside. Trees. Snow. Trees. Snow. More trees.

The rhythmic jiggle of the railway cars lulled him to sleep once again.

•

He awoke to a peculiar neuralgic sensation in his lips. Something between a tremble and a tickle. A tingle? Did every label begin with a t? Was this a quibble? Ah, a quiver, perhaps! It was not pain exactly, but very irritating. He'd experienced it before, but when? A year ago? Longer? The Cow Jumped Over the Moon. That nursery rhyme came back to him; what did it mean? *Arrggh! This tingle is very unpleasant!* He touched his finger to his lips to see if that would stop it. Sideswiped his lips as if brushing off a mosquito. Nothing. Fitting his glasses onto the bridge of his nose, he hauled himself out of his compartment and sought the railway car's shadowy bathroom mirror. The glass was dirty; he scrubbed it with his sleeve. Leaning close, he tried to detect movement in his lips. Could see nothing. Was it all in his head then? He worked his mouth back and forth a few times. No luck.

Ignore it! he told himself. Continue as if. He returned to his seat, seized suddenly by panic. He'd left everything valuable out in plain sight! Still, all was as he'd left it. And as soon as he realized this, he also realized his loping lips had stilled. Back to normal. Why did it come? Why did it stop? How did it leave? God help us. The Cow Jumped Over the Moon.

He lay his head back against the headrest. *Relax, Charles! You are turning into a kook! A crazy person!* Still: so much we don't have words for! A buzz. Had it been a buzz? No, buzzes made noise. Unless, of course, it was one of those that dogs could hear and humans couldn't? Absurd, perhaps, but really! So many sensations we can't describe! Yet we aspire to translate these ineffables into another language! Well, perhaps the next language would have the right words? Maybe it's only our own sad tongue that's deprived?

His mind galloped along, unstoppable. If you have no word for something you feel, do you actually feel it? If you call it a buzz, does that make it a buzz? In fact, who can be certain—when you confess your inmost thoughts to someone, say—that what they understand is the same as what you struggled to find words for?

Merde!

A porter passed through the car with coffee, and after Charles had warmed himself with it, he crawled back under a woolen blanket the porter had left him and wished for sleep. Sleep. Now there was a word.

14
MIXING MEMORY AND DESIRE

CHARLES DECIDED TO send a few emails.

Late December

To: Jonathan Belknap, Buffy St. Olaf, Orchid Lafitte, Xavier Krill, Jake Cash, Becky Weingarten, Trish Truex

Re: My Trip

Hey, Gang!

You'd never guess where I am right now! Sailing through the wilds of Siberia! Well, not sailing, actually, more like gently jouncing along on a coach on the Siberian railroad. This country is so vast that it's hard to keep track of, and each vista, glimpsed from the window, seems like a different view of the same scene, so the whole effect is hypnotic and soporific. Several times I've fallen asleep when I didn't intend to . . . and wakened convinced I hadn't traveled anywhere at all!

In any event, I'm loving it. I'm off to a great start, with my short story translated into Russian by—get this!—a mathematician with extreme literary gifts! Now I'm on my way to Beijing to get one of his friends (a physicist! go figure!) to translate the Russian version into Chinese!

So, enjoy your bloodletting rituals in the writing group. Struggle to get what you can out of it sans my sage criticism. I'll have lots to talk about when I get back. But that's months and multiple countries into the future. Wow!

My best to all of you,

Charlie

To: Marisol Lapinsky

Re: My Trip

Hey, Marcy!

You can't imagine how thrilled I am to be on the Trans-Siberian railroad right now! You've been here before, and now I've had the experience as well.

What you'd truly be amazed by is that I found someone who knows your mentor and buddy, Professor Hazard! Knows you as well! Do you recall Gennady Novgorodtsev, the mathematician? Says he met you in Akademgorodok when you and Hazard were conducting tours through that part of the country. Well, turns out Gennady is the fellow I finally found to translate my story! How, is a long tale, certainly too long for email.

But here's the kicker! I'm completely smitten with this guy's daughter! Svetlana's a lot younger, but seems to be really into me! We met on the plane over, where she works as an Aeroflot stewardess. We were flirting with each other during the flight, then she called me after at my hotel and, within minutes we were in the sack! Fantastic, no? So when I was having trouble with the translators I'd scheduled, Svyeta suggested her father do the translation. It's completed now, and it's (I think—haven't seen it, actually) a brilliant job. How cool is that!

By the way! I'm sure there's more I haven't heard about your Russian travels, but couldn't you at least have told me you met a scholar who looks just like Professor Hazard?

And how's by you and Anthony? It'll be so great to see you again. Some of my stories, only you would appreciate.

Love to yourself and Tony,

Charlie

To: Svetlana Novgorodtseva

Re: Here I am

Here I am, darling, still on the Trans-Siberian, still pitching and rolling with the motion of the train, still staring at the endless taiga, still excited by my project and the chance to meet Lu Chi, and still—most of all—wishing you were snuggled up beside me on the seat, your warm body pressed against—whoa!—better stop thinking that way, else I'll be carried away by my passion!

And thank you for your lovely sweater, Svyetochka. I know it will keep me warm through the many cold months ahead.

Miss you, Love, and dream about you.

All my best wishes, kisses, hugs and fond touches, your History Professor/Writer/Translation Freak,

Charlie

15

A SNEAK PEEK

AWAKE AGAIN, CHARLES glanced out of the window and sighed at the sameness. Guess what, he said to himself. Chekhov was right. I'm bored out of my frigging mind. After a few moments—not for the first time—he began thinking about his short story. He pulled it out of his briefcase and smoothed it across his lap.

The story was based on a precipitous religious conversion he'd experienced as a boy, a dramatic meltdown at a revival meeting when he was twelve. But that was only part of the story. It was also about how religion had gotten mixed up—conflated, in fact—with sex. The pull toward religion and the impulse toward the carnal act were both, he thought, marked by an existential longing. Add to that his confusion and guilt over succumbing to temptations of the flesh. What a curious crowd were the Southern Baptists of his boyhood!

For the sake of his narrative, he'd invented a mother for his alter ego, Jeffrey Hawkins, since he did not remember his own. Also a sister. A sister would have been nice in real life. How would his days on earth have been different? he wondered. Who knows? The siren of the piece—the Lilith, the Medusa, the temptress for both the sex and the religion in his story, and the immediate precipitant of his character's confusion—had been modeled on someone very real indeed. Though, at the time, the events had caused him much anxiety, he'd tried to write the story with humor, making frequent use of the budding sarcasm with which he'd equipped his youthful protagonist. Whether the story worked or didn't work (he gnashed his teeth each time he thought about this), it was the piece that would be making its way across multiple languages and cultures.

He blew out his cheeks and glanced, yet again, at the first two paragraphs:

We Shall Come Rejoicing

Foggy's New Bride—as everyone on the ranch referred to her—was in her late twenties, with loose black hair and full, pouting lips that opened over slightly crooked incisors. Young Jeffrey Hawkins was mesmerized by her long and shapely legs. She wore flimsy floral-print dresses that draped softly over her body. Though almost everyone on the ranch who wasn't Mexican was from Oklahoma or Arkansas, he suspected Earleen might be mail-order. She claimed to be a God-fearing Christian, and had called on Jeffrey's mama to talk about religion.

Jeffrey had heard enough tales of damnation and fiery furnaces to make him fearful. His mother had purchased leather-bound New Testaments for both himself and his sister, Lucy, and given them each crocheted crosses with ribbons threaded through to use as bookmarks. So the concept of the Savior's love redeeming a blighted soul was not a new one. But when Earleen sat and fanned herself in his mother's kitchen that hot Sunday in 1948, he felt something stirring, but was it Jesus?

Suddenly, Charles was overcome by curiosity. He had to look at the Russian translation, even though he'd promised himself he wouldn't. He reached into his briefcase and lifted it out carefully, as if he were handling a clay pot recovered from the tomb of Tutankhamen.

Возвратимся с радостью

Новой Жене Фогги – как ее тут же окрестили на ранчо – не было и тридцати, на плечи ей спадали черные локоны, а пухлые губы приоткрывались, обнажая ряд не совсем ровных резцов. Юный Джеффри Хокинс был заворожен ее длинными, стройными ногами. Под тонким ситцевым платьем в цветочек было нетрудно различить контуры лакомой фигурки. Хотя почти все на ранчо, кроме мексиканцев, были из Оклахомы либо Арканзаса, Джеффри заподозрил, что Ирлин выписали по почте. Выдавала она себя за набожную христианку и однажды даже заглянула к маме Джеффри, потолковать о вере.

Джеффри вдоволь наслышался о проклятии и пылающих котлах, и боялся. Мать его где-то приобрела два Евангелия в кожаном переплете, ему и сестре Люси, и к тому же выдала им вязанные кресты с ленточками на закладки. Так что, в сущности, представление о любви Господней, искупающей грешные души, не было для него новостью. И все же в тот жаркий воскресный полдень 48-го, когда Ирлин сидела у них на кухне и обмахивалась веером, он ощутил некое возбуждение. Но от Христа ли это?

Well. Not bad. Not bad at all. But did it have the same flavor? Certainly "*pukhlye guby*" for "pouting lips" was sexy, as intended. Gennady had chosen the word "*prokliatie*" for "damnation," and Charles thought that was perfect, wasn't sure, in fact, what other word might be used. Wasn't it Dostoyevsky who had talked about the "*prokliatie voprosy*," usually translated as "accursed questions?" But was the Russian passage as blazingly fearful? Could one smell the brimstone?

He glanced out the window again. They were rounding a bend, pulling into a station. He felt drowsy once again. Too much thinking. He slipped the two versions of his short story back into the briefcase, tucked his blanket around his shoulders, and once more fell asleep.

•

In a bathroom three cars forward, a stoutly built man—a rough, seen-it-all face on his squat neck and sturdy shoulders—sat on the toilet, warming a dose of heroin in a small, curved spoon. No use taking this job too seriously, the user thought. No one was getting off the train for some time. After all, why was he earning money these days if not for the ability to indulge in the sensations he craved? This job was such low-impact shit anyway. Not like the old days in Nam and Afghanistan. Might as well relax. He sucked the warm brown syrup into a syringe, tapped his needle and sought a vein between his toes. Ah! he sighed, a few seconds later. Nothing more to do until we reach Beijing. Piece of cake! There we go. Ah, lovely!

16
COLLAPSING IN CATHAY

FROM THE MOMENT he'd climbed down from the railway carriage, Charles had resolved to zip directly to the university in hopes of catching Lu Chi unawares. Although the arrangement with Gennady's friend seemed certain enough, Charles was still smarting from what had happened in Moscow and St. Petersburg. So he found a driver with a smattering of English and a gift for improvised sign language, impressed upon him that he needed to find the School of Physics of Beijing University, and together they sped off through the bustling city, choked with morning traffic, bicycles, three-wheelers, orangey-gray acidulous vapors, and enough people to keep a census taker busy for the rest of the century.

All Charles had time to notice was: no rickshaws, no coolie hats, no blue Mao pajamas. Just men and women in bulky coats struggling against a cold December day.

Carving a path through the crowds and the murk, his resourceful driver had found the building they sought after several fruitless crawls along other beautifully landscaped avenues. His round skull stuffed into what looked like a blue railroad cap, the driver darted his head this way and that as he peered at the inscriptions on buildings. Charles's head swiveled along with the driver's, though he was helpless to read any sign that would have offered him a clue as to where they were. Once arrived at what the driver convinced him was the right destination, Charles tipped him what he would have given a driver back home, and the cabbie stared at the American greenbacks as if wondering whether he'd been robbed or could now afford to take the rest of the week off. But at last he grinned and departed, amid a display of stylized exit-taking bows.

Inside the building, Charles found the school's secretary, a very cheerful young woman with arching black eyebrows and beautiful English, who introduced herself as Mei Ling and assured him that Professor Lu was indeed here, only in a meeting. Would he care to wait in Dr. Lu's office? He would.

Alone, surveying the office's contents, he decided that it resembled academic burrows the world over, with two exceptions: on one wall, a framed photograph of the CERN Collider with two white-helmeted figures examining a bank of microprocessors, and on the facing wall, a tranquil watercolor of a mountain stream, in which a tall man stood fishing, embroidered silk robe tucked in his sash, fat birds skittering through the branches of an apple orchard on the shore, a feeling of Ancient China about it. Strangely, the fisherman looked an awful lot like one of the helmeted men inside the Collider. Charles lowered his luggage to the floor beside a chair.

Books lay open on the desk, and Charles glanced down: two in Chinese, one in English. He leaned closer. Partially hidden by one of the books was a Xeroxed reprint of one of his short stories! The first story he had ever published, in fact, in a university literary journal called *Falling Leaves*. The one he'd discussed with Svetlana, "Doing Mama."

"Professor Baker!"

Charles jumped and whirled, feeling like he'd been caught

peeking through a keyhole. A slender fellow over six feet tall filled the doorway, wearing a dark suit and smiling broadly. He had aviator glasses, a full head of slicked-back hair, and carried himself like one born to privilege. Small patches of gray at the temples. The last Chinese emperor, thought Charles, as cast by Bernardo Bertolucci. Thirty years younger than Gennady at least. Maybe fifteen years younger than Charles.

Gesturing toward the desk, his host said, "As you see, I've been doing my homework, Professor Baker." Something about the quality of his voice, his delivery, his lack of accent. He could have been an actor!

"N*i hao*! Am I getting that right? Although I'm not a professor, these days, but a writer," said Charles, pumping Lu Chi's hand enthusiastically. "Wonderful to meet you, sir!"

Lu Chi swept off the glasses, tossed them on the desk. "A *good* writer! I've been enjoying your story."

"Flattery will get you everywhere. How on earth did you find a copy?"

The Last Chinese Emperor shrugged. "Please, Dr. Baker. My university has one of the finest libraries in the world. I did a search, snapped my fingers and asked the library to scan me a copy! Please sit down."

When they were seated, Lu Chi asked, "How long have you been in our fair country?"

His English was impeccable. Was that an Oxford tie?

Charles glanced at his watch. "About forty-five minutes, I'd say, unless you count all those hours since the train crossed your northern border."

"Impressions so far?"

Charles was unsure how to reply. He'd been pumped with adrenalin since he'd left the train, but now weariness was beginning to overtake him.

"Just kidding," laughed Lu Chi. "Didn't mean to give you the third degree. People are always confused, anyway, by their first glimpse of my very old, yet very new country. So, you've come to have your story translated, yes? Though from Russian, not English? A different story, I understand, than 'Doing Mama,' which I've been reading with great delight. So, tell me, Dr. Baker—"

"Please, call me Charles."

"Tell you what. I'll call you *Dr.* Charles until I've known you at least 24 hours, okay? I'm a bit stodgier than my Russian friends, and miles more formal than you Americans!"

To Charles, he didn't sound stodgy at all. How stodgy could he be if he enjoyed the impudicity of "Doing Mama," by far the most ribald story Charles had ever written? To Charles, Lu Chi seemed like twenty-first century man incarnate. Comfortable contributing to scientific journals, comfortable reading messy minor-league literature with a hint of the modern in it. Comfortable posing for the pages of GQ? But Charles only smiled.

"As you like, Dr. Lu."

"Good! So explain to me exactly what you have in mind, Dr. Charles. Neither your message nor Gennady's was entirely clear."

Charles reeled off the five-minute version of his project.

"Well! I find your project intriguing, and would very much like to contribute what I can! But are you asking me to *do* the translation or find someone? I'm eager to do it myself but I have friends in the Foreign Language Department who might be more logical candidates."

"You've done translations before, I understand. As well as written poetry. Not to mention your work in physics?"

"To be sure. I'm a high energy physicist, what they used to call particle physicist. Both terms have their disadvantages. On days when I'm sick or lethargic I don't much feel like calling myself a high energy physicist."

Charles smiled pleasantly.

"At any rate, my peers tell me I've made a few modest contributions in that field. But like Gennady, I do know several languages—French, Russian, German, Mandarin, Korean and Japanese."

"And English, obviously."

"Of course. I've published two books of poems and two novels. There. You have my résumé. I assume it's Mandarin you'd like your story translated into?"

"Are there other choices?"

He shrugged again. "It's best, I think. Actually, there's not that much difference in the characters themselves—only a few things that apply to pronunciation. Mandarin and Cantonese are differentiated mainly in how they're spoken, not how they're written. Mandarin has the most speakers, certainly. Seven hundred million or so. And now that we've lifted the one child per family rule, it will just keep climbing. Unfortunately, not all of them read! But, that's a separate problem, right?"

He looked searchingly at Charles, who suddenly felt as if his mind were being blanketed by pond-scum. It had been a long trip from Novosibirsk.

"Are you all right, Dr. Baker? You look tired. Tell you what. Why don't we get you situated? Then you can get a good night's sleep, and we'll talk tomorrow. Will that be all right? Why don't you leave your story with me?"

Charles smiled weakly. "I am a bit bushed, come to think of it. That actually sounds like a good plan."

"Splendid! You are not booked somewhere? Let me help you with that." He punched a button on his telephone and picked up the receiver. "Mei Ling? I would like you to find Dr. Baker lodging at the Shangri-La on Zhizhuan Road. Okay?"

The Shangri-La? "Oh, no!" said Charles. "It sounds wonderful, but I'm sure it's beyond my budget! Even the name makes my wallet flinch. I'm perfectly all right with—"

"Nonsense! You're an honored guest! My university has an arrangement with the hotel; it's where we hold our physics conferences, and scads more besides. Don't even think about it. It's on us."

"That's extraordinarily nice of you, but—"

"No buts. Let's get you some rest."

If he'd not been so tired, Charles might have danced and flailed in protest a bit longer, but after four days on the Trans Siberian, he did yearn for a comfortable bed. He stared straight into the knot of Lu Chi's Oxford tie and nodded in mute surrender.

•

A half hour later, however, adrift in the lobby of the Shangri-La, he gaped. The façade, with its twenty-four stories, had been pleasing enough, but the interior! It struck him as both tasteful and opulent. Two large counters faced him across an intricately designed parquet floor. Behind each walnut enclosure, dwarfed by the lobby's immensity, stood a dark-suited young man. Mentally tossing a coin, he veered left.

"*Ni hao*," he began, "do you speak—"

"Dr. Baker!" smiled the concierge. "We've been expecting you. Delighted you could stay with us!"

Charles looked confused.

"Dr. Lu called ahead. Your suite is ready."

"My what? Oh, but actually all I need—"

The concierge snapped his fingers and a bellboy appeared.

"Please escort Dr. Baker to the Temple of Heaven Suite, Kai. See to it he has everything he needs."

After a zippy trip aloft and a short walk down a corridor whose carpets swallowed his shoes, Charles experienced his second bout of awe. So this was how the other half lived! He groped in his pockets for money, remembering that he soon needed to change some dollars for more *renminbis*. Rummaging through assorted rubles and kopeks, he finally found an American five-dollar bill, which he pressed into the young man's hand. The youngster bowed and withdrew.

Alone now, he looked around. No, it couldn't be the other *half* who lived this way. The other one per cent, perhaps? The point-one percent? He picked up his laptop and valise, unsure where they should come to rest, and tiptoed forward, as if the carpet might conceal land mines. The entrance hall was a high-ceilinged marvel, and the living room a vast arena of sandalwood and beige: carpeting, drapes, and a plush semi-circular couch that could have accommodated a soccer team, with coordinated throw pillows in muted brown. A few yards beyond, plate glass windows more than twice his height offered a view of the Beijing cityscape. Several flotillas of smaller buildings were visible, as well as a space needle in the distance. He moved closer. A light snow was falling. What had happened to the smog he had floundered through all the way from the train station? Perhaps these windows were really giant screens playing a digital loop of urban charm? Turning, he glimpsed two chairs—in matching beige—placed at a modest remove from the couch. He imagined diplomats in creased pin-stripes conversing across the several yards of carpet. He blew out his cheeks. Soft lighting came from tiny bulbs along reticulated branches of trees growing down from the ceiling. Not real trees, surely? Turning again, he wandered through the master bedroom, with its mammoth bed and walk-in dressing room, past the fireplace, past the giant flat-screen television. Then into the bathroom, whose enormous built-in tub doubled as a Jacuzzi.

Good Lord! thought Charles. *From sleeping on the floor of a postage-stamp apartment in Siberia to this! If I were paying, my budget would be wiped out in one night.*

He drifted through the dining room, with its mahogany table and upholstered chairs, took note of the kitchenette, which he thought might be the envy of chefs at a high-end restaurant in New York. He completed the circuit by returning to the living room. *Could clouds form in this space?* he wondered. *Rain fall? Why not? One could play polo here!* "Farley, quick to the stable. Fetch me m' horse!" he muttered to himself.

Then, after a moment in which he appeared to fall into a trance, he lowered to the carpet the two pieces of luggage he'd forgotten he was carrying and steered his body once more toward the bedroom. Slipping off his shoes, he flung himself into the middle of the enormous bed, where he was asleep before the down comforter had finished adjusting to the weight of his body.

17
A WALK IN DOWNTOWN BEIJING

A COMPACT WESTERNER WITH football shoulders, only recently disembarked from the Trans Siberian, ambled along Beihuashi Street. The day was cold, but clean, bracing. He felt comfortable in his small waist-length down jacket. Hell, he'd known worse. Lots worse.

"Yum," he said softly, munching on a baked potato he'd bought from a street vendor. "God, I love this town." The Professor, he knew, was holed up in the Shangri-La. He'd be there for a while. No problem.

The Shangri-La! He chuckled. *How lucky can you get! That's all right. I'm nearby, and not paying a king's ransom. Who's he putting the touch on, I wonder? I know who's bankrolling* me. He stretched and looked around, turned onto Xihashi Street.

Everyone's always hustling here! Commerce! That's what this city is all about. Hell, it's what this whole country is all about! How'd they ever get sidetracked into communism? Oh, right! Imperial corruption, foreign dogs, Chairman Mao!

At an intersection up ahead, a small fellow balancing several huge, flattened cardboards—shells of refrigerators, perhaps? giant TV screens?—tottered along on a bicycle. Where was he headed? To a scrap heap? Closer to hand, on either side of him, birds for sale. Cockatoos, toucans, robins from America, wild doves, owls, herons, dozens he couldn't begin to name. And other animals as well: foxes, armadillos, lynxes, bears, boa constrictors. There were crickets in straw cages. *Hey, a bobcat! Where do they get this shit? Start a private zoo in the comfort of your own home!* Shop owners out in front of the stalls and cages, yammering, cajoling, tugging at people's sleeves. He shook his head, uttered a few negatives in Mandarin. Though around him he could hear Cantonese as well. You might hear anything in this town. French. Arabic. This was Beijing.

And around the bend, on the next block, what would you find? The same animals for sale, but now to eat! We clean 'em up, scoop out the entrails, dress 'em up nice, you eat 'em. Go ahead, roast an armadillo! A nice broiled tarantula anyone? Pets on one corner, meat on the next. Ah, China! He loved this town! When the butchers run out of meat, do they turn the corner for a fresh supply? When the animal hawkers find one of their beasts too old in the tooth to fetch a good price, do they ease around the bend and peddle him to the men with the sharp knives?

Also a country with a history, he thought. When you asked people here what was the worst thing that ever happened in this country, as he had asked many while still working for the Company, the answer depended on social class, time of day, but mostly the generation. An educated young man or woman might respond: 'The Cultural Revolution.' They'd tell you about denunciations. Hectoring loudspeakers. Fathers and mothers rounded up. Posters with slogans on every corner. People uprooted because the neighbors said something, or the children. Books, papers, household goods—all seized. Citizens whisked away into the countryside to labor on farms, get their hands dirty (learn a little humility, for Mao's Sake!), be re-educated, develop a proper appreciation for the Revolution and its blessings. And readings every day from *The Thoughts of Chairman Mao*. He'd seen all this when he worked for the Company.

He had now eaten the potato, skin and all; he licked his fingers clean and, finding no Kleenex in his pocket, wiped the fingers on the sleeve of his jacket, then stuffed his fists in his pockets.

Oh, yes! he said to himself, remembering his previous line of thought. But if you asked the old-timers, you'll get a different view. The worst thing? Unquestionably, 'The Great Leap Forward.' A whole generation earlier. Because people died. By the millions. A fucking tsunami of famine. Provinces decimated. Neighbors, fathers, mothers, daughters, sons, all vanished. That's what they remembered. And why not? The Great Leap Forward. And yet . . . in the sweep of Chinese history, what was any of these? An eye-blink. Did Mao know that? Someone once asked him, what did he think of the French Revolution? His answer: "Too early to tell."

He saw a Taco Bell up ahead and chuckled. *Now look what we have. Taco Bell, CVS, McDonald's. Commerce triumphant. Almost.*

Where Xihuashi became Donhugashi, just past an old woman using a treadle sewing machine in the street, he descended three steps to enter a small noodle shop, and nodded to the owner, a shrunken, bowed, but still vital-looking old man with a traditional Chinese beard.

"*Ni hao!*" said the rotund American. "*Ni hen mang ma?*" The shopkeeper, greeting him like a long-lost family member, replied that no, he was not *too* busy. Would he like lunch? A spot of Tiger's Breath?

You betcha! He nods to the shopkeeper and takes a chair at a small table by the window. Here he would sit for the rest of the morning, by God. A little Dim Sum, a little conversation. Wing knew everything. The road ahead was empty, unknown, but the Professor—that Baker guy—would be ensconced in his grand palazzo for a while, at least. And if he moves, I'll know. If anything happens that demands my attention, that requires . . . adjustment, I can sure as hell find a way.

18
SO WHERE ARE THOSE TASTY CHINESE VICTUALS?

"SO, DR. CHARLES, I gather that the boy in this story—certainly in the Russian translation I'm reading—is a teenager who is conflicted about many things: sexuality, religion, his attitude toward his parents, a confusion which gives rise to—"

It continued to amaze Charles that a man of Lu Chi's debonair appearance, polish, actorly tone of voice and obvious erudition, would occasionally address him as "Dr. Charles." A bush-league mistake, that, considering his certain awareness that, in Western languages, surnames—always used with titles—came last.

"Forgive my interruption, Dr. Lu, but I can't comment on that."

They faced each other across the acres of couch in Charles's Temple of Heaven Suite. He'd slept until early afternoon, when Lu Chi had phoned to suggest they meet in Charles's living quarters.

"Beg pardon?" Lu Chi's ivory forehead furrowed in puzzlement. "Didn't you write it? What am I missing?"

"Nothing. But if I tell you more than what's in the words, I'll be compromising my purpose."

"How so? Surely the more information I have about how you see your characters—not just your young hero but the minister's wife, not to mention the mother, the sister, and that other minister, the traveling one—the more accurate and nuanced I can make the translation. Wouldn't you agree?"

That other minister. He'd referred to one of the characters in his story—a fire-breathing Southern Baptist itinerant evangelist—as minister rather than preacher. Did such choice of English words signal that a characterization had already been altered? Charles hadn't read far enough into the Russian translation to know what word had been used for "preacher." But was it the Russian word that indicated a small shift? Or the Chinese cultural matrix in which his Chinese translator was immersed? Charles wondered—with some excitement—what other refractions might already have tilted the story? And what others were to come?

"Of course," he said. "But I'd like the translation done without my input. A cold read, if you take my meaning. I'm curious, you see, about what changes occur as a result of the logic and vocabulary of the receiving language. What differences a culture makes. That's why I'm keen on choosing languages and cultures worlds apart from one another."

Lu Chi looked as if he'd suddenly divined whether an electron was a wave or a particle. He leaned back against his cushions. "Ah! You are playing the American game of "telephone," only with literature! I think I understand. A book by my ancestor of the same name has been rendered into several different English versions, so I think I can finally say I get it. You want to see just what the translator comes up with, to see if its passage through many languages changes it fundamentally."

"Exactly."

"But then . . . ," he spread his upturned hands and raised his eyebrows, ". . . why bother to accompany your story? Why not simply email it to these various places?"

Charles chuckled, just short of embarrassment. "Partly for the lark, though I try to convince myself it's a lark with a purpose. I'd hoped I could assure the process wasn't contaminated if I traipsed along and explained my intentions each time. Is that overkill? It's certainly the reason I chose an unpublished story, since a published one would be available to any translator with a good library. Like you, obviously, since you've already read 'Doing Mama.' Looking at the English would be cheating."

"So you are both Author and Policeman."

"Well—"

"No, no, I completely understand now! Did my reading your earlier story botch things up?"

"I don't think so. But please approach the translation as though you didn't have me available."

Lu Chi smiled, obviously amused. Charles took advantage of his silence to ask a question.

"You spoke of your ancestor a moment ago. "Are you descended, then, from *the* Lu Chi?"

"Everyone seems to believe so. You are familiar with the *Wen Fu?*"

"First came across it in a poem by Howard Nemerov, who called it *Prose Poem on the Art of Letters*. And I've read Sam Hamill's translation."

"Know them both. Though Nemerov chose a better title than Hamill's *Art of Writing*, Hamill's translation is quite good. What's not clear in either one is that *Fu* refers to a particular form of prose poem that before Lu Chi's time was used mostly for military epics. It pleases me that those earlier military epics are mostly forgotten, while his poem—about language—seems immortal."

"It's a scary text. When you think of trying to live up to it, it's hard not to cringe."

"Quite so! A little Confucius, a little *Tao Te Ching*, a little Buddhism. And it adds up to a lot of great advice. I read it two or three times a year."

Wow! thought Charles. How could one fail to be intimidated by this man's erudition?

They were quiet a moment, then Lu Chi moved his arms apart, palms up. "You know, Dr. Charles, I'm suddenly thinking of my favorite verse from the *Tao Te Ching*. May I quote it for you in my own English translation?"

"Of course!"

"Thirty spokes share the wheel's hub;
It is the center hole that makes it useful.
Shape clay into a vessel;
It is the space within that makes it useful.
Cut doors and windows for a room;
It is the holes which make it useful.
Profit comes from what is there;
Usefulness from what is not there."

Charles raised his eyebrows high. "Nice," he said, and wordlessly proclaimed himself fully intimidated.

"I will be guided by that, Dr. Charles. I shall endeavor to make as *useful* a translation as I can."

"Can't ask for more. Thanks, Lu Chi! Now, have 24 hours passed? Can you please call me Charlie?"

"Of course, Charlie." He slipped Charles's story into his briefcase. "Is this your first visit to China?"

"Closest I got before was the Chinese Embassy in Moscow."

"How did that work out?"

"Thirty-some years ago I visited the Soviet Union, in my former incarnation as a Russian historian. I was traveling with an adventurous friend who was eager to get to China. You'll recall, no doubt, that borders weren't open much in those days."

"Yes. He was turned down, of course?"

"He was."

"You spoke of your friend as an adventurer. Seems like you were an adventurer too!"

"Are you kidding? I think of myself as a stick in the mud. Aside from that trip and a few visits to Mexico, I've not traveled much. What about you? Been abroad much?"

"One of the lucky ones."

"Oxford?"

His translator smiled. "Yesterday's tie? Sorry, Cambridge. That's where I learned to speak the King's English. And several times to the old Soviet Union and to Russia, hence my friendship with our mutual friend, Gennady."

These last words were uttered quickly, in a way that made it clear Lu Chi was eager to leave. As he fastened the clasp on his briefcase, Charles's stomach growled.

"On another subject," said Charles, rising along with his guest, "where can I find some good Chinese food?"

Making his way toward the entrance hall, Lu Chi chuckled, then paused and leaned against the doorway, thinking.

"Charlie, I have a splendid idea. Do you like Hunan, perhaps? Quite spicy fare?"

"My favorite."

"All right, then. It's going to take me about two weeks to do this translation. So I have a suggestion for what you do while waiting. I've a friend, Yuan Quinjian. Interesting fellow.

Somewhere between the thirtieth and fortieth richest man in China. His factory—and his hand-built palace—are near Changsha, in the southwest, but he flies back and forth all the time. Loves flying. I know him because he's having a sculpture of me done for his palace to add to his statues of Winston Churchill, Lao Tzu, and Martin Luther King."

As if Charles weren't intimidated enough.

"I believe the best Hunan cuisine in China will be found in my friend's cafeteria."

Seriously? wondered Charles.

"I can probably arrange for him to fly you down there, so you can sample his fare and see a different part of the country. Are you game?"

By now they had almost reached the elevator, having left the door of Charles's suite flung wide. Charles was trotting to keep up with the long strides of the Last Emperor of China.

His host was already in the elevator. "I'll set it up and call you tomorrow," he said. "Meanwhile, if you're hungry, call room service. They have excellent sauerbraten."

19

THE THIRTIETH OR FORTIETH RICHEST MAN IN CHINA

AT FIRST, CHARLES didn't take Lu Chi's suggestion seriously. To be personally escorted to Hunan by one of the richest men in China? In a private jet? To sample the meals he served his workers?

Though Charles was not an expert, he felt sure that Chinese was one of the great cuisines in the world. He himself preferred hot, sprightly dishes, but whatever the capsicum quotient or geographical provenance, surely logic dictated that the best meals were to be found in Beijing or Shanghai, or Hong Kong. That was where the high rollers did their business, took their pleasure, and spent their money, was it not? Which meant that everything delectable had long since been plucked from the provinces and funneled into the Big Cities. How and why should some late-blooming capitalist businessman, however beneficent—however rich!—provide four-star smoke-alarm meals for his factory workers? Absurd! And why would *he,* Charles, be invited to experience this?

Less than 36 hours later, however, he found himself in the cockpit of a Gulfstream G150, breasting the thin haze over

Beijing before escaping, with astonishing velocity, into a clean, cloudless blue sky.

Incredible! he thought, swiveling to get a glimpse out the window of the fabled Chinese city whose delights he had barely sampled, now retreating in the distance. The plane's wing dipped left, as the small, sprightly jet aircraft nosed south-southwest. To the north, he could just make out the Great Wall, lumbering its shadowy way across the landscape, looking like one of those large, serpentine dragons he had witnessed on Chinese New Years in New York. *This,* he came close to uttering aloud, *is beyond my wildest dreams.*

"So, I am in the presence of a famous American writer!"

Charles looked over at the man piloting the plane. Mockery? Yuan Quinjian was compactly handsome, neatly barbered. When they'd met in the airport's VIP lounge, he'd been wearing a pair of square-cut, black-framed glasses, which he'd now switched for aviator frames with silvered lenses. In his forties, with wide, smooth forehead and deep-set, appraising eyes, he exuded both confidence and competence. Upon entering the cockpit, he'd shed the jacket from his tailored suit. Now that they'd reached cruising altitude, he smiled and relaxed against the cushioned seatback.

"A writer, yes," said Charles, "but famous? Hardly. Famous is John Updike, God rest his soul. Famous is Philip Roth. Or Toni Morrison. Or . . . I don't know, Jocelyn Lynne Barley, perhaps?"

"Modest too, I see. Talent *and* humility is a rare combination."

His voice, while clear, had a sandpapery edge to it. He spoke in short bursts, enunciating carefully.

Charles's eyes sought the window. Did even the rich and famous long to meet the rich and famous? A Chinese millionaire is impressed by a writer with only a handful of published stories?

We are all star-fuckers, he remembered a long-ago girlfriend sharing with him. Marlynne had socialized with the Hollywood A-list for a time because of highly rated documentary films her ex-husband had made. *Every time I met George Clooney or Warren Beatty*, he could hear her confiding, *it made my panties wet.* The phrase had grabbed his attention, and he'd often wondered: Was she was speaking metaphorically?

"Mr. Yuan," Charles said earnestly, "I am so grateful for this. To be whisked off to Hunan for a meal and a visit? It's like a dream!"

"I am most happy to do it, Dr. Baker. I love flying and company. Did you know I was the first to ever fly a private jet in China? I also retain pilots who fly for me sometimes, when I'm too busy, but since I'm back and forth to Beijing two or three times a week, having friends accompany me is a pleasure."

"Was this the plane you learned in?"

Quinjian laughed. "Hardly! That one is out of date. Mechanics of flying stay much the same, but technology changes. Like cell phones. I own two Gulfstreams and a Cessna Citation X, which is, by a hair, the fastest private jet in the world. You can say this? 'By a hair?' I must watch my English now I am in the company of a famous writer."

Who am I, thought Charles, *to resist such a title?*

Below were hills lightly dusted with snow, baring a few outcroppings of gray rock, and Charles suddenly wondered if this was the country where Lu Chi had his summer home. He thought about asking, but his attention was diverted to the panel of blinking readouts in front of him.

"You examine my instruments," Quinjian noticed. "Would you like to know how they work?"

Charles brightened immediately, wondering, *How do you say "You bet your bippies!!" in Chinese?*

"Could I? They're more daunting than I imagined. Show me everything!"

Yuan spent the next half hour proudly explaining both the mechanics and electronics of his cherished Gulfstream to an enchanted Charles. Following which, a famous American writer—certainly a happy one—retired to the lounge area behind the cockpit to work on his email.

•

They ate nothing on the plane, though the flight took several hours, and Charles began to wonder whether this was a trip to sample food, after all? They eventually touched down at a place Quinjian called Swathtown. As Charles by now expected, the landing was flawless. There ensued a three-minute trip at nail-biting speeds in a gleaming silver Maserati, before they braked to a stop near a low-slung whitewashed building.

Following his host's directions, Charles preceded him into a gleaming kitchen, where he was introduced to a Paul Bunyan-sized man in restaurant whites and a chef's cap. Several others in kitchen whites bustled about. After a few minutes of small talk translated by Quinjian, they entered a large lunchroom, where dozens of colorful tables were arranged at artful angles to each other. Earlier, Charles had tried to imagine the "cafeteria," but *this* was unlike any vision he'd been able to conjure up. Very pleasing. Half the tables were occupied, mostly by women, each wearing smartly designed orange coveralls with tailored sleeves. Across the back of each jumpsuit Chinese characters were stenciled, while the front pockets were inscribed in words Charles could read: *Swath Industries*. Quinjian pointed to a table near the kitchen, where Charles sat alone for a few moments after a uniformed young man had touched Yuan's arm, whispered to him, and drawn him away. The two of them retreated to a corner of the room and engaged in animated conversation.

The spotless lunchroom was done in satisfying pastels. Nice acoustics. Muted conversations. A soft Bach partita drifted from hidden speakers. Five minutes after he'd been seated, while Yuan and his worker were still conversing in the corner, two waiters appeared with tea and food, their fluttery attentions making him feel like a visiting dignitary. Both dishes they offered were pork: the first they called *Mao Shi Hong Shao Rou,* and the second Charles was able to identify, through all the bowing, enunciating, gesturing and pointing at the menu, as *Jia Chang Dou Fu.* Charles had no idea what either name meant, of course; he hadn't understood a thing since his host had been thrust into a makeshift meeting. His attention became focused on a vegetable concoction that reminded him of a small sculpture garden. He dug in. Several dipping sauces tweaked his taste buds with their fiery tang. When the chortling waiter-chefs retreated to the kitchen, Charles was left alone with his chopsticks and his still formidable appetite.

"Sorry," Quinjian apologized, returning to seat himself beside Charles. "Rude of me, but necessary. Your food is enjoyable?"

"Sublime!" Charles said. "Truly! I would not have guessed. Where did you find your giant of a chef? I mean that metaphorically as well as physically! Why is he not cooking in Beijing?"

Quinjian chuckled. "Ah, yes. I believe he would also be a star in New York. Kong Wan is a childhood friend from my village. When he told me his ambition, I arranged his training. I pay him well and he seems happy. As long as he continues to prepare fine meals for my workers, I am happy too."

"Didn't they call one of the dishes *Mao* something?"

"'Mao's red-braised pork,' most likely. A favorite of our late Chairman. Mao the man was not a favorite of mine—you will see he has no place in my statue garden of dignitaries—but his food choices stand the test of time. He came from Hunan, you know. Born only a few miles from here."

Many small dishes followed over the next hour, each better than the last. Charles didn't intend to stuff himself, but the food was irresistible, and he kept thinking *just one more bite.* He feared they would need to roll him out of the room. *Who is this masked man?* he wondered. *This Chinese captain of industry who loves flying and adores food?*

"I'm impressed with your décor, as well," Charles said as he downed his last morsel. "Did you hire an expensive designer to do your cafeteria? Or another childhood friend?"

"Everything myself. Later on, you will see my palace, which I also designed. The flooring is assembled from recycled wooden shipping containers. You see, I started out to be an interior designer. It was through the accident of my brother's invention that I wound up an air conditioning industrialist."

"Invention?"

"A brilliant engineer, my brother. His first invention was a boiler that, contrary to what we had come to expect in China, did not explode. Yes! This was rare! So our boiler became much in demand. With a small stake I had saved from my decorating business, I backed him. We began building boilers on a grand scale. Made a fortune. But when demand lessened, I heard about an unusual design for air conditioners, and I decided: That is the future. Are you finished with your meal, Sir Charles? Come, I will show you my factory."

20

GEORGETOWN, GRAND CAYMAN

T HE STREETS OFF Hero's square were bustling, half with Speedo- and bikini-clad tourists and half with un-rumpled businessmen, most in the white suits so typical of the Cayman Islands, the rest in dark ones of silk or herringbone tweed, much too hot for the strong sun and gentle onshore breeze. These were men who'd just flown in from New York City or Sao Paulo or London or Zurich and would be taking the next plane back from the nearby airport, on much too tight a schedule to switch outfits or enjoy the Caribbean sunshine.

At a teller's window in the Banco Estafadores, SA on Dr. Roy's Drive was a portly fellow in classic Cayman whites, who smiled appreciatively at the lovely caramel-skinned teller and wished her a pleasant day. Across the blue and white Moorish tile floor, he ambled to an empty lobby desk, where he fingered a handful of crisp American hundred dollar bills from a manila envelope and began counting. Smiling to himself even more than he had at the teller, he fitted the envelope into his inside jacket pocket and left the bank.

The Grand Cayman Beach Suites, where he had his rooms, was only a pleasant fifteen minute saunter along Church Street, with the balmy Caribbean waves dancing off to his left and the breeze teasing the brim of his light straw hat. On previous occasions, he'd stayed at the Royal Palms, but he preferred his current accommodations, so close to the diamond-white beach. In front of the motel were scattered a handful of sparkling white tables with colorful beach umbrellas, where you could be served a frothy cappuccino or a stiff Jamaican rum punch to happily punctuate your day. Ah, Grand Cayman! After a month or two spent in the trenches, this was the life!

The man quickly changed into his bathing trunks—a bit more commodious than the skimpy outfits worn by the bronzed and highly muscled men striding along the beach—and hastened to one of those tables, where he ordered a beaker of white rum. He still wore his favored light straw, only now he sported amber shades. Before he left his room, he'd made a few quick calls, and two young women, chosen from a menu he carried around in his head from previous occasions, would arrive at his room at three to haul his ashes for him and share a little coke. In fact, he'd been able to arrange it so that they would be bringing the blow with them. A package deal, so to speak. He smiled at the prospect. One blonde and one dark-skinned beauty, as specified. Both under nineteen, as specified. My, but he was reaping just rewards for half a lifetime spent in the pressure cooker, performing deeds and living among men he could never talk about.

A shadow darkened his table, and he looked up. A man in his forties, dark hair, mustachioed, deeply tanned, with curly body hair that rivaled the undergrowth of a Brazilian rainforest. He carried a canvas beach bag with the imprint of a Greek airline. Both men were silent and expressionless for a full minute. Then both erupted into wide smiles.

"Cavafy!"

"You old sowbelly! How you doing, Beach Ball?" The man's

English was heavily accented, the voice resonant but furry, as if he had a growth of green mold on his tonsils.

The heavyset American nodded toward the other chair. They reached across the table and clasped hands.

"Doing splendidly, you Cypriot beachcomber. How about yourself?"

"Good! Good! In and out. Get to Cayman often as I can, of course. I surprised to hear from you. I t'ought you was retired."

"Oh, you know how it is, lad. Let's just say I'm a consultant. Still earning, but on my own terms. *Kapeesh?*"

The man called Cavafy nodded slowly, tweaked his long moustaches. "You not registered under your old name, Beach Ball. How come?"

Beach Ball's face hardened. "What's that to you? And how do you know?"

The Greek smiled secretively. "It don't matter, BB. I just curious. You know me, I gotta girl works at the motel."

Beach Ball drummed his fingers on the table and looked away. When he looked back he said, "You bring it?"

"Of course! Don't I always?" He unzipped the beach bag and pulled out a folded newspaper with a small, waterproof cigarette case slipped inside. His companion reached into a pocket of his swim trunks and withdrew a tiny white envelope. They made a quick exchange under the cover of the newspaper and all objects disappeared from the table so quickly it was possible to imagine it had never really happened.

"Thanks, Buddy," said the American.

"Anytime, Beach Ball. So, Beach Ball, how long you staying?"

"A few more days. Then on to Sao Paulo for a little more R&R."

"Ah! Man of leisure! I like that! I envy you!"

A waiter happened by, and Beach Ball signaled him for

an extra glass. For another fifteen minutes, they sipped white rum and looked at the Caribbean. Then Cavafy rose and said goodbye, striding strongly back across the island sand. Beach Ball watched him go. Well! Now he could contemplate how he intended to spend the time between 5 p.m. and midnight, after his two comely escorts had performed their services and departed. Now he had the means to induce in himself those astonishing, rococo dreams. He smiled once again. Lies came so easily these days. He had no intention of traveling to Brazil. His return flight to Beijing was booked; he would be on his way at thirty minutes past noon tomorrow.

21
UP, UP, INTO THE WILD BLUE YONDER!

CHARLES ENJOYED HIS time in Swathtown. He, of course, took the guided tour of the factory. He was not only impressed with its spotless condition, but soon learned why Quinjian was so rich. The cordless air conditioners he made—which ran on a solution of lithium bromide—were marketed quite widely, according to Yuan. The Philippines. East Asia. Central Asia. There had even been trial runs in the United States: samples had been purchased by Con Ed in New York, plus there was an extensive installation in Fort Bragg. He said they were also a part of some large, hush-hush project just underway with the American army in Texas. Curiously enough, very few takers in mainland China.

The palace, as both Lu Chi and Yuan Quinjian referred to Quinjian's sumptuous residence, was not only huge—a mélange of exquisitely wrought circles and angles that called to mind Frank Gehry—but was wreathed by elaborate gardens and a circle of sculptures. The sculptures were all realistic likenesses, though larger than life. It surprised Charles to find Churchill, Martin Luther King, Balzac, and Lao Tzu among the subject sculptures. Also portrayed were Alfred Nobel, Pepin the Short, and Sequoya, and yes—just as his translator Lu Chi had claimed—a pedestal had been set aside which would someday bear his likeness. Or was it to be the Lu Chi from A.D. 302? He recalled his translator remarking obliquely that he might be not only the spitting image but also possibly the reincarnation of the great master. So. That would make him, Charles supposed, both the quintessential twenty-first century man, as Charles had silently christened him, and the prototypical fourth century man, as well! Not too shabby.

The only rationale behind Quinjian's choices was, as his host repeatedly asserted, that each one harbored a unique and brilliant vision.

Another surprise of this baronial estate was that the Bach recording Charles had enjoyed over the loudspeakers at that first day's luncheon had been recorded by the homegrown Swathtown orchestra, which consisted exclusively of factory workers (again, mostly women). Their repertoire, in addition to Bach, included Albinoni, Gesualdo, Monteverdi, and—interspersed, without apparent irony—a soupçon of Bob Dylan. The foreman Charles had seen conferring with Quinjian in the cafeteria doubled as the conductor. As he listened to the full recording, Charles decided they played very credibly, equally adept with "Like a Rollin' Stone" and the "Partita in A Major."

In his plentiful spare time, Charles managed through email to firm up his plans for India, his next stop. As his days in Hunan drew to a close, however anxious he might have been to get back to Beijing and to his project (Lu Chi had emailed him that the translation was complete), he found himself a little reluctant to leave. When that moment arrived, however, it was on a day on which Yuan Quinjian had an important sales meeting in Macao. Thus, with many apologies for being an ungracious host, he designated another pilot to fly Charles back to the capital, a big beefy fellow named Shui Jiao, whose droopy eyelids made him look rather sleep-deprived. That made Charles nervous, but since he trusted his host, he did not object. Quinjian assured him that Shui was experienced and quite responsible.

On a crisp winter morning in late December, therefore, Charles became airborne in the same Gulfstream that had flown him to Hunan. After exhausting such topics of conversation as were available to him, given Shui Jiao's limited command of English, Charles quit the cockpit for the lounge, eager to compose email to Lu Chi about his impending arrival. Then he stretched out on the lounge's comfortable cushions and went to sleep.

Forty-five minutes later he woke and stretched. There was a bathroom in the rear of the plane, which he used before making his way forward to the cockpit to check on their progress. Through the windshield up ahead he could see that the plane was on a smooth, level course amid absolutely cloudless skies. But viewed from the back, there was something odd about Shui Jiao's posture. His spine was on a slant, head drooping to one side. Fuck! Had he actually gone to sleep?

Charles approached with a hearty, shouted, "Hey, Jiao! How's it going?" There was no reaction. And in fact, when Charles looked closely, the truth dawned. He reached for Jiao's neck and pulse. With growing alarm, he slapped Jiao across the face several times, an act born more from desperation than any need to confirm the truth. The truth was obvious. The man was utterly, irretrievably, undeniably dead.

•

Now a secret must be imparted. Charles Baker knew how to fly. As a youth, he had piloted a small propeller plane in the company of his father. When the senior Charles had been appointed foreman of that huge corporation farm in California, management had figured it was both prudent and efficient to buy a small Cessna from which he could look over the company's acreage each morning and evening. Young Charles had not only learned to fly alongside his father, but fallen head over heels in love with it. How exhilarating to be up above everyone and everything, soaring like the red-tailed hawks that split the desert air over the ranch! Such excitement! Such power! One hand on the wheel while the other clasped the small, red-knobbed throttle. Pushing the right rudder with your foot and easing the wheel around to achieve a nice, smooth bank. Shoving the throttle forward to collect speed, tugging it back to slow down—carefully! carefully!—too much, and you'll stall! Plummeting down to check on a ditch break, swerving, pulling up and banking hard away from the problem . . . .

However. As indubitably true as the Chinese pilot's indubitable demise, was the noteworthy fact that when Charles had acted as pilot—in that tiny, tiny, single-propeller plane, in that aluminum-bodied, fabric-winged aircraft whose fuselage, tail, struts, engine, and all weighed less than a thousand pounds, in an era forty-some years before, when there were no computers, no autopilot, no GPS, no iPhones, in fact before even the fucking transistor had been invented—he had done so *only while airborne.* Adept enough at banking and climbing, he had never landed a plane.

And now, as Charles studied in mute incomprehension the three-ring circus of accumulating data on the electronic display panel, he shuddered. *Charles, let's not kid ourselves,* he said. *You are going to fucking die!*

117

22
WHAT GOES UP MUST COME DOWN

H E SANK DOWN into the co-pilot's seat and took a deep breath. Having accepted the probability of absolute disaster, what good was fretting?

Let's take stock, he told himself. Ransacking the plane for a parachute? That made no sense to him. Instructions would be in Chinese and he'd probably get the harness on backwards. Would that make him float up instead of down? *Stay focused!* he commanded himself. Radio? He doubted he could connect with anyone that way, since (a) he wasn't really sure how to use it, and (b) if he reached someone, they'd likely be speaking a language he knew very few words in. After *Ni Hao!,* what? On the other hand, why reject even the slimmest chance when you're a high-wire walker on a strand spun out by a silkworm?

He removed the headset from the silent Shui Jiao and fitted it over his own ears, trying to remember what the plane's owner had explained to him on the flight from Beijing. Two weeks ago? It seemed like a lifetime!

He examined what Yuan Quinjian called the yoke or control column. Okay. Buttons, nubs, and knobs along its handles. If he remembered correctly, the white button was the "talk" button. The red one, further down, was the autopilot. Don't mess with that. He pushed the white.

A noise erupted like a convention of locusts revving up to attack a wheat field. When that cleared, he spoke loudly:

"May Day! May Day! Emergency! Does anyone speak English? Charles Abel Baker here. May Day! May Day!"

A nervous laugh as he remembered that his name was a slightly scrambled version of the U.S. military radio alphabet code used during World War Two. Able Baker Charlie. What would someone think who heard it over the radio? That they were in a time warp?

He tried again. Nothing. And again nothing. He'd been told that the console built into the flight deck's wall, with its metallic orchard of flip switches, was the radio. Different channels, he supposed. Different wavelengths? He flipped several, but had no better luck. He slapped the panel a few times, as if trying to dislodge his quarter from a jukebox that wouldn't play his song. Useless.

Okay, just as well, wasn't it? Which dialect of Mandarin that he didn't know how to speak would he have been required to converse in had he managed to make contact?

Suddenly he remembered something. Rising abruptly, he rushed back into the cabin and retrieved his briefcase and laptop. He opened his computer, brought it to life. Here were all the emails he had recently completed, but not sent. Right. Not sent because he hadn't been able to find a connection up here. So he could not email Lu Chi—or even his friend Jonathan in faraway New York—and seek help that way. If you get into trouble, call me, Jon had said. Right. Well. Would you call this trouble? He fished his cell phone out of the pocket of his jeans. A solid minute later, however, he was staring at the phone in consternation. No signal. So what good were those freaking phone numbers? He was tempted to dash the phone against the floorboard, but slipped it back into his pocket instead.

He peered over the jet's nose at the terrain below. Far, far ahead, he could see mountains. He spotted the compass. Due north. *How far north was Russia?* he wondered. *Focus, Charlie!* He looked down. Anyplace down there to land? A river, a highway?

He took a deep breath, squared his shoulders. *Okay, Charles,* he told himself. Fasten your seatbelt. His father's stern voice echoed in his head. *Let's see what you're made of.*

He took hold of the yoke with his right hand and the throttle with his left. He looked where Yuan Quinjian had told him the altimeter was. Gotcha! The airspeed indicator? Yes! Both instruments digital now, not the floppy red needles he remembered from yesteryear, but so what? He'd adjusted to electronic clocks, hadn't he? As long as those two guides were there—height and speed—forget the rest. *Take this baby downstairs, Charlie.* He exhaled sharply, reached down with his right thumb, and pressed the red button to release the autopilot.

•

Ten minutes later, he was having fun.

It was like a roller coaster, only he was driving! He decided where the bumps and curves came. The plane's instant response to each suggestion of his fingers became a thing of joy. You want to go left? Turn the yoke, apply the rudder gently and, by God, you peeled off to the left! If the aim was to bear right, same thing in reverse. If you wished to descend, you pushed the yoke gently forward and—because it picked up speed very quickly— eased back on the throttle. He overdid it at first but he learned, and gained confidence.

Within half an hour, he felt almost as much at home as he'd felt years ago in his father's Cessna. A teenager again. A sixteen-year old flyboy with thunder in his heart and a world of possibilities ahead of him.

"You're wasting time, Buddy," he told himself. "Time to go down." He eased back on the throttle, could feel the plane dropping immediately. It flashed through his mind from Yuan's lecture that the landing speed was two hundred miles per hour. He must remember that.

Fifteen thousand. Fourteen thousand. Twelve. At five thousand feet, he leveled off. It seemed a good height from which to survey the possibilities. But finding nothing that looked suitable for landing, he decided to go lower.

At three thousand, you could see more. But it was scarier because it made the ground real. You could really see the landscape in detail now, its curves and dips, its plateaus. What the rapidly shifting landscape also made plain to him was how much faster this plane was moving than that long-ago Cessna.

Roads, if any, should be visible now, he thought. *A road, please! Doesn't anyone drive in this frigging country?* What he saw was only bleak terrain, bare of anything save spotty sagebrush. The countryside seemed uninhabited.

Then suddenly, banking right, he spotted a road. A straight one, with no cars in sight. *Hallelujah!* But his elation was momentary. The road was narrow, and a flickering row of telephone poles ran alongside it. The plane's wings would be snapped off like matchsticks. He sighed. This was not going to be easy.

Amidst this discouragement, however, he looked straight ahead and: *voila*! A river appeared. How sweet was that? The river lay flat and straight, and on the near side of it was a lake. Couldn't be better. Now he wouldn't even have to lower the wheels. With a huge sigh, he banked the plane around to regroup and line it up properly for a good approach.

He told himself: "Land on the lake, Charlie. Let your momentum glide you up to the mouth of the river, where it will be easy enough to reach the shore on either side. You're almost home, boy."

He kept muttering as he fiddled with the approach. "Watch that gauge. No less than two hundred miles per. You have to make it to the water. Don't stall. You're dropping too fast, Charlie! Goose it, goose it! Woops! Too much! Back off, stretch out. Good, good. Piece of cake now. Straight ahead, here we are, here we are. My target. The near edge of the lake. Perfect. Just perfect. Water on the lake calm, white—WHITE? JESUS CHRIST! I'M LANDING ON ICE!"

His mind now raced like a computer, clacking out ones and zeros, searching for what Yuan Quinjian had told him about the landing gear. Suddenly, he remembered. Just as the plane swooped past the lake's front edge, a couple of hundred feet above the surface, he pulled a lever and the wheels deployed. *Sensational! Only a few seconds to touchdown.* He cut the power, fighting to keep the nose level. *Gently does it. Soon . . . soon . . . there!* The plane dropped, struck, bounced, settling at last on the hard surface. But though he cut the throttle immediately, the plane was still going fast. *Too fast?* Trees on either side a green blur. Did Yuan Quinjian tell him how to reverse the thrust? Yes! That tiny, baby throttle on top of the big one. He jerked it back, heard the roar and felt the deceleration.

Still too fast maybe? Now he remembered that the tops of the rudders, once on the ground, act as brakes. So he pushed down hard and, in milliseconds, realized his mistake. *THIS IS ICE!* He could feel the aircraft swerving to the right. He pressed the left pedal to shift direction, but it did no good. Control was a thing of the past. The plane continued its swerve, not heading for the middle of the river, but skidding toward a rocky promontory at the river's mouth.

Blood drained from his face. *SHIT OH SHIT OH SHIT!* As the rocks grew larger, he grew paralyzed, unable even to comply with the sensible command he'd heard over and over in movies about such emergencies: "Brace for impact!"

23
BETWEEN SOMEWHERE
AND SOMEWHERE ELSE

H E OPENED HIS eyes. Blurred figures, muted colors. Blue, green, gold passed back and forth before him. Were these shades? Silken ones, if so. Shades like the shades of his feelings. Now he could hear a soft hum in the air, rising and falling, gaining rhythm and pitch, supple, murmurous, gentle. Human speech. Those vaguely moving shapes were people. There it was: laughter! At him?

He tried to clear his throat, but it emerged as a groan. One of the shapes separated itself from the others and sank down beside him. He was lying in a bed, he realized. A face, a pretty face, assembled itself out of the mist. An oval face, narrowing toward the chin. A pair of large eyes with dark lashes. Black hair surrounding the face, like a fluffed pillow.

A musical chime issued from the small mouth. A pause. Then, in English, each word distinct, like a dropped lead weight: "How. Are. You. Feel. Better?"

Now that his pretty vision, if she was a vision, had asked, he did in fact begin to feel. His head throbbed. His ribs ached.

A sharp pain slithered down the side of his right leg, dived off into his toes.

"Too early to tell," he tried. "Where am I?"

"Stream of Wandering Spirits," said the voice slowly. "Our village." Even in English, the effect was musical. "I am Gou Ming. You remember who you?"

The blurred colors in the distance were in stasis now. Only this young woman was clear. Almost clear.

"Charles, I think. Yes, Charles. Charles Baker. American."

"We guess. Your driver license. You been long time sleep."

"Yes?"

"Oh, yes. Three day now."

"Oh, my! How did I get here?"

A blue color detached itself from the still life in the distance and moved closer. A pleasant-looking middle-aged man sank down beside the young woman.

"I am Gou Jin. This my daughter. She take care of you. We hear crash. Pick you out of wreck, bring you to Wandering Spirits."

Charles tried to smile, succeeding only feebly. He struggled to rise, and fell back. "Thank you," he managed. "I'm lucky to be alive."

"Yes," Mr. Gou said. "Plane smash up bad. Other man not so lucky."

"Umm," said Charles. "Yes, other man not lucky at all." He tried again to raise his head, but found the effort beyond him.

"Rest," said the sweet-voiced young woman. "When you awake up, we feed you."

•

He awoke the next day feeling better and managed to sit up. Through a straw, they fed him a clear broth distilled from a kind of mushroom they scraped (as he learned) from the side of their porch. Before the end of the day, he had managed to stumble out of bed and hobble a few steps. Nothing appeared to be broken, but he was sore all over and his head throbbed incessantly. He went back to bed, dozed and woke intermittently, was fed more broth. And the next day, a kind of whey or mush; he didn't ask. It was warm and sweet, and he began to eat with greater appetite. He had discovered that his briefcase and laptop were rescued along with him, and appeared to have survived the crash better than his own body. Thank God for plastics.

He wrote no one, called no one. The villagers asked no more questions, content to treat him as their guest. Charles had never known such kindness. Gou Ming was in constant attendance. She found him a sturdy tree branch, trimmed it of leaves and bark. With that, he could support his weight more bearably when he tried to walk, and he began to venture out farther and farther each day. On the third or fourth day of his reawakening, he had a visit from the leader of the village, a Director Tian. Here too there were no probing questions. Mr. Tian asked after his health, appeared sad that his plane had been destroyed, said they had buried the other man. Charles, in return, volunteered nothing about how he had come to be in the plane, or why.

Stream of Wandering Spirits. Where had he heard that name? This puzzle rose to his mind periodically, but he made no effort to tease it out. He was recovering; that was what was important, that was everything. Each day he grew stronger. Each day his hurts lessened. What else mattered? Everyone was so friendly. He began to speak Chinese phrases. *Hello. Goodbye. How are you? I'm fine. Thank you. I'm hungry. I'm thirsty.* If he went out walking, everyone bowed and doffed their caps. He bowed in return. He would accept this paradise until he felt completely healed and could find a way to thank them, for real.

One evening, snug in the cabin that had been his home for several weeks, he basked in the glow of a flickering fireplace and in the further warmth of Gou Ming, who was kneeling beside him. For the first time, he put his hand on her arm, worked it down until it brushed the top of her hand, took that hand in his own. He was aroused; his own heart was beating like a tom-tom; he could see her small breasts rising and falling under her kimono.

"Gou Ming," he whispered.

"Yes?" she said, her lashes still shielding her eyes.

"Please improve my vocabulary. How do you say 'You are so beautiful!' in Chinese?"

She made no answer, but did not object when, a moment later—trembling, almost sick with want—he kissed her.

•

The very next morning, out early and wandering farther afoot than he'd been, he was enjoying the unusual warmth of the day. Marveling at the mist that was now burning off as the sun climbed the sky, he limped joyously, with his stick, along a packed dirt path edging the river that flowed beside the village. He'd learned it was named the Zhou, and was the source of the lake into which he had crash-landed the plane, farther downstream. Now that the weather had warmed, the water coursed along freely enough, not a shred of ice to be seen. He rounded a bend. In the distance were the mountains he'd heard called Shaman. He spied a Buddhist monastery he'd been told about, resting on a promontory midway between the river and the distant peak. And there, in the river, beyond a small forest of reeds, he saw a man fishing.

But this was extraordinary! The man was Lu Chi! No question! Except this Lu Chi was older, much older. Beyond the robed figure with the ends of his garment tucked into his sash, on the far bank, was an apple orchard where fat birds dived and jostled with one another, uttering fierce, staccato shrieks. Were those waxwings, flitting about that tree on the left? How did he even know the name? Were those others grosbeaks? This sudden knowledge surprised him. Of course he knew sparrows, hawks, eagles, wild doves, crows—birds he'd seen in his youth on the ranch. But these? How would he have any idea what they were?

The opening lines of a poem—the Nemerov poem called "To Lu Chi"—came to him:

> *Old sir, I think of you in this tardy spring,*
> *Think of you for, maybe, no better reason*
> *Than that the apple branches in the orchard*
> *Bear snow, not blossoms, and that this somehow*
> *Seems oddly Chinese. I, too, when I walk*
> *Around the orchard, pretending to be a poet*
> *Walking around the orchard, feel Chinese,*
> *A silken figure on a silken screen*
> *Who tries out with his eye the apple branches,*
> *The last year's rotten apples capped with snow,*
> *The hungry birds. And then I think of you.*

That was it! He searched his mind now for other parts of the poem. Something about a stream, a pure, reed-hidden stream. Something about a heron "fishing in its own image?" Yes! He remembered now! He looked again at this older version of Lu Chi as the words came back to him:

I have a sight of you,
Your robes tucked in your belt, standing
Fishing that stream, where it is always dawn
With a mist beginning to be burned away
By the lonely sun. And soon you will turn back
To breakfast and the waking of the world
Where the contending war lords and the lords
Of money pay to form the public taste
For their derivative sonorities.
But yet that pure and hidden reach remains.

He called out, cupped his hands and called again. But though the day was still, and his voice should have carried easily, the man did not hear, or chose not to acknowledge that he did. The figure continued serenely on, casting his line again and again.

24
WHITE LIGHTS, BIG CITY

H E AWOKE TO the *thirp! thirp! thirp!* of an electronic machine. After a moment, his vision cleared and he could see, standing within spitting distance—though his mouth felt too dry to spit—two figures in white, a man and a woman. Much buzz and bustle in the background. Everything white, except for the tubes threaded into his arms. The woman he'd spotted, middle-aged and dumpy, with a nurse's cap on her broad forehead, noticed his alertness. Raising her eyebrows, she advanced, chirping.

"Mr. Baker! You are awake! Welcome back! All is well!" Her English was perfectly understandable, though heavily accented and a bit stilted, as if she had practiced its articulation for hours in front of a mirror.

"Excuse me? Where am I?"

"You are in the Xinhua Hospital of the Beijing Red Cross, Mr. Charles. We are delighted to see that you have returned to the world at last!"

"But . . . where's the village? I don't get it. Where's Gou Ming?"

"Gou who? I don't know any Gou Ming, Mr. Charles. Nobody who works here, certainly. I am Chen Hong. Perhaps a dream while you were out, no?" Her smile was broad and kind.

"No, no! This is impossible! Since I've been . . . what? How long have I been 'out,' as you say?"

"Well, let's see." She examined a chart at the side of the bed, tapping a pencil against her lips. "Your coma has lasted . . . almost ten weeks. Really! We are so happy to see you! I must call Doctor Li."

"Hold on! My coma? Ten weeks! But . . . I don't understand! That's impossible! I only—"

"Nevertheless, Mr. Baker. Ten weeks—" She checked the chart. "—tomorrow. It is late March now, you know? My goodness, you were banged up. But you are almost healed now. And awake at last. I go for the doctor."

"Wait! Wait! Hold on!" Charles was bewildered and close to despair. "Where's my stuff?"

"Stuff? Oh, would that be your briefcase and laptop? It is my understanding that when you were airlifted here those items came with you. Your friend Dr. Lu has them, over at Beijing University, I have heard. Would you like me to call him for you? He visits often. He will be so happy you have returned to the land of the living!"

Charles's confusion was being replaced by a physical anxiety. He could feel it begin in his toes with a tingle, then spread to his knees, thighs, groin. It danced along his stomach lining, then rose through his chest to his jawbone. His lips begin to vibrate.

Beijing! Where was Gou Ming? Where was Stream of Wandering Spirits? Had it all been a dream, then? Surely not. It was too real. He wanted to go back. To feel those soft lips of hers once more. The warmth of that special sun, near the apple trees and the reeds. And the stream! He wanted it all back. He blinked rapidly a few times, and then expelled a bellows-full of warm air from his chest. His eyes teared up.

A dream, then. This was the real world. Gou Ming and the Village had never been.

Or maybe . . . maybe *this* was the dream. If so, how could he wake himself up?

•

Two things made it evident the very next day that his current reality was not a dream: Lu Chi, and the Chinese translation. The valise and computer had been recovered, exactly as the nurse had said, and Lu Chi had taken them to his office for safekeeping. Smiling, but with a look of concern on his handsome face, Lu Chi now returned them to Charles's bedside. After making repeated apologies for the misfortune that had happened in his country, he showed Charles the translation, in print, and waved in the air the CD onto which the digital copy was written. He had labeled it clearly, in English, so it would be unmistakable. Charles squeezed his friend's hand feebly in thanks—he had a way to go to regain his full strength—and related the story of Shui Jiao's death and the airplane's crash as best he could remember. But he said nothing about Stream of Wandering Spirits, a name that was already beginning to sound ironic to him. Lu Chi told him that Yuan Quinjian was mortified at what had happened, and eager to make it up to him any way he could.

"I am so happy you are recovering, Dr. Baker. I was very worried, as was my friend, Quinjian. By the way, I noticed you had some unsent emails on your laptop. Would you like me to send them for you?"

"Thanks, but no. I'll take care of it. Thanks for the reminder, though."

When the nurse stepped in to announce that visiting hours

were over and he would need to leave, Lu Chi departed, assuring Charles he would be back the following day.

•

After Lu Chi had left, Charles found the Chinese translation in his computer case. He pursed his lips as he examined the first page:

喜悦回归

迷雾的**新媳妇**--农场上的人们马上就开始这么叫她--还不到三十岁，有一头披肩的黑发，她丰满的嘴唇微微张开着，露出一排不太整齐的门牙。年少的杰弗里-霍金斯被她修长，匀称的腿迷住了。在单薄的印花连衣裙下，不难看到她诱人的身体曲线。虽然除了墨西哥人，农场上几乎所有的人都是从俄克拉何马州或阿肯色州来的，杰弗里还是怀疑伊尔丽是通过邮件邮寄来的。她自己也**时不时地露出破绽**，**让人看**出她是个虔诚的基督教徒，有一天，甚至**来看**杰弗里的妈妈，跟她谈起了**宗教**信仰。

杰弗里听到过不少诅咒的话和**有关烧得很旺的锅炉的事**，他很害怕。他妈妈不知从哪里弄到两本皮装的福音书，给他和他姐姐露西，还给了他书签上的用缎带编织的十字。因此，实际上，上帝的能赎心灵之罪的爱，对杰弗里来说并不陌生。但是，在**第48**个炎热的礼拜天中午，当**看到**伊尔丽坐在他们的厨房里，不停地给自己扇扇子，他感到了一种不知名的**兴奋**。**不会**是因为基督的原因吧？

Well, there it was, wasn't it? The first translation into a language he knew nothing about and, obviously, could not read. He let his eyes slither among the slopes and curlicues, the swoops and crosshatchings, imagining he could understand them. What did they convey that was the same as, or different from, what he had written? A small bird fluttered in his chest as he realized he was truly on his way. Damaged, but on his way.

25

THE TWENTY-SEVENTH MOST SPOKEN LANGUAGE IN THE WORLD

"PROPERLY DONE, SIR, you are translating not just a story, but a whole culture! With all its trappings and subdivisions, with all its traps!"

Traps! The word jolted Charles, sending a small shudder through his body. He thought briefly of the traps for badger and coyote that had been set in the early days of the ranch where he grew up. Of animal carcasses strung out endlessly on fence posts along the road leading into the foothills.

The parchment-skinned man sitting in a tattered wicker chair in his office at Bangalore University leveled his gaze at Charles. He spoke with professorial authority, though his appearance—tangled white beard straggling down his blue tunic until it vanished behind the desk, loose-jointed thumbs circling each other like prizefighters looking for an opening—called to mind a photograph Charles had once seen, of an old hermit who'd lived some forty years in an Adirondack cave. Professor Pericles Mahanthappa's nose was thinner, perhaps, and longer, and, unlike the hermit's, looked as if it might be about to melt into the rest of his face.

"A culture, Mr. Charles, which is made up of its *own* stories, its own religions and superstitions, its high and low castes, its racism, its dress and mannerisms, its economics of waste, privilege, and privation, its attitudes towards art, towards mechanics, towards the natural world . . . towards butterflies! Towards dreams!" The rheumy eyes twinkled, but the cannon shots fired across the bow of Charles' drifting attention did not stop. "Its humanity and generosity, Mr. Charles. Its sense of the power and limits of the individual. Its attitudes towards *yoni* and *lingam*."

Wait! Charles thought. *Wasn't that . . . .*

"Its attitudes towards love, sir. And rain. And blowing wind." The last few sentences were accompanied by a series of robust hand- and arm-gestures, and a smile that advanced then ebbed like a beach tide at sunset.

"Towards melancholy, towards death."

With these last words, which even in their utterance had the feeling of finality, Mahanthappa's hands fell back into his lap. His eyes closed, his chin sank. Caught as he was in a shaft of sunlight burrowing through the tall, leaded window, he suddenly made Charles think of a dried apricot, all juice evaporated, nothing but withered orange skin remaining. As the moment grew longer, Charles began to fear the old gentleman had expired on the spot.

Charles had used the Internet while still in China, to read up on Mahanthappa. The professor's father, long since passed away, had also been a scholar, specializing in Athenian democracy; hence his selection of his son's name. Well, thought Charles, now what? He fretted as the moment continued. He furrowed his brow and pursed his lips. A Chinese pilot had perished in his presence. Had he become a bad-luck charm? A sort of inverse rabbit's foot?

He cleared his throat. No movement. Should he summon help? Just as he was rising to seek someone, he saw a small stir in the ancient's eyelids. Charles resettled himself, and decided to speak as if nothing unusual had happened.

"I couldn't agree more, Professor Mahanthappa. I guess that's the challenge a truly great translator sets himself. Working in those important cultural subtleties. I'm thrilled you're taking my project so seriously."

Mahanthappa beamed, full of energy once again, the sap returned. The brief siesta seemed to have done him good. He now looked—except for the beard—like a travel agent about to offer his prospective client a premium package.

"You have come to the right place, Mr. Charles! I will transmute your story from one culture to another with great pleasure and precision. Chinese to Indian, Mandarin to Kannada. You have chosen, in fact, a language most ancient and formidable. From the Dravidian family, one of the oldest! Kannada is, in my opinion, the finest of the twenty-two languages we officially recognize in India, a sublime vehicle for contemporary short stories."

Charles felt the urge to raise his hand, a student again in a freshman lecture course. "Excuse me, Professor Mahanthappa," he said rather timorously, "could I see what the alphabet looks like? Do you have a sample text of some sort? I'd just like to see it."

"Of course, of course!"

Mahanthappa swiveled in his chair and pointed to a blackboard at the side of the room. "Ummmm," he said, and again, "Oooff!" as he struggled to rise. "Uh, would you mind, sir, taking hold of that ring and yanking it down?"

Charles looked to where the professor's wobbly hand was pointing. It was like a wall map, he saw. He pulled it down all the way.

"And there you have it," Professor Mahanthappa said proudly from behind him.

ಎಲ್ಲಾ ಮಾನವರೂ ಸ್ವತಂತ್ರರಾಗಿಯೇ ಜನಿಸಿದ್ದಾರೆ. ಹಾಗೂ ಘನತೆ ಮತ್ತು ಹಕ್ಕು ಗಳಲ್ಲಿ ಸಮಾನರಾಗಿದ್ದಾರೆ. ವಿವೇಕ ಮತ್ತು ಅಂತಃಕರಣ ಗಳನ್ನು ಪಡೆದವರಾದ್ದರಿಂದ ಅವರು ಪರಸ್ಪರ ಸಹೋದರ ಭಾವದಿಂದ ವರ್ತಿಸಬೇಕು.

"My," said Charles simply, as he returned to his chair and studied the text. And repeated it. "My, my! It's beautiful! What does it say?"

He could hear the satisfaction, almost a smugness, creep into Mahanthappa's voice. "That is Article 1 of the Universal Declaration of Human Rights. Do you know it? 'All human beings are born free and equal in dignity and rights. They are endowed with reason and conscience and should act towards one another in a spirit of brotherhood.'"

"Yea, verily!" said Charles. "A noble sentiment, indeed!" He folded his lips inward in a gesture of satisfaction and turned back to face his story's next translator.

The latter was quiet again, eyes closed, posture relaxed. Drooping, in fact. Different from the previous silence, but still, Charles worried. A form of meditation? How did one spot the difference between relaxation and catalepsy? He decided to wait it out, and sure enough, a few moments later, the man's ghost took on flesh once more. Someone had reached out and given the Victrola's arm a yank.

"Thirty-five million people speak it, Mr. Charles, most here in Karnataka. Fewer than Hindi, but still. Not to be sneezed at, correct? The twenty-seventh most spoken language in the world."

"And, as I believe you told me in your email, winner of seven Jnanpith awards—am I pronouncing that correctly?"

"Yes, yes! Our Pulitzer. No language in India has produced fiction that has won so many accolades."

26
FENDING OFF THE FOOD WALLAHS

ALL THE WAY back to the Comfort Inn Vijay Residency, though the midday sun was bright and hot, Charles felt himself wading through a fog of exhaustion. If he hadn't been tired already, Mahanthappa's peroration would have been enough to drain him.

It had been a long trip from Beijing to Bangalore, and he'd barely had time to check into his hotel before rushing to his appointment at the University. Twenty-three hours, with three stopovers: Hong Kong, Bangkok, and Mumbai. Sweet Cheeks Airways (possibly a bad translation?) might be a puddle-jumper airline, but what choice did he have? A direct flight might have bankrupted him. Even this route had erased almost a thousand dollars from his dwindling budget. How fortunate that his China trip—he felt buoyant when he remembered—had been virtually expense-free. First the luxury hotel Lu Chi had booked him into, then being ferried back and forth to Hunan province (of course the return trip had nearly cost him his life), finally a prolonged hospital stay that had been paid for by . . . someone. The International Red Cross? The nation of China? The City of Beijing? His bet was Yuan Quinjian's insurance; all he knew was, he'd never seen a bill.

As he walked, he waved off the sporty yellow motorized rickshaws, ignoring as well the samosa-wallahs, the aloo tiki-wallahs, and all others who urged their savories on him from the street. Still others were selling lassi, that yogurt drink he'd once tried—and enjoyed—in New York. Although not bhang lassi, he thought, which he saw painted in crude lettering on the sides of their carts, having become recently aware of the Indian word for *cannabis*. Right! Welcome to India. At the moment, he yearned only for the American-style coffee bar he'd seen in the hotel, where he would revive himself with a cappuccino before flopping into bed. He could then sleep, he hoped, for the same number of hours it had taken him to get here.

A fly buzzed round his head and he batted it away. Too bad he couldn't have come overland, but a few mountains blocked the way. Should he have tried to backpack across the Hindu Kush? He'd spent so much time in Beijing—most of it unconscious—that it was now April. Time to start planning in earnest the trip to Mexico, which he'd already selected as the next stop, mainly because a fellow at Santa Teresa University named Amalfitano was conversant with Kannada. Choosing Kannada had a downside: it was hard finding anyone outside of India who knew it.

Suddenly—before awareness dawned as to why he had stopped—he found himself as still as the stacked boulders at Stonehenge. The smell had come first perhaps, pungent but familiar. In all events, there she was. A cow.

The beast stared directly at him from the middle of the street, wet nose shining, beautiful candelabrum ears batting at flies, loose-jointed jaws moving side to side in a motion older perhaps than mankind, big, long-lashed brown eyes unblinking. And Charles stared back. Not because of its horns, though they were striking. One had been painted turquoise, along with a sprinkle of other colors and an inverted teardrop pattern in white. The other had a similar design, but the base color was orange. However, it wasn't the cornucopia of colors that had stopped him. Not at all.

Cleo! he said to himself. He walked up to the cow, draped his arm across her withers, leaned his cheek against her neck, squeezed hard and began fondling her dewlap. "Hello, Cleo," he said. "Hello, good girl."

The cow was clearly not a Jersey, but a Brahman, *Bos Indicus*. Nevertheless, the feeling that grabbed him was sudden and reflexive. Had Cleo's soul somehow migrated into this body?

•

His father had purchased Cleo from a neighboring farmer when Charles was ten. No one but Charles had milked her. Once his buddy, Ignacio, had departed from the ranch, Cleo had become Charles's closest friend. He'd walked her every morning to Jonson's Well, near Dead Man's Creek, so she could eat fresh grass, returning her in the evening to the shelter he'd helped build. Sometimes he'd whisper his troubles to her, as they stood beside her lean-to gazing at the desert sunset.

Cleo had died when Charles was fifteen; it had been his fault. She'd eaten too much bran from a barrel whose cover he'd absent-mindedly left off. Once she'd drunk water, the flakes of bran had swollen, and thus her belly, beyond its capacity. She was in agony; they'd had to put her down.

•

Charles laid a kiss on *Bos Indicus*'s neck and moved on. Past the revolving doors of his hotel he paused to let his eyes adjust to the reduced lighting. He found the coffee lounge and ordered a cappuccino, ignoring a bustling clutch of people in conversation at the coffee bar, and a man fiddling with some kind of equipment in a dark corner. After stirring sweetener into his cappuccino, he leaned back in his chair and sighed.

The days he'd spent in China recovering from injuries still puzzled him. Stream of Wandering Spirits had seemed so real—as vivid as childhood, as memories of Ignacio or Cleo—yet the fact of his coma had compelled him to regard it as a dream. Yet how could Gou Ming not be real? He could still smell her hair. Hear the music of her voice. What sort of breathtaking opium dream had she been?

Svetlana was real, wasn't she? Of course she was. So why, if Gou Ming was a dream, would he invent her, and not simply dream of Svetlana? Damn! Was there anyone who could understand these things?

He sipped his beverage, bought a package of peanuts from a vending machine, and began munching. He'd not even been aware he was hungry.

Following his release from the hospital in Beijing, there'd been an inquest. A plethora of officials—including, he suspected, some insurance lawyers—had asked questions about the plane crash. Questions directed not only to him, but to Yuan Quinjian and Lu Chi, as well. Toward him, the questions seemed gentle and polite. Even the wife and children of the pilot, Shui Jiao—who'd wept openly in court—did not rise to demand some sort of punishment, as he'd feared they might. After all, they had only his word that Shui Jiao had died of natural causes. There'd been no autopsy, since Jiao had been buried earlier by the villagers from Stream of Wandering Spirits, and . . . no, wait! I'm getting this wrong! Wandering Spirits was a false memory!

To be perfectly honest, he had no idea where Shui Jiao was buried, or if he was buried at all. Most of the inquiry had been conducted in Chinese and—though someone had translated the questions put to him—most of what got said in court had escaped him.

Another curious thing. The hearing was conducted over five days, and throughout that entire time, a stout man of medium height, American by the look of him, had sat in the back of the court and said nothing. After the proceedings had concluded, Charles had asked Lu Chi about him, but his friend had said he could not even recall the man's presence. The stranger had taken no notes and was therefore, Charles thought, unlikely to have been a reporter. Nor did he offer testimony. Not once did he raise his hand or even clear his throat. Charles might not have remembered him at all had it not been for the small, slow smile the stranger conferred on him that last day, just before he slipped out of court.

27
CAUGHT!

CHARLES YAWNED AND stood, finally relaxed enough to retire upstairs.

Suddenly, there was a blinding flash of light, and three men burst into the room, black ski masks pulled over their heads and automatic weapons pointed. Orders were barked in an unfamiliar language as they began firing. Glass shattered. Table tops splintered and flew through the air. Customers were hurled against tables and walls, writhing and moaning. Or collapsed like rag dolls, silently. All this Charles saw in the one and a half seconds before he dove under his table.

Though out of sight now, he was convinced he'd be dead in a heartbeat. He scrunched himself into as small a space as possible. As the din of gunfire and all things shattering continued, he clenched his teeth, squeezed his eyes tight shut. He willed himself to become invisible.

For a while longer, chaos reigned. Then came a pause, a lacuna, a charged silence. He imagined his neck slipped into the lunette of a guillotine; this was the lull before the blade drops. He ached to draw a breath.

"CUT!"

It was a woman's voice. Charles shuddered. Here it comes,

then! Next would be the order to decapitate anyone who'd survived the gunfire.

A muffled conversation began instead. Next, a brisk crashing sound, as if shards of glass were being swept off a table. Eyes still shut, he felt a small rustle of air and realized that the tablecloth under which he'd sought refuge had been lifted.

Words he could not make out (muffled by a mask?) were directed at him. In English, but with a marked Indian accent. Was he being taken hostage?

He opened his eyes. He saw only two large legs at first, then raised his eyes along the trunk of a huge body. The assailant had no face, only a smooth black stump on top of immense shoulders.

Then the mask was swept off, revealing a boyish brown face—square-jawed, curly-headed, smiling—a high school football hero respectfully addressing his prom date's father. "Sir? You can come out now. It's okay. It's just a movie."

•

A moment later, heart threatening to burst out of his chest, he found himself escorted by the Uzi-wielding thug (or *actor*, perhaps, Charles was still unsure) to a table in an adjoining room. A sari-clad woman with blue-black hair sat talking with several earnestly gesticulating people. The moment he arrived in front of her, she swiveled to face him. She smiled and his mouth fell open.

"Arundhati Roy!'

She stared at him dead on for several seconds while her compatriots sniggered. "Well, I'm flattered you recognized me, sir. And I apologize that we got you embroiled in all this! Here's the truth. We noticed you shortly after you came in—we already had the scene organized and were just waiting for the lighting to be set up—and my DP asked me, should we let him stay or escort him off the set? I played a hunch. I decided, since you really looked like you needed a cup of coffee, that I didn't have the heart to ask them not to make one for you. Well, that part's not totally true. To be honest, I was curious how our scene would play out with a real potential victim. And a westerner at that! American, right?"

Charles could only stare at her. He should be furious, he knew, but this was Arundhati Roy!

"It seemed like such a good idea at the time," she continued. "Nevertheless, I do apologize! Did we scare you dreadfully?"

"I think I'm still scared. So all this was just a movie?"

"*Is* a movie, sir. *Is* a movie. But forgive me, I haven't asked your name." She extended her hand.

"Charles Baker, American writer. But are you really Arundhati Roy?"

She laughed, then looked up at her cohorts, all of whom were grinning.

"Actually, no, Mr. Baker. I'm her younger sister, Sejal."

She looked at her crew again and winked. "We've always looked like twins. So how do you know my sister?"

"I read *The God of Small Things* years ago and thought it brilliant!"

"How nice of you to say so. I'll pass that along, the next time I'm in Kerala, if I can tear her away from one of her political rallies long enough to say hi."

She shuffled some papers. "Now. Mr. Baker, some important questions. First, do you forgive me for including you in my movie? Second, can we use this footage, or must I ask them to destroy this room and all its glassware once again? If you're OK with it, would you be willing to attest to that decision with a waiver? Third, do I need to pay you?"

Charles was no longer terrified, but his mind was doing cartwheels. When he'd seen Arundhati's picture on the back of her book, all those years ago, he hadn't imagined anyone could look more beautiful. But that old saw was correct: *If you think a woman is beautiful, wait till you see her younger sister!*

"I saw her interviewed once," Charles began, "on Charlie Rose. Together with Salman Rushdie. She was stunning."

Sejal had wrinkled up her nose at the mention of Rushdie's name. "Ah, yes, Arundhati and Salman. On opposite sides of the political fence, these days. But anyway . . . ."

She looked down at some papers, tapped her fingernails, then looked back up. "Thank you again for your several compliments, Mr. Charles. Even though so far they're directed only at my sister, with whom I don't always see eye to eye. But we need to take care of some business here. I tell you what. Can you meet me tomorrow for lunch? We'll talk then. About your writing, and about my movie. Even about Arundhati, if you insist. How's that?"

Half an hour later, a new date scribbled into his appointments calendar in red ink, Charles stretched out on the bed in his small but comfy room, the excitement of the last hour finally beginning to wane, hoping against hope he would at last be able to sleep.

28

FALLING ASLEEP IN THE EAST; DREAMING OF THE WEST

C HARLES SLEPT FOR twelve hours, and dreamed of Indians. Not from the Punjab or the Deccan Plateau. Instead, he found himself unexpectedly in Oklahoma, in the cabin of Sequoya, the inventor of the Cherokee writing system. The year was 1829.

"I'm thrilled to meet you, sir. I've long admired you for developing a written language for the Cherokee."

This edition of Sequoya was tall. Why not? A tree had been named in his honor. He held himself comfortably erect, puffing contentedly on a slender, curved pipe. His eyes sparkled. An outsized turban exaggerated his height further, spinning wide swaths of alternating red and white bands around his head. A sweater of thick blue wool draped his upper body, its relaxed fit and loose weave suggesting a Christmas present one's aunt (or dear wife) might have knitted.

The effect was both formal and informal. The desk where he sat was cluttered with open books, papers, ink, quill pens. A fireplace in the cabin blazed, and the sounds and smells of a meal being prepared came from the kitchen. A radio playing Johnny Mathis caused Charles a moment of surprise, but when Tony Bennett came on, he shrugged his shoulders and relaxed.

Although his host appeared completely accommodated to the cabin's sweltering heat, Charles was sweating.

"It was an amazing accomplishment!" he continued. "I've heard that Cherokee tribe members without previous knowledge of letters found themselves able to read the Cherokee newspaper straightaway."

An almost imperceptible bow from Sequoya. He fingered a silver medallion he wore around his neck.

"I prefer not to boast. That lovely rumor exaggerates the facts somewhat."

Charles's eyes grew wide as he watched the smoke from his host's pipe form a large letter in the air. A capital R.

"People still needed teaching," said Sequoya, "but it didn't take long to make readers of them."

"Very impressive in any event. But excuse me! On your desktop there. Is that your syllabary?"

Sequoya was quick to respond. "Not *my* syllabary, *the* syllabary. The Cherokee syllabary!"

Charles scooted his cane chair closer to examine the paper more carefully. The first letter was an R. After that came a D and a W, each in a distinctive font. Other letters suggested different borrowings, though additional Latin letters emerged: a second R turned up, its right leg thicker than the first, and without an upward thrust at the end, clearly not in the same font as the first. Wait! Here was a recognizable P and here an M! There were other familiar letters, and just as many that were not.

RDWIrG♉℘℘
ᴧꙅᵞᴧᏏᏏᏢꙅᎷ
ᵭᵱℰᖴᏔᏴꙅᎯ
ᏬᏱᏆᎯᎫᵞᏞᏔ
ᏟᏁᏝᎻᏆᏃᎾᏀ
ᏒᏂᏕᏙᏆᏞᎬᎾ
ᎢᏱᏰᏝ☌ᏯᎫᏦᏦᏉ
ᗺᎾᏟᏀᏙᏨᏰᏕ
ꙅᏀᎥᏪᏞ☀ᏸᏰ
ᏡᏝᎻᏝ☍ᏟᏒᏝ
ᏝᏫ☍☍ꝊᏝᏋ

"Interesting," he said finally, uncertain what to say next, for at that moment, he witnessed another wispy but perfectly formed letter—this one a D—lifting off from Sequoya's pipe. It joined the first letter, and they began to frolic around their creator's head.

Charles looked back at the syllabary, trying hard to ignore the distraction. "I see Latin, maybe Cyrillic, maybe Greek and—could that be Arabic? Or is it Persian?"

Sequoya smiled cagily and puffed a Persian-looking letter into the space above his head. "You have divined my sources. Perhaps you are unaware, however: each letter is not merely the building block of a word, as in English; it represents instead a different *syllable* of the eighty-six that make up the Cherokee tongue. That was my master stroke!"

Charles beamed but secretly wondered, *Didn't I already identify it as a syllabary?*

All at once, a tremor began under the burlap-colored skin

of Sequoya's eyelids. Soon it had spread to his cheeks, his lips, and, after that, his entire body, his placid demeanor crumbling like a year-old cookie. *What on earth?* wondered Charles.

"It took so long for my tribal elders to accept it!" Sequoya rasped, his rage barely controlled.

Rising from his chair, he paced the room, limping slightly. Agitated, he waved his pipe in huge arcs, as the tobacco continued to spawn letters—all copies of those Charles had seen on the page.

"So many times I was sure I would not succeed!" he shouted. He stopped at the window, where, though it was still early morning, light was beginning to flood the cabin. The entourage of smoky letters danced around his head. A muscle in his cheek twitched.

"FOOLS!" he exploded. "I would show it to this elder, to that one. They turned up their noses! Stubborn people!" He was ranting now. "Who is as mulish as a Cherokee chieftain? The Eastern elders . . . aaggghhh! It took years! Years!"

Suddenly, the great man began to spin about on his bad leg. Again and again he twirled, smoky letters darting and swooping about his head like a squadron of World War I fighter planes.

Abruptly, the dance stopped. The letters rested, as well. Sequoya sank back into his chair, looking old and exhausted.

At that point, obedient to some unspoken message, the letters—now swarming again around Sequoya's head—took off in a V formation, heading for the window. There, they reformed into a single writhing torso (*with fingers!*) that tugged the sash halfway up.

A cool breeze filled the room. Sequoya remained motionless a moment longer, shoulders drooping, then straightened in his chair. Spine erect, shoulders lifting, he had recovered. Only the turban, slightly askew, betrayed his former agitation. "Now," he said. "Any questions?"

He thinks I work for a newspaper! "I'm not a reporter sir. I'm actually here with a different request. I wonder if you would mind translating this story of mine from Kannada into Cherokee?"

Sequoya was clearly puzzled. "From what?"

"My story is now in a language called Kannada. An Indian tongue."

Sequoya's face darkened. "Well, of course I don't know *all* Indian languages. I can get by in Choctaw and Pawnee. A little Seminole, in a pinch. But those tribes don't yet have written languages! Are you trying to trick me? There *is* no written Indian language except Cherokee! Who or what, may I ask, is this . . . Kannada?"

Not waiting for an answer, he strode to a corner, snatched a greatcoat off the wall and drew it on. "I must go now," he said stiffly. "Thank you for stopping by." He bowed, as he had once before, but grimly this time.

"You're welcome, sir, but I wish—"

"You see my horse outside the window?"

Charles looked. A roan horse, small and gaunt, stood saddled and ready to go. It shook its mane impatiently.

"I am off to Mexico, my impertinent friend, to find a lost Cherokee tribe. In fact, I am attempting to unify all the tribes in the Southwest." He made a broad gesture with his hands.

"And if that succeeds, perhaps *all the Indian tribes in America*! The first step, of course, is a common language! A single written language for all Indians! I'd like to see the United States government turn aside our petitions then! Perhaps we could even bring this—how do you call it?—Kannada into the fold." He glared at Charles. "If it truly exists! Farewell!"

Charles watched from the doorway as Sequoya limped down the path, mounted his nag, and rode off down the hill. As he watched, from the surrounding forest, every few meters or so, came other horsemen, until there were hundreds—thousands even—riding south to Mexico.

29
BEWITCHED BY A GODDESS

"HAVE YOU READ *Don Quixote*, Dr. Baker?"

"Some time ago, yes. And please, call me Charlie."

They were seated in a restaurant in the outskirts of Bangalore. Whisked there an hour earlier by a car Sejal had dispatched to his hotel (actually, an old station wagon with a young driver), Charles had been tingling to the *frisson* of sitting across a table from a creature who was, in his opinion, one of the world's most beautiful women—even more stunning than her sister—but he was also alive to this opportunity to take pleasure in Karnataka cuisine. While Sejal asked many probing questions, he'd been nibbling away, with her encouragement, at a variety of vegetable fritters called *bhaji,* plus a fermented rice-and-lentil crepe known as *masala dosa*, and was now eyeing a tantalizing lamb curry.

Which was more enthralling, this meal or his gorgeous host? Sejal, who seemed to relish his enjoyment of the meal, nibbled on carrot sticks while she sipped a glass of American chardonnay. The combined aromas of the dishes and her perfume were intoxicating.

Sejal crunched down on a bit of carrot and said, "Do you remember the passage in *Don Quixote* where a priest from his village talks about an Italian poet's having been translated into Castilian? The priest argues that being translated has robbed Ariosto the poet's verses of a good deal of their original value, and adds that all such attempts are doomed. He says, 'no matter the care they use and the skill they show, they will never achieve the quality the verses had in their first birth.' Something like that. Is that how you feel, as well?"

"Well . . . no, I don't think so," Charles temporized. "Poetry is the worst, of course, more difficult to translate and less perfect in the end. Auden once said he thought prose could be translated and poetry could not, that was the difference between them. Yet he also admitted his debt to Cavafy, even though he didn't know Greek and only read him in English. So yes, something is lost, but surely something is gained, as well? Take, for instance, your sister's book *The God of Small Things*. I read it in English! And thought the language was exquisite! Also, consider this: the line you just quoted from Cervantes was in English. Which means it had been translated from seventeenth century Spanish. Surely our conversation would have suffered, had that line never been translated?"

She smiled. "Good point, Charlie. Dirty Little Secret, however. Jhumpa wrote *The God of Small Things* in English."

"Ah! Really! Well, I'm sure it's been translated into a bunch of languages, and all the people who read it are lucky to have done so, even if they haven't read quite what I've read."

He was quiet a moment, crunching on a savory papadum.

"Do you know many languages yourself?" he asked, when the crumbs had vanished down his throat. "You grew up in Kerala also, I suppose."

"I did." Sejal took another carrot stick and wetted the length of it with her lips. The full length of it. Charles's libido noticed. He looked away a moment as an image of Svetlana in that Petersburg hotel flashed into his mind.

"And Kerala," she continued, "it goes without saying, has the best educational system in India."

"Really?"

"Really. Even my sister would admit to that, I believe. I speak Malayalam, of course, which is what they speak in Kerala, when they're not speaking English. But I also know Kannada, Telugu, Gujurati, Bengali, Sanskrit, Hindi, Urdu (pretty simple if you know Hindi), plus French and German. And some Tamil, as well. Read and speak each."

"Wow! You and your sister are both amazing. How is it possible to know so many languages?"

She laughed. "They're all around me, silly! India hums with language. You said you grew up on a farm, right? Do you not know the names of your crops? All the animals and insects and birds where you were raised? Languages are like this to me. They surrounded me when I grew up. I made them my friends, played with them, embraced them, toyed with them. But with respect to translation: a black-haired child cannot be made into a blonde one. Both are equally beautiful and both are equally themselves."

Charles nodded but did not stop eating. *Why don't I weigh three hundred pounds?* he wondered. The lamb curry was extraordinary. Cardamom, ginger and cinnamon competed with each other for top billing in his mouth, which also sizzled with the heat of many talented peppers. He took spoonful after spoonful of *raita*, trying to de-incinerate his throbbing tongue, then dabbed at his mouth and tried to reply through the pain.

"So you're not opposed to translation?" he asked.

"Not at all. Great thoughts and great stories must be shared with other cultures. As you already guessed, my sister's book has been translated into 36 languages. And that's great. For her."

"So, with respect to my project: ten languages, then back into English. What do you think my story will become in the end?"

She looked away a moment, then back into his eyes. "Scrambled eggs?"

Charles sprayed the table not only with laughter but a dandelion pod of curried rice. Sejal laughed with him.

30

WHAT HAPPENS IN VEGAS
STAYS IN VEGAS

A FEW DAYS LATER, Charles was once again in Sejal's company, this time speeding east out of Bangalore on a macadam pathway through palm trees and low-lying hills, then along bouncy dirt roads, where withered grassland soon gave way to a smattering of low scrubs that seemed incapable of sprouting fresh shoots. They crossed a small river where a loose cluster of old men in loin-cloths waded, perhaps bathing or performing some kind of ritual, while unyoked oxen searched for grasses nearby. Further on, a series of low-slung, charcoal-colored escarpments rode the perimeter on the northern flange. From there, the route took them into parched-looking country where lumbering sandstone rocks dominated an otherwise lunar landscape. Except for the markedly undulating terrain and the white-bearded Indians in fast-rushing streams, rather than Mexicans with shovels and rolled-up khakis in irrigation ditches, much of the journey reminded Charles of the California desert where he'd grown up.

"Where exactly are we going?" he asked for what seemed

the third or fourth time. Sejal was keeping their destination a mystery.

As before, she'd picked him up at his hotel, this time in a jeep, with a huge, black-bearded, white-turbaned Sikh behind the wheel. A single pickup, loaded with cameras, tripods, and other cinematographic paraphernalia, bouncing as noticeably as they were, brought up the rear. Charles, who had bought a hat the previous afternoon, spent most of his time clutching it tight to his head, as their vehicle jolted along and the wind tore past. Although a bit puzzled as to why Sejal had taken such an apparent shine to him, he was willing, as long as Mahanthappa was still working on his story, to be a party to her plans.

"Am I being kidnapped?" he asked, amused. "If so, I'm a willing captive."

She smiled. "Good. Now I'll tell you. We're heading for the Marabar Caves."

"Aren't they a long way off? Way up north? Forgive me— correct me if I'm wrong—but aren't the real caves called Barabar? That's what my guidebook said. Marabar was just what Forster called them in his novel. Or do I have it backwards?"

She was quiet, as the driver nervously skirted a pothole.

"If you're planning to take me that far," he added, "I *do* object. I'll fetch just as much ransom here as there, you know. Which is exactly nothing."

Her only answer was, "My, my, Charlie Baker. You are better informed than I thought." She looked at him and smiled.

The wind was playing games with her sari, now and then offering him a glimpse of brown thigh. She did not seem in any hurry to secure its edges. Once again, his libido noticed.

"I am calling the caves what Forster called them in *A Passage to India,*" she said finally, "because my movie is based on his book. Yes, the real caves are in the state of Bihar, but so what? This countryside is similar enough, so just out of town a ways, I've had my very own Marabar Caves built. Would you believe from chicken wire and Plaster of Paris? Hollywood is not the only city that can construct sets to look like whatever you please. The great Japanese set designer Tsuburaya built a miniature replica of the entire city of Tokyo for the Godzilla films. The *entire city*."

"Interesting. But—excuse me—didn't David Lean already make a movie of Forster's book?"

Sejal's voice was sharp. "So what? So bloody what? Mine will be ten times better. Mine is contemporary. Twenty-first century. I call it *The Final Passage*."

"But how is updating it possible? So much has happened since then. World War II, Ghandi, independence, partition, constitutional government, modern technology, terrorism. And since the British no longer rule India, who would be your Mrs. Moore, your Adela? Who would be your Dr. Aziz? Would he still be Muslim? What will be your incident, or should we say non-incident, in the Marabar Caves? What will it trigger?"

She sighed. "You're beginning to tire me, Baker. Be careful, or I'll leave you in the middle of the road here. You've already had a taste of one thing it triggered. You wandered right into the middle of it."

"Oh—so I did. Sorry, didn't mean to offend you. But isn't Forster's book about the clash between East and West, and the impossibility of real friendship between the two? Are those themes still as important today?"

"Are you suggesting there no longer is a clash between East and West? In India and elsewhere? America? Europe? Everywhere on the globe, in fact? Aziz's background is more relevant than ever, wouldn't you say?"

"Well, when you put it that way—"

"One change in my film is it's more violent, Charlie. Like the times we live in. The court's decision involving *my* Adela and *my* Aziz provokes real riots, not near riots. This is my vision. I am a filmmaker without fear. All over India people will be slaughtered in eruptions between Muslims and non-Muslims, including Westerners. Mumbai, by comparison, will seem like the bite of a gnat. It will resemble more the separation into India and Pakistan once independence had been declared. You read about that?"

"I was a boy. But I remember reading about it in the newspaper. Yes. Very painful. *Very* painful."

She was quiet, but he could almost hear her fuming.

"Sounds more interesting by the minute, I have to say. But I still don't see—"

"Of *COURSE* YOU DON'T *SEE!*" Her vehemence silenced him.

After a moment, she added more quietly, "But only because you haven't yet seen my film. My film will *make* you see!"

He wondered what to say next. Or whether he should say anything. "Well. It sounds very passionate and very scary. I'll be awfully interested to see how you pull it off."

"Sit back and enjoy the scenery, Dr. Baker. We still have another ten miles."

It wasn't just her film that was scary, Charles decided. *Sejal was scary, as well.*

•

They'd arrived at the set only moments before. Sejal had invited Charles to look around and then had disappeared, no doubt to attend to some technical details of the scene that would be shot here.

He took a few steps into the middle cave of the three he saw before him. He moved forward one slow step at a time.

Before the light had dissolved completely, he sidestepped to a wall, palmed it, then inched forward using its surface as a guide. *Should he light a match?* he wondered. Then remembered that he carried no matches. *Oh, never mind! What to do now?*

He decided to see whether Sejal's technicians had reproduced the strange echo he'd read about in Forster's fictional recreation of the caves. What words should he speak to test it? Alone as he was, he felt safe to say, "I wonder where the beautiful and sexy Sejal is at this moment?" Although he hadn't expected to hear his own words come back to him in the thrumming overtones Forster had described, what did come back was a shock: the voice of his hostess.

"So you think I am sexy, hey?"

A trick? He hadn't seen her come in. In fact, no one had followed him! Charles was embarrassed. "OmiGod! Sejal! I'm so sorry! I had no idea you were here." A pause. Mortified, he whispered, "*Are* you here?" His face burned so hotly he feared it might generate a visible glow. He tried to discern the direction the voice had come from.

"I really didn't mean to insult you," he tried again. "I—"

"Hush!"

A whispered command. But from where? Could she be behind him?

She was. A moment later he had no doubt of this, as a pair of warm arms encircled his waist and joined themselves together across his stomach. Her full breasts pushed against his back. *OmiGod!* he thought. *Is this really happening?* At the same time, he made an unconscious effort to tighten his stomach muscles in a futile effort to eliminate his paunch.

"Have you been fantasizing about Adela's experience in the cave, Charlie Baker?" Her voice was soft, teasing. "Mr. Abel Baker Charlie Dog? The experience that did *not* happen to

Adela? That did *not* happen to Dr. Aziz? But whose reality is so palpable you imagine that it happened anyway?" She tightened her hold, pressing herself harder against him.

"No, of course not! Nothing like that! I never thought of such a thing."

"Of course you did, Dr. Baker! You are a man, are you not? All men think about such things."

"Well, yes, but—"

"Hush now!" she said again. And her hands began moving. All over.

"Perhaps I have thought about such an encounter in these caves myself?" she whispered, a gathering tension in her voice. "Perhaps I have created them for precisely that reason? What do you think? We are totally in the dark now, Charlie. And no one will know, unless one of us tells? Correct?" One soft hand had moved upward to his chest. Unbuttoning his shirt, it slipped inside. The other dropped lower, found his hardness, traced its outline.

"Sejal, I . . . we—"

"Shhh."

He could, of course, overpower her. Pry her arms loose, spin around, force her away, demand—in his most imposing voice—that she stop.

Right. Like that was going to happen.

Then, just when her fingers started toying with his zipper, when he felt his defenses totally breached, the hands stopped moving. The arms disappeared.

Abruptly, with a strength that surprised him, she spun him about and placed his other arm, then his hand, against the wall. He was now turned toward the way he had entered the dark.

"A non-event, Dr. Baker." Her voice was cold. "Just as in the novel. We must follow the script, correct? Nothing happened.

All in the head. Walk forward, close to the wall. Soon you will see the light."

•

When he emerged into the shattering sunlight, he found the meager camera crew milling about. A kind of picnic seemed to be in progress. Some snacked on papadums, samosas, and pakoras that lay scattered across paper plates at a small folding table. Others fiddled with tripods, banks of lights. Sejal was nowhere to be seen. When she did appear, a half hour later, it was from somewhere else. He never saw her exit the cave. She joked for a while with her crew, then began barking orders. It was as if she'd forgotten he was there.

On the return trip to Bangalore, they rode in a silence as vast as the Deccan Plateau. His lip began to twitch, but there was nothing he could do about it, so he did his best to ignore it. Two thoughts kept circling in his head, as if searching for somewhere safe to land. The first, fueled by a bubbling anger, was that he had been played. He had not seen that coming. He'd been duped, soiled, tossed away like a used dust rag. The second, totally incompatible, was that maybe he had fantasized the whole thing. It was dark; he couldn't see a thing, so maybe it was wish fulfillment? But, if that were the case, wouldn't he have wished for consummation?

At the door of his hotel, she flashed him a coquettish smile, then roared off into the night as if nothing had happened.

31

IN EINSTEIN'S UNIVERSE, STRAIGHT LINES DO NOT EXIST

LATER THAT EVENING, as he emptied his pants pockets, Charles discovered that his flash drive was missing. This was the drive that contained his short story, including its English, Russian, and Chinese variations. He'd never kept it anywhere but in his pocket. Now it was gone.

His thoughts went immediately to Sejal, to how her hands had moved over him in the cave. Was it possible she'd slipped it out of his trousers during those moments? Surely not. At the time, his flash drive had possibly been the furthest thing from his mind. But what other explanation was possible? *OhmiGod!*

In a panic, he pulled his trousers back on and shot downstairs. Rajif Pandit, the clerk who had checked him into the hotel days ago, was again on duty. In his thirties, he was a handsome man with crisply ironed black hair, deep-set brown eyes, and a small gold ring in his left ear. Unfailingly courteous. He'd been on duty every time Charles had been in the lobby. So much so that Charles had wondered several times where, and whether, he slept. Yet he always looked as if he'd just stepped out of a commercial for Burberry evening wear.

As Charles arrived at the counter, Rajif was busy sketching a route on a map for an elderly French couple. Standing in place, Charles danced from foot to foot, like a man with a bursting bladder. After wishing his other guests a pleasant evening in perfect French, the clerk turned to Charles and smiled politely.

"Good evening, Dr. Baker. You are enjoying your stay?"

"By and large, yes. Very much. But I need to know. Has anyone left something for me? A package, perhaps? An envelope?"

Rajif turned to search the mailboxes, then back again. "Sorry, Dr. Baker. Nothing. You were expecting a message of some sort? A package from abroad?"

Charles dropped his eyes and sighed deeply. Looking up again, he said, "No, actually, I've lost something, Mr. Pandit. I was hoping someone might have recovered it and . . . dropped it off. Though how they would have known it was mine, I'm not sure." He tapped his hands to the sides of his head several times. "Let me ask you this. Do you remember the lady you've seen me with the past few days, Ms. Roy? Did she mention anything about me?"

"Ms. Roy, sir?" Rajif looked puzzled. "You mean the woman who waited outside for you, once in a station wagon and once in a jeep? The filmmaker."

"Right. What I'm asking is—"

"Did you say her name was Roy, Dr. Baker?"

"Yes, Rajif. Sejal Roy. The filmmaker. The sister of Arundhati Roy. She and I—"

"Arundhati Roy's sister?"

A noise of squealing brakes came from the street.

"Quite right, and she—"

"Arundhati Roy, the novelist?"

Charles lay his hands on the desk. What was wrong? Arundhati Roy was a celebrity. Surely she was as recognizable to others as to him? He sighed. "Quite so."

"Dr. Baker, begging your pardon, sir, but I know a bit about Ms. Roy. I've met her, in fact. And our mothers were childhood friends in Kerala. I'm sorry to be the one to tell you this, sir. But Arundhati Roy does not have a sister. She is an only child."

Charles tried a smile, but was defeated by his now twitching lips. "That's impossible!" he said. "In fact, I met her here! In this hotel! When she was filming in your coffee bar. Right over there, beyond those drapes!"

Rajif looked troubled. "I am sorry that you are mistaken about this, Dr. Baker," he said gently. "I can see how important it is to you. But the lady you are referring to is a young film student. At our Bangalore Film Institute. I understand she is doing her thesis now. On a grant, I believe. Since she's on such a tight budget, our management agreed to let her film that one scene at this hotel at no charge. So long as her grant paid for the breakage."

"Her name is not Sejal?"

Rajif's tone was apologetic.

"I'm afraid not, Dr. Baker. She goes by the name Adela."

"Adela!"

Charles's look was so stricken, that the clerk began to fear he was ill. "I can understand your confusion," he said hesitantly.

He paused, observing Charles's crestfallen slump against the counter.

"Come to think of it," Rajif began, choosing his words

carefully, "she does look a lot like Ms. Roy. Like Arundhati. Or at least like Ms. Roy as she looked in that photograph on her book cover. But that was . . . ummm . . . 1997, I believe? And very likely it was taken even earlier, when she was in her twenties. Ms. Roy is nearing fifty now, and her hair may be getting grayer by the minute. But you're quite right, of course. I can see the resemblance when I think about it. An easy mistake."

When Charles remained silent, Rajif fiddled with the notepaper on his counter.

"She is a very good-looking woman, no?" he added, guessing that this was important to his guest.

"She is a good-looking woman, *yes*," said Charles dryly, then turned to walk away.

The clerk cried, "Wait!" and held up one hand in a traffic-cop gesture that never failed to rankle Charles.

"Yes?" said Charles, turning back, eyebrows arched.

"Sorry. Didn't mean to startle you. It's just that . . . I only now remembered something. That first evening, after you had retired, I believe, Adela was here, in the lobby. Her camera crew had packed and left, but she was talking for a while with a stocky man—a stranger to me—who wound up passing her a fat white envelope. It may have been nothing, of course, just an admirer offering to help finance her movie, but I thought maybe . . . . Anyway, I thought you should know."

Charles could think of nothing to say. He thanked Rajif and took the elevator to his room.

•

When he woke the next morning, panic no longer occluding his brain, Charles realized that the situation wasn't the complete disaster he'd feared. The two translations were stored on his laptop and on CDs, both of which were still with him. And, of course, there was his fail-safe: he had mailed the Russian and Chinese translations to a safe-deposit box in New York. That was the one part of his planning that seemed to be holding up. Hopefully. Who the hell knew what the bank was up to?

Although the cave experience and the discovery that Sejal was a fraud had unnerved him and dropped him into a temporary despond, he began to toy with the idea that it had all been his imagination anyway—that sequence in the cave. After a few days, he could scarcely remember it, and he soon recovered his purpose and his energy. The fact that, at the end of the week, Professor Mahanthappa called to say that the translation was complete did a lot to revive his spirits.

The professor had been chipper on the phone, but when Charles saw him at the university he again wondered: *How long can this man last? He's not only knocking at Death's Door; he's swinging back and forth on its hinges!* When Charles reached across the desk to collect the CD, the professor's arm trembled like a palm frond in a stiff breeze. Fortunately, Charles managed to trap the thin wafer before it dropped to the parquet floor, tucking it quickly into a sleeve in his briefcase. Shaking Mahanthappa's hand afterwards was equally dicey; it was like grasping a thin strip of flypaper. The arm was limp at all joints from shoulder to wrist, yet the grip didn't want to let go.

Back in his hotel room, Charles stood for a moment looking out the window. From this high floor, in a truncated, triangular view of the crowded thoroughfare that fronted the hotel, he could see food wallahs and cows. Were those the images he was to carry away from Bangalore? Oh, there was more, he supposed, that he might remember from the few days he'd been free to roam the city: the Durga Temple, with its intricate carvings of many-armed gods and goddesses, the lovely purple flowers in the Ladbagh Gardens, the ubiquitous yellow bicycle jitneys that zigged and zagged this way and that through the traffic. But, no. For him, it was food wallahs and cows. Caves, or wild, brutal terrain seen from a bouncing, careening jeep, or rapid gunfire splattering the walls while he cowered under a chair, these were evidently not things he wanted to remember. Where, oh where was Svetlana when you needed her? He sighed.

Was nothing in the world straightforward and simple? He glanced at his laptop, open on the bed. He'd just received an email from Óscar Amalfitano in Mexico, saying he wanted to put off translating Charles's story. Now he needed to find someone else fluent in Kannada. Was Amalfitano's message a brush-off, as had happened in Russia? It didn't feel like it, and Amalfitano did know a number of languages, so if he could schedule him at the right time, and his story was then in the right language, Charles still might be able to take advantage of his kind offer.

No, not a brush-off, he decided, just a postponement. You can't mistrust everyone, can you?

He sank down on the bed again, hoisted his laptop, noted the languages Amalfitano's email had said he was fluent in, and began to work out a timetable. It was still April, after all, and adjustments could always be made. Look what amendments had been forced on him already! Wasn't a more or less constant tinkering with the schedule an expectation he'd begun with in the first place? This was an adventure, after all, and isn't unpredictability the very heart of adventuring?

•

The next morning, Charles went straight to the airport and left India.

The incident in the caves, it seemed, could not be obliterated. One corner of Charles's mind held onto images he'd done his best to sweep under the rug. No matter how carefully he patted down that corner of the carpet, its softness and puffiness couldn't be ignored. He could remember, yet not remember he was remembering. Dostoyevsky's title would suffice: *Zapiski Podpol'e*. Notes from Under the Floor. As the plane picked up speed that morning for its liftoff from the Bangalore airport, a fellow passenger from across the aisle might have overheard Charles muttering: "Adela. Perfect. Just perfect."

PART THREE

32

A MID-COURSE (DO WE MEAN CURSE?) CORRECTION

I T WAS THE hottest July on record in Greece, and one of the scariest. Lying as it does in the middle of a geological triple play, astride the intersections of the Eurasian, Aegean and African tectonic plates, Greece is at the mercy of seismic forces. So much so, that hard-bitten old fisherman joke that they can't tell if it's an earthquake that's giving them the shakes, or too many drams of *ouzo* the night before. In ancient times, folks credited such upheavals to violent squabbles among the dignitaries of Mount Olympus. But when, on July 14 of the current year, the African Plate—perhaps suffering its own case of dyspepsia—subducted sharply, the wrenching tremor was felt all along the complex undersea boundaries.

Not as large as the one that toppled the Colossus of Rhodes in 226 BC, nor that which in AD 365 elevated Crete by nine meters and triggered a tsunami that devastated Alexandria, this quake still managed 6.9 on the Richter scale. Since the tectonic slippage was in the middle of the Aegean, it opened its major wounds in northeastern Greece, sending ripples into Athens sufficient to topple a few of the less substantial buildings. The wave it unleashed also converted a handful of fishing boats along the coast to kindling, while swamping dozens more along the eastern coast of Crete.

Plus it transformed to a feathery powder one whole wall of the cheap hotel in Athens where Charles Abel Baker was staying. He'd been out when it happened, seeing the sights from a downtown trolley. Though his conveyance was jounced around a bit and ripped from its electrical moorings, it had remained upright, and the only damage Charles suffered was a bit lip.

Several times over the course of the past months he had wished that Svetlana was with him, both to assuage his loneliness and to share joy in each successive translation, but scary moments like this quake made him immensely grateful she was not travelling with him.

Fortunately for his translation project, the earthquake also skipped the Vallianos National Library in Athens, where Themistocles Poggioli—himself a poet influenced by Cavafy—was busy pouring the music of the Italian version of Charles's story into the flat but precise language of modern Greek. Poggioli, son of a Greek mother and an Italian father who had been killed while fighting in the underground during World War Two, knew both languages fluently and had made his living doing translations from Italian to Greek. Down in level thirteen underground, Poggioli would have become only a buried artifact had the quake toppled the *biblioteka*, but it did not, and Poggioli had finished his work in good time and delivered the required copies to Charles.

•

Two weeks after the quake, in late July, shards of light ricocheted off the white terraced walls of a small cafe on Corfu. A relaxed and thoroughly recovered Charles sat alone at an outdoor table, sipping an iced cappuccino. The table's huge parasol sheltered him from the sun's bravado, as he reveled in the Mediterranean breeze that tossed his beard and ruffled the hairs along the back of his neck. He stared across the water at a coastline that included Greece and Albania, and wondered idly, was there any substantial Albanian literature? Perhaps he should have his story translated next into Albanian? Rather than Japanese, as was his current plan? It would certainly save on travel costs!

So many languages! So much he didn't know!

There were other patrons on the patio. An elderly lady in a smart-looking suit, too hot for the weather, drank tea a few tables away, and a heavy-set gentleman in khaki walking shorts relaxed at another table, his nose buried in a newspaper. Charles, too preoccupied with deconstructing his journey thus far, paid scant attention.

Despite hiccups and hesitations, as Charles now thought of them, he had every reason to believe his project was going splendidly. Translations from Russia, China, India, Iceland, Italy—and now Greece—had been achieved. He'd been very lucky in Iceland. What good fortune to find Halldór Laxness III, a grandson of the man who'd won the Nobel Prize for literature in 1950, to translate his story.

Charles had suffered a jolt of panic in India when his Mexican correspondent, Óscar Amalfitano, had written he was taking the summer off from the University of Santa Teresa. Something about "needing to get away from the madness for a while." Happy to do the translation in the fall, Professor Amalfitano had told him, but that hadn't fitted Charles's timetable. So, a frantic scramble to find another soul knowledgeable in Kannada in the next country on his list had led at last to young Halldór. After he'd flown to Iceland, he'd found Halldór to be a bright, quick-moving fellow in his mid-thirties, with long, stringy hair and twinkling blue eyes, who lived not in Reykjavik but in the remote northern city of Akureyri. Laxness, he learned, had spent several years of his youth in India learning languages, including Kannada. In a show of diligence he was quite proud of, Charles consulted all three major universities in Iceland and learned that language departments in each held Mr. Laxness's skills in high regard. Problem averted.

There'd been other setbacks, as well. Not just the Greek earthquake. The first, he supposed, was the glacier mishap in Iceland. Then there was that lost laptop in Italy. But no grand scheme goes off without a hitch, right? Troubling though these events might have been at one time—discouraging, even— Charles was aware of a shift in his outlook. No longer would he wring his hands and curse his fate; he saw such reversals now as mere wrinkles in the complex tapestry he was weaving. As Vladimir Ilyich Ulyanov—alias Nicolai Lenin—had once proclaimed: two steps forward, one step back. That's the way it went. Progress, any way you looked at it.

He took a sip of his drink and chuckled, remembering the old joke about Disraeli and Gladstone. The one he'd told all his classes. The thought of his teaching days (or rather his abrupt separation from them years ago) darkened his mood for a second, but his mind rolled out the familiar story anyway. A staff member had approached Disraeli, asking him to distinguish between misfortune and disaster. Disraeli had replied, "Certainly! If Mr. Gladstone should fall into the Thames, that would be a misfortune. If someone fished him out, that would be a disaster." So. The difficulties Charles had experienced were, he felt certain, misfortunes.

Although! Charles fiddled with the ice in his glass and looked thoughtful. Iceland had been *almost* a disaster, had it not? For him, personally? While Laxness ground away at his story, Charles had gone glacier climbing (an outing suggested by the translator himself), and had barely skirted death, almost tumbling headlong into a frozen gorge. A deep one. The kind one sees in documentaries on the National Geographic Channel.

He'd almost slipped through a split in the ice cube, is the way he put it in emails to Jonathan Belknap and other members of the writing group in New York. Last-minute rescue from behind by a stout fellow he'd not even known was along on the climbing party. With this gentleman's help, he'd clambered to safety in a perfect terror. Firm hand on his collar, that fellow. Didn't even look like a professional climber. Such a shame he'd vanished before he could even be properly thanked. The Icelandic guide, to whom his rescuer was apparently also a stranger, put the mishap down to "global warming, don't you know? Early melt. Makes the damned ice extra slippery, see?" Perhaps. But how, Charles later wondered, did global warming account for the damaged fastener on his climbing harness?

Charles took another sip of his cappuccino, laughed to himself, and shook his head. In Italy, it had been a different problem altogether. His life was never in danger, but his project's success was certainly threatened. His laptop had vanished on the train bound from Naples to Rome. Since his new flash drive had been tucked into a sleeve of the computer case, rather than in his pocket, that had disappeared as well. He chided himself later for "putting all his eggs in one basket." Although storing the flash drive in his pocket had led to earlier difficulties, hadn't it? Whatever the case, recovery was right around the corner! The laptop and all its accoutrements had turned up the next day at his Rome hotel with a scribbled note: "Found this under an empty seat in a third-class carriage on the Naples-to-Rome line. Thought you'd like to have it back." Written in English. Go figure. And no indication of how the finder knew where he was staying. The concierge seemed equally puzzled. Charles had wondered about it for a while, but then, such an unforeseen ending was part of what had helped him develop his new attitude. *All's well that end's well*, he'd told himself, and promptly stopped worrying.

After all, that evanescent *agita* could hardly erase the good parts of his Italian adventure. The food! The lodgings! The bulk of his time had been spent neither in Naples nor Rome, but in Positano. The man he'd found to do the translation (Halldor's suggestion) happened to be an expat Icelander living on the Amalfi Coast. As a result, Charles had spent two weeks in the best hotel in Positano because that translator, one Snori Laxdaela, had a close friend who was not only a hotel proprietor but a devotee of literature, particularly American.

What a piece of luck! thought Charles. A translator himself, the hotel owner had seemed so entranced by Charles's project that he'd invited Charles to stay in the hotel for free.

The scion of an ancient baronial family, Italo Moravia was now operating—as a hotel—the family's splendidly renovated mansion. It perched, like a modern-day marble castle, on a cliff overlooking a black sand beach several hundred feet below, reachable only by a narrow stone street winding down the cliff through the town. White marble was everywhere in the hotel, yet the structure seemed so merged with its environment that one fantasized it had been carved out of the cliff itself. Every apartment had a terrace with Moorish floors and wrought-iron guard rails, from which one could see dozens and dozens of other terra cotta roofs like the one on the building where Charles had often stood looking. Out to sea was the island of Capri. Immediately below his balcony was a fifteenth century church with a red, white, green and gold cupola, whose bells woke him each morning. The church's interior, once its gloom had been penetrated, sheltered dozens of Renaissance paintings on biblical themes. And the hotel's dining room could still make his mouth water, even in memory while sitting here contentedly on the island of Corfu. Over meals of tortellini with wild boar sauce, or venison in a Barolo wine reduction, Charles had spent hours talking with the knowledgeable Mr. Moravia about literature and translation.

He heaved a sigh and looked at the calm stretch of beautiful green water he could see from his terrace. A single fishing boat entered his vision, putt-putting north to south, imprinting a transient, churning V on the otherwise mirrored sheen. He shook his head as another memory occurred. The earthquake had crippled the hotel where he'd stayed in Athens, reducing his room to rubble. Fortunately, no one was hurt, save the hotel manager, who sustained a broken arm. Charles's laptop, a victim—though hardly a target—of that event, had been discovered a few days later at the police station, where someone who left no name had turned it in.

Wouldn't anyone be forced to admit that his project so far was a success?

33

WAS THAT A PAPER PLANE I SAW FLUTTERING WILDLY INTO THE VOID?

T HE DOOR TO the terrace opened, and out walked the second reason for Charles's extremely chipper mood. The blonde woman moved confidently, hips swaying, dark glasses anchored firmly on her lovely nose, long legs reaching out to grasp as much of the tiled floor as she could with each stride. Her loose white frock rustled gently above her knees, reminding Charlie of a frothy ice cream confection.

"Good morning, *kotik*," she said, sinking into the chair next to Charles. She swept off her glasses and leaned in to kiss him on the cheek.

A small shift of his head rerouted her kiss to his lips. "*Dobroe utro, dusha.*"

Svetlana had arrived on his birthday, now a few days past, just as she'd told him she would at their tearful parting in Siberia. They had stayed that first night in one of the districts suffering the least damage, in a cheap hotel in Athens to which Charles had fled after the collapse of his own hotel's wall.

Despite the shoddiness of the surroundings, it had been an astonishing reunion. Svetlana seemed unchanged. She wore her hair shorter, but the eyes he'd fallen into at that hotel in Moscow eight months earlier were just as blue, just as clear. Over the next few days, Charles noticed shadows crossing her face at odd moments, but he dismissed this. She was Russian, he reasoned; weren't all Russians moody? He was overwhelmed by the pleasures of their lovemaking. And soothed by the tenderness that tiptoed in after the frenzy. He imagined himself a veteran soldier gathered from the battlefield; she was a nurse spreading balm on his wounds.

It was she who had urged him to leave Athens for a more vacation-like atmosphere after his story's translation into Greek, and Charles—remembering fondly the Durrells' descriptions of Corfu that he'd read as a young man—had chosen that island. Fortunately, Corfu, on the far side of Greece from the earthquake's epicenter, had remained untouched, and Svetlana's flying perks could shift them there for nothing.

The sun was warm on the terrace. A waiter arrived with the glass of white wine Svetlana had ordered while inside, and adjusted the huge umbrella to better shade their chairs. After the waiter left, she said: "You do not mind, *dusha*? I have wine while you drink only coffee?"

"Only! I love coffee. And, of course, I'm hopeful that your glass of wine will wash away some of your sexual inhibitions."

She drew back, looked at him uncertainly, and blushed. "You are kidding with me, no?"

"I am kidding with you, *yes*. Of course! I'm teasing! I mean to imply that you are anything *but* inhibited and I am lucky to be the one who reaps the benefit. I love our sex together. It is beautiful."

She made a wry face at him, drummed her fingers on the

table. "Okay. So, last night, *dusha*, you said was more about Italy you want to tell. What were you trying to tell me before you fell asleep and began snoring?"

"Did I snore? Oh! Sorry, love. Yes, yes! I wanted to tell you about Mr. Moravia, the man who gave me a room in his swank hotel. Wonderful fellow! He has this small dog, a Yorkie, with a boxy face and bushy eyebrows. Cute little fellow. Tan and white. Very intelligent looking."

"*Sobachka*. Lap dog. Like in Chekhov story."

"Exactly! Well, this dog was quite a character. Mischievous and mysterious. You never knew quite what he would do next. He called him Calvino. The dog was a real actor, could feign sadness or joy, depending on what he wanted from you. Such twinkling eyes! Well, this little fellow livened up our dinners together, because Italo would often feed him morsels from his plate in the dining room, while holding him in his arms."

Svetlana made a face. "Disgusting! In Novosibirsk I had dog when little girl, but bigger one. Papa would have spank my bottom if I let him in the house, let alone feed him from table."

"My father, too, actually. But that's not the point. I mean, imagine how unconventional! In one of Italy's finest hotel restaurants, in the dining room. White tablecloths. Fine china and glassware. Attentive waiters in starched white jackets, napkins draped over their arms, displaying the fanciest bottles from the hotel's superlative wine cellar to a spiffed-up, *haute-bourgeois* clientele. And here *we* are, the two of us, sitting at a table as elegant as any other in the room, while Italo is feeding tidbits of veal *puttanesca* to his dog!"

She shrugged. "If you say so. Or perhaps is piece of indulgence by, what you call it, upper crust? For ordinary guest in his dining room, would he permit this? I do not think so. But this is it? This is big news you could hardly wait to tell me? That in Italy you got to feed a dog?"

Chastened, Charles shrugged and muttered, "Maybe you had to be there." Then added, "Just an anecdote I thought might amuse you." Privately, he decided it would get a better reception from members of his writing group. Except for Jake, of course, who would mock it pitilessly. In any event, it was probably a better anecdote to share with Svetlana than his experience with Sejal or his dream while in a coma.

He swirled his coffee around in his glass, drank the last swallow. "Well, never mind. Mostly we were talking about translation. Italo is a translator of English language fiction into Italian, and vice versa. Not what I required at the moment, of course, since my story needed translating from Icelandic into Italian. Nevertheless, he was a dedicated professional, and I enjoyed listening to him trying to convey what it felt like. The process. I've never heard anyone speak of translation in such—almost mystical—terms. He quoted me some comments by another translator whose spirit he identified with strongly. I thought the descriptions so marvelous, I wrote them down. Here."

He fumbled in his pocket, retrieved a crinkled piece of notepaper. Moving his empty glass aside, he smoothed the paper as best he could against the surface of the table. While he did this, Svetlana looked into the distance—toward Albania, perhaps—and sighed. Almost, but not quite, inaudibly.

"Okay. Here we are. The translator's name is Wallis Wilde-Menozzi, and Ms. Menozzi says: 'One is breathing, breathing, as if with a lover. A long conversation starts, an intense dialogue goes on. A rough patch. A startling, gifted uncovering. A return to peace and the satisfaction of fitting.' Isn't that a nice description of what it feels like to translate? Even rather sexy, no? It goes on, 'In that special breathing, there is the life of another, so mysteriously alive and beckoning.' I like that! 'Mysteriously alive!'"

He beamed, a bit forced. Svetlana, staring straight ahead, her chin resting in the palm of her hand, fingers toying idly with an earlobe, said: "Very poetical. But awkward too, *nyet*? Maybe was translation from another language."

While she returned her gaze to the sea, he sipped his drink thoughtfully, one foot moving impatiently up and down. He was oblivious to the fact that her foot was moving up and down as well.

After a moment, she said, "Is not just sex, you know?"

Charles's foot stopped moving. "Excuse me?"

"Is not just sex. I don't travel halfway around the world just for good sex. You are special to me, Charlie."

His mouth was still open. He closed it, trying to decide what to say. His sheltered tongue slid its way along his teeth, then back the other way, "As you are to me, Svyeta. I didn't mean to offend you. I was just teasing. But what brings this on? It seems so . . . out of left field."

She sighed and raised a hand to the back of his neck, smoothing the hairs along its nape. "I don't know about what field is in. But tell me, Charlie, you are enjoying your trip around world? Is turning out like you expect?"

He cleared his throat. "Both better—and sometimes worse—than I'd imagined, I suppose. Win or lose, a real eye-opener. I get weary sometimes, but all in all, yes, it's been extremely satisfying. Six languages so far! And, *dusha*, it would never have happened without you. I was about to give up back in November, without even achieving my first translation."

She withdrew her hand, fiddled with the silverware that had been placed on the table to no purpose, since they weren't eating.

"You were very sad then, I remember. So tell me, Charlie. Have there been other women on this trip to take your mind off your sadness? How many you shack up with since Svetlana?"

He laughed and shook his head, quick to answer. "None, my love. Only you."

He thought once more of Sejal—Adela?—the incident in the cave, but as before decided against that revelation. That was an almost, right? Hardly worth mentioning. Now Stream of Wandering Spirits—and Gou Ming—that was another matter. But, wait! That had never happened! Surely he wasn't responsible for what he'd imagined while in a coma? One day he might tell her, but surely not now? Why complicate matters with a trivial fantasy?

So he bounced the question back to her.

Her brow contracted; she glanced away.

"There is man who wants to marry me," she said at last. "He is doctor. Of medicine. In Novosibirsk. He is say he love me very much."

Uncoiling his fingers from his cappuccino, Charles placed them carefully in his lap, to keep them from squeezing the glass so hard it might shatter. Whence came that boot pressing down on his heart?

"And you? Have you agreed to this?"

"*Nyet*. Not yet. I tell him only I would think about it. I would consider."

"I see. So where has this 'considering' led you, so far?"

She shrugged as she had earlier and looked away. "I am not a person with property or money, Charlie. Not like your Italo. I want to quit airline one day. Soon, perhaps. Has given me pleasant life for a while, mainly because of good travel. But I have forty-three years, *dusha*. Travel seems now sometimes heavy. *Tiazhyolii*. Not like adventure anymore. And my father also is not getting younger. I am all his family. How long will papa have his health? *Ya ne znaiu.* Who can tell? This is what I think about when I am 'considering.'"

He wanted to say something, felt desperate to say anything, but found himself unable to speak.

•

The next morning, they made love, an act that seemed abstract and passionless, though tinged with desperation, as if they were floating in a hot air balloon miles above the earth, turbulence rocking them, where they clung to one another to keep from falling out of the gondola. Afterward, abruptly, Svetlana turned her head away and began to cry. Charles sighed and laid a hand on her shoulder.

"What's wrong, love?"

She sobbed as children sob: wailing, moaning. Each time she stopped, she blew her nose and began again. *Might she be ill?* he wondered, but felt helpless to ask. As if he had no right. At last she grew quiet, lay back on her pillow, stared at the ceiling.

"I have betrayed you, Charlie. You are my great love, and I betray you. I destroy everything."

He lay back alongside her, staring at the ceiling himself. Knowing he needed to be strong. He thought briefly of the Marabar cave incident, but took another tack. "Svyeta, if you're referring to this other man, this doctor—"

"*Nyet!* Being with doctor is not what I done!"

"Then . . . what?"

She raised herself on her elbow, clamped a hand over his mouth. He watched a single tear leave the corner of her eye and work its way to her chin. "Charlie, is worse than that. Much worse. *Slushaytye mne, pazhalsta.* Listen to me. What I feel in my heart for you is very true. But is built on lie. No, don't speak. Just listen."

She fell back. Charles remained silent. *What on earth was coming?*

"*Akh*, Charlie, *bozhe moi!* I am so ashame! I meet you, I call you, I come to you in hotel, because I am paid to do it. They come to me, Charlie. They offer me five thousand *Amerikanskii* dollars to seduce you. To . . . how they put it . . . throw you off the course. 'Handcuff him with passion,' they say, so you will lose interest in your project."

The air seemed to have left the room. He opened his mouth to speak, closed it again. Finally, "Who? Who came to you? Who is *they*?"

She sighed, raised herself on one elbow. "I don't know who is they. It was one man. He contact me in New York before plane takes off. Big man. Well, not so big. Short but . . . broad. Speak Russian well, but like American. I don't know how he knows about you, Charlie. I don't know why he care."

They lay there a while without speaking. Then, "I don't know why I do this, Charlie. I never do anything like this before. But these people, they have their ways."

These people?

"Reminds me KGB. I think these other men who fail to translate your story—these other Russians—were maybe bought, as well. I bet my bottom dollars."

Charles, eyes closed, shook his head. "But, Svetlana. This can't be true! You were the one who helped me! You led me to your father to translate my story!"

"Yes!" She fell back again, looked down toward her navel, then over at the window, through whose shade a tiny sliver of morning sunlight was beginning to probe.

"Of course I help you, Charlie. Because I feel so bad for

you. Because I fall for you. So much. So, so much. When you call me and you are so sad, I must to help. I feel so terrible. I feel, what have I did? I love you, Charlie! And I cannot live with this lie—I must tell you! I am so, so, so sorry for what I done!"

Again, silence. Charles felt drained, stunned. Abruptly, she rose, began drawing on her clothes. She was crying again, but more softly now. "I go now, Charlie. Don't try to stop."

How could he stop her? A paralyzing drug had spread throughout his body.

When she had finished dressing, finished closing her suitcase, finished straightening her uniform and adjusting her cap, she withdrew an envelope from her purse, laid it on the bedside table. "Here is birthday present from me, Charlie. Is your ticket to Japan."

Later, when he finally opened the envelope, he saw that it also held five thousand crisp American dollars in one-hundred-dollar denominations, still secured around the middle by a paper tape.

34

A LOCOMOTIVE SLIPS
UNDER THE RADAR

DEREK WAINSCOT COULD not believe his project was tanking. Digging a yellow pad out of his desk drawer, he prepared to enumerate some points. Three lines later, he furiously crossed out what he'd written, ripped the paper into tiny shreds, and fingered the confetti into the wastebasket. He sank back into his chair and tapped his pencil against his teeth.

First—and worst—was the problem with Jocelyn. It had begun well enough. Lunch at Per Se, where they'd lavished upon her their supreme culinary gifts. He'd plied her with a 2004 Leflaive Chevalier-Montrachet Grand Cru, and, once she was in a receptive—nay, a joyous—mood, outlined his project. "Yes, of course!" she'd replied, so things were off to a fine start. She'd selected the story on the spot, and later he'd called his good friend, Pierre Médoc, to see if he was available to do the first translation, into French. That, too, was easily agreed upon.

Then, out of the blue, Jocelyn had called to renege. Moreover, she was irate! She'd somehow heard that someone (she didn't know the name, thank goodness) had come to him earlier and laid out the idea for the same project he'd proposed to her, and had heard as well that he'd turned it down flat. (All the while she was talking he wondered who the mole might be.) His behavior, in her razor-sharp opinion, struck her as "ripping off" a fellow writer, and she wanted no part of it. Not only had she withdrawn her permission to use the story, but she'd threatened to publish her next book (which meant, in all likelihood, her next *dozen* books) with Knopf. It had taken every nuance of his most accomplished groveling to avert the unthinkable.

Why would Jocelyn Lynne Barley be so sensitive about a nobody like Baker? (She may not have known his name, but must have inferred he was a cipher, a wannabe.) More to the point, what was the source of her intel? It had not been even whispered about outside his sanctuary, Roberto's. Even his secretary knew absolutely nothing. So how did Jocelyn find out?

And that was only stage one of the meltdown. He'd finally gotten the project reignited in early February, when, after being rebuffed by two writers who couldn't or wouldn't see the point, he'd finally scored with another writer from his stable, Tobias Foxx. After a week or two waiting for a reply—Foxx was on a book tour—Derek at last received the go-ahead, and Tobias had shipped him a brand new story that had never seen the light of day. Back in business!

But then! After Tobias's story had been whisked through three separate translations—French, German, and Russian—Toby had withdrawn as well. Abruptly. Didn't say he'd heard anything negative, didn't berate Derek or call him names (as Jocelyn had done—goodness, what a vocabulary that woman had). He simply squelched the deal with a polite one-line email. Their agreement had been verbal, of course, so no chance of suing him. Besides, why would he risk losing Toby as an author, as well?

What a royal cock-up! Derek had paid four top-of-the-line translators substantial sums, and now he was stuck with a nonstarter. Well, to hell with it! No good-money-after-bad for him. The project was dead. Looking out the window of corporate headquarters at their sleek, fifties-modern building on Fifth Avenue, he drummed his pencil against his desk and sighed. Who knew this undertaking would be so fraught?

Derek had told no one at his parent company what he was trying to accomplish, fearing they would nix it. That was both a good and a bad thing. It meant he'd wasted a lot of time. It meant he'd paid tidy sums out of his own pocket to his translators, and *huge* sums to his buddy Pig, who'd been circling the globe on a mission to torpedo Baker's project. And here was the worst part: without success! Derek had been getting regular reports. He knew all the incidents that had befallen Baker, and knew the man had somehow scraped through. It was astonishing that this piker and his project were still alive!

Derek walked away from the window, circled around his colonial-sized office, and sat back down again. So he'd finally concluded: enough is enough. Having already paid a small fortune without discernible results, he'd decided to call off his attempt to derail Baker. But how?

Every day this week he'd sought fruitlessly to contact Pig. Where had the fat flake vamoosed to? No email from him, hours of voice mail unreturned. Insupportable! Not only because Derek was hemorrhaging money. Much worse than that.

Beneath his armpits Derek could feel the perspiration gather. Had he started a locomotive down a track toward a frighteningly dark tunnel? Or a steep cliff? An out-of-control train he was no longer able to stop?

35
THE PAST IS PROLOGUE

THE FLIGHT FROM Athens to Tokyo took 704 minutes. Only in the last twenty-nine, the long descent into the Tokyo airport, was Charles thinking about Japan and the translator he was scheduled to meet there. One hundred eighty minutes had been spent in fitful sleep, and for almost all of the remaining five hundred or so, his thoughts circled around Svetlana and whatever sidebar memories their relationship conjured up. His dreamtime, as well (a sizable portion of the one hundred eighty), had mostly been taken hostage by her: Svetlana on an ice floe floating out to sea, while he hopped from foot to foot and semaphored helplessly from a rocky coast; Svetlana tumbling down a deep well, while the rope she clung to ripped through his palms until he was no longer able to hold on, and so on.

He felt scraped raw by regret and self-recrimination. How could he have behaved so badly? Why had he fallen mum during her marathon of pain and remorse? Although knowing he needed to be strong, stunned into silence, he had failed her.

Until she mentioned the Novosibirsk medicine man, he'd never even considered a rival. That he could lose her. He'd assumed . . . well, hard to say what he'd assumed. She was just there, his gift from the gods, an angel sent down when he needed her. Pleasuring his body and breathing life into his spirit, not to mention helping him in practical ways large and small. Can't get your story translated? My father can do it. Can't afford a St. Petersburg hotel? Stay with me. Can't afford to eat out? I'll cook for you. Need to fly to Novosibirsk cheaply? How about free? And she was still helping. Just as his coffers were nearing exhaustion, she'd arranged free air travel to Japan in pursuit of his goals. A perk she got from Aeroflot no doubt, but still.

Yet who wouldn't have been pole-axed by her admission? She had betrayed him. And he, like a fool, had been taken in. It wasn't his good looks, charm, or authorial persona that had pushed her buttons; she'd been *paid* to fuck him silly. And he'd fallen into it like a bear into a honeypot. Whenever he remembered her knife-edge moment of revelation, he fumed. How did she put it? "Charlie, I fuck you for money."

Was that it? She had flattered him, teased him, used her beautiful body to eclipse his senses completely, and it was all a lie. She'd done it for money! Whether she was a two-dollar whore or a five-thousand-dollar whore, did it really matter? He'd been rejected before, maybe even two-timed once or twice, but for *money*? She'd accepted a bribe to undermine him and his mission; didn't that taint all her subsequent declarations of caring and ardor? Wasn't her avowal that she adored him now critically suspect?

Charles breathed deeply for a moment, trying to get his anger under control.

Well, actually, that wasn't as clear as it might be, was it? What, after all, had she gained by confessing to him now? And there was the matter of the five thousand dollars she'd been paid to seduce him. Not only had she failed to spend it; she'd given it to him for the next leg of his journey. What better proof of her loyalty? Of her love?

This all seemed strange—like an unknown language. Charles's romantic past had been curiously bleak. Married at twenty, he'd been divorced at twenty-six. The years he and Celeste had spent together were weighted more toward intellectual stimulation, rather than carnal, and noticeably short on joy.

They'd met in college when he'd felt, as one often does at that age, at the center of roads forking in many possible directions. There had been a nagging urge to write—but he'd felt unworthy, since he saw others all around him who had better skills, people who'd gone to prep schools where they'd read widely among the A-list authors. In short, he'd had neither compass nor map.

Celeste, on the other hand, had known exactly what she wanted. She was a bang-on devotee of the life of the mind, with a will forged from pure titanium. Since she was working hard to be a scholar, he—reluctantly, tentatively—had gravitated toward that, as well. Scholarship became what they did together, how they defined themselves. But in the back of his mind, there fibrillated the sense that it was *she* who was defining *him*, and after a while, that rankled. In a few years, Celeste was an anthropologist, carving out Linguistics and shamanistic societies as her bailiwick. He was a Russian historian, sleepwalking through the political chronology but growing fat on Russian literature and philosophy.

In their prenuptial courtship, they had sometimes made love, but more often, they talked. Not long after they were married, carnal encounters wandered out the door on little cat feet, becoming, for the most part, a memory. When sexual excitement wandered in again through the back door, it was not—for Celeste—with Charles, but with a psychologist who taught at the same small college in the Pacific Northwest where Charles and Celeste had both accepted positions. With the psychologist—so Charles had learned from Celeste's need to unpack—there had been swelling crescendos and clashing cymbals as there had rarely been with Charles. And very shortly, for Charles, the sexual clamor—that ardor, that fervor—had been re-claimed with a senior coed from his Russian history class. Their affair had proved sweet, lovely, white-hot, and brief.

He and Celeste divorced soon afterward, and he'd left that Northwestern college for a minor university in New York City. Since then, over the years, he'd had only scattered and skittish liaisons, some lasting longer than others, but each overlaid with a patina of nebulous gloom. A few lightning bolts, but not many. And never any association long enough to develop rust.

And now? Quite frankly, love was a word he'd never expected to hear again. From anyone. And when Svyeta had voiced it, he'd been unable to reciprocate.

Was love what he was feeling now? Could he imagine a life with Svyeta? What kind of life would it be? An Okie, California dirt-farmer, ex-college professor, minor writer living in New York, partnered with the beautiful daughter of a brilliant mathematician, motherless and raised in the wilds of Khrushchev's Siberia? And twenty years' difference in their ages. Uh, make that twenty-two.

36
IF THIS IS JAPAN,
WHAT TIME IS IT?

CHARLES'S TRANSLATOR, CRETA Kano, lived in an unpretentious middle-class Tokyo neighborhood of small, tightly spaced bungalows not far from the train station and just around the corner from a dry cleaners. Equipped with these directions, Charles had been able to find the right door without too much difficulty. So he hoped, at least. He took out his handkerchief and wiped the back of his neck before ringing the bell. So August was hot in Tokyo as well?

After three rings, a woman of perhaps Svetlana's age came to the door dressed in an orange blouse and off-white linen skirt, each reminiscent somehow of the early nineteen-sixties. Bouffant hair-do, white pumps. Where was the pillbox hat? Something butch about her, he thought, in the broad forehead and square jaw, the hard eyes below woolly eyebrows. Were it not for the eyes' pronounced epicanthic fold and the fact that she was standing on a doorstep in the middle of Tokyo, he would not have guessed she was Japanese.

And she soon gave cause to doubt it further. She thrust her hand forward like a Texas oilman greeting a neighboring millionaire. Charles half expected to be grabbed and hugged, but the handshake ended after one downward yank, an elevator hitting the bottom of the shaft. *Howdy, pard!* he almost said.

Then came the bow, which he returned.

She stepped back. "Dr. Baker," she said. "Won't you come in?"

He smiled and slipped off his shoes at her signal, following her into a modest, tastefully furnished living room. A Naugahyde couch and two matching chairs surrounded a glass-topped table. Off to one side lay a breakfast nook, and beyond it a row of low-slung windows.

Another woman stood quietly beside the couch.

"Dr. Baker, I would like you to meet my sister, Malta," said Ms. Kano.

"Ah! Very pleased to meet you, Ms. Kano and . . . Ms. Kano," he said. "Very pleased indeed."

He smiled and bowed, suppressing an urge to inquire about the names. His bow, however, set off a chain reaction. First Malta bowed, then Creta, then he bowed again, after which they bowed together. Then, mercifully, it stopped.

Malta's resemblance to her sister was striking, although she was shorter than Creta and was dressed in a kimono. Her hair was done up Geisha style, a high chignon held in place by either a comb or a long pin, as if she were prepared to rush off to a rehearsal of *The Mikado*. Perhaps it was his jet lag, he thought, but both sisters struck him somehow as caricatures.

"Please," said Creta, indicating the couch.

As he lowered himself to the cushions, Malta, whom he had come to think of as Kano Number Two, moved to fluff a pillow for him, while Creta asked if he'd like a cup of tea.

"Wonderful!" exclaimed Charles, too loudly for the small space. "Yes," he muttered, more softly this time. "I'd love a cup." And the first Ms. Kano—his translator—went off to the kitchen, while Kano Number Two sank down next to him on the couch. So close he could smell her perfume. Shalimar, was it?

"You are probably wondering about our names," she said.

"Well—"

"Made-up, of course. Mine because I spent some time earlier on the island of Malta. That's in the Mediterranean."

"Yes, I know. In fact I've just come from—"

She cut him off. "I spent some time in Malta in my youth. And Creta spent time on Crete. Hence the names. Creta we spell with a C in English, but it is pronounced not like Greta but like Krita—with a K—because the Greek name for Crete is Kriti. Understand?"

"Ah! Well . . . that makes sense, I suppose."

"I speak almost no Greek. I speak Maltese. And Japanese. And English." She paused.

"Yes! Quite well, as a matter of fact!" Charles replied, a bit addled. "The English, I mean."

"Creta, growing up in Crete, speaks Greek. And reads it. Very well. She's the one who's skilled as a translator."

"So I gathered. My correspondence with her suggested that she's connected to the University of Tokyo. Is that correct?"

"She teaches modern Greek in the graduate school. Department of South European Languages and Literatures. I barely know Greek. A few words only. I speak Maltese."

It's like being a squash ball careening among multiple strangely-angled walls, Charles thought. Was Malta on some roundabout campaign to get his story translated into the language of an island nation that over 5,000-plus tumultuous years had been ruled by everyone from the Phoenicians to the Knights of St.

John? "Well, since it's Greek I need right now, I'm certainly pleased that she's agreed to translate my story."

Creta returned to the living room with a tray, a teapot, and three cups. They drank in silence for a while.

Eventually, small talk began. After a few minutes, Creta asked about his short story, and Charles, as was his custom, gave her a printed copy of the Greek text, plus a CD with the story its only contents. During the next several minutes, he outlined the nature of the project, as he had to Lu Chi, Professor Mahanthappa, and each of the other translators.

"Good," she said. "When do you need this, Dr. Baker?"

"Within two weeks, if you can manage it," he said.

"No problem. I have some time now. Perhaps I can finish in one! But no promises, now." She gave a startling little laugh.

"Fair enough. Well, I suppose I should be going. Thank you for the tea. I'll let you get to it then."

They all rose together, but before he could turn toward the door, Creta said, "Dr. Baker, I need to ask a favor. Could you perhaps help us find our cat?"

"Beg pardon?"

"We have an orange-and-white tabby, who seems to have gone missing. Do you suppose you could help us find him?"

Charles was surprised. *This is very odd*, he thought. "Well, I'm not sure. What did you have in mind?"

"I believe he is out in the alley somewhere. Would you very much mind looking for him?"

"Well, no. I mean, sure, I'll give it a try. How do I make my way into the alley?"

"Through the window."

"You mean—"

"Through the window. Here. I'll show you."

She moved to the row of windows behind the breakfast

nook. With a mighty heave, she slid back one pane and motioned for him to climb out into the alleyway.

He hesitated. The window sill was low enough for him to swing his leg over, but he could see that outside, the paving stones were several feet below the floor he was standing on. He looked back at Creta to confirm that this was what his translator really expected of him. Malta, who had brought him his shoes, smiled beatifically.

"Hah! Well, okay." He slipped on his shoes, bent to tie them, straightened back up. "Well! Here goes! Not as limber as in my younger days, but hey! I'm game! Shouldn't take long, I suppose. Say, I believe I'll take my computer case with me, if you don't mind. Could you hand it to me through the window once I'm outside?"

"Of course," from Creta. "And thank you, Dr. Baker. This is very kind of you."

"Very kind," echoed Malta.

He clambered over the windowsill and let himself down into the alleyway. He thought he might have scuffed his shoes, but there was no other damage. When he'd dusted himself off and adjusted his clothing, he reached back and took the case Creta was offering him.

"So, what's the cat's name?" he said.

"Timothy. He answers to Timothy."

"Okay, then. I'll just go look for Timothy. Oh, when I come back—"

"Just knock on the window, Dr. Baker. And thank you again." She closed the pane and disappeared from view.

37

THE WIND-UP BIRD

CREEEAK!

Charles looked up. It was a bird, he was sure of it. But he didn't see any. He cleared his throat, looked around, and discovered the alleyway was quite narrow, certainly not wide enough for cars to pass through. There was a fence opposite the window he'd just struggled out of, and beyond it, flowers growing in a back yard. Begonias. He looked one way and then the other. To his right, the alley appeared to end fifty or sixty yards along, any exit blocked by the rear wall of a building. In the other direction, it extended further, at least a lengthy city block. He failed to see many hiding places for a cat, but what the hell. Might as well try.

"Timothy!" he yelled. "Oh, Timothy!" He stopped, feeling ridiculous. He didn't know this cat. In fact, he didn't know any cats in Japan. Was his voice too loud, too soft? Should he be saying "Here, kitty-kitty!" instead? He began walking, choosing the way left, still calling the cat's name. There was no reaction, except for the infernal creaking of that damned bird, which he still couldn't see. Irritating.

Why, he wondered, would a cat that didn't know him, that had never heard his voice before, respond to him at all? Wouldn't the cat be repelled, instead? Suspicious? Alarmed? Scared out of its fucking mind? This is not my master! Nor either of my mistresses, each of whom dresses as if she's in a time warp! Or did cats think like that? (Well, surely not the time warp.) Did cats think at all? He had no idea.

After he had wandered along the alley for about fifty yards, crying out an absurd English schoolboy moniker two Japanese sisters he hardly knew had conferred on their missing feline companion, he stopped and leaned against the corner post of a chain-link fence. He lowered his computer case between his legs and sighed. *I've become a fishmonger,* he thought, *in some nineteenth-century waterfront folk ditty:*

"Oh, Timothy! Oh, Timothy,
Alive, alive-oh!"

Or, no, no—even worse—it was as if he were in the middle of some bent tale, a novel, perhaps, with a baffling, mysterious plot, a kind of literary aporia, where—if there was a resolution—it was an invisible one, hanging there in the morning air, just out of reach, high in the bird-squeaky sky.

The real question, of course, was why was he doing this? Had he traveled halfway around the world to chase down a cat in an alley? (Another thought interrupted: even if Timothy was a registered breed, had he now become—ha! ha!—an alley cat?) The answer to why he was doing it was, of course, because they'd asked. And because he felt he owed them, since translating his story seemed more a favor on Creta's part than a business transaction, given what he was able to offer as payment.

The bird screeched again, and Charles looked up. Still invisible. *Anywhere you look,* he thought. *Invisible bird. Invisible cat.*

38
THE BIRD WINDS DOWN

"HEY, THERE!"

Startled out of his reverie, Charles looked up. A Japanese girl of perhaps seventeen or eighteen stood in a yard a few feet away. She was dressed in form-fitting yellow shorts and a flowered cotton blouse whose ends were tied in front, leaving her midriff bare. Slender, with short-cut black hair. Surprisingly large breasts spilling over the top of her blouse. Still, something tomboyish about her, he thought.

"Oh! Hello! You startled me."

"I can see that."

They stood there a moment. Her gaze did not waver. "What are you looking for?" she asked. Her English was flawless American.

"How do you know I'm looking for something?"

"Sixty-something white dude roaming through a closed-off alley on the outskirts of Tokyo?"

She paused, apparently for effect, then added, "Last four or five of those were looking for something."

"I see. What about the four or five before that?"

"My guess is they all were."

"Since you put it that way, I'm looking for a cat."

The bird screeched. They both looked up.

"I'm glad you heard it too," he said. "I was beginning to think that bird was only in my imagination."

"What bird?"

"The one that . . . oh, never mind."

"Just kidding, grandpa. Say, what do I call you?"

"My name is Charles Abel Baker."

"Hi. I'm April. Kawabata."

"Nice to meet you, April."

"I'm not going to call you Charles Abel Baker. Don't you have a nickname?"

The bird's one-note shriek came again, and Charles shook his head, frustrated at not being able to locate it.

"I'll call you Wind-Up Bird," she said.

"Excuse me?"

"That's what you're hearing." She gave a loose wave of her hand toward somewhere in the sky.

"What kind of bird is a wind-up bird?"

"It's the bird that signals spring."

Charles contracted his eyebrows. "A little late, isn't it? Last time I checked, it was August, and hotter than hell."

She laughed.

"Do *you* have a nickname?" he asked.

"April."

"Should have known." He was quiet a moment. "So why can't I see him?" he said at last. "Since you know so much about the neighborhood."

"I should. I live here. Right there." She pointed to a small white house just behind her. The grass under her feet, he noticed, had not been cut in weeks.

"Don't worry, Mr. Wind-Up Bird. No one can see him."

"Really? He's truly invisible?"

"Truly."

They stood there a moment. She was pretty, in a saucy way. Certainly clever. *Must drive the boys mad*, he thought.

"Shouldn't you be in school?"

"I *am* in school. University of Tokyo. And in case you hadn't noticed, Mr. Wind-Up Bird, it's August. No classes until next month. I have a part-time job counting bald men."

His hand went instinctively to his hair.

"I knew that would get you. It's part of a survey. Some people want to know how many bald men there are in Tokyo. For an advertising campaign I suppose. Whether for hairpieces or tonic, I haven't a clue. I just go to subways and peer over the stairway at the men coming up. I have a clipboard and a clicker. Divide them into A, B and C depending on how much hair they've got. And, hey. Don't worry. You barely qualify for a C. It's an okay job, but you can't stand it for more than a couple of hours at a stretch. And it's hard to do it fast enough, unless you're with another person. You wanna count heads with me?"

"I don't think so. Thanks, though."

"Okay, no counting heads for us. Then, listen. You wanna see a well?"

"A well?"

"Yes. Like for drinking water. At least once upon a time it was. It's dry now. I can't figure out who owns it. But it's right over there, where the grass ends, behind that large house."

He looked where she was pointing but, feeling slightly uneasy, said, "Why would I want to see a well? I'm looking for a cat."

"Maybe the cat fell down the well. Ever think of that?"

He pondered a moment, then sighed. The bird screeched. He did not even look up this time.

"Lead on," he said.

39
THE WELL

S HE LED THE way to a large yard with a statue of a bird in one corner. Perhaps the wind-up bird? The house in front of the yard was abandoned, April explained. She had no idea to whom it belonged, if it belonged to anybody. Certainly the property was overgrown with weeds reaching right up to the side of the house, where there was an even larger lot, vacant and equally overrun. At its center was—as promised—a well. It extended out of the ground a few feet and was capped by a round, wooden board. Two medium-sized stones had been laid atop the board to secure it. The well was concrete, but an outer layer of small stones had been pressed into the surface before it dried. Whether a structural decision or an aesthetic one, Charles couldn't be sure.

April removed a stone from the well's cap. A slight girl, she needed both hands to do it, and, since it seemed only fair that he should help, he removed the other. They slid the wooden cap off together. He felt uncomfortably complicit, as if he were now implicated in a clandestine and possibly illegal act.

"It's deep," she said.

He looked in. Beyond the rapidly diminishing light that stretched only a yard or two into the ground, only darkness loomed. "Timothy! Oh, Timothy!" he called dutifully, remembering his purpose. That task seemed so distant now, somehow inconsequential. Still he persisted. "Here, kitty-kitty!"

"He could be dead you know? Down at the bottom? Lying there dead as a doornail."

How was it, he wondered, that a Japanese girl in the middle of Tokyo was so at home with American expressions? Almost without realizing it, he began to examine her cliché. How was it that a doornail could be dead? Were there live doornails? What the hell was a doornail, anyway? Just a nail hammered into a door?

He gave up and answered her question. "Unlikely," he said. "Cats are remarkable in that way; they can fall quite some distance and land on their feet, with little or no injury."

"You know cats?" she asked.

"Just read it somewhere."

A moment of silence, then Charles made a little gasp and slapped his hand to his forehead. He felt he'd been scammed.

"Hey!" he said. "What am I thinking of? The cat couldn't have gone down the well. There was a board over it! I doubt the cat could have heaved the board aside before jumping to its death in the well."

April nodded. "Maybe. But it could have been off when the cat got here. Then someone covered it up again. You never know."

They fell quiet. "You think you should go down?" she asked finally.

Charles felt himself tense. "Go down? Why would I go down?" His voice rose what seemed to him an octave or two; he could feel a slight quiver begin in his lip. "Why would I climb down a dark well looking for a cat I have no genuine interest in? I'm doing this search as a favor. What on earth are you suggesting?"

"Hey, Wind-Up Bird!" she responded. "Don't get so excited. I'm just asking."

She was right, of course. The panic was all his. However ludicrous it would be for him to shimmy down to the bottom of a well to recover the pet, possibly dead, of two odd sisters he'd only just met, it was hardly a reason for his palms to be sweating. Or for that annoying lip-twitch to return.

"Anyway," he said, still defensive. "Look around you. No means of getting down and back."

She looked thoughtful. "You'd need a rope ladder," she said. "A long one."

After a moment, she said, "Have you ever heard the saying, 'When you're supposed to go down, find the deepest well and go to the bottom?'"

He smiled at her. "Can't say that I have. What's it supposed to mean?"

"Haven't the foggiest. Someone said it in one of my classes at the university. I forget who. Relates to Buddhism or something."

Charles shook his head and peered into the well again. He started to speak, but changed his mind. He felt a stirring beside him, like a gentle breeze blowing past.

"Well, Mr. Wind-Up Bird, I have to get going. I need to count bald heads this afternoon."

He drew himself up to his full height and looked at her, struck once again by her composure, her self-possession. She was the queen of direct looks, no question. Hands comfortably at her sides, she stood there giving him a syrupy look that wouldn't quit. He had no idea how to interpret it, but had the spooky thought she might know exactly what he was feeling, even if he didn't.

"Sure you don't wanna go with me?" she asked. Her half-smile never wavered.

"Thank you, April. But I think I'll take one more look for the cat before heading back into the city."

Her smiled deepened, then she curtsied, pirouetted smartly, and left. He watched her walk off, then turned immediately toward the well, not so much to inspect it as to defeat the image of her retreating buttocks in those tight yellow shorts. Now the yard's only human inhabitant, he looked around. Scattered weeds, a few rocks, the occasional empty candy wrapper or potato chip bag, the ugly stub of an abandoned water well.

Only then did he realize he was done searching for Timothy. Nor did he feel like making his way back to the two sisters' window to report on the failure of his mission. A phone call later would have to do. He capped the well, clutched his computer bag firmly, and made his way toward a fence beside the abandoned house. There was an opening, which led, he hoped, to the street.

40
IS IT ZEN THEN?

HIS ROOM AT the Smile Hotel in downtown Tokyo was so tiny that Charles could not take three strides in one direction before needing to pivot and walk the other way. In either direction, he brushed his calves, on one side against the bed, which seemed built for an undernourished jockey, and on the other a plywood platform, which supported a futon the width of a pipe cleaner.

It was an unsuitable place for pacing, yet the next morning, he found himself pacing, agitated by something he couldn't put his finger on. Something about the encounter he'd stumbled into yesterday. Occasionally it was images of the girl, April, that flickered through his mind. *But maybe that was camouflage?* he thought, hopefully. Surfacing just as often, without any tantalizing sexual overtones—or was he fooling himself about that?—were images of the well. Why?

He stopped by the narrow window and moved the curtain aside so a little light could make it through the smudged panes. They were just clear enough for him to see the restless, aggressive traffic six stories down, as well as the giant neon Daiwa sign, several meters tall, on an adjacent building. Daiwa. Was that a restaurant, a camera, a car, or a fishing rod? Christ, he knew so little about Japanese commerce. The windows were not clean enough to take pictures, if you wanted to take pictures, if you had a camera, if—

His thoughts broke off. He sighed and shook his head. What was it about the well? There'd been a well on the ranch, hadn't there? Also dry. Quite near the place he'd staked out Cleo every morning. Like yesterday's well, it was on the site of an abandoned property, formerly that of an old codger—part farmer, part painter—who'd once owned a few acres of desert near the dry arroyo known as Dead Man's Creek. There was an old two-story house on the property, too, built right next to the ravine, which Charles had once sneaked through, telling no one about the paintings, the books, and the huge copper pots and pans he'd found there.

But the well. That was another matter. Several times he'd folded his arms on its rocky sides and peered into it while Cleo munched placidly on the nearby grass. You could see only as far as the light went, of course. And then, as now—there was no escaping it—something had tugged at him to go down. Pins and needles traveled along the back of his neck. What was it April had said, that supposed distillation of Buddhist or Taoist or Shinto or some other kind of received wisdom? "When you're supposed to go down, find the deepest well and go to the bottom." Not even when you *needed to*, but when you were *supposed to*. Was something trying to tell him something?

He'd been pretty much a straight arrow as a teenager, but there'd been a flaky streak. Something foolhardy, adventurous, wild. Once he'd lain down in a cotton field that was being sprayed by a biplane. Face up, eyes wide-open, as several thousand pounds of flying machine thundered past three feet above his nose, its wheels tickling the tops of cotton stalks, while a vaporous cloud of sulfur settled around him. Yet the pull of that old well on the ranch he'd resisted. And now?

The phone rang suddenly, making him jump. Who could that be? He'd given the hotel's number to only one person, his translator, Creta Kano. Could she be experiencing difficulty with the translation? He'd already explained he didn't want to intervene in the process. Did she want to renegotiate her fee? *Hah! Nothing left in the cookie jar, lady!*

The room was so small he could pick up the receiver without moving from the window.

"Hello, Dr. Baker. How are you? Beautiful day outside, isn't it?" A woman's voice: soft, breathy. No trace of an accent, Japanese or anything else.

"Who is this, please?"

"Never you mind who I am, Dr. Baker. Although you will come to know me in time. But, rest assured. I know you."

"How is it you know me? What's your name, please?"

"I know, for example, that you are a writer seeking to get his short story translated from Greek into Japanese. I know that you've had interesting adventures in different countries."

"What? This is not amusing. Who are you? "

"Don't be alarmed, Dr. Baker. May I call you Charlie? I think I should call you Charlie, Charlie."

"But how do you . . . is this April? Are you April Kawabata, playing a joke on me?"

"April? Nice young girl, Charlie. But no dice. I'm not April."

"Then who? How can you possibly know these things?"

"I know your experiences in these countries haven't always gone as smoothly as you'd hoped. I know you have a Russian girlfriend who is causing you some grief at the moment. And you have salacious thoughts about that young piece of jailbait,

Miss Kawabata. She's only seventeen, Charlie, regardless of what she may say. But relax. You'll know who I am in time. I'm surprised you haven't guessed already. In time, you'll come to know me rather well."

"I'm sorry, but this is ridiculous. Why are you calling? Either tell me what you want or get off the line!"

"My, my, we are up tight, aren't we, Charlie." The last was uttered in a comically, almost threateningly, sultry voice. "Wanna know what I'm wearing right now, Charlie? What do you think I'm wearing at the moment?"

Ah, so it was phone sex. But how did she know about—

"Look," he said. "I'm not really interested in anything right now. I don't know how you got this number, or how you were able to dig this stuff up, but—"

"Charlie! You think I'm 'digging it up,' as you put it? I know you better than that. Let me relax you. I'm wearing a transparent blue negligee and matching panties, and I'm lying on my bed at this moment. The negligee ties at the top with a blue silk ribbon and has come undone, so that one of my breasts is exposed. So what are you wearing, Charlie? Are you naked? Is your thingamabob getting hard?"

My thingamabob! Good grief!

He hung up, sweating. Now his damnable lip was twitching again. He went to the window and punched at the buttons on the air conditioner, but it must have been jammed into the duct just for show.

So who in the hell was that? What a strange universe he had fallen into.

He collapsed onto the narrow bed, lying back with his arms folded behind his head, one elbow jammed against the wall. He had planned to go sightseeing today. Wander through downtown Tokyo. See the Imperial Gardens, visit the Meji

Jingu Shinto temple grounds. And tomorrow, perhaps take a train south to pay his respects to Mt. Fuji. But invisible forces were nudging him in unaccustomed directions.

And odd though it was, he viewed the phone call as just a diversion. He had decided. What he needed to do was *go down*.

41

CAN YOU APPRECIATE LIGHT WITHOUT KNOWING THE DARKNESS?

BY THE TIME Charles arrived at the well, it was after 2 p.m., and the sun was very hot. Having inquired of everyone he met in downtown Tokyo, either in English or fractured guidebook Japanese, he'd finally found a store selling the appropriate gear, and now he felt prepared. He'd bought a rope ladder, the longest they sold, choosing one with wooden rungs. He had three plastic bottles of water, several energy bars to stave off hunger, and a couple of packets of Kleenex. Never know when you might need to blow your nose.

He had no idea how long he planned to remain underground, but decided he was adequately provisioned. Alongside the well, he found anchoring grommets (apparently it was not the first time a rope ladder had been attached) and—feeling like a bungee-jumper preparing to hurl himself off the George Washington Bridge—he tossed the unanchored end of the rope into the hole. A line from an old Southern blues ditty came to him: "Gotta kee-eep the de-villll . . . down in the hole!" He chuckled, paused a moment, then heaved himself over the side.

The rope ladder's flexibility caught him off guard. His weight stretched and warped the rope as he descended each rung, making it difficult to find his footing on the next rung down. His foot slipped—twice—but each time he recovered and continued. His computer, which he'd been reluctant to leave behind, was shoulder-strapped to his body, water bottles stuffed securely in one outside pouch, energy bars in the other.

A few rungs down, he could see nothing below, not even the next foothold. From here it would be strictly by feel. The only thing visible was the white disk of the opening above, now growing smaller and smaller. The ladder was his only connection to the outside world. He found himself breathing heavily, more from anxiety, he suspected, than physical stress. He continued anyway.

It's not just stubbornness, he told himself. Nor some inner resistance to reversing direction, which some had accused him of in the past. His ex-wife, for example. But no. It was because he needed to go down. Was *supposed* to go down.

His foot touched the graveled surface at the bottom of the well, and he sighed with relief. Thank God the ladder had been long enough!

After resting a moment, he sloughed off his bag and positioned it carefully against the wall. It was peculiar to be operating only by feel. *Rather like the cave in India*, he thought, *though thank goodness there will be no Adela this time*. He stayed upright a moment longer, feeling the well's cold sides with the flat of his palms, then slid down slowly, coming to rest beside his bag.

Sides. In a thought that struck him as belonging somewhere in a Samuel Beckett play, he wondered if it was proper to refer to the inner surface of this cylinder as having sides. Didn't the idea of a side presume an opposing side? Here there was no "on the one side," or "on the other side," because it was all continuous surface, was it not? But if you didn't call these walls "sides" what could you call them (it)? Did other languages have the same problem as English? *Oh, horseshit!*

He exhaled sharply and looked straight ahead. The dark ahead was as dense as that to either side of him.

Now what? he wondered. *Well,* he began, and smiled, remembering his father, who'd been notorious for quipping "That's a deep subject!" whenever someone used the word "well" in a sentence. Not very funny, in Charles' opinion—in fact, veritable schoolyard humor—but it always drove his father into a cackle, and Charles shook his head as he remembered. No one to whom his father had ever addressed that remark had laughed along with him (unless they had to; he was the foreman, after all), but it never stopped him from repeating it. Charles had always thought of his father as bereft of humor. Why, he wondered, had the man clung so tightly to that morsel? That tiny pun. Like a man possessed. Was he, like his father, a man possessed? Just as driven, but by different things?

In any event, here we now are, he thought to himself. *So. Why are we here? And while we're at it, what's this royal "we" bullshit? Who's down here with you, Charlie? Your father, clearly. But who else?*

He leaned back against the wall and closed his eyes. No darker, of course, but more tranquil, anyway. After perhaps a minute, he barked a laugh. Because he suddenly realized that he needed to pee, and just as suddenly realized he'd neglected to prepare for it. Game over? *No!* he decided. *Absolutely not.* He was determined to stay a while. Nerves could be driving his need. *Once you put it out of your mind,* he told himself, *you'll be fine.*

•

A few minutes later, he began to cry.

Ah, Svyeta! he breathed. She'd poured her heart out to him. She'd confessed her feelings, while he lay there like a wooden dummy, a fence post. Now look how the fence post is splintering!

Realizing he was unlikely to ever see her again, he was struck by a crippling sense of loss. A hole seemed to open in his chest, and widen until it was larger than his entire body, deeper than the well that now contained him.

Here he was, careening around the world on an obsessive mission to do this stupid translation project, while—right at the outset, on that plane flight to Moscow—he had stumbled into one of the most, maybe *the* most, bounteous experiences of his life and . . . failed to recognize it. Had he ever been happier than those two weeks in Siberia? Had he ever stopped to ask why? To consider what her feelings about him might be? Or his for her? No. He'd plunged ahead like a child playing blind man's bluff. Everything was about his "important" project. His next language, his next translator, his next plane flight, his next hotel. About *him,* and how he would complete the next leg of this stupid, compulsive game he was playing.

Had he ever asked her about *her?* What did he know of *her* dreams, *her* wishes? Well, a little. But very little. He'd wanted to do something extraordinary and daring, something life-changing. And meanwhile, some self-willed blindness had kept him from seeing his connection with Svyeta for the extraordinary, fundamentally daring thing that it was.

Two weeks ago, in that Corfu hotel room—however

shocked he might have been—could he not have tried to prize out of her what it was that had driven her to take a step that now shamed her? He could have. He should have. But he didn't.

"Paralyzed, dumb-dick Charles Abel Baker—that's who I've been," he muttered to himself. "Make that Dis-Abled Baker."

42
SACKCLOTH AND ASHES

H E DIDN'T KNOW how long he'd been sitting there, adrift in his thoughts. Had he been asleep? Suddenly he felt parched. At the same time, his bladder was screaming, *empty me or burst*. How long had he been ignoring *that*? Quickly, he downed a whole bottle of water, used the empty container to relieve his bladder. Replacing the cap, he moved the bottle as far away from his person as he could manage.

He looked up. The small disk at the crest of the well was white no longer, but a deep, dark blue. Evening had come. Up there, beyond this well and the vacant lot surrounding it, people were sitting down to a meal of chicken yakitori, or ordering a mojito in a crowded bar, or going bowling perhaps, or just settling into an easy chair to read. What might they be reading? In an alternate universe, perhaps, a collection of stories by Charles Abel Baker. Yes! Beginning with the title story, "We Shall Come Rejoicing." Hmmm. But in what language?

He laughed, then relaxed back against the concrete to think some more. And the mood of weighty regret dropped down upon him once again, like some kind of inescapable companion.

Charlie, Charlie, Charlie, he admonished himself. *Did you fuck up, or did they?*

What he was remembering was his abrupt separation from the university, some thirty years before. The pain was like tearing a bandage off a wound insufficiently healed.

Writing might have been his first choice, back in college days—such was his memory nowadays, at least. But long after his marriage withered and was sundered, he'd continued teaching, moving from a small college in a western state to a more ballyhooed university in New York City, expanding his course offerings, working on several articles peeled off from his dissertation. (But not completing them, his writing time leaning increasingly toward fiction.)

It was the teaching he loved, not academia in general. He'd enjoyed only a few of his colleagues; others he made no effort to know. Only too late did he become aware of an intradepartmental pecking order, never thinking twice about whom it might be useful to cultivate a friendly relationship with. Nor did he think about how his indifference might risk alienating senior faculty members. He fraternized more with actors, poets and dancers than with academics. So he never saw the axe blade falling.

Down in the well, Charles began to consider another label for his naïveté: he'd considered himself above it all. *Let others participate in the rat race*, he'd thought. *I have autonomy here in academia. I teach my courses however I want, choose my own books, give whatever lectures I want. So long as I'm faithful to my own vision, I'm okay.*

He'd been proud of that attitude, right up to the moment a faculty committee had denied him tenure.

Three decades past that event, Charles still hears his inner voice cry out: *Foul! Wrong! Unfair!*

When he'd appealed to his department chairman, the response had been, "Frankly, Charlie, you're considered a loose cannon. Old-timers—those on the tenure committee—don't know you very well, and what they know they don't like. You're supposed to be a historian, yet you mostly dabble in the art of letters instead." His chairman had actually chuckled then, switching his cigar from one side of his mouth to the other with an adroit motion of his tongue, before adding, "Sorry, Charlie."

It had come at a time when jobs in history departments were few and getting fewer. To this day, it had all felt to him insupportably unfair.

But.

His mind having reached the rear platform of the train he was on, he somehow managed to swing aboard a car on a parallel track heading in the opposite direction.

Maybe they were right, after all. Scribbling stories into the wee hours of the night did subtract from the time he'd had available to do serious scholarship, right? Maybe he should have spent more time whittling down his two-volume dissertation into a publishable book? Was it unfair of them to expect *that*?

And there was little doubt, as he now saw it, that he'd had a chip on his shoulder. "Contumacious" was a word he remembered overhearing another faculty member whisper once, as he'd walked past in the hall, and he'd wondered, *me*? Am I balky? Contrary? Willful? Refractory? *Well, maybe*, he thought now. Maybe he shouldn't have been so vocal about the deadening ennui of faculty meetings, or dodged committee assignments as if they were the incubators of infectious disease. Had his gripes been overheard? He'd read enough nineteenth-century British novels to know that when the heroine passes a private note in the village bookstore, the whole town will know its contents before midnight.

Does it follow, Charlie wondered down in his black hole, that he'd never been cut out for academia in the first place? At least unsuitable for a university that valued scholarly publication above all else? In fact, it might be argued they'd done him a favor. Once out of academia, he'd been free to pursue his writing as best he could, limited only by the need to make a living.

But that, of course, had not been easy! Plenty cold outside the warmth of Philosophy Hall. What had he been trained for? Nothing. Eventually, he'd managed to find a civil service job, curtail his urge to cavil at every shortcoming, keep his nose clean, and cooperate alike with fellow staff members and bosses, like normal people. Along the way, he'd given up drinking, saved a little money, earned a small pension, and used his spare time to write.

Charles shrugged and sighed. Strangely, he began to feel as if a load had been lifted. At least a little bit. He scrambled in his bag for an energy bar, began to eat it hungrily. Perhaps it was time to return to the upstairs world? He took a swig of water, relieved himself once more into the bottle he'd set aside for urine, packed everything securely, put the computer bag's strap around his shoulder, and felt for the ladder.

He felt again. Since the ladder was not where he expected it, he now went carefully around the well's entire circumference, palms to the concrete, slowly. He went around again. And again.

There was no question. The ladder was gone.

43
ONLY THE PASTA IS REAL

E DUARDO ENJOYED BEING a waiter. The efficiency of his movements, the alertness to detail, the energizing tug of his sixth sense. Who needs water? Who needs a drink? Who wants to pay their bill but doesn't know it yet? These were capacities he manifested with pride. He did think it a bit odd that Roberto's was packed on a Thursday evening, but you couldn't always predict.

Standing now in his starched white shirt, black vest, and black tie against the blue velvet drapes dividing the garlic-redolent kitchen from the sedate and carpeted dining area, he was alive to everything in the room. He sensed that the family of four at Table 3 needed water, and noodled Julio into action with a modest dip of his chin. He noticed that among the large family dining early this evening—they occupied Table 10, the big round one in the far corner—the children were restless and about to become rambunctious. That bore watching; he knew with mounting certainty that, within the next five minutes, the eight-year old would upset his mother's glass and flood the tablecloth with blood-red wine. Perhaps a subtle intervention now would save both the waitstaff's burden and the family's laundry bill.

At the same time, he sensed that the couple at Table 7, either newlyweds or recently engaged (he had seated them at the most discreet and least visible location), were keen to abandon the restaurant for their hotel room and rip off each other's clothes in a white-hot rush of passion. Quickly he began to weave his way through the tables, knowing the man would be signaling for the check by the time he reached them. He'd been observing the man's restless right hand beneath the tablecloth, on a stealth mission to explore the underside of the woman's Bendel skirt. Bowing slightly, smiling subtly, Eduardo made sure to drain the remaining ounces of the Huerhuero Vineyard Cabernet Sauvignon (his suggestion) into each of their glasses before producing the check and accepting the platinum credit card.

Eduardo Montalbán was Mexican, born into a Teotihuacan family that was prosperous or insolvent, depending on who was husband of the month. His mother was a hot-looking go-getter who had had many lovers over as many years, but bore only two sons. ("And *gracias a Dios* for that!" she had often exclaimed.) Who his father was, was not entirely clear, though she'd claimed it was Ricardo Montalbán and had conferred that surname on Eduardo. To her elder son, Juan, she gave the name Negrete, after Jorge Negrete, an earlier and older film star. She apparently loved actors. They'd been back and forth between Hollywood and Mexico City many times.

Certainly, Eduardo had the looks. Even in his sixties, his strong-jawed, handsome face resembled his putative father's: the Apollonian nose, the chiseled brow, the broad mouth always with its hint of a smile, the dancing brown eyes. The wavy black hair had eventually become pepper-and-salt, as had the small, neatly trimmed moustache.

But good looks and waitering creds figured only slightly in Eduardo's story. He had other skills. He was a computer maven who was uncommonly adept at disguise. (Code name: Mandrake.) He'd been recalled to the States twenty years ago, after a brilliant undercover career on four continents, because his high-tech skills were needed in New York. Even now, the largest room of his fourth-floor walkup on East Fifty-Fourth Street resembled a sophisticated computer lab. Head-waitering at Roberto's had at first been a cover, but when he'd retired from the Company five years earlier, he'd decided he enjoyed it, so why not?

Past 11:30 p.m., the restaurant emptied out. Singly or in couples, the late-night diners vanished into the humid August evening. Other waitstaff and busboys had already departed, one by one. The chef had left, as well; kitchen staff was in its final stages of cleanup. Only one tall gentleman remained in the dining room, hunched over an espresso at a corner table, face buried in the *International Herald Tribune*. Scattered copies of the *New York Times*, the *Times of London,* and *Le Monde Diplomatique* bespoke a long tenure at the table. A faint click from the back of the restaurant told both Eduardo and his customer that Julio—always the last out—had departed, and Eduardo began walking as the man lowered his newspaper. It was Jonathan Belknap.

Eduardo sank down, relaxing at last, discarding his waiterly aspect with a sigh. Jonathan scooted over to make room on the banquette. He tossed the *Trib* atop the other papers and folded his hands.

"So, Eddie. What word?"

"Frankly, I'm worried."

"Really? Why?"

"I've lost track. I don't know where he is."

"I thought you'd given him a GPS bud."

Months ago, shortly after he and Jonathan had their

first meeting in years, and as soon as Jonathan had outlined his concerns, Eduardo had recruited another friend to keep track of Charles Baker's whereabouts at close range, and to intervene as inconspicuously as possible if help was needed— Roger Wawrinka, formerly with the Company, who lived in Berne. Smilin' Jack, as he was known, had flown to Moscow, then Siberia, following hard on the heels of his target. At Eduardo's request, he had let himself into the apartment in Akademgorodok one night when all were asleep, and planted a GPS device in Charles's shoe. That apparatus had kept track of Charles's location when he'd crash-landed in northern China. It had been Smilin' Jack who had alerted the Chinese branch of the International Red Cross to the wreckage; with help from Eduardo's high-tech equipment, he'd been able to guide helicopters to the precise location and they had ferried Charles to the hospital in Beijing.

Eduardo allowed himself a sigh. "I had. I did. And it's performed flawlessly up to now. Smilin' Jack follows him around, and I'm the one who alerts him to where his target is when the tail doesn't work. The only gap was India, because Jack was off the scent at that moment, but he's saved your guy's bacon several times. Notably in Iceland, where he was about to take a tumble into a gorge. Somebody had monkeyed with his harness, we suspect."

Jonathan nodded. "I remember a brief reference to it in the encrypted email you sent. That was a close one! Is there more?"

"Oh, yeah! In Italy, Jack was on his tail on the train when our adversary swiped the target's computer case out from underneath your guy's seat while he was in the loo and tossed it off the platform of the car. That would have really fucked up your friend's project. Fortunately, our scuzzball was too hasty; the train was passing over a viaduct all right, but it was too close to the end of the bridge when he let fly. Or maybe it was just a bad toss. You know Cruikshank. Smart as a shark, but coked-up most of the time. Or worse. Anyway, the case landed in some soft sand and bushes right next to a girder, not in the water he was aiming for. Jack spotted it, got off at the next stop, and recovered it. Once I'd told him your friend's location, thanks to the GPS unit, he got it back to him. Anonymously, of course."

"Was that the last time he needed to step in?"

"Nope. That earthquake in Greece? Your friend was out in the city—lucky bastard!—when his hotel wall collapsed. Fortunately, Smilin' Jack was just across the street in a hotel that had better luck. So, being on the spot, he just saunters over, pokes through the rubble like any other Good Samaritan, and comes up with your friend's—what's his name? Charlie? Anyway, he rescued Charlie's computer case. Once again. Got it back to the hotel authorities, who passed it along."

"Sounds like he's been useful. Like you say, I do know Pig—Cruikshank—who's a royal bastard. But I don't know Smilin' Jack. What made you pick him?"

Eduardo grinned. "Oh, I worked with Jack many times back in the day. Particularly in Libya. He's an all-around good operator. Lives in Berne now, and he was bored. We actually didn't expect as much trouble as you were worried about, but your dude seems to have a knack for getting in over his head, with or without Pig's help."

"Okay. So what happened in India?"

"Well, Jack was away at that moment. I can tell you your boy went to some weird places. I mean, into a cave, for Christ's sake? As far as I can tell. I know for sure the signal disappeared for about twenty minutes, then popped right back, pretty as you please. By the way, no caves listed in that location. I have no idea."

"So why was your boy not around?"

"Well, let me ask you a question. Who do you think is paying for this junket? All those plane flights and hotel bills, all that chow? You never offered to contribute, right?"

Jonathan played his tongue over his teeth, poking at something caught between two molars. He'd eaten penne Bolognese and a salad; probably the salad was the culprit. "Well," he said finally, "I would have, of course! And will, if necessary. You didn't ask."

Eduardo laughed. "Just yanking your chain, Jon. It's paid for. The same guy who hired Pig to spike the project? He's the one providing the funding."

"Excuse me? How is that possible? The fellow who's paying Cruikshank to sabotage the project, is also bankrolling Smilin' Jack to keep it clean? You're using Wainscot's money?"

Eduardo grinned. "Exactly. Only he doesn't know it. The reason Smilin' Jack was not around for part of the India trip is he was in Georgetown picking up funds."

"Georgetown! I don't follow."

A delighted chuckle. "Well, you don't know Smilin' Jack, but you do know Pig. Let me tell you, these dudes are somatic twins so to speak: same height, broad-shouldered, solidly built, tubby. Even their faces aren't that different. Close enough that, with a little artistic doctoring—Jack's almost as good at disguises as I am—he was able to pull off a little banking scam. He knows his way around banks, anyway. Lives in *Berne*, for Christ's sake."

An appreciative grunt from Jonathan.

"So here's how it worked. Wainscot dumped a ton of money in an offshore account in Cayman for Pig to draw on whenever he needs it. I was waiting on their table when they hatched the plot. That was dumb luck, of course—I didn't know it was your friend they were talking about until later. Took me no more than two hours to break into the *Banco Estafadores* server and identify the account number, and after that, it was a cinch. Smilin' Jack is tapping the same account Pig is, and Wainscot is paying for the whole thing."

Jonathan managed a smile. "Sheer genius, Eddie. And I appreciate the update. But what's gone wrong now?"

"Beats me. The signal's stopped. And Smilin' Jack, who's usually on top of things, didn't see where Charlie went. We've lost the scent. Sorry, Jon. Last we know he's in Tokyo, been there a few days. We know he's registered at the Smile Hotel. We know the broad he's getting to do the translation. But Charlie has vanished."

"Device malfunction?"

"Unlikely. My equipment is state of the art. It's like he's fallen into a hole somewhere."

Jonathan was frowning. He removed his glasses and rubbed the bridge of his nose. "Well," he said. Then repeated it. "Well."

He rose slowly, collected his newspapers into a bundle.

"You'll keep me informed? If anything changes?"

"My computer at home is on 24/7. And Smilin' Jack can get in touch with me anytime too, by encrypted phone. I'll keep you posted."

They looked at each other a long moment, and Jonathan let out a breath he didn't even know he was holding.

Eduardo raised his eyebrows. "Regards to your wife, Jon."

"Don't be daft. You don't know my wife. For that matter, you don't even know me."

They smiled, briefly shook hands, and clasped each other's shoulder. Then Jonathan let himself out the door. Five minutes later, Eduardo followed.

44
ROUND AND ROUND THE MULBERRY BUSH

CHARLES HAD LONG ago discovered that neither of his devices worked. His smart phone was not smart enough to connect from below ground with anyone, nor was his computer able to find a link to the Internet. By now, indeed, both batteries were dead, a fact which did not fail to remind him he'd forgotten to charge them before embarking on this venture.

Hunger pangs, once the power bars had been exhausted, had come on strong, in waves. They had finally backgrounded themselves, a low-decibel hum from somewhere you couldn't name, annoying but ignorable. Quite early on, he'd decided, intelligently enough, to ration his intake of water, and had drunk only a capful at a time of the two pints remaining to him. Now that was gone too, and he was thirsty, his tongue fuzzy. He'd lost track of how many times the small disc at the top of the well (his only visual focal point) had brightened then darkened, only to disappear altogether until next time.

Now he lolled motionless in the dark, at the bottom of the well, waiting for what would come next.

•

At some point, the horses took over. He found himself unaccountably astride a strong mount, riding at full gallop over a flat plain. It was not the horse of his youth on the ranch, the one he'd cared for but not owned. The horse he was riding this time, at a breakneck pace across the prairie, was a roan, like the one they came to call Secretariat.

Amazing! Galloping over the plains on perhaps the greatest racehorse of all time! Bouncing painfully, riding bareback, clinging desperately to the horse's mane.

Ahead of him, a cloud of dust that proves to be—as he draws near—the ragtag horde of Indians and soldiers that Sequoya led into the Mexican desert in pursuit of his lost tribe. He is chasing Sequoya! "Hey, Chief!" He tries to shout. He spots him up front, head held erect, as if leading a regiment into battle. In the air he can recognize the letters of the Cherokee alphabet still dancing around Sequoya's turban-wrapped head, drifting back his way, swirling, becoming ephemeral, disappearing. Suddenly, Charles hears hoofbeats from behind. Swiveling as best he can, he sees he is being pursued. A cluster of fat-bottomed men on horseback. Shouting, but what are they shouting? Is this threatening, or do they mean to rescue him? He tightens his grip on Secretariat's mane, tries to keep his eyes on Sequoya.

Then Sequoya and his army vanish. A ravine has swallowed them. Charles's horse stumbles. Charles is catapulted into the air, lands hard on the dirt, tumbles end over end. Coming to rest facing his pursuers, he sits, arms stretched behind him for support. On the fat men come. Now they've dismounted;

now they advance like a small forest moving. Fanatical smiles. Fangs. Each man carries a scimitar, brandished high. Unable to rise, Charles scrambles backward, crablike. The ground beneath him softens, becomes quicksand. He starts to sink. The marauders stop at the edge, grinning. Now he is up to his waist, now to his shoulders, his chin. He closes his eyes, accepting the inevitable.

•

"Mr. Wind-Up Bird? Mr. Wind-Up Bird! Halloo! Are you down there?"

He hears the sounds indistinctly at first. The image of sucking sand fades. Someone is calling him. *This is real! Someone is really calling!*

He struggles to raise himself to a sitting position, trying to answer but finding he can squeeze out only the scratchiest of sounds. He coughs. The call comes again:

"Mr. Wind-Up Bird! Are you there?"

"Yes!" he croaks. "Yes! I'm here! It's me, Baker! I'm down at the bottom of the well!"

"Well, Mr. Wind-Up Bird, what on earth are you doing down there?"

"Never mind. Someone pulled up the ladder. Can you toss it down?"

"Of course, Mr. Wind-Up Bird. But why did you go down there in the first place? Who pulled it up?"

It was she who had put the idea in his head to go down, but he was too exhausted to remind her. "Listen, April! It's you, isn't it? April Kawabata?"

"Of course it's me!"

"April! Someone was playing a trick, I guess. But listen!

Please! I can't hold out much longer. Please send me down the rope ladder?"

"Of course, Mr. Wind-Up Bird. But I hope you'll tell me how you got yourself in such a pickle! Here it comes!"

With a small clatter the ladder fell, all the way to the bottom. Breathing heavily—panting actually—Charles gathered up his belongings and fastened them around him, only now understanding how weak he was. Positioning his hands and feet on the ladder nearly required more than he could give. His muscles trembled. He took a deep breath and slowly began to climb. Ten minutes later, with April's help at the very top, he stumbled out of the well and collapsed against its side.

"My goodness, Mr. Wind-Up Bird, you don't look so good."

"Water. You have water?"

"I live right over there, Mr. Wind-Up Bird. You stay here now. I'll be back with water in just a moment."

"Don't worry . . . too weak to move."

A short while later—Charles couldn't have said how long—she was back, extending a quart of bottled water.

"Take it easy is what I suggest," she said softly. "Don't drink too fast. That's what they tell you after marathons. I've seen it on TV."

Charles tried to drink slowly, but found it difficult. He kept returning the bottle to his mouth, kept gulping.

"*OmiGod*, that tastes good."

"I should think so. Now. What happened, Mr. Wind-Up Bird?"

"I went down to the bottom of the well. And someone pulled the ladder up. I'm lucky they didn't carry it off!"

"Not sure I would call this lucky, Mr. Wind-Up Bird.

More like one of those 'If it weren't for bad luck, I wouldn't have any luck at all' kind of deals, if you ask me." She smiled and patted his hand. "So why did you decide to go down there in the first place?"

He sighed, almost a groan. "Remember what you told me? That quote about 'when you are supposed to go down, find the deepest well you can and go to the bottom'?'"

"Wow, you took that seriously?"

"I felt like I was supposed to go down, so I did."

"Wow! You're a real philosopher."

"Hardly. I just. Well. Never mind. Listen, April. Thank you for coming to my rescue. Thank you so much for noticing the rope ladder . . . but, listen, can you please call me . . . Charles?"

"Of course, Mr. Charles. And you're welcome. No problem."

"Thanks. Whoa! I feel faint. You don't have anything to eat over at your house, do you? I can pay you for it."

"Not an issue. I can make you a sandwich, real quick. Hang on."

While she was gone, he remained motionless, half sitting, half lying, propped against the wall. He fell asleep in the short time she was gone. She woke him, sat beside him, and was quiet while he ate his sandwich. Halfway through, he smiled for the first time in days. Here he was in Tokyo, center of one of the world's great cuisines, eating a ham and cheese sandwich!

When he had finished, he allowed his head to droop onto her shoulder. She took his hand. "Feel better, Mr. Charles?"

"Still weak, but I need to get back to my hotel. How can I repay you?"

She squeezed his hand. "You're sweet, Mr. Charles. You just feel better, okay?"

"Do my best. Listen, you ever spot that cat I was searching for?"

"No sign of him. Though I've been so busy back and forth counting bald heads that I've barely had time to notice anything around here. Need help getting back to your hotel?"

"I'll manage, thanks. Thanks for everything, April."

"You take care, Mr. Charles."

He struggled up, shouldered his pack and started off. Wobbled a bit at first, but kept going. He could feel April's eyes on him as he struggled toward the break in the fence. When he reached the street he looked back, but she had already disappeared.

45

WORRY BEADS

CHARLES LAY ON his coffin-like bed in the Smile Hotel, slipping in and out of sleep like a needle stitching up an endless bolt of cloth. There were no dreams this time, or if there were, none reached the tricky crossroads in his brain where they would be processed, organized, witnessed, and remembered. If interludes of wakefulness lasted long enough, he would rise, use the toilet, splash water on his face, and descend the rickety stairs to seek food at the cheap ramen noodle shop across the street. Then he would return, taking the six flights slowly, each time resting a few minutes on the third floor landing, sprawled out against the railing. When he reached his room, he would crawl into bed to sleep some more.

After three days of this, he awoke to realize he was perspiring. Up to now, he'd been unaware of the weather, inside his room or out. He'd been oblivious to the gentle rain that three days ago had cracked the fierce August heat, unaware that a cold front had settled in for a day or two. But now he was fully aware that the heat had returned. Covered with a fine gloss of sweat, feeling like a strip of barbecue roasting slowly in the oven, he eased himself into a seated position, stretched, blinked, and yawned. That a shower ought to be high on his list of aspirations was not lost to him, but he decided there was a task of an even greater priority. Of overweening importance. After wiping his face as best he could with the damp sheet, he struggled up, found a pen and a notebook.

And there he sat, still as a mummy arisen from its tomb, meditating about his trip. Across from him, on the futon, lay a note he'd picked up from the front desk on his last climb up the stairs. Creta Kano had called. His story was nearly ready.

Admit it! he said suddenly to himself. *Something is deeply screwy. All this negative shit could not be happening accidentally.*

Consider: You've been turned down twice by translators after they'd assured you they would do the job. You've crashed a plane because its pilot died unexpectedly, spent weeks in a coma. Your flash drive was stolen in a make-believe cave in India. You almost slipped down a crevasse in Iceland because your harness was probably tampered with. You lost both laptop and flash drive on the rail line between Naples and Rome. You survived an earthquake in Greece. And, as if that weren't enough, a ladder you'd bought to climb back out of a well you were exploring vanished into thin air, not to be returned until a young lady named April went looking for you. Now. Accidents? Or deliberate attempts at sabotage?

Svyeta was living proof, he admitted to himself, that some sort of intrigue was underfoot. According to her, the Russian scholars who didn't perform were probably bought off. But by whom? For what? Who had such a stake in this? It was still hard for him to believe that Murmantsev, whom he'd never met, had been bought. And Pnin—that wonderfully eccentric character who provided some of the most stimulating conversation he'd enjoyed during the entire trip? Pnin, too? That was really so damned sad!

A torpor began to creep over Charles, but he forced

himself out of it and tried to focus. Mishaps. Intrigue. Had he wandered into the middle of a novel by John Le Carré?

A list! When in doubt make a list. He looked down at his hand, still clutching the pen he had yet to use. Lists always brought things into sharper relief. He'd make a list of the bad and the good that had happened on this trip. That should do it. A column for each. If there was no good to balance what he entered in the bad column, he'd insert a question mark. *Okay:*

BAD—a. lost 2 translators. GOOD—a. found Svetlana (tho she was paid).

He wondered: *Negative? Positive?* He moved on.

BAD	GOOD
a. lost 2 translators	a. found Svetlana (tho she was paid)
b. pilot died	b. ?
c. plane crashed	c. ?
d. coma	d. ?
e. scammed by Sejal	e. ?
f. robbed by Sejal	f. ?
g. stout man payoff to Sejal?	g. ?
h. accident on ice cliff	h. saved by stout man
i. lost computer & flash drive	i. found by anonymous person
j. earthquake buried laptop	j. found by anonymous person
k. ladder removed from well	k. ladder found by April

Well, there it was, wasn't it? Pretty lopsided. To be fair, the negatives of b, c, and d (the dead pilot and plane crash and coma) might be squeezed into one, which would make it less imbalanced. And maybe e, f, and g (the Sejal fiasco) could be similarly grouped. On the other hand, Bad-a could have been split into two parts, Bad-a1, Murmantsev, and Bad-a2, Pnin. Which would weight it even more toward the negative.

Come to think of it, were the items he'd listed as good really products of the bad? If the bad incidents (loss of flash drive and laptop) had never occurred, then the actions listed on the good side (their safe return) would not have been necessary.

Hmmm. The misfortunes were clearly not all accidents, though some could be. But any way you looked at it, the good things were no more easily explained than the bad.

And another thing! If one regarded them as deliberate, another pattern arose. Halfway through his trip, some sort of counterweight had come into being. But that made no sense, either. He could not explain why anyone should want to protect him, anymore than he could explain why anyone would want to sabotage his trip or put him in danger.

He shook his head to clear it. Why was any of this happening?

He struggled off the bed and went to the window, tossing back the curtain for a good look. The Daiwa sign was still there, blinking on and off from the high building to which it was affixed. Well, that was good, wasn't it? Reality was still reality. Even in Japan.

He dropped his bearded chin to his chest and sighed. It was time to take a shower.

46

TAXING THE HEAD, TWEAKING THE HEART

C HARLES HAD EMAILED Óscar Amalfitano so often during the past few months—even from Greece, after the earthquake, when the Mexican professor had written Charles to express his concern—that he was beginning to think of him as a friend.

Dear *Señor* Óscar,

My translator, Ms. Kano, tells me the Japanese version of my story is almost complete. So now I'm wondering whether to come to Santa Teresa immediately so you can translate my *mss.* from Japanese into Spanish, or wait to pick up two other languages first.

I'd originally intended to see "Rejoicing" translated successively into ten languages, and if you translated it into Spanish now (which I think of as the *last* step before re-Englishing it), I will have collected only eight. The others that I'm considering are French and Arabic. If I decide on that course, I'm not sure where to get the French-into-Arabic done.

I'm also a bit weary. I've been away from my beloved New York for almost a year now and am growing eager to sleep in my own bed again. Much as I love France—one of the only two countries I've been to before this trip—I'm not sure I want to go there now. And where I might go for the Arabic I'm still uncertain. Much of the Middle East seems a powder box right now. Where can one go to feel completely safe?

In any event, I would appreciate your advice. Should I come to Mexico posthaste, you think?

All the best,

Charles Abel Baker

Another email was long overdue.

Dear Marcy,

Sorry it's been so long without a letter. But I've something to tell you. I'm depressed. Or at least regretful and bewildered. Shit! Sad will do.

It's about Svetlana. You remember before how elated I was? How thrilled and amazed to have found her? How un-lonely?

Well, when she joined me again on my birthday in Greece, she told me something that floored me. Made me question her loyalty and her love. She cried when she confessed to me what she'd done, then did something so generous that it completely overwhelmed me. And before I could gather myself to react, she vanished back into the wilds of Siberia.

So now I'm feeling—well, crippled. Furious with myself. I responded to her remorse with mere silence. I guess I was simply unable to come to terms with what she'd told me.

While she was miserable, I was a piece of wood. She may have failed me once, but now I'm the one who has ruined everything.

I'll never see her again. She said she'd had an offer of marriage from some sawbones in Siberia. End of story.

And now I'll need to resign myself to a life of loneliness. What's left of it.

As far as my project is concerned, I'm still committed. In Japan at the moment, but my next country may be Mexico. Or France. Or somewhere else. Right now, I've no idea.

Say hello to Tony and the kids,

Charlie

Estimado Professor Baker,

You are of two minds, clearly. We've all been there.

Let me offer some suggestions, and you can take your pick.

First of all, coming now is certainly not out of the question. It might take a couple of days longer because it's the beginning of the semester, but that's no big deal. On the other hand, should you wish to get to ten before re-Englishing it, as you put it, I can be of some help there as well.

I've a very close friend in Paris, Jean-Claude Pelletier, who, like me is proficient in many languages. I think you will remember my telling you that I am primarily an Archimboldi scholar, and have translated many of his works into Spanish from the original German. As has Jean-Claude into French. But he also knows Japanese, and I'm quite sure would agree to do your short story, which would give you a French version.

From there, for the Arabic—or Fusha—version, you could go to Lebanon, one of the more stable Middle Eastern countries at the moment. I have a friend there as well, who teaches at the American University in Beirut. Faisal is a brilliant linguist and translating the French into Arabic would not be problem. As you probably do not yet know, I'm also fluent in Arabic, so could render that version into Spanish to complete your program.

If that alternative appeals to you, let me know.

Respectfully,

Óscar Amalfitano

Hey, Charlie!

Aren't you the one! Did anyone ever tell you you're a hopeless romantic? Oh, right, that was me, a dozen times or more.

I haven't heard you so down in the dumps since you lost your job at the university. Well, you got over that, or pretty much, and I'm sure you can get over this, as well. If getting past it is what you need to do.

But ask yourself. Are you in love with her? It sounds like you are, you know. And if you are in love with her, why aren't you doing something about it?

If the answer is yes, does it really matter what she did? I mean, if you feel her remorse is genuine? Love forgives a lot of sorry shit, Charlie. She's in her early forties, you tell me. Does she want kids? Is that something her Siberian medicine man can give her that you wouldn't want? Think practical, Charlie. You'd be surprised how thinking that way can put the emotional Sturm und Drang—real though it may be—in perspective.

But, remember! This chick is from Russia, Charlie! You and I both know what that means, right? Does the word emotional come to mind? I love Russians, but damned if I could live with one! Don't forget: I had a Russian father and a Puerto Rican mother.

But if you love her, you'd better go after her, Buddy. Before it's *really* too late.

Your friend in good times and bad,

Marcy

Dear *Señor* Óscar,

May I call you Óscar? Thank you for your suggestions. I'll give you my answer in a couple of days, as to whether you should reach out to those fellows as you described.

Visited Mt. Fuji today, and it cheered me a little. But only a little. Perhaps I should visit a Shinto shrine; I've heard that's sometimes comforting.

Ciao,

Charlie

Dear Charlie,

Take as much time as you like. I'll be here.

By all means, call me Óscar.

Óscar

Dear Óscar,

Thank you for your patience. Weather's a bit cooler now,

which is refreshing. Now that I'm of clearer mind, here's what I think.

Frankly, I'm bone-weary. I think I'd like to settle for eight languages, and come to Mexico now. Mexico is a place where I feel comfortable, actually. Somehow, when I said I'd only been to France and the USSR, my several visits to Mexico had slipped my mind. I was there twice as a young man, the first time in a Russian village (of all things) in Colonia Guadalupe, in Baja, near Ensenada. Then in Mexico City a few years later, and even Cancun, five or six years after that. I even speak the language a little, having spent most of my boyhood in the San Joaquin Valley in California, where Mexican youngsters were often my closest pals.

So if it's all right with you, I'll come directly to Mexico at the earliest opportunity and request that you translate "Rejoicing" while I'm there. Is that still an acceptable plan?

Fondly,

Charlie

My dear Charlie,

Absolutely. Looking forward to your visit.

All the best,

Óscar

PART FOUR

47

THE LAST TIME I WAS SOUTH
OF THE BORDER . . .

Ó SCAR PROVED TO be a lanky giant of a man, six-six or six-seven, as Charles first glimpsed him when he unfolded himself from a very small, older model Toyota at the pickup row of the airport. Even without having seen a picture or heard a description, Charles somehow knew it was he. He had bony, broad shoulders and a large, angular head that seemed sculpted by a chisel; no one had bothered to sand it smooth. All his features were large; the nose gave him the look almost of a bird of prey. The word "acromegaly" crossed Charles's mind but even with larger-than-life features, Óscar was strikingly handsome. Most dramatic of all was the shock of wavy white hair—seeming both coiffed and untamed at the same time—that made the large head even larger. He wore no hat, and the aggressive Mexican sun had bronzed his face and neck. Charles, happy to have made it at last through customs after a long flight, shouldered his bags and went to meet him.

"*Holá, amigo!*" said Óscar. "*Qué tal?*"

"*Buenos días*, Óscar! *Yo soy* tired . . . *cansado* . . . *poquito, pero* . . . otherwise, I'm okay."

They hugged.

"Good to hear it, my friend. Is this it, your luggage? I'm glad, actually, because my vehicle is—" he gestured "—as you see."

They took a large, broad road from the airport until they entered the city environs. Then along narrow streets and wide ones, past mom-and-pop stores as well as Walmart superstores. Traffic seemed brisk, cars were of all sizes, trucks were common, and many seemed focused on beating the scrambling pedestrians to the intersections. Honking was so frequent it was almost like music, a staccato, tinny symphony of continuous surprise. They were silent until Óscar took a left onto something called the Avenida Plutaroco Elias, and Charles, who had been thinking, *So this is what Santa Teresa looks like*, suddenly blurted out, "I've been here before."

Absorbed in shifting gears, Óscar was silent a moment, and then said, "Oh?"

"I've no idea what jacked my memory, but yes, I have been here before."

"And when was that?"

Charles shook his head in disbelief. "Decades ago. Late sixties, I suppose. No! 1971! Flew here from the Pacific Northwest to divorce myself."

"Excuse me? This is a clever Americanism I am not familiar with?"

Charles chuckled. "Sounds odd, I know. I was teaching at a small college and living in the state of Washington when my wife and I agreed to a divorce."

When he paused, Óscar asked, "How does that lead to 'divorcing oneself?'"

"Well, we'd agreed on the division of our meager spoils, and also decided to let a single lawyer handle it. No dueling lawyers in court doing he-said, she-said. The problem was that Washington's marriage laws required divorcing couples to sign a separation agreement and live apart for one year after that, and during that year, submit to 'couples counseling.' Something Celeste and I didn't want. So the lawyer offered us a shorter, sweeter way: a Mexican divorce. Which was fine with us. But Celeste wanted to have it in the court record that she was the injured party—that she was the one divorcing *me*. I didn't mind that. I just wanted out of the marriage. Then she balked at flying to Mexico. Wanted *me* to do it. I was surprised at first. I remember asking her in the lawyer's office: 'Let me get this straight. You want me to fly down to Mexico, and stand in for you divorcing me, on the grounds of *my* mental cruelty to *you*?' Without missing a beat, she said 'Yes.' So I shrugged and agreed, and that's what happened."

It crossed his mind that he would have done anything to end that relationship. If he'd needed to stand on his head in front of the judge, he would've done that too.

They were now passing buildings that could only be part of a university: large, monumental structures with columnar facades, sculptured lawns, gnarled old trees, flagstone walkways, scattered statues. But they were merely passing by, looking at them from the highway, so to speak. Óscar did not turn into either of the two wrought-iron gates available from the roadway.

"A bit bizarre, my friend," said Óscar, smiling slightly. "But then, I never understood the American legal system, anyway."

"Yeah. Funniest part was—picture it!—I had to stand in front of the judge and affirm that I was Charles Abel Baker, standing in for Celeste Antonia Baker and, in that capacity, wished a divorce from Mr. Baker. Then I stepped two paces to one side (that was *my* idea, hamming it up, I suppose) and swore that I was Charles Abel Baker, representing myself, and I was not contesting the divorce!"

Óscar smiled and shook his head. "Well, law in Mexico is strange too. And down here it's so seldom followed that it may not make a difference anyway. In fact, Charlie, I have some deep and dark things to tell you about the lawlessness that grips my city. But why don't we save that for tomorrow? Because . . . we are here."

At his words, they turned right off the Avenida Plutaroco Elias, up a long driveway clotted with clumps of grass, coming to rest at last beside a small, two-story bungalow. It looked as if it hadn't been whitewashed in a decade, nor the grass along its edges trimmed in months. But there was something about it that told Charles—correctly, as it turned out—that the inside would be tidy and snug.

48
LEARNING TO CONJUGATE
THE GHOSTS

THE NEXT MORNING, after Charles had showered and shaved, he descended the stairs to find Óscar just finishing preparations for breakfast. Over eggs and chorizo, toast, and strong coffee, Charles thanked his host profusely for his hospitality, remarking that he'd not enjoyed a better rest during his entire journey. After the meal, they retired to Óscar's study, a book-lined cubbyhole off the living room, with a large desk looking out a window into a small garden. Scrunched against the opposite wall, beside a second window, two comfortable armchairs were arranged, separated by a worn but colorful braided rug. Óscar settled his large frame into one of them, tucking a purple folder into the space between the chair's arm and the seat cushion. Charles took the other chair. His host folded his hands and looked at his guest with great seriousness.

"*Mi amigo*, we should review what it is that you want from me with respect to translating your document—your short story—from the Japanese. But first, there is something of great importance I must tell you about your stay here in Santa Teresa. Let me give you some background.

"First of all, I love Santa Teresa. I was born and grew up here. I've traveled very widely—Spain and Portugal, Germany, India, Japan, England, Italy, quite a few other places, as well. Lived abroad for years, at different times, studied at Cambridge and the Universities of Toledo, Madrid, Gottingen, Milano . . . . I may even be forgetting a few. All this by way of saying I was delighted—ten years ago—when I was offered an appointment at Santa Teresa University, because coming back here was, indeed, returning home."

Although his résumé was impressive, Óscar's tone was so matter-of-fact it seemed entirely devoid of conceit, and somehow welcoming. Charles liked it.

"Nothing like getting back to the home town, I guess," he said. "Like Kant and Königsberg, I suppose."

Óscar raised his eyebrows, and then looked amused. "Well, glad to be placed in Kant's company, but of course, he never left town at all. Hardly similar in that respect."

Charles blushed. "Sorry. Just chatting. A bit nervous, I think. Rather intimidated by your credentials. And envious."

"Oh, don't be, please. I wasn't offering my résumé for that reason. Let me say, Charlie, that I'm quite impressed with you! With your perseverance, your doggedness, your willingness to take chances. And from what you've told me, it's been quite a journey! I'm not sure I know what the end result of your project is going to be, though, or why, in this Internet age, it was necessary to travel so far for it. Is there a book of some sort in the offing?"

Charles laughed nervously. "Some would just call me obsessive and let it go at that. I . . . I'm not even sure why I embarked on it, to tell the truth. Just curious, I guess.

What shape would my story—*any* story—assume after all those translations? Some languages strike me as so different structurally, that it's like . . . I don't know . . . being plowed under and reseeded, regrown. You know? Well, listen to me! I mean, you know much more about translating than I do."

"Please, don't downplay your curiosity, Charlie. And any interest in language and translation is obviously something I admire. You are to be commended for your hypothesis that something strange may happen to a story when it goes through all those languages."

"And what you're about to do now! Japanese into Spanish! That must be quite a leap, right?"

"Well, yes. There can be many challenges, but not more so than English, I think. I'll mention one or two, if you like. I'll use English in my examples because, from a structural or grammatical point of view, it's not that different from Spanish. Not only are English and Spanish Indo-European, but also, even though one is a Germanic language and the other Romance, there's been so much borrowing and mingling that I consider them kissing cousins."

Charles had always liked that expression. He smiled, inviting Óscar to continue.

"Spanish and English both have indefinite as well as definite articles, like a, an, and the," his host explained. "Spanish has more than English, but that shouldn't detain us now. Suppose I say in English: 'The children will eat the fish.' Well, there's no equivalent in Japanese to the article *the*. One usually has to use *kono*, *sono*, or *ano*, which mean respectively *these*, *those*, and *those over there*. Now. If you try to translate that literally, as best you can, it would be '**Kono** *kodomotachi wa* **kono** *sakana o tabe deshyo*' (these children these fish eat). But a more suitable, more common translation might be

'*Kodomotachi wa sakana o tabe masu.*' Which, if you translate it back into understandable English, would be 'Children eat fish.' And that's a different statement, is it not? First of all, lost is the future tense of the original, but also lost is the sense of specificity with respect to *which* children."

He smiled. "And that illustration barely scratches the surface. In fact, to carry it a bit further, *sakana*, besides fish, can also refer to 'a snack served with drinks,' which may or may not be fish at all."

Charles chuckled. "So how do you overcome that?"

"Other than looking at the context, you don't. Not really. You simply do the best you can to render the meaning of the original, as you understand it. In the particular case we mentioned, you might stick some articles back in. Or not. Because you wouldn't have a clue that the statement— encountered in Japanese—wasn't simply describing a characteristic of all children: Children eat fish! Nor would you suspect that the future tense was involved."

"Hah! And the story you're translating—my story, as I wrote it in English—has now gone through a lot of languages, each of which has its own grammatical hurdles and water traps. That's why I'm so intrigued to see what it might look like when it's all done! A paté we can spread on bread? Will the story still be there? The basic narrative line? If so, will the style be there, which supports a particular interpretation of the story?"

He almost added, *Will the humor still be there?* But caught himself because he realized that would tell Óscar more about the story than he wanted to reveal.

"Hard to say," said Óscar. "But I'll do my best with the Japanese story I have in front of me. And we'll see what comes out of the sausage grinder!"

Charles shook his head. "I'm so impressed with how many languages you know! To think you could have translated it from Kannada, as well! It's hard for me to even imagine such mastery."

Óscar shrugged modestly. "Well, I've traveled widely, and—yes, I suppose I do have a certain native facility with languages. But the bulk of my activity has been translating from German into Spanish."

Charles stared at Óscar's bony knees a moment, a smile playing on his lips. "Let me ask you," he said, "what's the single most interesting fact about translation you know? Anything come to mind?"

Óscar scratched his chin. "Hmm! Let me see." He looked out the window a moment, then turned to face Charles once more, his fingers playing with the edges of the purple folder beside him in the chair. "Do you know why the Irish claim that the word *mañana* can't be translated into Gaelic?"

"I don't think so."

"Because the Irish don't have a word that conveys that degree of urgency."

Óscar smiled, and Charles chortled. "Marvelous!" he said. "Thank you for that."

•

They sat for a moment in companionable silence. Despite the awe in which he held Óscar, Charles had never felt so comfortable with any of his translators. Then Óscar continued.

"My pleasure. But, listen, Charlie. Time out! *Mi amigo*, I love talking about translation, but I have a mission this morning. What I was trying to get at with my preamble about choosing to live in Santa Teresa is . . . ." He paused, rubbed his chin and sighed.

"Okay. One of the reasons I've invited you to stay with me here, at my home, is that Santa Teresa—my beloved community—is currently not a very safe place in which to roam about. Have you heard about our violence of recent years?"

Charles was still silently reviewing Óscar's Irish joke. Coming to attention, he shook his head. "Can't say that I have. I apologize if I've been unaware—"

Óscar waved his hands in the air, a gesture which caused Charles to notice how beautifully formed they were, classic long-fingered hands that might have been sculpted by Rodin.

"It is not important what you know," Óscar said, "and there is certainly no reason to apologize. But I do feel it's important to impress upon you the seriousness of our present circumstances, and why I'm suggesting that while you're here, you don't venture into town but remain in my modest home until I've finished the translation."

He folded his hands again and looked away for a moment. Charles frowned slightly but remained quiet.

"Let me do it this way." He slid the purple folder from its resting place beside the seat cushion and extracted several thumb-worn pages. "I teach philosophy, and in one of my graduate seminars in ethics I begin my introductory remarks in a way I would like to repeat for you this morning. Is that all right with you? It won't make you too uncomfortable to hear my little lecture for a few moments?"

Charles shrugged and smiled. "Of course not. I'd be delighted to hear what you have to say."

"Well, delight is not the emotion you will probably

experience from this telling, but here goes. I begin my remarks to my students in this way."

He glanced at the papers in his lap and began reading:

Her name was Maria Angelina Lopez. She was 16, and she was found by the railroad tracks on the outskirts of town. She was dressed in bra and panties, and her body was badly bruised: thighs, shoulders, belly, and buttocks all showing discoloration from repeated blows. She had been raped, even cruelly raped, to judge by the torn vaginal lips and the blood, and her throat had been cut. She was a worker at a *fábrica* that put together small goodies for the American market.

Marta Isabella Terranova was nineteen, a secretary at a different *maquiladora* in a different part of town. When found, she was naked from the waist up, but still wearing a dark, silk skirt. There was no sign of rape or bruising, but she'd been strangled with her own stockings. Her blouse was never found. Some boys riding their bicycles in the area discovered her body on the garbage dump, three miles outside of town.

Another young girl, never identified, was found in an alleyway just off the main street of Santa Teresa, fully clothed in peasant skirt and blouse. An out-of-towner, they supposed. A country girl. Her legs had been pried apart with such force that one hipbone had been wrenched from its socket, so that her legs were pointing in opposite directions. She'd also been raped and her throat had been cut so severely that the head was almost severed from the body.

Alongside the road leading westward out of town a woman in her early twenties was discovered by a passing motorist. She was dressed in a smart suit of an expensive cut, but her blouse was ripped and her body was already bloated with gases. She'd been dead for days. No one knows why she wasn't noticed before, but the authorities speculated that she'd been murdered elsewhere and transported to that location. Her panties were missing, but there was no sign of rape. Her throat was also cut. She was identified as Hortencia Veronica Rubirosa and lived in one of the better parts of Santa Teresa, out by the Jardín Porfirio Diaz.

Óscar set his notes aside. Charles was looking at him in openmouthed horror.

"Charlie, for several years before the present day, murders of women, mostly young, have been occurring here with depressing regularity. Probably upwards of three thousand, by now. Only a few of these murders have been solved; the rest are unexplained. From time to time the authorities would arrest someone and claim that it was over at last, but it never was. *El depredador psicópata*, some have said. A mad serial killer on the loose on a wild spree. But it started back in 2003. Or perhaps even earlier. Depending on which murder you date it from. One man? One *depredador*? Some murders look like the signature of a single individual. Others do not. A rash of serial killers, perhaps? Copycats? A dark, hidden army of copycats, descending on the city like locusts? Drug violence was another theory in the early days. But why those victims? It did not make sense. However . . . ."

He paused and shook his head. "These murders were but a bleak foretaste of what goes on in Santa Teresa today, where the problem is mostly drugs. Or their purveyors. Now it is no longer just women who are raped and strangled and maimed, anonymously and with no clear purpose. Now others are being killed, every day. Men, women, and children. Policemen, ordinary citizens, shopkeepers. These latest atrocities—at least in large part—are certainly the work of a drug cartel. The drug cartel. Our drug cartel. Trying to keep itself in power. The army has been brought in, but the killing continues. The cartel calls itself *Los Avispones*."

Charles cocked his head. "Hornets?"

"Yes. I call them *Los Moscas Inmundos*."

"Uh . . . flies?"

"'The Filthy Flies.' 'Unclean Flies,' if you prefer. Nasty, dangerous people, Charlie. Without conscience and very well organized, from what I can see. The *policía* has been thoroughly infiltrated. It is hard to know who, if anyone, is protecting you."

Charles rearranged himself in his chair.

"Wow! That does not sound good."

"Does not, and is not. So my advice to you, Charlie, is to stay in my house, here, near the university. If you do so, no one will bother you. I have a large library. I'm sure you can find enough good reading material to occupy your time. Your room was comfortable?"

"Quite. Slept like a log."

"Good. I go to the university for my classes on Tuesdays and Thursdays. The other three days, and the weekends, I shall spend here and work in my study to translate your story. I look forward to it."

49
ENNUI AND CONSEQUENCES

ON THE FOURTH day after their breakfast conversation, Charles, ensconced in the comfortable armchair in Óscar's cubbyhole of a study, set aside the book he was reading and sighed. He was restless. Óscar was at the university, and had called to say he would be tied up in committee meetings until quite late. Charles had wandered through the house, upstairs and down, looked at a picture here, thumbed a bookcover there, finally sunk into this plush armchair, and tried to read. Óscar certainly had many interesting books, in many languages. But today Charles found himself quickly bored.

Hey, he mused, launching himself from the armchair for yet another amble around the room, in every other country he'd been in, he'd tried to immerse himself—to a degree, at least—in its culture. To hear the songs, the chatter, the street music, to visit the sites of historic or cultural interest, to wander about in the shops. And wasn't this likely to be his last stop before heading home? Why, the United States was just across a bridge that spanned a river not a mile or so from where he stood! Not that he was planning to *walk* into his native country, but . . . .

His thoughts seemed to dissolve, as he crossed a threshold and turned right, then up the staircase leading to the second floor, making this trip for the third or fourth time this morning. One step, two steps, three . . . . What was the name of Beckett's character in *Stories and Texts for Nothing*? The fellow who could never decide how many steps there were in a staircase because he couldn't be sure whether you were supposed to count the level of the floor where you began to climb as "one" and the platform of the first riser as "two," or whether the first time you raised your leg to step up, *that* was considered "one"? Beckett's guy had the same trouble, if Charles remembered correctly, at the top of the stairs: Count that final step, when you achieve the platform of the hallway? Or don't count it, because it isn't really a step? Where to begin, where to end? Charles had always identified with Beckett's alter ego.

He sighed again, as he attained the landing and walked toward Óscar's bedroom. Wouldn't it be nice to buy presents for a few people, now that he was almost on his way back? Christ, should he have nothing at all to show for his year abroad? And suddenly, as he drew up in front of a framed, Emil Nolde-like pen-and-ink sketch of Óscar, hanging just inside his room above a dresser, he said to himself, aloud, "This is absurd. I'm an adult. I do respect Óscar's warning about the dangers of Santa Teresa, but really! I've lived in the middle of a city plagued by its own street troubles from time to time, but I'm careful and prudent, and I've never been mugged."

From the doorway to the bedroom, Charles spotted a somewhat faded photograph in a silver frame. A beautiful woman and—no doubt—her daughter, taken outside the doorway of this very house. Their clothing suggested the sixties. He picked it up, running his fingers over the glassed-in image, whose inhabitants faced the camera but did not smile. The photograph's age emanated a sense of sadness, absence, a forgotten world. He returned it to its spot on the dresser. *Besides*, he mused silently, picking up his thought where he had left it, *although Santa Teresa seems to have had a lot of fatalities recently, a ton of raw, bad stuff happening, it's still a city of something over a million souls who go to jobs, go to restaurants, go to shops, go to schools every day, right? Not everyone gets killed! No, it was good of Óscar to warn me, and noble of him to think my safety his responsibility. But to stay cooped up in this house for another week or so—it's just too much!*

He glanced out the small bedroom window. Nothing. From here, nothing but the broad *avenida* leading past the university.

He stared at the emptiness only a few seconds before abruptly nodding his head in vigorous agreement with his own decision and making his way downstairs to the wall phone in the kitchen. Beside the phone were pieces of paper thumb-tacked to the wall, many of which had numbers scrawled on them, and one of which, torn from a newspaper or telephone book, was an ad for a taxi service. Charles picked up the phone and dialed.

·

The cab came fifteen minutes later, its *taxista* a small, slender fellow with a wide moustache and a wider grin below his New York Yankees baseball cap. He greeted Charles both in Spanish and English, then to Charles's surprise, swept off his cap and dipped gracefully into a bow as he opened the cab door.

"*Bievenidos à Santa Teresa, señor.*" He smiled warmly.

Charles crawled into the cab, an old peach-colored Chrysler (painted many times, Charles suspected) with a broad green stripe down its side and the word "taxi" painted on the door in the same green paint. *Quaint*, Charles decided. *The real Mexico. Now, this is more like it!*

Off they took down the lane leading to the Avenida Plutaroco Elias, where they turned left and headed back toward the center of town. Charles had told his driver, in the best

Spanish he could muster, that he was interested in shopping, and wished to go where there were lots of crafts, but in a store, not on the street. The *taxista* nodded appreciatively. Charles relaxed and sat back.

"*Es un día muy bonito, si?*" asked the cheerful Mexican. "*El cielo, el sol?*"

"Uh, *si*, the sun and the sky are very beautiful, *señor*. It's desert country. I love the desert."

A few minutes into the trip, the driver picked up his cell phone, which had been lying on the seat beside him. After punching in a number on his speed dial, he began speaking in tones too low for Charles to pick up. Charles ignored this and looked out the window, taking in the sights, reveling in his escape. Trucks large and small (*troques,* Charles remembered) lumbered along the highway, most of them outperforming the lazily moving cab, almost all sporting the Mercedes Benz logo in their grillwork. He did not notice the driver glance at him in the rearview mirror as he listened to the voice on the other end of his iPhone, failed to observe the quicksilver smirk that flashed across the driver's face.

•

"Where are we going? *Señor, adonde vámos?*"

During the last few minutes, they had wound their way through progressively less savory neighborhoods.

"*No hay problema, señor,*" said the driver, smiling. "Do not be alarmed. This is shortcut. Also, I need to pick up a friend of mine who needs a lift into town. It will take one minute only. *Un minuto.*"

At the next corner they found the friend. A fellow the size of a howitzer, with rounded shoulders and a head like a bowling ball, climbed into the back seat beside Charles, who had to slide over to accommodate the new passenger's bulk. The man smiled, grunted "*Hola*," and looked out the window.

A minute later they were on a *camino* that seemed to be leading out of town, not toward the central business district Charles had hoped they were headed for at last. Out the window, houses were thinning out. A scrawny Mexican adolescent chased a dog around an adobe shack. *How could this be a shortcut?* he wondered.

"*Estás seguro?* You're sure this is the way?"

"*No hay problema, señor.*" The driver nodded his head vigorously and kept smiling. "*Dos cerquitas.*"

Charles had encountered this expression decades earlier, on his first trip to Mexico. He'd translated it then as "down the road a piece." Could be any distance.

Really, this is too much! he thought. *Time to take the reins.* He leaned forward again. "You're taking me out of my way, and I'm paying for this. I want to go to the center of town at once!"

Casually, the large man in the back seat leaned across Charles's body to depress the lock button, while the driver stomped on the accelerator as if trying to obliterate a pesky insect from the face of the earth. "*No hay problema ninguna, señor,*" the big man drawled. "*Y no es necessario pagar.*" He grinned hugely.

Not necessary to pay? As the old Chrysler gained speed along the road's rutted surface, rattling and shaking, raising dust clouds, spraying gravel, Charles felt the large man's arm settle around his shoulders, and understood. He felt as if he'd swallowed one of those Russian potato dumplings that drop to the bottom of the stomach like lead fishing weights. His chin sank down against his chest. *Holy Mother of God!* he said to himself, as much a prayer as an oath. *I'm being kidnapped.*

50
A SWARMING OF GNATS

C HARLES AWOKE WITH an ache near his collarbone and the beginnings of a cramp in his left calf. He shook his leg in an effort to forestall the cramp, and cast his eyes around the dark cellar. He needed to urinate. He wriggled his arms, which were still handcuffed behind the cane-bottomed chair he sat in. *Shit!* He swiveled his neck back and forth, hoping to relieve the pain. It felt as if a log had been repeatedly rolled over it during the night. He hadn't been tortured, thank God, but sleeping in a chair with your hands hobbled behind you was no picnic. *Jesus, what a nightmare!*

The deepest shock yesterday had been the moment a man of medium build and neatly trimmed beard had strolled into the room and demanded: "*Quita los zapatos!*"

Though he'd been shoved rather dramatically into the chair when brought to this room by his two Mutt and Jeff kidnappers, his hands, at that point, were still free. Thus, obediently, he'd leaned down and begun removing his shoes.

Then *el lídero,* the leader, standing directly in front of Charles with his hands on his hips, had nodded to the *taxista,* who probed at the shoes, first the left one, then the right. With the aid of a jackknife, he'd dislodged the heel of the right shoe and brought forth a small metal gadget, tossing it immediately to his leader. Grinning, the man had waved the device before Charles's uncomprehending eyes.

"Now you're going to tell me you didn't know anything about *this*—right, Dr. Baker?" he had said, in perfect, unaccented English.

Utterly astonished, Charles had gasped, "How do you know my name? And what on earth *is* that?"

The man had swept off his aviator glasses and looked at Charles. One brown eye, one blue. He had chuckled, appealing to his two henchmen to share his mirth, which they did. He'd sustained his amusement long enough for Charles to notice a small gold ring in his right ear, long enough to observe the dark hollows below his cheekbones, in which a pulse could be seen beating. Then, with a scowl, he'd dropped the mysterious apparatus to the floor and stomped it. When he lifted his foot, tiny fragments stippled the concrete. The man's smile had returned: ominous, magnanimous, condescending. Charles remembered thinking he had beautiful teeth.

"I have trashed your GPS, *mi amigo.* How people know where you are. Not any more."

And quickly, before the sputtering Charles had had time to ask more questions, he had barked, in Spanish, "Take him to the toilet! Feed him! And handcuff him to his chair!"

Fully awake now, Charles shook his head at the disturbing memory. He wondered why it felt like morning. There was no window in the cellar from which to see daylight.

He began casting about in his mind for some explanation of this unfathomable turn of events. Why had he been kidnapped? What did they want with him? How did they know his name? Who had planted a tracking device in his shoe? Who in hell could possibly be that interested in him? Preposterous! An oath came back to him from his youth in the San Joaquin Valley, in the days when he'd jabbered with his Mexican comrades. *Roto cabrón!* he screamed in his mind. *Chínga tu mádre!* He was remembering a potent oath he'd heard repeatedly from friends in his youth on the ranch, something about goats and one's mother.

The people who had captured him, it seemed obvious to him now, were likely the *Avispones* Óscar had warned him about. But who was it that—even *before* he'd been seized by these *ladrones,* these . . . jackals!—had been monitoring his every move?

He could ask, but of course he had no answers.

•

Around noon, his wait was over. In swept the man who had demanded he remove his shoes, followed by a train of sour-looking cronies. The two who had kidnapped him yesterday were there, and three others as well, each one, to Charles, looking tougher than the next. Today the leader wore a handsome, tailored suit, as did several of his henchmen. But, surprise! He carried Charles's shoes, which had been repaired and even shined. He flourished them expansively in front of Charles, as if they were a present he was offering a duke or an earl, as if they were resting on a velvet pillow, and set them down gently in front of him. At the leader's nod, one of the men he hadn't seen before undid the handcuffs. Charles wriggled his arms in their sockets a few times and wordlessly began to draw on his shoes.

"Allow me to introduce myself, Dr. Baker, if you *are* Dr. Baker. No doubt you have guessed that I am Felipe Ortega and you are now in the hands of my merry band of gentlemen. I say that because you are a professor, are you not? Or 'profess' to be."

Señor Ortega allowed himself a smile at his own witticism.

"*Si*, you have guessed it. We are a drug cartel. *Los Avispones*. But so much more. Everything you have heard about us is true, and more you haven't heard. One thing is for certain, Dr. Baker. We are the most powerful governing body in Mexico. Others—the Mexican State, for example—have multiple tasks. The Roman Catholic Church—again, many tasks. It is easy for us, you see. We have only one aim, one goal. To become rich by moving our product into the hands of those who crave it. We are already rich, but we wish to be richer. And we shall. For we have absolutely no qualms about how we get there. Anyone who stands in our way is snuffed out like the puny cockroaches they are."

He paused, waited for some kind of reaction.

"How do you know my name?" asked Charles.

"Oh, my! You think that is difficult? That is not difficult. To know who you say you are, whom you profess to be, is not difficult. What we don't know is who you really are. Who are you, Dr. So-Called Charles Abel Baker?"

Charles knitted his eyebrows together and stared at his interrogator. At both his blue eye and his brown eye, briefly distracted by his use of "whom," so rare these days. *He knows and doesn't know at the same time? What nonsense is this?* "I haven't the faintest idea what you mean."

Ortega shrugged. "Make it easy, make it hard, it doesn't matter. We will find out."

Charles heard a cell phone ring. A man in the doorway, by the stairway leading up, attended long enough to identify the caller, then walked to Ortega and handed him the phone. Ortega listened in silence for a minute without changing his expression, then clapped the cell phone back together and tossed it to its owner. He began giving orders rapidly in Spanish.

Mutt and Jeff moved quickly to Charles's sides and helped him to rise to his feet. They cuffed his hands again and slipped a bandage over his eyes.

"You are being moved, Dr. Baker. For that's what I will call you for now. Until we get the real goods, correct? You will be accompanied to the latrine and then you will be taking a trip. You will be fed on the plane. I will not be with you, but no matter. I have others who will be most persuasive, I assure you, in extracting the information we require. Have a good day, Dr. Baker."

Ortega began striding toward the stairway, shouting as he went: "*Jesús! Carlos! Vámanos!*"

As Charles stumbled along beside the two gentlemen who were guiding him to his long-awaited appointment with the *pissoir*, he thought, *Extracting. Such an awful word.*

51
COLLOQUY AT MARBURG

AT 10:30 ON a crystal-clear September morning, Morton Cruickshank, known to a select few as Pig, sat on a bar stool in the Tokyo Airport, sipping a *Tazawako Ji Bīru* and crunching a mouthful of beer nuts. Beside him on the floor, secured safely behind the bar rail, was a medium-sized beige suitcase with a collapsible handle, only suits, ties, hankies, and underwear inside, no contraband. He took a slug of beer, rolled it around inside his mouth before swallowing. He sighed. Now *this* was beer! Totally unavailable in the States. First and only beer brewed in Akita Prefecture. Town of Senboku. Dark malty taste, smoky even, with highlights of . . . who knows? . . . clover, maybe? Juniper berries? He sniffed at the glass and took another swallow. Christ, he hated to leave Japan! One of his favorite countries. He not only loved their beer; he was crazy about the women.

He glanced at his watch. A half hour to boarding. He really wasn't looking forward to this, had almost decided to bag it, but finally agreed. Proving he was an all around nice guy, right? Down deep? But, Jesus! The Marburg Hotel? He'd never heard of it. What kind of a dump was that?

The flight would take thirteen and one-half hours. Too

bad he wouldn't have time to stop off in Frisco. He knew a wonderful bordello there. And that supple brunette. What was her name? Toffee? Right. How likely is that? Real name probably Dolores and she hailed from Dubuque. But she was something, no matter what her name was. Eager and enthusiastic, with ding-dong tits. Almost a keeper, that girl. Claimed she'd been a dancer, and certainly was flexible.

He sighed again, once more consulted his Rolex. "Bartender," he called out, "Hit me one more time, will you?"

•

The subtle, faint ting-ting-ting of Roger Wawrinka's alarm sounded, and he sat up in his bed in Berne immediately, as if he had never been asleep. He switched off the alarm with a practiced twist and climbed out of bed. He drew on his pants, neatly laid out on a nearby armchair. The trousers were a cream-colored Haggar Mynx Gabardine, Hidden Expandable Waist, Pleated Dress Pant. Given his bulk, the expandable waist was important if he wanted to look presentable. Suspenders helped as well, and across the armchair they lay, black with pink trim. But those were later. He strode to his closet, and after a moment's study, selected a pink herringbone shirt with a Windsor collar, and a black tie with discreet pink diagonals. Despite the fact that he lived in Berne, Wawrinka—known to a few as Smilin' Jack—traveled widely, and bought his shirts on Savile Row.

Having knotted his tie before the full-length mirror in the bedroom, he slipped on his handmade all-weather walkers (Orvis), and tied the laces firmly. Next, he reached his suitcase from the top shelf of the closet and began to pack.

Fifteen minutes later, he was in his kitchen eating toast and jelly. A banana and a chocolate-chip muffin stood in readiness beside the small plate. It was enough, he figured; he would have another breakfast on the plane. In first class he could get most anything he wanted, and Wawrinka did like to eat.

After rinsing his plate and fitting it into the drainer, drying his hands on the soft, white Anichini Lorenzo hand towel affixed to his refrigerator with a magnet, he twist-tied his small bag of garbage, glanced at his Breguet Classique to check the time, and reached for the handle of his luggage, parked—as it ever was—beside his breakfast chair. The flight would take seven hours, fifty-one minutes. He had made it many times before.

•

It was Saturday, and Derek Wainscot tried desperately to avoid the office on weekends these days; the pressure was huge, and he needed an occasional break from the routine. Most of the manuscript reading was done on the weekends anyway, but away from the office, in bed or stretched out on one of his two comfy divans, with a drink nearby and subdued strains of Pablo Casals or Murray Perahia coming from the speakers. The softer sonatas, good background music. Mozart. Rodrigo. Sometimes he would even drop off and catch a few winks.

But this Saturday he had chosen to come to the office to try to dispose of a logjam of paperwork the parent company had forced on him. It was all becoming too bureaucratic, this job. What was he, an editor or a number cruncher?

Besides, it was a shorter walk to where he had to be. The Marburg. Across Fifth Avenue, up a few blocks, east to Madison.

Derek waved his head back and forth in abject misery, laid his forehead on his desk, and kept it there awhile. Insufferable. The whole thing was insufferable. How had it come to this? Had there ever been a more humiliating experience in his sixty-three years? Not even close.

But he raised his head again and shook his head and

shoulders vigorously. *You narcissist!* he accused himself. *This shouldn't be about you, Derek! It should be about the person your foolishness has harmed. And about what can be done to make it right. If anything. This is not a quagmire the responsibility for which you can fob off on someone else, Derek.* He clenched his teeth and shook his head like a Labrador emerging from a lake.

He raised his eyes to the clock on the wall. Ten minutes to four. He gathered papers into his briefcase and took his topcoat off the coat rack in the corner. It was early September, but there was an unexpected chill in the air.

•

Fortunately, the luncheon crowds had cleared out of Roberto's, and the fellow whom Eduardo had asked to work the dinner shift this evening, a young actor, had arrived in plenty of time to do setup.

Smiling at Antonio, one of the water boys, Eduardo went back to the cloakroom and retrieved his briefcase and laptop. He opened the case a moment and leafed through the papers contained in the folder he'd put there this morning. He had everything. Everything he thought they might need from him. He snapped it shut and stood silent a moment, thinking.

He'd been in some unholy snarls in his life, truly awful and life-threatening situations. And no one to tell the stories to, not having a woman in his life, or never for very long. Not that he would have been able to tell her anyway. Like Libya, for example. Spying on Khadafy. Needing to know the exact magnitude and breakdown of his armed forces. And later, arranging with Khadafy's colonels to transfer prisoners to that North African cesspool for interrogation. Or, like what he'd done in Chile. God, he'd hated that! But it was what one did. One followed orders; one did not make policy decisions. A loyal trooper, he'd left calling the shots to the puppet masters in Washington. Very few of his operations were things he was proud of. Most missions he'd been in charge of had been successful, to one degree or another, but that didn't mean he was proud. But this! Nothing had ever been so personal.

There was a mirror in the cloakroom, a small, round shaving mirror, propped up against the back wall on the lowest shelf. In the dim light of the overhead forty-watt bulb, Eduardo studied his features. He still had his Montalbán good looks, he thought, though his full, wavy hair had prominent streaks of gray around the ears now. Much of that, it seemed to him, had accumulated in the last few months.

A name suddenly popped into his mind. Mandrake. That was his code name for most of the time he'd been in service. Mandrake the Magician. Well. Some kind of magic was needed now. Or a whole lot of luck.

His replacement stepped behind the curtain into the cloakroom, having completed his preparations for the dinner rush. "You all right, Eddie?"

Eduardo glanced at the clock.

"I'm fine, Ward. Have a good evening. Make lots of tips."

He slipped the laptop into its case and walked across the empty restaurant, carrying his two bags.

•

Jonathan Belknap shook his head in a world-weary fashion, and stared out the picture window of his Madison Avenue Office. He hadn't expected it to come to this. Who could? When he'd unveiled to Charlie his former association with the CIA in the men's room of this very building back in—when was it? Last November? He'd offered him a private phone number and a potential network for a leg up, just in case. But he hadn't really expected anything to happen. And then later, when he decided it might just do to have Charlie tailed to see that he didn't get into trouble, his hunch never extended to the serious danger Charlie was apparently in now. Who could have imagined it?

He'd called the meeting at the Marburg to bring together the parties who had a stake in Charlie's dilemma, to fashion a solution.

Truth to tell, he was getting too old for this shit. He'd be eighty-four next birthday. He should be finishing up his spy novel, which he'd been chipping away at for years. And he had to admit, Charlie's real-life drama might be keeping pace with anything his imagination or memory had to offer.

He probed a tooth with his tongue. Felt like something still stuck in there from lunch. Dammit, I should see a dentist, get that fixed.

That was his final thought before glancing at the clock, grabbing briefcase, hat and coat, and quitting his office for the elevator and the short walk uptown.

52

DOWN AND UP TO SOMEWHERE

C HARLES WAS HUSTLED down a flight of stairs, then another, still blindfolded. *Why, why, why?* he wondered. *Why is this happening to me?* Then a new thought struck him. They were going down! He'd expected to go up, since his interrogation had taken place in a basement. After a few minutes of forced walking, he was loaded onto a small cart of some sort. The cart was on rails, for he stumbled over them; someone should have told him to lift his feet. Next he was being whipped along on this motorized handcart, both ruffians still holding onto his arms to steady him. They were obviously passing through a tunnel of some sort. It smelled dank, but some light leaked in around his blindfold, so it must have been a lighted tunnel. An underground corridor to where?

Well, he'd been in a lot of dark places on this trip, hadn't he? Down in that well he'd once given up hope of being rescued from. In a pitch-dark man-made cave in India. What would it feel like, he wondered, to spend your whole life underground? His mind went to Dostoyevsky, to *Zapiski Podpol'e*, usually rendered as *Notes from the Underground*. But that was a mistranslation, of sorts, wasn't it? "Notes from under the floor," literally, or "between the floorboards," more accurately. *Pol* meant floor in Russian, and *pod* meant under, beneath—the title referred to that space in apartment buildings between the ceiling of the apartment below you and your own floor, where the vermin, the creepy crawlies, hung out: cockroaches, mice, rats—others, perhaps. "Notes from creepy-crawly land." He wondered whether there were bugs in this tunnel.

"Out! *Vámanos! Ándale!*"

He was forcibly lifted off the cart and, once more, propelled forward.

Up two flights, he smelled oil, gasoline. The flooring was concrete. An airplane hangar. He knew this even before he was half-lifted, half-dragged, half-pushed over some aluminum wing struts (these he could see, below the blindfold) and into a small plane. Thrust into the back seat, a four-passenger job, then. An old Cessna, he'd bet, even without being able to see it. A 140 or 170, or maybe a later model. One of the old workhorses, anyway. Keep them in parts, they could last forever. This was a plane he could *fly*, by God, he suddenly realized. Not like that stupid jet he crash-landed in China! If they'd only unhook his hands and tear off the blindfold, if only he could subdue his captors, crawl into the front seat unencumbered, like some Ian Fleming or Robert Ludlum hero, then—*voila!*—he could escape! Well, maybe later. Something to keep in mind, anyway.

Before you could count from one hundred backwards, they were airborne. And that sound! That sound! The purring engine and the air blowing past, the familiar lift and dip of small air pockets, the faint vibration you could feel through your whole body! It was so familiar to him; he was back on the ranch, he was young, he was looking over crops. Those were not his captors in the front seats. Instead that was his father and . . . perhaps Musgrove, the big boss. The two talking quietly. Consulting about productivity. Next year, they would plant cotton on Section Ten and wheat on Section Nineteen. Now they would be passing over Dead Man's Creek, which must have been . . . oh, three hundred feet below, no more, as they . . . in low, murmurous voices . . . discussed tumbleweeds and ditch breaks and the acreage they would agree to keep fallow. The voices drowsed and lulled. Blindfolded, exhausted, Charles fell into a deep sleep.

•

When he awoke they were still in the air. The pressure on his bladder told him they'd been up awhile. Logic told him they were flying south. If north, they'd have been in the United States before they'd even gained good flying altitude, and he was sure that wouldn't suit their purposes. If east, they would have been somewhere above the Caribbean; if west, out over the Pacific by now. So, south.

Sequoya had gone south into Mexico looking for the lost tribe of Cherokees. *How far did he get?* Charles wondered. The Tarahumara were in the north, he'd read, and they certainly weren't Cherokee. And if you went all the way south, you'd encounter the Aztec tribes, or their descendants. *They* weren't Cherokee. How could that rumor that drove Sequoya have started? The Cherokee were an Iriquois language tribe dwelling in the Carolinas, later driven west to Oklahoma along the Trail of Tears, he remembered. Why would any of them have wound up in Mexico?

Nevertheless, the conviction had seized Sequoya, and he went. Maybe he knew something the history books didn't. Or maybe it was just the idea of a lost tribe that got him? Like the "lost tribe of Israel"? Sequoya had translated the Bible into Cherokee. *Hmm. Obsessions about language can kill you,* thought

Charles. *Witness my own. I can't really predict my fate, but it doesn't look promising.*

He swiveled his head to the right and leaned it alongside the plexiglas window. Slowly, steadily, he pressed his forehead against the plastic and moved his head downward. Carefully. Quietly. Sure enough, the blindfold's bottom edge began to slide up. He inched it up just enough for him to be able to peek below its folds and look out, hoping no one in the front had noticed.

Jungle! Wow! They had traversed the length of Mexico; they must be above Chiapas or Campeche. Charles had never traveled down so far, but he had studied maps on other trips into Mexico. Somewhere in the South, anyway. What had awakened him might have been the lighter sound of the engine as they cut power, or the change in air pressure in his sinuses; they were flying no more than a couple of hundred feet above the tree tops.

So shockingly green! A profusion of shades, densities, shadows and shapes. All green. He could see a choked tangle of branches and leaves; occasionally an ambitious palm tree thrust its shoulders above the canopies of its neighbors. Beautiful. *There must be jaguars, pumas, magueys, and ocelots down there! Cats galore. Hey, maybe even Timothy! Could that be where Timothy had gotten to? O, Timothy! O, Timothy!*

And there was certainly—somewhere down there (fear began to gnaw at his insides once again)—a hideout for the members of *Los Avispones*. Up ahead he spied a clearing, a grass runway. He worked his head against the plexiglas once more, in the other direction, nudging the blindfold back down, trying to obliterate the evidence that he had seen. Then they were on the ground, and the door was open. He could smell the jungle.

53

NEARING ZUGZWANG

THE HOTEL WAS new and sturdily built, a tribute to German engineering and American interior design. The conference room was on the fourth floor, in a part of the hotel without windows. The room was finished in cedar paneling. As requested, security cameras had been masked, and the high-tech video and audio recording devices customarily provided had been removed. Legal tablets and pencils sat at each of the ten positions around the rectangular oak table, as did empty water glasses; twin cut-glass pitchers full of ice water were spaced conveniently. A temperature and humidity control system operated below the threshold of human hearing. Three walls were wood; along the fourth stretched a colorful map, a modified Mercator projection of the world.

The first man through the door was Eduardo, who, glancing briefly at the map, took a chair on the far side of the conference table. A minute later, a broad, slightly rotund figure entered the room. He, too, shot a quick look at the map, then stopped and looked at Eduardo pointedly.

"You're Pig," said Eduardo.

Cruikshank stared at him sourly. "You have the advantage of me. Who the hell are you?"

"Name's Eduardo."

"Okay." Cruikshank picked out a chair directly across from him.

"Sometimes known as Mandrake."

About to sit, Cruikshank stopped himself abruptly. A different look came across his face. "No shit!" he said. "The Canadian Caper, in '80. That was you? Rescued the six American diplomats captured by Iran? Disguises and false passports?"

"Me and Tony Mendez, yes. I trained Tony in disguise, and backed him up. Served as liaison with Hollywood."

"Weren't you also involved in shoveling ground-to-air missiles to the Taliban, back when they were fighting the Soviets?"

"Not so pleased about it now."

"Also a computer nerd of some sort?"

"A techie, yes."

Pig shrugged and lowered his broad bottom into the chair. "Well, pleased tameetcha. And glad to have those rumors confirmed." He thought a moment. "We all did some crazy shit, back in the day."

"Some of us still do."

Cruikshank narrowed his eyes. "What's that supposed to mean?"

Before Eduardo could answer, the door opened and Wainscot entered. He nodded to Cruikshank at once, but barely glanced at the man to his left. He took a seat at one end of the conference table, perhaps from force of habit.

"Pig," he said tonelessly.

"Hello, Louisa."

Cruikshank nodded toward Eduardo as Derek turned to look at him.

"This here's—"

"*EDUARDO!*" The blood drained from Derek's face. "How can

this be? I hardly recognized you outside of—what on earth are you doing here?"

Eduardo smiled. "Long story, I'm afraid. Suffice it to say Pig and I know each other—know *of* each other—from long service to the Company."

"You're CIA?" Derek's incomprehension seemed bottomless. "But this is preposterous!" he said. "How could you . . . ? You mean you were listening when—"

"Don't worry about it," admonished Eduardo. "Almost nobody knows what anyone else does. Pig and I just met, though we've heard about the high points of each other's careers. Or low points. And, of course, I saw him with you at Roberto's."

"*El correcto*, Louisa," said Pig. "And who knows anything for sure, anyway? Life's fulla surprises, right? Gotta get used to it. The more you know, the less you know, isn't that what they say?"

"Much of the time," sighed Mandrake, taking up the mantle, still trying to cushion the shock of his and Derek's mutually altered status, "my front pocket doesn't know what my back pocket is doing."

As Derek continued to appear stupefied, he added, "And that was true even back in the day, right, Pig? Everything on a need-to-know basis? In our old business, Mr. Wainscot—may I call you Derek?—people were tight-lipped. If I worked in one theatre and Pig worked in another theatre, zero got out. Oh, when an operation went absurdly south, there were rumors. Eh, Pig? Or if a caper unintentionally made headlines or found its way into a report you had access to—then maybe you'd learn something about your fellow masked crusaders. Until then, it was our default position that nobody knows nothing about nothing."

Pig nodded excitedly, happy with the shoptalk. They were riffing now. "Afraid he's right, Louisa." A dramatic pause. "Except in Abkhazia. If you were in Abkhazia these days, you'd know things. No, if you were in Abkhazia, you'd know *everything*." He grinned.

Derek had passed through shock into puzzlement. Was he being played? He'd known Pig a long time, but maybe that didn't mean as much as he'd supposed. He hadn't seen him since well before he'd started sending Pig those frantic messages to scuttle the operation and return home. How had that Belknap fellow been able to bring him back when Derek couldn't? Speaking of Belknap, where the hell was he? Suddenly he registered what had just been said.

"Where in the world is . . . Abkhazia? Did you just make that up?"

Eduardo and Pig laughed together, cognoscenti now. "You don't know about the domino capital of the world?" Pig asked, in mock incredulity. "It's like Istanbul in the forties, or Berlin after the war. Anything you wanna find out, you can learn in Abkhazia. More intel there than Brighton Beach."

Derek looked petulant, suspecting—then certain—they were blowing smoke. How dull. Showoffs, both of them, engaged in a pissing contest that was also an effort to demonstrate their joint superiority to him. "So why aren't you guys in Abkhazia looking for answers?"

The door swung open, and Smilin' Jack ambled in on pudgy, well-tailored legs. Despite his bulk, he looked like a mannequin in a Burberry window. He was followed seconds later by Jonathan Belknap. Pig and Mandrake had resumed their back-and-forth about Abkhazia as Belknap was taking his seat at the opposite end of the table from Wainscot. Smilin' Jack had chosen a chair to the right of Eduardo, one seat removed.

Jonathan immediately brought his palms down hard on the table. "Gentlemen!" he exclaimed. "Your Company chit-chat might be enlightening to the one among us who is not now nor has ever been a member of the CIA, but—"

"I was Skull & Crossbones in college," Derek offered, like a child volunteering that he'd read the first page of the class assignment.

Everyone fell silent.

Jonathan spoke in a quiet voice. "We're not discussing the clandestine perpetrators of Old Ely panty-raids, Mr. Wainscot. We have serious business to conduct. We are trying to decide what happened to Charles Baker in Mexico, where he has disappeared from view. We suspect he's being held captive by some of the most dangerous idiots on the planet. And I want to hear some suggestions."

"Excuse me!" Smilin' Jack interrupted, rather forcefully. "I haven't been properly introduced. If I'm to contribute anything to this discussion, I need to know who you all are, and you need to know who I am."

"Sorry!" said Eduardo. "My bad. Gentlemen, this is Roger Wawrinka, from Berne, also known as . . . ." He went around the table, introducing Smilin' Jack to each man in turn.

Pig studied the new arrival with considerable interest. He'd rarely seen an agent more nattily attired. Even at Langley.

"Now I got it," he said finally. "You were the guy who planted that GPS in Baker's shoe. Smooth job. Hope you didn't crease your pants in the process."

The two men eyed each other, both now aware that others, at least, might consider their appearances twin-like. Wawrinka wondered whether Pig knew that they had both been using Wainscot's bank account to finance their activities. Pig, for his part, was nodding, having begun to realize that, with a little makeup . . . .

Jonathan sighed and deliberately cleared his throat. "Well,

now that we are all bosom buddies, the question is, what do we know about Charlie's disappearance? Eduardo? Anything?"

"I can tell you the exact time it happened. At 4:10 p.m. three days ago, the GPS stopped sending signals. At that point, it would appear that our subject was sixty-five miles south of Santa Teresa, a point to which he had moved by car. What kind of car, or whether of his own volition—"

"It wasn't of his own volition," broke in Jonathan.

Smilin' Jack, who had acquired his nickname not because of an excess of *bonhomie* but because he almost never smiled, spoke up next, sounding as if he were reading a message into a tape recorder. "I was in Mexico with our subject. I can tell you that Baker was staying with Óscar Amalfitano, a professor of philosophy at Santa Teresa University, who was apparently the individual he'd commissioned to translate his story from Japanese into Spanish. Three days ago, Mr. Baker entered a cab outside Professor Amalfitano's house, across from the university. I imagine he intended to go downtown, but the cab took a seldom-used road in a southerly direction. I was tailing them, but chose not to follow, as I would be too easily observed. I decided to bide my time until I could learn from Eduardo of his location, from the GPS. When that device stopped sending signals—as I was advised by Eduardo—I decided to return to Berne, where I had other business, and was almost immediately summoned here."

"Mr. Cruikshank?" Jonathan eyed him balefully.

"In Japan," said Pig, in a barely audible voice. "That's when I last saw him. I'd been taken off the case. So I decided to do a little R&R, you know?"

"I spoke to Amalfitano by telephone," said Jonathan, "once I'd heard from Eduardo about the GPS cock-up and he'd heard from Smilin' Jack where Charlie was staying. Professor

Amalfitano told me he'd warned Charlie that going into town could prove dangerous, warned him emphatically about *Los Avispones*, but was pretty sure he'd taken a cab into town to do shopping. The number of a car service was missing from his kitchen wall. So. Gentlemen. That's the last we know."

Derek was having trouble keeping his mind in order. He knew none of this. It was as if he'd opened his terrace door to discover not a terrace but a thirty-floor drop-off. The focus of his shock was Eduardo, to whom he appealed now in genuine bewilderment.

"My trusted waiter-friend! You mean all this time you—"

"Wainscot, we don't have time for this!" bellowed Jonathan. "You can sort out your personal relationships later. What we need now are answers!"

Eduardo nodded his head in agreement. "Absolutely. Information. Before we can know what to do, we must confirm whether it's the cartel that's grabbed him. I have a DEA friend in Mexico who's infiltrated *Los Avispones*. It'll probably take me a couple of days to find out. I suggest we meet back here in two days' time, and then we can plan how to handle it."

Jonathan stared into the silence that followed.

"So be it, then. Gentlemen, day after tomorrow. Same hour. My friend's life may depend on it. Until then, silence."

Derek, alone and isolated at his end of the table, threw his hands in the air in an expression of hopeless guilt. "Gentlemen," he said. "I am so sorry." He looked as if he were near weeping. "Even though my representative here, Mr. Cruikshank, was never *in* Mexico, I feel as if I'm partly to blame."

"You are!" thundered Jonathan, leaning so far forward in his chair, he almost raised himself off its bottom. "You damned sure are."

54
INFORMATION OVERLOAD

HE TALL, BOYISH-LOOKING fellow who entered the interrogation room where Charles sat unshackled at a small table had a red-tinted mop of flyaway hair. He could have been a young man on a football scholarship to a small college in the Midwest. *Middle linebacker*, thought Charles. *Doesn't even look Mexican.* But these days, who looked how you expected them to? Migration, immigration, emigration, intermarriage. Cross-pollination yields infinite variety.

On closer inspection, the youthful image crumbled. When the man's eyes fell on Charles, it was with an experienced, flint-hard gaze, and a crow's nest of wrinkles around the eyes completely jettisoned the barely-past-Clearasil impression. Charles inferred a fierce intelligence. The man circled the room twice before stopping in front of the table. His gait was peculiar, as if something were chafing him. Also, his trunk arched backwards from the hips to a degree that made it seem he was straining to become a question mark. When he paused in front of Charles, he joined his hands behind his back and smiled. It was now clear to Charles he'd had a face-lift. Judging by those wrinkles, he was due again.

"*Buenos días*, Dr. Baker. I am Colonel Porfirio Cartagena. I trust you spent a comfortable night? Anything you need? More pillows, perhaps?"

Yesterday Charles had been escorted from the plane to a room with a bunk bed and a toilet, a small sink, even a shower. The door was solid, heavy oak. Once his handcuffs and blindfold had been removed, he'd tried the lock and pushed hard at the door, all to no avail. Since he liked a hard bed, he'd managed to fall asleep, before waking from turbulent dreams around four in the morning.

"No complaints on that score. My complaint is that I was kidnapped in the first place. What in hell am I doing here?"

Cartagena made a tsk-tsk sound with his teeth. "I am endeavoring to be polite, Dr. Baker. It is in your interest to do the same. However, you have asked a legitimate question. You want to know why you are being held in captivity? Like a caged animal, you must think, however comfortable we make your cage. Perhaps you even imagine you are being treated like a spy?"

Cartagena waited, but Charles said nothing.

"It is because we believe you are a spy. We just don't know for whom you are gathering intelligence, or for what. Who are you, *so-called* Dr. Baker?"

Charles shook his head wearily.

"As I've already told others, I'm an American writer. You must know that about me. You already know my name, for Christ's sake. And a lot more, I would guess. Though how much, and why, I have no idea."

The colonel smiled and sat down in the chair across from Charles. He began to whistle softly, looking up at the corners of the room. The tune was one Charles recognized, remembered from summer evenings on the ranch, when he and other *trabajadores del campos* (Chicanos all, except Charles), would be driven home from the fields in the back of a pickup, singing

"Cielito Lindo." When the colonel decided to bring his whistling to an end, he broke it off mid-stanza and frowned at Charles.

"Let me ask you something, Dr. Baker. If it came to your attention that someone was traveling from one country to another, purportedly getting a short story translated from one language to another, again and again—a man who wears a GPS device in his shoe!—and that this same person was in contact with a former member of the CIA, while two others, also ex-CIA, traveled alongside him, marking his every move, wouldn't you be a little suspicious?"

Cartagena leaned across the table. "And now this guy shows up in *México*, on *my* turf?"

Charles shrugged. "I am who I say I am. And who are these three ex-CIA agents? This is crap! I'm not aware of any of this!"

"Aren't you now?"

Among the things that puzzled Charles, foremost, for some reason, was why this Cartagena fellow spoke such beautiful English. So he asked.

"Hah! I studied at MIT, *señor*. As did my *jefe*, *Señor* Ortega. That's where we met. As fellow graduate students, we both became aware of the bottomless enthusiasm you *norteamericanos* have for drugs. Which is why we decided that an obscene amount of money, a grotesque amount of money, could be made by supplying those cravings."

"And now you kill anybody in sight to maintain your control."

Charles realized he was in no position to offend, but out it had come nonetheless. His interrogator smiled.

"A bit naïve, wouldn't you say? Who sends those drones into the Somali badlands? Hmm? Who kills innocent people along the Pakistani border? Christ, don't you suspect your CIA is involved in the same business we are, in Afghanistan? As they unquestionably once were in Colombia?"

Charles had grown silent. His lip was twitching.

"But you know that. I must say, your cloak of naïveté has a certain charm. You do sincerity and indignation very well, Dr. Baker. But whom do you really work for?"

Cartagena rose and began to pace. With his odd gait, it looked more like a dance. A cowboy strut choreographed by George Balanchine. "Let me tell you who *I* am, Dr. so-called Baker. I am in charge of intelligence and security. After MIT, I became the assistant director of national intelligence for the Mexican government. But it was then that I realized how vastly more profitable it would be to go into business with Felipe."

Around the room he tramped, careening slightly.

"So, tell me now, are you CIA? FBI? DEA?"

Charles shook his head wearily. Cartagena stopped and studied his captive.

"Personally, I'm guessing DEA. We're not sure what your mission is. But trust me, I will find out."

Charles was breathing unevenly. How could any of this nonsense possibly be believed? He felt faint. But he was brought to attention again as Cartagena moved in closer, stomped his foot and glared.

"We'll get it out of you by asking you nicely. And if that fails, we will ask you *not* so nicely."

He sat down again and leaned back in his chair.

"Because everything leaves a footprint. Hmm?"

Charles's mind was swirling. *Everything leaves a footprint.*

Cartagena signaled to one of his minions, standing mute at the door. This one looked quite young, a boy, for sure.

At a gesture from Cartagena, the boy bent down to let the colonel whisper something in his ear. With a small, puzzled smile on his face, the lad knelt on the floor beside the colonel.

Cartagena reached out and tousled the boy's dark hair, smiling warmly at him. He ran his hand over his cheeks, his ears.

"Abejundio is a nice boy. Loyal and brave, Dr. Baker. Sweet. Pliable. A good worker." He turned his smile on Charles.

Then, with a swift motion, Cartagena withdrew a pistol from his boot, placed its muzzle against the forehead of Abejundio, and pulled the trigger. The boy slumped to the concrete floor, blood streaming from the back of his head, the quizzical smile frozen on his face.

Charles jumped up and back in horror. His chair clattered to the concrete. Cartagena pressed a buzzer on the side of the table and two workers emerged from the anteroom and wordlessly dragged the body out, leaving behind a clean towel, which the colonel draped over the pooled blood.

"I wished to impress upon you, Dr. Baker, that I am not averse to taking any steps necessary to protect our organization."

He indicated the overturned chair. Charles righted it and sank down upon it, his chest still heaving.

The colonel laughed. "Actually, I lied about the boy. He was loyal all right, but to an upstart bunch of filthy Oxacans who are trying to muscle in on our operation. We found this out only yesterday. Spies come in all ages."

He shrugged and glanced at his watch. "So. We've been at this awhile, *señor*. What say we get you some rice and beans for lunch, okay? And I'll speak to you again after you've had a nice meal and a chance to mull it over. When—if you insist on being stubborn—I can introduce you to all sorts of modern methods for extracting the information I require."

Extracting. There was that word again. The moment Charles got back to his room, he took a quick shower and tried to clean his pants as best he could.

55
LOOKING FOR A LIFEBOAT

THERE THEY ALL were again: Smilin' Jack, portly, dapper, dour as always; Eduardo, who'd entered the room with one eyebrow raised and never lowered it; Jonathan, poker-faced; Derek, drawn and glum in his three-piece suit and Valentino Garavani silk tie; and Pig, chubby, cheerful, looking like a gunnysack full of unlucky kittens someone had decided to drown.

"Your meeting, Eduardo," Jonathan said, the moment he sat down.

"Well, they've definitely got him. Got word from my friend in the DEA. Took him to one of their southerly safe places. A secluded, out-of-the-way, difficult-to-reach hideout in a mountainous jungle area known as the Chiapas Sierra. Accessible by plane, motorcar, helicopter, or tough hiking. Not even reachable by boat, too many rapids."

He stood and walked to the big map on the wall. He'd planted a red pushpin on a spot in southern Mexico, and now tapped his finger beside it.

"It appears they think he's a spy," he continued. "How long that will play out, I've no idea. They should—repeat, *should*—discover that it's not so, but there's no safe way for us to help them confirm it that I'm aware of. If our luck holds, they'll figure it out in time. Provided they don't just get itchy and decide to snuff him whether or not he's a proven threat. But we'd better move fast, whatever we decide."

Eduardo resumed his chair within a charged silence. Jonathan shuffled some papers in front of him, looked around the room.

"But I can tell you right now," Eduardo added, smoothing his moustache. "The only way you're going to get him back is with a ransom. If it's not too late. If he's not been shot already, or isn't by the time we finish this meeting."

"We could try a little wet work," said Pig, grinning. "Get together a special ops team, try to rescue him. Do the Mexican government a favor, shoot a few of their druggie *vaqueros* into the bargain."

Eduardo was firm. "No. Money is the only way."

"Or perhaps we could—"

"Listen, Piglet!" Eduardo barked. "Are you presuming to know more about Mexico than me? I was fucking born there! I'm telling you ransom is our only hope. We want our boy alive, OK?"

Pig's glare suggested he was ready to leap the table and strangle Eduardo.

Jonathan cleared his throat, waited a beat, then spoke into the charged silence. "I think Eduardo is right." He paused again, to let the tension dissolve. "But how much money are we talking about here? Where will we find it? How do we make contact? With whom do we negotiate?"

All heads but one turned, nearly in unison, toward the end of the table where Derek was sitting. The editor sighed and shook his head. "Hey, wait a minute, fellows! Really! I understand that I'm considered the banker here. But, gentlemen! My money supply is not inexhaustible! I mean I do feel a trifle responsible, but—"

"A trifle, my ass!" Jonathan shouted. "If you hadn't had Charlie trailed and messed with by your boy Pig here, we'd never have had to put somebody else on him to unravel whatever mess you got him into." Even as he said it, Jonathan realized he wasn't being completely fair; he'd entered the fray only on a hunch, unaware of Pig's assignment. It wasn't sabotage he was expecting, but naïveté: Charlie's own suspected talent for dunking himself in whatever hot water was available.

Derek was indignant. "Oh, please! *I* didn't tell him to go to Mexico! And I'd already asked Cruikshank to step down long before he went there." Pig was rolling his eyes. "Charles Abel Baker was the one who decided to go to Santa Teresa! *He* was the one who chose to take himself downtown on some ill-considered shopping spree, and despite the fact he'd been warned against it—*you* told us that. Getting picked up by the cartel is on *him*. Surely!"

Jonathan placed both hands flat on the table and leaned forward, his jaw working back and forth. "Don't you get it, Wainscot? It's an unbroken chain of causation. If your boy hadn't rigged it with those Russian professors, we'd never have planted a GPS. There wouldn't have been spooks like Pig and Mandrake and Smilin' Jack and me following Charlie around like dogs trailing a bitch in heat. We left a scent, Wainscot! Why, of course they thought he was a spy! I'll warrant they already had Charlie on their radar before he ever hit Santa Teresa!"

He leaned back, trying to adjust his tone to something calmer, more judicious. "I mean, I agree that there's enough fault to go around, but I don't know anyone who bears a greater responsibility than you. Tempers have gotten a little hot here, and for my part, I apologize, but now we're all sitting in a room together, trying to rectify the situation, to get our buddy back, and you, Derek, are the only person with the wherewithal to bankroll our operation. Charlie doesn't have any rich relatives. Hell, he doesn't have any family at all."

Visibly chastened, Derek sighed and closed his eyes a moment. Pig looked down at the table and blew out a long, controlled breath.

When Derek opened his eyes again, he asked, "How much money are we talking about here?"

Eduardo spoke first. "My guess—a million, at least."

"More," said Smilin' Jack. "Probably a million and a half."

"But I don't have that much!" protested Derek.

A smirk appeared on the faces of everyone else at the table.

"Beg to differ, Mr. Wainscot," said Smilin' Jack. "Don't forget, we've been drawing on *Banco Estafadores* just like Pig has. We tapped into your account, ah-mee-go. We know what's there."

Wainscot levitated from his chair. "You what?"

"There's no point hiding it any more, Louisa," said Pig. "They found out, apart from anything I did, then went in as me and withdrew just what they needed—Jack, here, did—so they know pretty much what's in there."

"We know exactly how much is in there," corrected Eduardo.

"And we assume," added Jonathan, "that's not your only nest egg."

"I can confirm that," said Smilin' Jack. "I don't know about any American accounts, Derek, but I've looked at your holdings in Switzerland. I live in Berne, and I have my ways."

Derek sat speechless for a moment, though his mouth was open wide.

Finally, he said, "All right. I'll try to meet whatever their demands are. I suppose I owe Mr. Baker that. No, make that I *do* owe Charles Baker that. And I apologize most profoundly for my role in this."

Thoroughly deflated, he glanced around the table. "But we don't really know what the amount is, do we?" he added hopefully.

"No," said Eduardo. "We're just guessing. And the first step is to find an intermediary. Someone impeccable. Someone the cartel will trust to arrange things. I have an idea about that, so I'll start to work on it immediately."

His declaration hung there in the air for several seconds, a heavy chandelier dangling above the table by a thread.

"Were you planning to tell us at some point?" asked Derek.

Eduardo tapped his splayed fingers together a time or two, frowning. "Derek, you are the only one among us who is not professionally trained in keeping secrets. Do you think you can keep this one under your hat?"

"If I'm laying out that kind of money, I can keep anything under my hat."

"All right, then. The guy we're trying to get is the Archbishop of Mexico. Somehow he's a guy they can trust."

"The Archbishop of Mexico!" Smilin' Jack looked astounded. "How does he know people in the drug cartel?"

"From the confessional, I would guess," Jonathan interjected. "Talk about someone who can keep secrets, it's a Catholic priest."

"Look, I know from nothing about the man's background," Eduardo continued. "The most I know—this comes from my buddy in the DEA—is that this dude was appointed right after they sacked Antonio Barabasto. Remember that? The pope canned the former head of the Legacy of Christ because of pedophilia, graft, and corruption, and ordered a top-to-bottom restructuring of the Legacy. Sentenced Barabasto to prayer and penance of some kind. Which was a tough loss, considering that Barabasto had found ways to channel *mucho dinero* into the papal coffers. In any event, apparently the newly elevated archbishop had a good rep, and a mandate to clean things up."

"But can *we* trust this guy?"

"What choice do we have?"

Hardly anything was said after that; it appeared that the business of the meeting had been completed. Jonathan asked everyone to please stay in town or in touch, in case there was anything more they could do, and all save one filed out of the conference room.

Derek continued to sit at the table in a state of shock. *How did this happen?* he asked himself. *How did I get myself into this? All I ever wanted really was to be a poet and a translator.*

He looked down at the table and shook his head slowly. *Well, this will be the most difficult translation problem I've ever encountered, translating my money into a lifeboat. And I hope I survive this,* he said to himself. Then he thought a moment more and whispered aloud, to no one but the water glasses or the map on the wall, "No. I hope Charles Baker survives it."

That was when he saw it. The giant red pushpin Eduardo had stuck in the presumed location of the cartel's hideout was still in the map. He crossed the room, removed it, slipped it into his pocket. The sense that he was being raped financially remained, but now he managed a small quiver of moral superiority.

"Call themselves operatives!" he said aloud. "Professionally trained! And they leave their tracks for me to smooth over."

56
IF ONLY THIS WERE REALITY TV

CHARLES SPENT A restless night. The hard, narrow bunk bed, which he'd had no trouble adjusting to the previous night, was like a bed of brambles now; it pricked and pained him no matter which way he turned. Came a time when he was sure it was morning, when he could not wait to be lifted from this cell and taken to another location.

Although he feared that destination equally. That interrogation room. That altogether different world, where he had witnessed—like being thrust into the middle of a Hollywood slasher film—the cold-blooded murder of a young boy.

Although not a film. This was not a movie, not TV. Not the set of a half-nutty film student's remake of *A Passage to India*. Scary though that café scene in India had been—explosions, gunfire, shattered glass—that was fantasy. That was cinematic art, or a stab at it. That was pretend. What he had witnessed yesterday was real life. Or should he say real death?

He had looked so young, Abejundio. So innocent. What did his name mean? Wasn't it "bee?" He'd never heard "bee" used as a boy's name before. The boys he'd grown up with were named Carlos, Alfonso, Ignacio. Never Abejundio.

Cartagena had placed the barrel right against that alabaster, wrinkle-free forehead and blown out the back of the boy's skull. Blood and brains splattering over the floor, instantly. Dead, instantly. One minute smiling openly, though not understanding why he'd been asked to kneel. The next moment, oblivion.

Done for no other reason than to convince Charles that the same fate awaited him if he didn't cooperate. Well, they said he was a spy, but weren't they saying the same thing about him? And how could he cooperate? *He was not a spy!*

•

A short while later, Charles was led back into the interrogation room. He struggled to keep from trembling. When they seated him across from the Colonel, he glanced at his face. That same sly smile. He decided not to wait for questions.

"*Señor* Cartagena, Colonel, please allow me to tell you something right off the bat. Okay? I have been—"

"Of course, of course! Talk to me! I love to hear you talk!"

"Listen, I beg of you. I am not a hero. I am not courageous or brave or anything of the kind. But I have to tell you, because it is the truth, because there is nothing else I can tell you. I am not a spy. I am a writer. The story seems so absurd to you, so suspicious, but it's absolutely true. I'm just a writer who got this idea—maybe silly, maybe profound—to see one of his own short stories translated into ten different languages, then back into English. I simply wanted to see the end result!"

Charles could hear his words cascading out, but was that his voice? So very high? Slow down, he told himself. Slow down.

"Sir, I would make a terrible spy! I don't know how to keep information to myself! What I know, I usually tell to whoever will listen as soon as I discover what it is."

Someone laughed. *Was that me?* he wondered in panic.

The colonel sat across from Charles unmoving, his smile etched in stone. His hair seemed redder today. A color lift?

"Boring, right?" said Charles. "So irrelevant that it's boring. Well, hey, that's my point! I'm just a writer, a former academic. What could be more humdrum than that?"

Cartagena hadn't moved. *Is he a hologram?*

The colonel tuned his head away slightly and yawned, covering his mouth with a relaxed hand. "Forgive me," he said, shaking his head. "Late night. Too much tequila."

After a further pause, he said, "Now. Thank you for your lovely speech, *Señor* Baker. Your passion is admirable. Have you ever been on stage? Your speech was a bit actorly in parts, I thought. The makings of a thespian, perhaps? And yet—yes, a bit dull. But boring is not the question, Dr. Baker. The question is, how much of it is true?"

Abruptly, a cell phone rang in the pocket of a guard standing at the door. Immediately, the colonel stopped speaking. The guard listened for a moment, then, without a word, crossed the room and handed over the phone. Cartagena listened alertly for perhaps a minute and a half. Then he grunted incomprehensibly, snapped the phone shut, and tossed it back to his guard.

He looked down for a moment, his hands flattened against the table. Then he looked up again, at Charles. Another smile on his face. A different smile.

"And I have my answer," he said.

57
ME AND DOSTOYEVSKY

WEEKS HAD PASSED since that day in the interrogation room when the colonel had been interrupted by a phone call. Charles had been treated well enough. The food was passable; he was allowed to wash out his meager wardrobe once a week; he'd grown used to his narrow bunk bed.

He'd also begun exercising. Strange, he'd never worked out in his former life. Why now? Well, nothing but time, he supposed. No books, no paper, no pens, no computer, no cell phones. No TV. Nothing but time. And keeping fit seemed important. Not letting oneself go to seed.

Early on, a Russian proverb he'd encountered in his studies started threading its way though his consciousness repeatedly. "*Tsar ispuglal'sya,*" it went. "*I dal manifest. Myortvym sbovodnym, zhivir pod arest.*" ("The Tsar became frightened, and issued a manifesto: The dead should go free, and the living should be put under arrest.") How far off was that from illustrating the absurdity of his situation? Apparently, they'd concluded he was not a spy, but he was still a captive, with no idea what was to become of him.

He also thought, from time to time, of *Zapiski iz Myortvovo*

Doma, Dostoyevsky's memoir-cum-novel about life in "the house of the dead," modeled after a prison in Siberia where he'd been sent to serve a four-year sentence after being convicted of belonging to a banned, underground reading circle, a collection of young intellectuals who were studying French socialism. Come to think of it—Charles's thought arrived in a blinding, and not unpleasing, epiphany—his experience *was* like Dostoyevksy's, wasn't it? Tsar Nicholas the First, who made early nineteenth century Russia a police state, had at first staged a mock execution, with the prisoners of the Petrashevsky Circle lashed to posts in a snowy courtyard, facing a firing squad. Only at the last minute were their sentences commuted to time in that harsh Siberian prison. Dostoyevsky had become convinced—as had Charles—that he was about to be shot to death. Nor was Charles sure, even now, that such an outcome had been entirely rejected. In his captors' shoes, thought Charles, what would he do?

Rumor was he was being put up for ransom. He had overheard his jailers talking in Spanish when they changed shifts outside his cell door and pieced it together. Ransom! For him? What were they thinking of? What were they supposing? What were they *smoking*? Had they become victims of their own product? Had someone conceived this idea in a drug-addled haze?

How could the *Avispones* possibly expect anyone to pay enough ransom to make it worth their while to make the attempt? Cheaper to shoot him and be done with it. He was just a writer, and not a very important one; his government—however active it might be in "assisting" the Mexican government to bring its drug syndicate maniacs to heel—would never lift a finger to save him.

So who, in the private sector, would pay? He had no family. He had very few friends: a couple of members of the writing group, his buddy, Marcy—that was about it. Friends had been hard to hold onto for Charles, over the years. Had he *ever* had a true friend? A bosom buddy? Someone he cared really deeply about? At least since childhood?

He stood and stretched, walked around the cell a bit. Almost time for his exercises. His daily routine. After a few tours around the small room, he stopped and leaned back against the wall.

Svetlana was a friend, of course. Or had been. Not only a lover, but a profound friend, despite the raw commercial nature (for her) of how they'd met. She had proved her friendship over and over. The fact that their initial meeting was based on the payment of a fee seemed to recede now further and further into the distance.

Did it really matter how they'd met? Some people meet because they are negotiating the buyout of a business, he thought, and eye each other as enemies across a conference table. Some because they are attorneys on opposing sides of a criminal case, brought together because of a heinous crime against society that the courts are seeking to rectify. Some because they are each engaged in a political campaign for opposing candidates. Some are hooked up through dating services. Some are thrown together while backing up in opposite directions with drinks in each hand in a crowded bar, and jolt into each other and slosh their drinks all over the floor and themselves, and fire daggers at each other with their eyes until—the very next moment—they fall in love. He'd seen that in a movie.

Does it really matter? he wondered. What mattered, surely—in all cases—was what took place after whatever happenstance had brought them together. What sparks flew. What tender chemistry evolved. Surely what mattered now was how he felt about Svetlana *now*. And what she felt about him.

What good was that anyway? He realized, with a regret that

grew each night as he tossed and turned on his narrow bunk bed, that he loved her. That there had never been, and would never be, anyone in his life like Svetlana.

If there was to be a life, after all this.

He pushed himself away from the wall, and began his workout routine.

58
PLAYING A LONG SHOT

JONATHAN AND EDUARDO sat at the window counter of a busy restaurant on 23rd Street, a fast-food emporium of carefully prepared organic meals. They'd picked it because, between 11:30 a.m. and 1:30 p.m. its customers were clerks, secretaries, receptionists, hairdressers, bank tellers, and bureaucrats, all harried and pressed for time, who were disgorged from their surrounding workplaces then sucked back in as if they'd never been away. The resulting pace, clamor, and rapid turnover conferred on the pair of conspirators, they hoped, a certain anonymity and privacy. Hiding in plain sight.

"Got back from Mexico City last night at midnight," Eduardo said between bites of a chicken fajita panini. "Still a bit wiped."

They sat facing each other on stools, the large window displaying Park Avenue and its passing parade of pedestrians. The nearest table to their position was beyond the fixings bar, a good six yards away. Still, they leaned toward each other, speaking in low tones.

"I met with His Eminence," Eduardo continued, "and all systems are go. Contact with the cartel has already been established; the face-to-face meeting should take place in a matter of days. I'm told Dr. Baker is alive and well, so I'm very hopeful."

Jonathan probed the left side of his mouth with his tongue. *Damned arugula*, he thought. To Eduardo, he said: "Good! That's excellent!" He heaved a sigh and laid his tuna sandwich aside a moment. "Now. Any talk of funds we need to get ready? Anything I can convey to Derek?"

Eduardo found himself looking at a young woman just beyond the fixings bar, sitting sideways to him. Pretty. She had evidently finished eating and was writing something, a determined look on her face. The bulk of her very dark hair was so tight it looked captured by a sock, but one stray lock had fallen forward until it described a parabola down her cheek, almost obscuring her black lashes. He returned his mind to the conversation.

"Yes. They want a million and a quarter. It's a negotiation, of course, so it could cost less, but not much. How much should we quibble, do you think?"

"Fuck negotiation. As long as Derek's willing, let's pay them their price. I don't want anything screwing this up and putting Charlie in danger."

"So be it."

Eduardo took his wallet out of his pocket, extracted a business card with the name of a Mexican bank, and slid it across the countertop. On the back was a number written in pencil. "Tell Derek to wire the full amount from his Cayman bank to this account immediately." He grinned. "Unless you'd like me to send Smilin' Jack to do it."

Jonathan took the card without looking and slipped it into the inside pocket of his jacket. He waved off the suggestion. "No need. Derek'll come through now."

A minute later, he finished his sandwich and licked his fingers. "Y'know," he said, "you and I have been around the block many times in this business. Yet this has got to be pretty goddamned strange, when you think about it. Am I right? The guy attempting to secure Charlie's release—our bagman, if you will—is actually the Archbishop of Mexico?"

Eduardo smiled. "Odd as hell, Jon. I agree. Seems like a nice guy, too. Medium-built dude, rather short. Well-spoken. Bunch of protocol before I could get through to him, but that's the Church for you, the Mexican Episcopate. The trappings, the rigamarole. The guy himself is another matter. No airs. Down to earth."

He paused, looked away a moment. "But it took a really peculiar alignment of the stars to elevate this guy to top dog in the Mexican hierarchy, you can be sure of that. If Barrabasto hadn't been so corrupt, or if his skullduggery hadn't come to light during a period when the whole church hierarchy was bleeding from revelations of child abuse, it would clearly never have happened. And yet, stranger still, this straight arrow has agreed to negotiate with a drug cartel in order to get Charlie back! Strange indeed."

Jonathan wiped his mouth with his napkin and stood. He was still CEO of a midtown public relations firm (something he'd been neglecting of late), and his board had a meeting scheduled. "Okay. Back to the rat race for me. Coming?"

Eduardo hesitated, glanced again at the girl. "I may hang here for a while, Jon. Could use another cuppa coffee."

Jonathan had noticed him noticing the young woman.

"We still need to stay buttoned up, you know."

"I know, Jon. Don't worry." After a half second, "Good luck with Derek. Keep the communication lines open. I'm yours at the drop of a hat."

59
LISTENING TO THE FROGS

CHARLES AWOKE FROM a disturbing dream to an airless room. He'd not cried out this time, but was breathing heavily. After a few moments of pondering, his breath having returned to normal, he raised himself to a sitting position, pushed off from the bed, and walked, a little wobbly, to the window. Fortunately, it could be raised easily enough, and he did so now. Very early on, after he was moved to this room, he'd entertained a fantasy of escaping through this narrow window. Crawl through the space at night, find the airstrip, fly out of here. Right. The moment he looked down he realized this room was in a kind of third floor tower. Moreover, the concrete surface below was on the same level with an underground garage. So. Four floors down. If he'd tried wriggling through and dropping to the surface below, he would surely have crippled himself beyond any possibility of a successful getaway. If he didn't land wrong and die from the fall.

It was late afternoon. The air outside was sticky, but there was something refreshing about it as well. A soft breeze caressed his face.

A concert of high-pitched squeaking came from the jungle— tiny tree frogs, he'd been told by the women who cleaned his room—punctuated periodically by a heavier, scratchy pop with a split-second echo. A larger frog, perhaps. Bullfrog? He didn't know their names, either common or scientific. Pity. He would like to be able to see them, but that was unlikely, wasn't it? Even if he were free to walk out the door, down to whatever stream flowed by out there, to cross it, to stride deep into the forest where the frogs were roosting in the treetops.

The sound itself was rather comforting. As if one species of frog were providing a chirrupy choral drone for the other's sporadic bass notes. Every once in a while the pitch of the background buzz would change, shifting up or down by a single note.

What were they signaling? he wondered. Was it an actual conversation? A language? Perhaps he should have his story translated into frog?

As he stood listening, his fingers stroked his beard. He hadn't shaved since he'd been captured. Perhaps tomorrow he would give himself a trim.

He turned away and found the bed again, still a little shaky. This was the first time he'd gotten out of bed voluntarily in a while. He lay down once more, hands folded beneath his neck, staring at a spot in the ceiling. Not that he saw it; everything he saw was on the inside of his head.

He'd been sick awhile. For how long, he wasn't sure. Days? Weeks? Now he was almost recovered; for two days, he'd been without the fever. His body had done all the work: no drugs. They'd offered him what they'd claimed were antibiotics, but he'd refused. Who knew what they might be trying to feed him?

There'd been an endless string of attentive young women during his illness, and one portly, sweet-looking older one, who'd visited his sickbed several times a day, laid cold cloths across his forehead, and surrounded him with additional blankets, even as he sweated and twitched and occasionally sighed. After the fever broke, he'd begun eating broth. Yesterday, some soft, mashed cactus. Today, a full breakfast they'd prepared for him: *huevos rancheros*. He felt he was beginning to regain his strength.

During the long while he'd lain hot and delirious on that bed, the oven of his mind had baked terrifying dreams. One was of Svetlana in a building with many doorways, from which she would appear and into which she would disappear, repeatedly. Another was of Sequoya on a horse, galloping, galloping, disappearing into a sandstorm, then reappearing as a gigantic face, before being sucked back into those dancing, swirling grains. In another, Charles was executed by a pistol shot to the forehead. The moment his head touched the concrete floor, however, it was yanked back up, only to receive another pistol shot. After each of these nightmares, he would scream, jerk himself upright, and soon, thankfully, attendants would come flooding in.

But the most sobering dream of all (too labored and methodical to be actually frightening) was the one he had awakened from only a few minutes ago. This was an execution dream with a twist: a brawny butcher with an axe the size of a car door kept positioning himself to strike off Charles's head.

Remembering this, Charles found his mind diverted onto a siding, one that caused him to smile for the first time in days. He was recalling what Nabokov had said in a preface to the English translation of his novel *Invitation to a Beheading*. He'd said he first considered the name *Invitation to a Decapitation*, but was put off by the un-euphonious verbal "stutter" of that title. He then noted the odd fact that he'd wished at first to name his Russian original *Priglashenie na otnoshenie (beheading)*, but was brought up short by the analogous disturbing repetition of sounds. He had therefore chosen *Priglashenie na kazn'* (decapitation), instead. And so the final, translated-into-English title was—paradoxically—more in line with his initial idea!

Charles brought his mind back to his dream. His smile faded as he grew thoughtful, almost analytical. In the dream, he'd been on his knees, hands bound behind his back. Despite the outsize biceps, triceps, and hams of the executioner, despite his disturbing medieval attire, his face was recognizable. It was not the brilliant Mexican psycho Cartagena, who had interrogated Charles for hours, had murdered a young boy just to make a point. No, it was Charles's old department chairman, a face he hadn't seen in years, who stood poised to deliver the decapitating blow.

Lying on his cot now, Charles felt himself on the brink of an understanding. This journey he'd been on for the better part of a year—this whole, damned trip—had been an attempt to assuage the humiliation he'd felt thirty years before, when he'd been booted out of the university.

He put his fingers to the sides of his head and rubbed it, trying to coax a narrative out of his brain. That blow to his ego all those years ago, Charles realized, was something he'd never recovered from, not entirely. He'd moved on, but he hadn't recovered. Instead, he'd yearned to do something spectacular, something grand, startling, meaningful. An achievement. A way of getting back. Of thumbing his nose at them. Of saying, "So there. *Now* you see."

He chuckled quietly and exhaled a long breath. And as he lay on his bed while the frogs' chorus continued to flow through the window on that freshening breeze, he decided: *How silly. How very silly.*

60
THE PRESENT IS PAST, THE PAST PRESENT

"*S*EÑOR, USTED TIENE *un visitante.*"

Charles rose from his bunk bed, groggy. It was the middle of the afternoon, but he'd been taking a nap. Why not? Everybody else did. It had surprised him at first; he'd never have suspected that members of a vicious drug cartel, who prided themselves on their "modern" methods, still clung to the Mexican custom of the siesta.

Still groggy, however, he struggled to comb traces of a vivid dream from his mind, and concentrate on what the boy was telling him. The hard afternoon sunlight slanted through the one narrow window in his small room, making him squint and shield his eyes with a cupped hand.

"A visitor?" he said. "*Para me?*"

"*Sí.*" The young man, a bit disheveled himself (had he been napping too?), bore a look Charles found difficult to fathom. Respect, was it?

"*El arzobispo de México quiere hablar con Usted.*"

Charles's jaw dropped, then he grinned, and chuckled. "Of

course," he said. "The Archbishop of Mexico. Why not the Pope? *Porque no es la Papa?*"

His rouser, whom he knew to be called Pepe, looked concerned. "*Es verdad,*" he said. The boy was trying to remain composed, but Charles thought he could discern an air of excitement.

Seriously? thought Charles, as he tugged on his trousers and tucked in his shirt. Then his skin grew clammy. Were they going to shoot him, after all? Was this to be Last Rites? Wouldn't a simple priest do?

"I'm not a Catholic," he said. "*Yo no soy Católico.*"

Pepe shrugged. "*No es importa,*" he whispered. "Come with me, please."

Puzzled, apprehensive, Charles followed the boy out the door of his room. Their path led along a corridor, then left through another, then right along still another.

•

Charles had been out of his room only a handful of times since his interrogation—weeks and weeks ago—and was aware that the building had many dimensions to it. But now he was ushered into a large room he'd never seen, with a carpeted floor, a desk, and several upholstered chairs. A few mirrors hung here and there, as well, and several portraits. Even a couple of bookcases, heavy with leather-bound volumes. The room had warmth to it, and the fireplace along one wall added to its sense of comfort and warmth.

He stood in the middle of the room and turned to face the door. "I am ready to receive," he announced pompously. His posture would have fooled no one, of course. Whatever this was, he was hardly ready for it.

Pepe departed. (Was that a little bow he had executed as

he left?) Several moments later he returned, escorting what was surely an hallucination. Or the first-to-arrive guest at a costume party? Before Charles stood a man of modest stature, outfitted in a scarlet cassock, with a lace-trimmed, knee-length white *rochet* over that, and finally a red cape, all of which, Charles remembered from reading about the medieval Church during his graduate school days, was the habit of a cardinal. The cape was called a *mozzeta,* he believed. And sure enough, a red skullcap completed the outfit. Wasn't that called a *zucchetto* or a *biretta?* He could no longer remember. In any event, someone had certainly gone all out to give him a moment's amusement.

But then he spied the bishop's ring, and something changed. A little thrill ran through him: *This guy could be real.*

"*Señor* Baker," said his hallucination. Or, possibly, his actual visitor. Because when he heard the voice, three cherries clicked into place on the face of some imaginary slot machine. He could never forget that voice.

"Holy Mother of God!" exclaimed Charles. "Nacho?"

Out of the corner of his eye, he noticed that Pepe was as puzzled by his outburst as Charles was confounded by what he saw.

The man smiled ever so slightly, then lifted one of his beautifully costumed arms and gestured toward the door and its young guardian. In a gentle but authoritative voice, he said in Spanish, "Leave us, please."

The door closed, and they were alone.

"Holy Mother of God, indeed," said Ignacio. "Yes, Charlie, it's me."

"But . . . but . . . I mean, Christamighty! Excuse me, Nacho. No disrespect intended but, I mean, wow! Why *are* you dressed this way? I had a feeling, when we were kids—you know, just before you moved away—that you were headed toward becoming a priest, but . . . but, wow! Are these vestments for real? Are you really a bishop? And a Mexican bishop, at that?"

"I am for real, Charlie. Not just a bishop, excuse me very much, but a cardinal. Goodness, are you color blind, my old friend? My official title is *Cardinal Titular de Santo Francesco d'Assisi a Ripa Grande*. Though I'm referred to most often as 'Primate Archbishop of Mexico.'"

As he spoke, Ignacio had begun removing his various outer garments. When he had stripped down to the more familiar black garb and white collar, he looked at Charles once more, and smiled. Despite the streaks of gray throughout his straight black hair, he had the same square face, the same mischievous eyes, the same broad dimples Charles had known when they were youngsters on the ranch. Deep lines radiated from the corners of his eyes, but they didn't make him look old, just like someone who smiled a lot.

The Archbishop touched his chest. "Now I am again a simple priest from the parish of Tepehuanes, where I was born. May I hug my good friend?"

They embraced warmly in the middle of the room. There were tears in the eyes of both men as they drew back, then hugged again. "I've missed you, Nacho," said Charles.

"And I you," Ignacio said. "You've been in my thoughts and my prayers for fifty years, Charlie. I'm so glad to see you again."

Charles's face suddenly grew deeply puzzled once again. "Wait! Nacho, why and how are you here? What brings about this extraordinary visit? To a man imprisoned by a drug cartel?"

"They didn't tell you? Charlie, I am here as your rescuer. In a few minutes, we will leave this place. You are free now, Charlie. I am both authorized and directed to accompany you back to the United States, where my stated purpose—my newspaper purpose—is to have a conversation with the Archbishop of New

York City about the growing number of Mexicans in his care. But in fact, it's the agreement with *Los Avispones* that I accompany you back to the United States. First to Oaxaca in my limousine, then we fly to Mexico City and connect to a direct flight to New York. All arranged."

Charles could not speak for a moment. Surely this was a dream? Perhaps he had never really awakened from his afternoon nap? He gripped the arms of his chair so tightly he feared they might crumble to sawdust beneath his fingers. "You're telling me I'm *free*? As in . . . *free*?"

"Please God, I should hope so. I just paid your jailers one and a quarter million dollars to ransom you."

Shock registered on Charles's face, but Ignacio was already glancing at his watch. "We must go, my friend. Let's make our getaway before they change their very expensive minds! We can talk in the car; it's a long drive."

•

They left without incident or deterrence. A mere smile and nod from Ignacio, once he had rolled down his window, was sufficient for the armed guards at the entrance gate to wave them on through. The primate had donned his cardinal's garb once more, and Charles saw that the guards were clearly impressed. Hell, so was he!

Once past the gate, they drove down a rutted road with many potholes. The driver guided the long limousine carefully and slowly, but it was a jouncing, rolling ride. A few miles past the fortress *hacienda* where Charles had been kept, the road's surface smoothed out a bit, but it continued to curve and twist, snaking its way through the deep jungle that reached in on both sides. After an hour or so, they reached a wider, gravel-covered road, and abruptly the ride got smoother. Charles finally relaxed back against the limo's soft cushions, excited and oddly sleepy at the same time.

But instead of nodding off, he wanted to talk. To catch up. It turned out that Ignacio had studied first at the seminary in Mexico, and later in Rome and Germany, as well. Even at the Sorbonne. He was surprised to learn that the current pope was a friend with whom Ignacio had studied in Germany.

At one point in their conversation, Charles asked how it could be possible that his friend knew members of a drug cartel? That had struck him as particularly unlikely for a prelate, he said, especially one of Ignacio's rank! How, Charles wondered, could a group that had fashioned paranoia into an art form bring themselves to trust a Catholic cardinal?

Among the comestibles Ignacio had brought along for the journey was a tin of Mexican chocolates he was fond of. He opened it now, offered one to Charles, and selected a cayenne-laced morsel for himself. Then he answered his friend's question. "You see, Charlie, many years ago, when I was the priest in Tepehuanes, Felipe Ortega was one of my parishioners. Long before he became involved with drugs. In fact, before he even went to college in the States. I was the one who recommended MIT. And I was not wrong to do so! He had such a brilliant engineering mind."

Ignacio sighed and shrugged. "One can only suggest a path, of course, not guarantee that someone will take it. At any rate, whatever someone tells you in the confessional booth is sacrosanct, Charlie, as I'm sure you're aware. For better or for worse. To me, it's more solemn than marriage. I consider it an unbreakable cornerstone of the Catholic faith. Felipe knew I would never betray that trust, and he's right. I never would. So he continued to trust me. Whatever you may think of *Señor* Ortega, my friend, 'all God's children' means *all* God's children."

He leaned back against the cushions and sighed again. "It's widespread knowledge, of course, that Felipe has committed horrendous crimes against both God and man. In point of fact, he was a rather peculiar boy. Perhaps one could have seen this coming." He sighed. "But still, he is a human being, with a human soul. And he was one of my early flock. Eventually, of course, as I moved up in the hierarchy, I went one way, he another; I hadn't seen him in years when he made contact recently, through an emissary. I'm not even sure who arranged it, nor do I know who paid the money that was wired to my account. But when I first heard about your captivity, weeks and weeks ago—"

"Wait!" Charles interrupted. "You heard about it weeks ago? How?"

The priest smiled enigmatically. Outside, the ride had smoothed a bit more, as a patchy macadam had been reached. "How, indeed?" he said. "Well, not through the newspapers, for sure. Let me put it this way. The government and the cartels have their surveillance capabilities—they grow every day—but a man in my position is not without resources. I keep 'feelers' out, you may be sure. I know a lot of what goes on—in various circles of society—a good deal earlier than the general population."

He continued with his earlier train of thought. "The moment I heard about your imprisonment, Charlie, I felt something in my bones. I prayed for guidance, but even before my prayers, I knew God had granted me a part to play in rescuing you. So, when I was contacted, I didn't hesitate. That I was called to this did not strike me as an accident. It was God's will."

Charles grew pensive. He selected another chocolate from the tin, one with an almond at its center. He chewed it thoughtfully. It was growing dark outside; the coarse road slicing its corrugated path through dense foliage had given way to a pavement descending through rolling hills, whose slight elevations cast blanketing shadows on the adjacent flatland.

"I'm very grateful to you, Nacho," he said finally. "Good Lord! I owe you my life! But we are pretty likely to interpret some things differently. As you might or might not suspect, I am not a man of faith. Haven't been for a long time."

"Does that matter? Would you expect that fact to make a difference to me? Or to change how *I* see things? Your faith is not what was at stake, here, Charlie. Your *life* was. You can call my intervention Fate, if you like. You can call it Destiny. You can even call it an 'accident' if you dare, but it doesn't alter my conviction that I was selected—no, *commanded*—by God to be your rescuer."

They were both silent for a minute or two, then Charles suddenly said, "Man, these are good chocolates, Nacho!" They looked at each other and broke up laughing.

"I know! I know! I'm addicted to them! Cayenne, cinnamon, other secret things I can't identify. What's not to like?"

•

Eventually, the tin gave out. The two couldn't have been giddier had they been swilling tequila in the back seat. Ignacio turned the empty container upside down and put on a tragic face. "No more!" he lamented. "No more!" They both laughed again.

Now that the road had grown easier, the tires' hum was a comfort. A crosswind had imparted a gentle rocking to the limo. Charles began to actually accept that he had been liberated. His incarceration was over.

Ignacio looked out at the dark, then back at his friend. "I don't know if you remember this, Charlie, but back on the ranch, when we were both twelve or thereabouts, we started working during the summer. Do you remember? And our first job together was chasing crows and sparrows out of a recently planted wheat field. To keep them from eating up the grain. First we tried your Daisy Air Rifle, but neither of us could hit anything, so we eventually resorted to tossing clods of dirt at them. Just to frighten them away." He chuckled at that point, remembering the moment. "Can't say their alarm was more than momentary."

Charles laughed. "I certainly remember that!"

"Well, do you remember that your father caught us sitting down on the job? How embarrassing that must have been for him! He was responsible, and there was his son loafing when he should have been working? As I recall, our taking a long break had been my idea, but when your father spied us, you insisted it was yours. I think you knew my father would beat me very brutally if he thought I was the promoter of our laziness. So you took the rap. And I said nothing, just watched as your father's wrath came down on you. He must have whipped you, too—I believe you told me he did—but you knew that *my* father . . . well, I would have been lucky to survive it. If it had been one of the evenings he'd been drinking, I might *not* have survived."

Charles was noticing how, because of the surrounding darkness, the limousine's windows had become mirrors reflecting back only what was in the car itself, the two of them, their faces in shadows thrown by the limo's overhead light. "I knew he beat you," he said, "but I didn't know he was *that* bad."

"It doesn't matter. What does matter is that this event changed my life, Charlie. I brooded over it. I marveled at your bravery. Such a selfless act. And I swore that I would never be passive like that again, never leave someone else to take the blame. That act, Charlie, was my proof that human kindness—concern for another person, and a willingness to sacrifice to ease another's burden—was alive in the world. I'd already become a believing Catholic, even an ardent one, as you know. But I think it was then I resolved, privately, to become a priest."

Charles was embarrassed, but also warmed by this revelation. During the flight to Mexico City, and then on the longer flight to New York, his embarrassment gave way to pride, but the warmth remained.

PART FIVE

61

NEW YORK FUCKING CITY

NOVEMBER. ALWAYS A chill wind off the Hudson. The moment Charles turned west on ninetieth Street, he remembered that fact. Why, he wondered, did it never fail to surprise him? Even when he'd been gone a day or a week, he'd forget. Now he'd been gone, what? A year? Yes. A year. *Forgive yourself your porous memory!* he admonished himself. The surprise is not that surprising.

From the doorman, round-faced Emilio, cheerfully at his post, he weathered effusive greetings, smiling wanly, trying to enjoy the warmth of the moment. Out of the corner of his eye, he espied the super, Horace, who came out of his office briefly to pump both of Charles's hands enthusiastically, with vociferous exclamations of welcome. A moment later, Emilio delivered an avalanche of mail to him, tugging a dark green garbage bag out of the package closet, of a size better purposed for collecting leaves in the fall. Charles lugged it upstairs on the elevator, then down the hall and into a corner of his apartment, to be dealt with later. Then he sank into an armchair, already tuckered out from this brief exercise.

After a moment, he dug his cell phone out of his pocket. It had been returned to him via Ignacio. Ignacio! He smiled. God, how wonderfully strange! From an irrigator's son to Your Highness, Your Worship, Your Eminence, or whatever it was appropriate to call him now. And there he was, Johnny-on-the-spot, the most fortunate coincidence in Charles's life by far. Charles's rescue and the trip to New York City had taken just over a day. Nacho had dropped Charles off at Columbus Circle on the way to the residence of the Archbishop of New York, and Charles had taken an uptown train three stops.

He thumbed his iPhone on and off a few times. How thoroughly had his captors pored over its contents before returning it to him? He imagined them meticulously scrutinizing every string of ones and zeros in its underbelly, dissecting the code that meant nothing to him but provided their astute hackers with a blueprint of his comings and goings, conversations and text messages, including every location where each of them had taken place.

Did the cartel really have the capability that its brilliant, sharp-eyed interrogator claimed? He looked at the smartphone again. Smart, sure. But not loyal; an incredible snitch when it fell into the wrong hands. Strange that it was even functioning! They must have charged it just before handing it to Ignacio. He awakened the phone again to see what was available to his less discriminating intelligence. There were page after page of unlooked-at emails, for sure, and—could that be right?—a registered count, inside a bright red circle, of 239 voicemails.

Well, he would deal with those later, too. Meanwhile, what of his laptop? he wondered. What of all those CDs, all the digital versions of manuscripts he'd spent a year wresting from translators around the globe? Had Óscar held onto them? Was his project, that which had sent him on his pixilated jaunt around the world, still intact? *Well, that too*, he thought, *I'll deal with later.* At least he had his life.

Restless despite his exhaustion, he repaired to the terrace, where he hadn't been in almost a year. Sinking down into his single outdoor chair, he looked out fondly on the man-made hollows, buttes, ravines and plateaus of Manhattan. *Eight floors up. What would it feel like to fall?* he wondered. For some reason, he suddenly recalled another terrace, a much lower one, no more than a porch, really, outside a cabin he'd rented one summer on Lake Champlain, where he'd gone to write. The couple next door—teachers up from the City on summer vacation—had had a habit of returning home from their day's drive around Vermont or upstate New York, and calling out, "Drink time, Charlie!" And he'd sit on their identical terrace for a half-hour's pleasant fellowship and conversation, sipping gin and tonics while gazing at the lake, which he remembered struck all three of them—on its calm days—as *fraudulently* peaceful. Because they knew the waters of Lake Champlain to be mysteriously, almost unfathomably deep; and local lore held that monsters lurked below its surface.

Looking out over Columbus Avenue, Charles shook his head and sighed. Home. All monsters presumably left behind. So why this formless discontent? Perhaps he was just tired. So much in the last few days, the last many weeks. He quit the terrace for the bedroom, where he collapsed on the bed, pulled the covers over his head, and went to sleep.

•

Hours later, Charles's landline was ringing. He struggled to emerge from sleep and from a deep, disturbing dream in which Sequoya, the great Cherokee alphabet-giver, rode his quivering mount alone through northern Mexico. Sometimes it was Sequoya; sometimes it was Charles himself. But instead of inquiring after his lost band of Cherokees, Sequoya tried to persuade each tribe he encountered to translate his syllabary into its language. And when each refused, this outsize figure, too big for his overburdened horse, selected a young boy from the tribe, bade him kneel, and to the horror of the assembled tribe members, drew a pistol from his belt and shot the lad in the head.

The dream had registered *plop!* after bloody *plop!* of fallen boys. Crawling out of the dream, Charles managed to find his phone in the dark and answer after ten rings.

"Hey, Big Guy! When were you going to call me?"

"Hey, Marcy. Good to hear your voice. How did you know I'm home?"

"What an ordeal, Charlie! I got the lowdown from your buddy Jon Belknap. When you stopped emailing me, I started tracking down your other friends to see what they could dig up about your whereabouts."

"Then you must know more than I do. I've been sleeping since I got back, and you're the first person in New York I've talked to. I'm eager to hear the whole story myself."

"Was it awful, Charlie? I'll bet it was awful. From what your friend Belknap said—Charlie, I just can't imagine."

"Well, I spent an awful lot of time thinking about Dostoyevsky's *House of the Dead*."

Marisol, who understood the reference, chuckled and groaned simultaneously. "I'll bet you did. Wow, Charlie. So glad to see you made it."

Charles yawned. He felt dull, yet somehow raw, as if his mind had been abraded by sandpaper. Maybe part of him was still in the dream? Or even back in the "house of the dead"? He'd been to so many distant locations on the globe. He was finding it hard to believe that his friend Marcy was only twenty blocks away. New York. He was actually back in New York.

There was a pause, and then she said, "So, Charlie. How did you leave it with Svetlana?"

Svetlana. His mind fuzzed over even more at the mention of her name. He yawned again.

"I haven't gone there, Marcy. I mean, there's nothing new. I haven't spoken to her since you and I last emailed each other. How many months ago is that? I don't know, Marcy. I don't know what to say."

"But you love her, right? It's not a memory that's faded after all you've gone through and you really couldn't give a toss? Am I right about that?"

"Yes, of course. You're right. I do love her. Maybe even more than before. No, definitely more."

After a moment or two, she said, "Well, Charlie, remember. Faint heart and all that shit. Personally, I think your soul's never going to be at rest until you've at least spoken to her."

Another pause. "You may be right, Marcy. I'm just not up to it right now."

"Hey, I didn't say right now. Did I say right now? Listen, my friend, I didn't mean to bring you down. If I spoke out of turn here, I apologize. Just think about it, Charlie. Meanwhile, welcome back to the land of the living! Call me. Let's get together soon, okay? Soon soon soon. I'll crack open a bottle of Veuve Clicquot. Or, in your case, sparkling cider. Okay? Love you, Buddy. Great to know you're safe. Just wanted to hear your voice. Over and out."

"*Ciao*, Marcy. Regards to Tony and the kids. Thanks for calling."

•

After hanging up, Marisol—twenty blocks uptown from Charlie—stared at her phone for several minutes. Did she dare? After all, she'd known Gennady years before Charlie ever did.

62

THE NEW NORMAL

AWAKE OR ASLEEP, his life felt like a dream. He kept resisting the urge to pinch himself. He called Jonathan the morning after he spoke to Marcy and heard the whole troubled, shoddy, grueling, heroic story, all that Jon knew, at least. It was an account roiled with intrigue, shenanigans, dirty tricks, subterfuge, daring and dramatic rescue attempts and, of course, an extraordinary amount of ransom money paid from—to Charles, at least—a totally unexpected source.

In fact, it seemed to Charles a saga verging on fable. Derek Wainscot, the force behind many of his troubles, morphing in the end into the agent of his salvation? The irony was mind-boggling. So should he love him or hate him? The question shuffled Svetlana into his mind, as one image follows another in a slide show. He supposed because that question applied to her, as well.

Despite his slippery sense of reality, he managed to plough through all his emails, sitting at a nearby Internet café. Most he dismissed as spam. Only a smattering of what remained required answers; nearly all were absurdly out-of-date. He also fielded phone calls from every member of the writing group. He was elated—thrilled even—to talk to each of them, but grew weary of repeating the same story. He began to experience his own voice as a tape-recorded message, an endless audio loop. Which did nothing to diminish his feeling of unreality. The tale sounded more fictional each time he spun it out to a new listener.

The third day back, he received the email he'd been waiting for. Jonathan had told him he'd called Óscar Amalfitano the moment he knew Charles was back in New York. Óscar had said that all his possessions were safe, and had told him a coming email would explain everything that had transpired with his project.

Charlie read eagerly:

Estimado Professor Charlie,

You are alive and well! How delightful!! You did not become one more casualty in my record of the shame of Santa Teresa. How I prayed for you during this dark, dark time! Well, not *prayed*, exactly, but kept my fingers, toes and everything else crossed. (I don't pray; I am a freethinker, like yourself.) (Or do I presume?) Never mind. The important thing is that you are safe and sound and back in your beloved New York, and I am delighted beyond words to hear it.

I very much fear that part of your ordeal can be laid at my door; I did not explain to you with sufficient strength, perhaps, the profound dangers of life in my beloved country at this moment. And, particularly, in my city.

I understand that you were rescued by the Archbishop of All Mexico! Or through his intervention. I do not know the gentleman; I hear he is a very nice man, and, non-praying man or not, I envy you!

Charlie, my friend, let me tell you what I have done. First of all, don't worry, I have everything you left at my house when you were spirited away: your computer, its case, all your disks, even a few clothing items (you travel quite light, it seems), one of which is a beautiful sweater which you may already find some need for now in New York, though it looks like it was made for some place *really* cold, like Siberia!

"Svetlana's sweater!" Charles cried aloud.

Every eye at the café turned to look at him. He grinned sheepishly and returned his attention to Óscar's email.

I, of course, quite some time ago completed my translation of your story from Japanese into Spanish, and, after learning what had become of you, I decided to do the following. Please understand that you can, of course, simply take the Japanese-into-Spanish manuscript I have done (which I will send you immediately), have it rendered back into English and be done with it. Period, end of report. (I love that American phrase!) However, there is an alternative. (As you've probably figured out by now, I'm a fan of alternatives.) I took the liberty, since you were not available to pursue this, of procuring *two* additional translations. (Sorry if this is seen as a transgression!) First of all, I sent my Spanish translation to that colleague I told you about in Lebanon, Faisal Shaheen. (You remember that he teaches at the American University in Beirut?) I hoped he could find the time to translate it into Arabic, in case that would be of use to you. Well, not only did he have time, but he did it quite quickly and—I believe—expertly, so that when it came back to me, and you had not been heard from yet, I had still *more* time.

Not knowing how long it was going to be before your escape was accomplished (or even—God forbid!—whether!) I decided to take one more step. I had mentioned Jean-Claude Pelletier in France as a possible translator, but Jean-Claude was unable to do it (he is in the middle of a *terrible* divorce right now!), so I then submitted Faisal's Arabic version to another friend, Anatole Popescu, who lives in Bucharest but has spent a lot of time in the Middle East, and whose principal source of income is in translating articles and stories from Arabic into Rumanian! Long story short, Charlie, he did it, and, if you should want it, you now have the ten successive languages. Wasn't that your original idea? I will send you *all of this* and you will decide what to do with it. If you want to go with all ten (I was very careful in my instructions to them, mindful of how you explained to me your purpose), and if you can find someone in New York to translate the Rumanian into English, you will have completed your project with all ten of the original languages, as planned!

Of course if you do not want to use these additional translations—since you did not authorize them in advance—no harm done. You are under no obligation to pay either of these gentlemen. When I explained the situation to them, they were happy to do your project gratis. Really, Charlie. No obligations whatsoever.

So, my friend! To borrow the words of your late Dr. Martin Luther King, whom your country rightly celebrates, "Free at last!" Olé!

I hope to see you one of these days very soon, and I remain,

Yours sincerely,
Óscar Amalifitano

Charles could hardly reply quickly enough.

Óscar! Thank you! Thank you! Thank you!
Sincerely,
Charles Abel (Charlie) Baker

Launching his reply with a percussive click, Charles leaned back in his café chair and took stock. Perhaps things were returning to normal. Whatever that was. Normal was very different now, wasn't it? Normal has been totally transformed. The important thing: soon he would have his materials back, and the world would be right side up once again.

63

VERSION ONE, TWO, THREE, FOUR . . .

THE DAY ÓSCAR'S package arrived from Mexico, Charles whipped out his computer case and whisked the CD from its pocket. Even Svetlana's sweater fell prey to his free-wheeling deconstruction of the cardboard box's contents, winding up with one cable-knit arm flung out along the top of his armchair while the remainder puddled in the middle of the cushion.

He rushed his cherished disks to a professional service he'd identified earlier, and bade them print out paper copies of each. Despite the noted firm's expertise, they had to scramble for software that could handle Kannada and Icelandic—but managed—and he willingly paid extra for both their search and the software, which they obligingly copied onto his flash drive after they'd used it. At his urging, it became a rush order, for which he also paid extra. The two employees who were assigned the job grumbled and growled a bit, indignant that they were being held past their dinner hour, but by 7:05 p.m. the job was done.

That evening, at home at his desk, Charles sifted through

his new-smelling manuscripts with care, assigning to each, in deep black swirls of ink, its numerical order, and inscribing on the top of each first page the date, time, "language from," "language to," and so on. He then entered this information into a small notebook. Finally, he created on his computer a database file that included, for each version, this same information, plus the translator, country of origin, and such contact information as he'd managed to hold on to.

Next he fanned the manuscripts out on the floor of his carpet and, sitting in his easy chair, regarded lovingly each front page in turn. It was a moment of almost incandescent joy. He found romance simply in letting his eyes sweep over the diversity of scripts: some cursive, others boxy, some razor-thin, still others hefty. Some letters stood up straight and saluted, others loped along girlishly, trailing off into delicate curlicues. He admired both the heavyweight strokes and the spindly ones. He lingered over dots, underscores, and accent marks. In short, his mind juiced at every squiggle. He felt like Silas Marner sifting his hoard of coins through bony fingers.

Charles studied his treasures and sighed. It was, after all, his deep-seated reverence for language that had, in large part, inspired his quest. The very idea of it, as well as how each of its almost infinite variations might reflect a heritage, the successes and limitations of a culture attained over time. More than six thousand languages in the world. And disappearing fast. Half might vanish in the next 100 years. Can you imagine it? Not even a vapor trail. Once the last native speaker expired, *poof!*

However much his lingering resentment and shame about losing his position at the university might have been the force driving his need to do something as dramatic as his cockamamie round-the-world trip, the *nature* of his quest had been about language.

He wondered if his reverence for language might even approach a religious feeling. What would his *amigo* Ignacio (now a Catholic cardinal!) think about that? All that remained in Charles's mind, really, from the intense religious preoccupation of his youth—part of which was recorded in the short story that was now arrayed on his carpet in eight different languages—was the statement at the beginning of the King James version of the Gospel of John: "In the beginning was the Word, and the Word was with God, and the *Word was* God."

A notion he'd meditated on often. Of course, the rest of John's chapter was a crazy-quilt of stunning apocalyptic visions that Charles both marveled at and dismissed, in equal measure. But a question lingered in his mind about the pivotal word in that sentence: *Logos*. The Word. Was it a good translation?

Charles was no biblical scholar, but he seemed to recall that the King James Version of the Bible was translated (at least the New Testament) mostly from Greek sources, and that John wrote his text in Aramaic. He then recalled, as he searched his memory further, that the Aramaic word was *Memra*. So *Memra* became *Logos* became *Word*.

All those seventeenth century scribes and scholars—as well as their sixteenth century predecessors, like William Tyndale—were doing the same thing he'd just finished doing! Only, he'd taken his text through even more languages, right? And when you considered that both *logos* and *memra* had other meanings? He remembered from his historical studies that the Greeks had used *logos* in many different ways: Heraclitus used it as a principle of thought and order; to Aristotle it meant "reasoned discourse" or "argument." And who knew which meaning of *memra* was in John's mind when he selected that particular word?

"Arrrgghhh!" he uttered aloud, and shook his head to relieve his frustration and clear his mind of its endless spinning off in all directions.

Back to the point, he thought, surveying once more his horde of linguistic treasure (or folly). *The question is, what now?*

His first decision was about what Óscar had raised in his email. Call a halt at eight versions and translate Óscar's Spanish into English? Or work to get that tenth version translated into Rumanian?

Ten was better than eight, right? But ten was more work for him, and eight was not too shabby. He was pretty sure he already knew someone who could translate Óscar's version from Spanish, while he'd need to search further for someone who could translate from Rumanian. And even if he could find a Rumanian translator without booking a flight to Bucharest, Charles was tired of searching, tired of trekking. Just plain tired. He settled on eight.

By calling Columbia University's Spanish Department, Charles found someone who could translate his manuscript from the Spanish, so three weeks after Óscar's package arrived from Mexico, the newly minted English version was complete. He picked up the finished manuscript from graduate student Lydia Bustamonte the same night Marisol had finally found time in her schedule to invite him to dinner, and—halfway down the elevator in Bustamonte's building—remembered that, as she'd handed him the envelope, she'd been hard-pressed to keep from laughing.

64
COMFORT FOOD

CHARLES HAD BEEN to Marisol's penthouse apartment near Columbia many times, though not, of course, during the past year. It was Tony who greeted him at the door. A tall, spare fellow whose spindly frame belied hefty engineering ideas.

While teaching full-time at a City university, Tony was also designing bridges whose revolutionary support structures were not only safer but cheaper, if only he could find someone who was willing to build them. Marisol had asked for her old friend Charles's blessing before they were married, fifteen years ago, and Charles had thought him an excellent choice. One of the things Charles found particularly engaging was that Tony remained quite respectful of his and Marisol's longstanding relationship, never trying to insert himself into their shared memories, which they would refresh and embellish almost every time they met.

The moment Charles crossed the threshold, they pumped hands and hugged each other, while Tony uttered condolences about Charles's Mexican incarceration. When Charles asked about the kids, he was told they both had overnight stays with friends; it was an adults-only evening. He followed Tony down the narrow hallway. Low-slung windows framed vistas of the

Hudson River. The view from these windows always reminded Charles of Independence Day in 1976, the two hundredth anniversary of America's birth. Charles had been one among many of Marisol's friends in this apartment during that gigantic celebration, watching schooners, battleships, brigantines, windjammers, catamarans, and a yawl or two parade up and down the Hudson River.

They found Marisol in the kitchen, a small, quirky space that Charles invaded immediately. He spread his arms to envelop her, but wound up dropping them and staring, astonished to see her dressed in a full-length gown, her best strand of pearls, and opalescent earrings. Her hair was swept into a shape that could only have been achieved in a beauty salon. It looked, to Charles, rather like a building designed by Frank Gehry. Around her waist was an apron.

"Whoa, Marcy, why are you so tarted up? This isn't New Years' Eve!"

"That's what *you* think, Buddy." She ignored his arms, continuing to stir the contents of a saucepan. "Don't you realize how special this occasion is? We're celebrating your return from the 'house of the dead,' remember? I've lain in a couple of magnums of Veuve Clicquot so we can toast you later. Why shouldn't I dress for the occasion?"

Charles looked at Tony, who wore an open-neck white shirt, with rolled cuffs. Charles, having shed his jacket, was dressed in jeans and a V-neck T-shirt. Tony shrugged.

"If you'd said something," Charles smiled, "I'd have taken my tux out of mothballs. Maybe. Don't think I've worn it since your wedding."

"Relax, Charlie. I don't expect my men to wear tuxedos. I just love to be in a gown when I drink the bubbly. Okay? So saying, she stripped off her apron, snuffed the flame under the saucepan, and delivered herself at last into Charles's arms. "Welcome back, Big Guy." She hugged him and planted a big kiss on his lips. "Champagne notwithstanding, my friend, your meal will be pork loin, mashed potatoes, candied yams, etcetera. Home cookin'. Just like your mama used to make, Oklahoma boy."

"You forget. I never had a mama," Charles said.

"Ouch! Right. Well, I'm sure it's what your mother would have made if she'd been around. At any rate—"

The last three words were delivered with force, but left dangling. Charles waited, puzzled both by the nature of her words and her drama-queen smile. It felt as if she'd just blown one of those long trumpets one sees in cartoons of medieval jousting tournaments, with a cloth tied to it and a message on the cloth. So what was the message?

He cast a quizzical look at Tony, who shrugged and looked away. When he reengaged with Marcy, she squeezed his hands and eyed him benignly.

"We have a surprise for you, Charlie. In the master bedroom. Close the door. Take your time. The meal can wait."

Charles was suspicious. "What on earth have you cooked up now?"

She turned him and pushed him gently. "Go, Charlie. Go claim your surprise."

Well, he thought, making his way along the hallway he'd just come down, this is an odd beginning! With Marcy, to be sure, weird is rarely more than a whisker away. He pulled up short in front of the door, his hand hovering over the knob. Then he twisted it and stepped inside.

A lamp on the other side of the bed was the only illumination, casting a penumbra of light over the armchair beside it. He was fumbling for the wall switch when he realized the chair was in use. Its occupant stood and turned to face him. His heart stopped.

"Svetlana!"

"*Zdravtstvuyte, kotik,*" she said. Her voice was soft and shy.

Having just come from the airport apparently, she wore the sky blue Aeroflot uniform he'd first seen her in.

"*OmiGod!*" he said. He forgot the light switch and stumbled toward her. They came together, two preconscious beings desperate to merge with one another. She was crying, an act he interfered with by planting kisses on her cheeks, mouth and eyelids.

"*OmiGod,*" he said again. "*Svetlana moya!* I've missed you so much. *Ya vas liubliu,* Svyeta. I love you madly."

He pulled back and looked at her. Then, taking hold of her shoulders, he gently urged her down to the bed. They sat there looking at one another.

"Svyetochka, how . . . ? What are you doing here?"

•

In the living room, far from the fibrillations of lovers encountering one another after a painful absence, Marisol and Anthony had taken seats in adjoining armchairs, fingers loosely intertwined. Anthony wore a neutral expression; Marisol looked smug. She leaned her head back against an embroidered pillow. No need to rush things, she thought. A good loaf of bread takes time to rise. But if the right ingredients are there, rise it will.

•

Back in the bedroom, Charles had managed to find a box of tissues, which he'd placed on the bed beside Svetlana. The area around them had come to resemble a field of white poppies.

"Charlie, I am so bad! Because I am feeling I have no right to email you, I was without knowing that drug lords snagged you! This is correct? Snagged?"

Not waiting, she continued: "So I don't even know when

you disappear! *Akh, Bozhe Moi!* Instead of feeling sad for myself, I should have worry for you! Such an idiot! I am so, so sorry. When I hear from Marcy what happen, I almost die."

She called her Marcy, Charles realized. Had they become that close? He took both her hands in his. "It's all right, *dusha*. You're here now. I'm here now. We're together, and that's all that matters. I love you, Svyeta, and I want to be with you. I hope you want that as much as I do."

"You are kidding me? More! *More* than you! Ever since I meet you, I want you, Charlie."

He cleared his throat. "What about your doctor? I thought for sure you were going to get married. I thought . . . under the circumstances, there was no chance for us."

"You are kidding, yes? My doctor—well, I exaggerate a little because I guess I try to make you jealous—but, *dusha*, was never anything big. *Da*, I think about it, for sure, for security and all that: quit airline, just do my artwork, get some help for papa's health. But I could never do this. *Nikogda*. Is either you or old maid."

"Can't imagine you as an old maid. You're much too beautiful."

"You have no idea, silly man. You think I am one way, but I am quite another. Thank you, though, for calling me beautiful."

He kissed her.

"You mentioned your artwork. Are you doing your art again? I'm so happy about that. You're very good, you know."

"I starting to realize. Publisher in Moscow is bringing out new Russian edition of *Prestuplenie i Nakazanie*; is wanting me to do illustrations."

"Illustrations for *Crime and Punishment*! You're kidding! That's wonderful! How did you make that connection?"

"Well, sometimes I meet interesting men on plane, Charlie."

"Svyeta!"

She laughed for the first time that evening. "I am kid you, Charlie. Teasing. You are only man for me."

He looked away a moment. "*Dusha*, there's something else I should bring up," he said. "You realize I'm quite a bit older than you, yes? *Ya budu starik skoro.* Is that how you say it? 'I'll be an old man soon'?"

"How do you say—is it bullshit—in English? With my help you will be like Benjamin Button, get younger every year. You see that movie, Charlie?"

"I read the book. But, think, Svyetochka. All things considered, I'll be the first to go. You'll be left a widow."

"Don't even think about it."

They kissed again.

"So, Charlie," she asked, "what we do now?"

"Live together? Here in America? I want you with me, Svyeta. Will you consider it?"

She looked down. Her shoulders slumped, and a serious expression overtook her that he remembered from when she was asleep beside him in that Moscow hotel. "But how we manage? We must be practical, *da*? *Voprosy mnogie!* Many questions. There is question of visas. Is legal issues. Is question of my father."

For the first time in months, he felt a burgeoning confidence.

"We can work it out. Everything. We'll talk about it, we'll discuss, we'll figure it out. The main thing is if you want to be with me as much as I want to be with you."

"I want it, Charlie. More than anything. More than the dinner that is growing cold in the next room."

He laughed. "Then we'll do it."

•

By the time they'd returned to the living room, Anthony was

dozing and Marisol was yawning, but they managed to bestir themselves and soon brought forth Marisol's succulent victuals. Toasts were made that night, not only to Charles for having returned alive from the clutches of 'The Hornets,' not only to the fresh-found joy that animated the faces of both Charles and Svetlana, but also to the crafty, behind-the-scenes machinations of Marisol, the *éminence grise* without whom—as Charles readily conceded—he would still be the lovelorn, lifeless husk he'd been a short hour before.

As befits such occasions, the conversation around the table was both inconsequential and riotously funny. Every bad pun was treated with the reverence of a papal encyclical. The pork roast, crisp from its warming, dripping with fat, and surrounded by succulent vegetables and tubers, was consumed avidly by one hungry Russian and three famished Americans, and Charles agreed that it was just like his mother would have made, if he'd only had a mother. On the stroke of midnight, Charles and Svetlana left Marisol's apartment to walk the twenty blocks to his, and at six o'clock the next morning, sleep-deprived and still drunk on love, they arose for a round of coffee and toast before Charles packed her into a cab bound for JFK.

65
PARTY TIME

THEY COULD HEAR the music all the way down the hall. The receptionist at Belknap & Ogilvy, whom Charles knew, had informed them the event was not being held in the small conference room where the writing group usually met, but in one of the larger conference rooms. Charles smiled at the receptionist and took Svetlana's hand. They'd been told not to arrive before eight, but the party had obviously been going awhile.

When they opened the door, they discovered a solid oak table large enough to seat a football team, including its coaching staff, with a smaller table at the far end laden with food and drink. The gap between was tight with bodies, mostly standing and chatting, drinks in hand, but a small space had been hollowed out where several couples were dancing to swing era big band music. "Ah, Benny Goodman!" Charles told Svetlana with an air of authority.

"*Nyet*, is Artie Shaw! I know this piece!"

Charles kissed her appreciatively. "I stand corrected."

Jonathan—their host—waved them over from the other end of the conference table. They laid their coats across two chairs and walked toward him.

He waited for them nervously. It had taken Jonathan a month to plan this party. Besides ramping up for the reading—the heart of the party—he'd intended it to celebrate Charles's safe return. A closetful of booze, wine, beer and mixers had been laid in, and in addition to the usual cold cuts, cheeses and olives, he'd prearranged delivery of a three-tiered, wedding-sized Favori cake (molten chocolate, hazelnut mousse, Frangelico liqueur) from Bruno's, his favorite Italian bakery, along with that *pasticceria*'s premier assortment of tarts, biscotti, sfogliatelle, cannoli, shortbreads and seven-layer cookies. The cake had an appropriate inscription, which he'd dictated to the decorator over the phone.

The most anxiety-laden task, however, had been gathering the guests. Members of the writing group were not a problem; they lived in New York. It was the out-of-the-country people whose schedules created challenges. Their myriad obligations required constant amendments. Plane flights were arranged, canceled, and rearranged. Jonathan had kept the identities of that portion of his guest list secret from Charles. Loretta, his secretary of seventeen years, on whose sturdy shoulders these preparations had descended, grew so frazzled by the constant reshuffling that she threatened to resign if she wasn't offered a raise. To which he'd conceded at once.

As Charles and Svetlana edged along the wall to join their host, someone stepped aside long enough for Charles to glimpse a patch of scarlet. He stopped, grabbed Svetlana's arm and gawked as his suspicion became fact: a Cardinal's full regalia came into view.

A moment later they were hugging. "Nacho! Incredible! Thank you for coming, *amigo*. All the way from Mexico?"

"Peru, actually. It wasn't easy, Charlie, but I didn't want to miss your party. I understand your Mr. Belknap here shuffled it several times to accommodate me, and I thank him for that."

Jonathan glowed. "We almost missed him because, day before yesterday, he got a summons from Rome. Thank God that was canceled. I worried that his visit with the Pope might have to do with your rescue. Our unscripted performance in spiriting you out was a bit dicey from the church's point of view, I suspect. But the Vatican postponed his visit at the last minute."

Charles grinned. "Kind of the Pope to put our party first, wasn't it?"

The Cardinal smiled. "You may be sure there are one or two other matters on the Holy See's agenda besides seeing that your rescue is properly fêted," he said. "Unorthodox though my intervention was, he knows about it and is okay with it. But whatever he wants to talk about, it won't be to slap my wrist, Charlie. As I think I told you, he's an old friend.

"While we're at it," he continued, "maybe we *should* be thanking God, as Mr. Belknap said. I certainly do. For the rescue, that is, not the party."

"Well, Your Reverence," said Jonathan. "In my mouth, that's just a common expression, I'm afraid. If we're going to thank Him, perhaps we should also thank the CIA, or at least its Old Boys' network of retirees. And, of course, a certain editor."

Charles looked around. "I half expected him to be here."

"Which half?" asked Jonathan dryly. "I invited him. He sent regrets."

"Umm. I see!"

"Well, I don't. In any event, let me run down the missing invitees, Charlie. Óscar Amalfitano is chief on that list. *His* regrets I believe. He strikes me as a wonderful soul. A *mensch*."

"He certainly is."

"Also . . . let's see. Professor Mahan . . . Mahan . . . you'll have to help me out with that name, Charlie! Anyway, I am sorry to inform you, your Kannadian translator is now in that Great Language Lab in the Sky. A peaceful death, they told me."

"Rest his soul!" said Charles. "Brilliant fellow, you know. But at many points, he looked to be barely holding on. I must send condolences to the university. No idea if he has a family."

Jonathan continued with his list of no-shows. "There was also that fellow from Iceland," he said. "Halldór, was it? Eager to come but sideswiped by the flu, he said. And the 'Pointer Sisters'—those strangely named Japanese women—I was never able to reach. Disappeared down some rabbit hole, I suspect."

"Along with their cat, no doubt," said Charles.

Ignacio, listening to their conversation even though he did not understand the reference, waited a beat before swinging his attention to Svetlana. "And so! This is the beautiful lady you jabbered about all the way from Mexico City to New York!"

Svetlana blushed before taking the Cardinal's proffered hand, suddenly engulfed by indecision. Genuflect? Kneel? Kiss his ring?

"Your Eminence," she managed. "Is correct term?"

He chuckled. "Well, that's the way your man here should address me." He poked Charles in the ribs. "But *you*, my dear, may call me Ignacio!"

Svetlana brightened. "Ignacio!" she said, louder than intended, as others turned to look. "Can cardinals dance?" The slow strains of a song, "Long Ago and Far Away," had begun to fill the room.

"You mean the bird, or me? *This* one can."

•

When does a collection of individuals become a crowd? Charles wondered. Someone had stuffed a drink in his hand; he couldn't say who. Svetlana had been spirited away to dance; later, he had danced with her himself; now she was off talking to someone else. The glass in his hand proved to be vodka, not water. He set it aside, made his way to the refreshments table, and opened a Perrier from a collection of small bottles.

He spotted a three-tiered cake with the legend, "Welcome Back From the House of the Dead!" *Hmm*, he thought. *How that phrase gets around.* He hoped the cake was as tasty as it looked. Since it had yet to be cut, he grabbed several olives, a roll, and a few morsels of spicy jack cheese. Next, he tried a pear tart, which he found scrumptious.

Looking around while wiping his lips with a napkin, he saw Jake Cash dancing cheek to cheek with another member of the writing group, Becky Weingarten. The mole on her cheek winked on and off as they wheeled around, snuggled tight. Hmm! Had a writing group romance bloomed in his absence?

So many people in this room that he knew and was fond of, but a few whose identity he was still guessing at. Someone laughed loudly at another's joke; he wondered what was funny, and suddenly grew anxious about how they all might react to the story he was reading this evening.

•

He found himself once more with Jonathan.

"This is Eduardo," said Jonathan, pulling a handsome fellow near him by his sleeve. "Mandrake."

"*Ah!*" exclaimed Charles. "*Very* pleased to meet you! Heard what you did for me. Thank you for your magic!"

"Jon's the one," Eduardo said, taking a sip of Scotch and smoothing his moustache with a manicured finger. "I just did as I was asked."

"I *have* thanked *him*," said Charles, "though obviously not enough." He gave his host a one-armed hug. "But I doubt I could ever thank him enough."

Eduardo's date was Clarice, a very pretty dark-haired woman, a wisp of whose hair kept falling over her face. Charles smiled and shook her hand. She returned his smile, but said nothing.

"A writer, I'm told," said Jonathan, when they'd drifted away. "Perhaps we can ask her to join the group?" And Charles learned that Eduardo had met Clarice at the little restaurant where the two ex-spooks had made final plans for his rescue.

Jonathan gripped Charles's shoulder to rotate him a quarter turn to the right. "And that," he said, pointing to a man on the crowded dance floor, "is Roger Wawrinka. Flew over from Switzerland in your honor." *How to describe Wawrinka?* Charles wondered. *A blimp? A shmoo?* He was certainly the best-dressed teletubby Charles had ever seen. And what moves! He was dancing with another writing group member, Buffy St. Olaf, who was dressed in a black mini. Well, she was the prettiest of the bunch, head of her own cosmetics company.

Suddenly the name Wawrinka registered. "Smilin' Jack?" he asked in amazement.

"The guy who saved your bacon many a time. Be sure you thank him later. He's the one who stuffed the GPS in your shoe. Also the one who grabbed you by your shirt collar and kept you from becoming an icicle. Never underestimate Jack, Charlie. He's strong as a bull. And fast."

Charles watched in fascination. The man's spins and leaps rivaled Gene Kelly in *Singin' in the Rain.*

"Isn't he also the guy who recovered my laptop?"

"Twice. In Rome, and again in Greece."

Despite the din, Charles heard the door open and turned

in time to see a new figure enter the party. Tall and handsome, wearing a black topcoat.

"OmiGod!" exclaimed Charles. "The Last Emperor of China!"

Lu Chi overheard Charles, and laughed. He quickly draped his coat over a chair and made his way over, where they grasped each other's hands and grinned hugely.

"This is Lu Chi!" said Charles, turning to Jonathan.

"I know! I invited him!" said Jonathan, taking Dr. Lu's outstretched hand. "Nice to meet you in the flesh, sir!"

"Svetlana!" Charles boomed out, waving her over. "This is Lu Chi! All the way from Beijing."

She joined them, beaming. "I met you as little girl," she said. "I am Gennady's daughter."

"Of course! But not so little! I remember you as a girl of fourteen. In pigtails."

"You wore pigtails?" asked Charles.

She shrugged and blushed.

"I understand that you and she," said Lu Chi, "are an item now? Congratulations to you both. But let me tell you something, Charlie. Your beloved was a dish, even as a young teen."

Charles frowned. "I suppose she must have been."

Svetlana turned a deeper crimson, while Charles pursued in his mind the implications of Lu Chi's statement, wondering how to formulate the questions he would want to ask her later.

Svetlana, after Lu Chi had turned his attention to meeting others, disappeared to fetch Charles another Perrier and herself a glass of wine. "You are man of hour," she whispered proudly upon her return, kissing him quickly on the ear. Charles had no idea what to say. But he could sense tears behind his eyes, ready to spring forth if someone said one more kind thing.

Marisol and Anthony arrived late, and no sooner had he greeted them than he noticed Jonathan attempting to urge everyone toward the conference table.

As Charles took his place at the head of the table, despite the fact that Jonathan had already begun speaking, his thoughts drifted to Gennady. He found himself wishing Svetlana's father were here. Charles had grown fond of him, and for the first time in many years he was to have a family.

No matter; Gennady would be here soon. With Marisol's help, Charles had managed to procure for him an adjunct professorship at the university where she taught. The pay wouldn't be great, but "compared to what I have here," Gennady had told him over the phone from Akademgorodok only last week, "it will seem like a king's ransom." Charles had smiled into his iPhone. He knew about ransoms!

The rest of Gennady's words came back to him. "I can't thank you enough, Charlie. You're going to make it possible for me to live out the rest of my days in comfort, in the midst of what I expect to be considerable intellectual stimulation, and— at the same time— surrounded by people I love."

"It's all you, sir," Charles had replied. "I certainly didn't have to beg. The university jumped at the chance."

•

Jonathan's introduction was winding down. Charles shook his head to clear it. Time to read his story.

He'd thought about this moment often, but now it had arrived, he struggled with how to begin. He cleared his throat.

"Thank you all for coming," he said. "You truly honor me by your presence. Well, I know you're curious about the fate of my story, so let's get to it. But first, you should understand that

I didn't manage to get all ten languages I had planned on. I, uh, got a little detained in Mexico."

A smattering of laughter.

"So, I only took my story through eight languages before it was translated back into English. But the result is still interesting. Most of you have read my story "We Shall Come Rejoicing," or at least all the members of my writing group have. If not, you have copies in front of you that Jon has been kind enough to run off. You can take them home and read them later, if you like. I also have copies—which I'll distribute after the reading, if you're interested—of the very new shape my story has assumed after passing through the medium of those eight languages."

He paused a moment and stroked his beard, neatly trimmed once again after his ordeal in Mexico.

"What's interesting to me," he continued, "what totally surprises me, is that the story that emerged at the end is reasonably coherent, and still shares some characteristics of the tale I originally told. Frankly, I'd expected verbal confetti. I'd expected something weird and incomprehensible. And it certainly has been altered.

"But I guess what surprises me most is how hard good translators work to make the whole story succeed in the language they're fitting it into. Whatever changes they've made, my translators seem to have done so in order to achieve the integrity they think the story had in the language they read it in. The good ones are too conscientious as *writers*—over and above their translations—not to deliver a product that makes sense.

"So—"

"Charlie, *please!*" It was Jake Cash. "Spare us the long-winded preamble. Why don't you just read the damned thing and let us draw our own conclusions?"

Charles smiled. "You're right, of course, Jake. Okay, here goes."

He began to read.

It didn't take long for the chuckling to begin.

And again it was Jake, whose outright laughter could be heard at many points during the reading, who was the first to speak when Charles had finished.

"Charlie, I have to hand it to you. Frankly, I always thought your attempts at humor were a little lame. But now you have a recipe: Write whatever you want in your bleak and humorless prose, then send it through all those linguistic transmutations. If it winds up sounding like Murakami strained through a sieve of Pynchon and Cortázar, with Calvino thrown in, well, so much the better!"

"Not Nabokov? I was hoping for Nabokov."

"*Please*, Charlie! Not even close!"

66
RECONNOITERING
WITH THE ENEMY

ESS THAN A week after the party, Charles received a call from Derek Wainscot. The call was brief and bumpy—neither party seemed to know exactly what to say—but its purpose finally emerged: Charles was invited to meet with Derek, not at his office, but at his apartment.

Charles paused in front of the apartment door on a high floor of a posh East River building, much as he'd hesitated outside the door of Random & O'Malley just over a year ago. He stared at the carpet, which was even deeper than that which had covered the hallway of Derek's midtown office. His lower lip began to twitch; he slapped at it. Obediently, it stopped. Well, that was something, wasn't it? Maybe he'd found the right technique at last! He sighed, turned away from the door, turned back.

Why was he dithering? He'd been asked here; he was expected. The doorman had already announced him. Still, katydids chirped in his gut. He felt anxious, angry, resentful, and—dammit!—grateful beyond belief. A disquieting mélange of conflicting emotions. He took a deep breath, swallowed hard, and rang the bell.

Derek, whose suit coat had been swapped for a silk smoking jacket the color of claret, admitted him with a nod and a wide but somewhat sheepish smile. Relinquishing his coat at Derek's invitation, Charles moved warily into the living room, and yes, there were the paintings he'd somehow expected, beautiful and obviously quite valuable canvases. Charles smiled in admiration. Not only good taste, but a shrewd collector.

"Please sit, Dr. Baker. Relax," said the editor. "Would you like a drink? A little brandy, perhaps?"

"Thank you, no. Water will do fine, if you have it. Oh, do you have sparkling water?"

Charles eased himself into a comfortable armchair alongside a Swedish Modern glass coffee table. Though he hadn't been told where to sit, it was the right location, he surmised. Another chair was placed just beyond the table, angled slightly. The intimacy of the arrangement brought to mind Óscar's modest study in Santa Theresa, as well as Gennady's cramped living space in Akademgorodok. The same coziness, he thought, but three different levels of income. He glanced at the sofa, large enough to sleep two people foot to foot, and again at the paintings. Only once before had he been surrounded by such luxury: that hotel in Beijing. But a man—not a corporation—owned this!

His host returned with their drinks. After Derek had seated himself and each had taken a swig from his respective glass, they smiled nervously and lowered their glasses to the table. A tense Charles looked at the editor expectantly. Which one was he: the man who had nearly gotten him killed? Or the one who had paid an enormous sum to snatch him from almost certain death?

Derek cleared his throat, hung his head, folded his hands, and then sought his guest's eyes. He began to speak in a low voice. "First of all, Mr. Baker—Dr. Baker—I am deeply, deeply sorry for my behavior over the past year. I apologize from the bottom of my heart. To say I conducted myself in a most underhanded manner toward you is an understatement. No confession, expression of regret, or request for forgiveness can possibly expunge what I did to undermine your project and advance my own. Without actually willing it, I put you in danger. And nothing can atone for that wrong I have done you. I am ashamed beyond my ability to express it."

You express it pretty well, thought Charles. *Is there a teleprompter behind me?*

Derek paused and took a sip of his drink. Charles looked at the ceiling, down at the table. *Am I expected to respond?*

"Well," he said. "I—" He stopped, wondered if he could continue at all. His impulse was to leap up and flee the premises, after hurling his water glass at Wainscot's head. But he tried to collect himself. He even managed a smile.

"Hey!" he began again. "You certainly made up for it in a spectacular way. If anyone, in all my past decades, had told me that my life would come to be valued at one-and a quarter-million dollars, I would've told them to go stuff it. On balance, I'd have to say you made up for it, Mr. Wainscot. I owe you my life."

The editor compressed his lips. "Not as much as I owe you for the opportunity to realize how badly I was conducting my own. As well as why, and how, I might change. I feel quite fortunate that I had the wherewithal to respond to the danger you found yourself in. And I apologize again for any part I may have played in bringing it about."

Charles leaned back in the armchair. Well, the ice had been broken. Was that all there was, then? Should he smile politely, shake hands, and leave? Or stay long enough to finish his Perrier? *What the hell.* He took a sip.

Wainscot rocked back, then forward again, held his hands

out to the side in a gesture almost of helplessness, finally placed them on his knees. "Charles. May I call you Charles?"

"Of course. Make it Charlie. Shall I call you Derek?"

"I wish you would. Only. Okay. Charles—Charlie—I have something that I want to tell you, then something I want to ask of you. First of all—and you are one of the very first persons to know this—I've decided to leave Random & O'Malley, where I've run my own imprint for a couple of decades. I'm planning to start a small press of my own, which I'll call Zalmoxis. I even have a logo all picked out. Here!" He rose. "Let me show you."

He approached one wall of the living room, removed a small, framed engraving and handed it to Charles.

"A butterfly?"

When Derek did not reply right away, Charles examined it more closely. It was certainly a beautiful creature: turquoise, its outstretched wings edged with black, and light brushstrokes of a deeper black on the upper wings, wider bands on the lower. Its thorax was a light honey color, though darker toward the head. The accompanying notation—done in striking calligraphy in deep black ink—declared that the insect had a five-inch wingspan.

"A big butterfly." he added.

"Not just any butterfly," smiled Derek. "It's called *papilio zalmoxis*."

"I see. And so your press is named after . . . a butterfly. I confess the word 'zalmoxis' is new to me."

"Not surprising. As you surmised, the butterfly will be the logo, but the press is really named for a Rumanian god. Part of Rumanian folklore. Zalmoxis was a Gataean-Dacian-Thracian god, worshipped primarily within the geographical territory corresponding to modern-day Rumania, as described by Herodotus and a few others. Well-known principally to those who specialize in Rumanian culture and language."

"Really? You know Rumanian?"

"Oh, dear me, yes. I translate Rumanian poetry. Specialize in one of the more famous poets, Nichita Stănescu.

"Now," he continued, warming to his task, "I have a number of writers who've been in my stable for a long time, and I hope to bring them over to Zalmoxis when it's up and running, which will be very soon. Very soon. Even though it's a small press—I expect to publish perhaps five or six books a year—it's not being done on a shoestring, Charlie. As you may suspect by now, I do have a little money."

Charles was unable to suppress a smile. *Enlisting the Archbishop of Mexico to bail me out of the clutches of a drug cartel is a pretty good hint,* he thought. *And those paintings on the wall? You could sell any one of those puppies at auction and have the geldt to operate your press at a loss for years.* He drained his glass and returned it to the table, deciding it was probably time for him to find a gracious way to say goodbye. Talking about money did not put the katydids in his stomach to sleep.

"Well . . . congratulations, Derek," he managed. "Sounds like a great idea. I'm sure you'll be able to publish a few titles of Rumanian poetry, right?"

"Oh, quite so! I certainly shall. And proudly. I can't conceal that that's a significant factor in my decision. But it wasn't the only one."

Charles, who had glanced around the room and settled his features finally into an 'awfully nice of you to ask me over' mode, had his hands on his knees and was preparing to rise, when Derek said, "Here's where you come in, Charlie. I'd like you to become one of my authors."

Charles's weight relapsed abruptly into his chair. "Excuse me?"

"I would very much like it if you would join my coterie of writers. My stable."

"Uh, I'm not so sure—"

"It means I'd like to offer you a contract, Charlie. Specifically, a three-book deal. First, I would like to publish this project on which you have been collecting the data for an entire year, for which you would write a foreword, as well as separate pieces introducing each version of the story."

Charles opened his mouth as if to speak, but Derek held up his hand, so Charles closed his mouth and raised his eyebrows instead.

"Second, I would like to suggest that you write—this will take a while, of course—the story of your trip around the world in pursuit of these translations. I think there's room for a nice memoir here. Not a scholarly tome, but an adventure story. Your adventures, Charlie. Ah . . . we might amend it a little to leave out some of the more . . . incriminating parts? Those that might reflect so terribly on . . . yours truly? Or we could change names? Or not. I don't know. That's definitely a discussable point. Perhaps you'd prefer to make it into a *roman à clef,* possibly titled *Problems of Translation*?"

Charles was sinking into himself. He opened his mouth again and silently placed his tongue against one side of his lips, as Derek continued.

"Or perhaps that would be the name of the book of—what is it now—eight translations? Anyway, we'll discuss the titles. As for the third book, don't you have other stories, like 'Doing Mama?' Actually, I know you do, Charlie; I've done my homework. I've read all your published stories. Every one. Some are better than others. In my opinion, you need a good editor, but you show real talent. You just require someone to snip and shape a bit. Someone who has a good ear, and an experienced eye. Someone to make it 'tight and right,' as I like to say. I'm no Gordon Lish—thank God for that!—but I think I may be just that person. I hope you'll give me that chance."

The room had grown quiet. Charles felt as if he'd driven into a fogbank and was unable to see a foot ahead of him. The tom-tom of his heart reminded him of the bass notes of those jungle frogs in Mexico.

Derek rose to replenish his drink while Charles continued to sit, angling his head this way and that like a parrot trying to achieve binocular vision. When his host returned, he gestured inquiringly toward Charles's bottle, but Charles shook his head, scarcely aware he was doing so.

"I owe you this, Charlie, but I'm not doing this just to palliate my guilt," Derek said, still standing. "This is not a mercy fuck, as the expression goes. It's important you understand that. I've reached a point in my life at which I want to publish what *I* want to publish. How much money my books earn or do not earn is not my primary focus anymore. *This* is."

Charles found himself staring at Derek with his mouth open. He closed it. "I don't know what to say!"

"What I suggest is 'yes.' I've yet to draw up the paperwork, Charlie. But that can be done quickly enough. I'm thinking . . . an advance in the neighborhood of a quarter-million? But that's negotiable."

"Hold on!" said Charles, excitedly. He was seized by a sudden unrelated epiphany, the money offer not even registering. He almost leaped from his chair. "I just remembered something. You said you translated Rumanian, right?"

"I did. I do."

"Listen! You may have heard that the other night, at a party—the one you couldn't come to—I read a version of my story that was re-Englished after eight translations. It had actually been translated twice more, but I hadn't found the right person to— Well, here's the thing. Number ten was Rumanian! How would you like to translate it from Rumanian back into English? That way, I—and this book you're talking about—would have all ten languages, just as I set out to do!"

Derek paused, threw back his head, and laughed, sinking once again into his accustomed armchair. "Excellent! Extraordinary! Yes, yes, I would! This is . . . well, extraordinary!"

They sat for a moment, each a bit stunned by the enormous changes that seemed to be ahead of them. Then Charles burst out: "I've always wanted to do a book on Sequoya!"

"Beg pardon?" Derek leaned forward in his seat.

"I'd like to write a historical novel about the great nineteenth-century Cherokee George Guess, Indian name Sequoya. Single-handedly designed a syllabary that all Cherokees could instantly understand. Years later, he wandered into Mexico—like me, I guess—looking for a lost Cherokee tribe. And was never seen again. I had better luck. But I would like to write a book about Sequoya."

The editor sat a moment thinking, then a wide smile broke over his face. "It sounds very possible, Charlie. We can throw that into the mix as well. Hmm. With the right push, a potential moneymaker. Well. If you are agreeable, shall we work out a plan? Something that takes into consideration both what you feel most strongly about and what would be the best use of your time from Zalmoxis's standpoint. It's all negotiable, Charlie. So. What do you think of my offer?"

The two men looked at each other. Charles couldn't tell what Derek was thinking, but what sprang to his mind were Bogart's closing words in *Casablanca*. "Derek," he paraphrased, "I think this may be the beginning of a beautiful friendship."

HELLO, NACHO!

MONTHS LATER, ON the first warm day of spring, Charles and Svetlana sat side by side on their terrace on the Upper West Side, looking over what felt to them like their own Empire. Two steaming mugs of coffee sat on matching side tables, but for the moment, they were holding hands.

Svetlana's father had long since been plucked from Siberia and ensconced in a small apartment in the Village. The Mathematics and Physics Institute at the university that had granted him an adjunct professorship (the same one where Marcy taught) was a ten-minute walk from his apartment. The department had already begun to use his name, and had incorporated the phrase "Home to the distinguished Winner of the Crayfish Prize" into its letterhead.

A month earlier, Svetlana had given notice to Aeroflot, after landing a position in the Russian Verbatim Reporting Services Department of the United Nations. Her visa now permitted her to live in the States, and she was aiming at eventual citizenship. In the evenings she had available, she was busy with her artwork, much of it spent on charcoals, pastels, and ink-drawings of Charles: Charles at his desk, looking thoughtful, searching for the right word; Charles asleep in the bedroom they shared; Charles as a haggard, care-worn prisoner (this from his tales of Mexico, enhanced by her imagination). The *Crime and Punishment* portfolio had been completed and, in fact—a dubious honor, Charles thought—*his* face had now been worked into several illustrations for a soon-to-be-published brand new Russian edition of Dostoyevsky's *The House of the Dead*.

As for Charles, the ten introductions plus the foreword to *Problems of Translation* had been completed; he was about to begin work on Sequoya.

Inside the apartment behind these two city-gazers, staring beseechingly through the glass of the terrace door, was a dog—a large dog. It was a Borzoi, which he and Svetlana had rescued only last week from an animal shelter. A dog that, on Svyeta's very explicit instructions, they did *not* feed from the table. This beast had been eagerly whining and wet-nosing the glass for some time, but now it collapsed into a shaggy heap on the carpet, crossing its forepaws to create a nest for its nose.

Outside, Svetlana took a sip of her coffee and said, "So what we are calling our new dog, Charlie? Is about time we name it, no?"

Charles pursed his lips and thought a moment. "Yes," he said. "I think I'll call him Nacho."

"Nacho? I am not familiar. What means Nacho?"

"You don't remember? Short for Ignacio?"

Her eyebrows achieved maximum liftoff. "You are naming our dog after the Archbishop of All Mexico?"

He did not answer right away because his thoughts had already jumped the rails. *How*, he was wondering, *would you translate "Archbishop of All Mexico" into . . . Mongolian?*

CHARLIE GRANTS AN INTERVIEW

ITERARY TRENDS QUARTERLY'S interview with Charles Abel Baker, author of *Problems Of Translation*:

Interviewer: Can you give us an example, Dr. Baker, of how—as you claim—reality can be altered by translation from one language to another?

Dr. Baker: Well, consider Johann Sebastian Bach.

I: What about him?

B: Bach once became furious with a fellow musician and referred to him quite pejoratively.

I: And?

B: Well, how serious scholars translate what Bach called the poor bugger ranges from "nanny-goat bassoonist" to "bassoonist breaking wind after eating a green onion." The only thing common to the two translations, of course, is the instrument, and it's my contention that if you translated Bach's insult successively into ten different languages before returning it to the eighteenth century German he spoke, that too would be gone. Like as not, the bassoon would become a mandolin.

ACKNOWLEDGMENTS

A WORK LIKE this requires thanks to so many people, some of whom I know personally and whose critiques, ideas, and expertise have helped make this novel possible. Others, equally important, I know only from their fine works of literature.

First, an especial thanks to Ben Fountain, whose sage advice and encouragement continue to be of profound importance to me, and to Jim Shepard, whose guidance in a workshop at Sirenland suggested directions for the manuscript that continued to influence my thinking.

A second, larger group includes authors whose comments I have quoted—with quotation marks but without citations, for this is a novel, not a scholarly account—as well as those I have paraphrased. They include Miguel de Cervantes (*Don Quixote*), Anton Chekhov (*A Journey to the End of the Russian Empire*), Edith Grossman (*Why Translation Matters*), James Merrill ("Lost in Translation"), Arundhati Roy (*The God of Small Things*), and Wallis Wilde-Menozzi ("Translation: When Asked to Write About Style").

"Good writers borrow; great writers steal" goes the old trope. I lay no claim to greatness, but nevertheless feel obliged to pay tribute to a third group of writers whose works I have deliberately mined for settings, names, the ghosts of characters—even a few plot points!—as a way of paying homage, because they have stimulated me in ways I thought germane to the purposes of this book, or simply because I thought it would be enormous fun to do so. This list includes Roberto Bolaño (*2666*), Fyodor Dostoyevsky (*The House of the*

Dead, Crime and Punishment, Notes from the Underground), James Fallows (*Postcards from Tomorrow Square*), E. M. Forster (*A Passage to India*), Jia Pingwa (*Turbulence*), Lao-Tzu (*Tao: The Way*), Lu Chi (*Wen Fu*, or *Prose Poem on the Art of Letters*), Haruki Murakami (*The Wind-Up Bird Chronicle),* Vladimir Nabokov (*Pnin*), and Howard Nemerov ("To Lu Chi").

Still others are those whose help on many levels has been so generously given. Such a list must include Serge Levchin, translator into Russian of the excerpt from "We Shall Come Rejoicing"; Ling Chen, for accomplishing the same feat in Chinese; Professor Emeritus Loren Graham of MIT and Harvard, for early suggestions about Akademgorodok and other matters; and Susan Heuman, college professor, Russianist and historian, for reading and double-checking my Russian words and phrases.

Finally, my thanks to those who have read all or parts of the manuscript and offered their cogent criticism: Angela Ajayi, Bob Bachner, Thais Barry, Portia Bohn, Elizabeth Bradbury, Leslie Dormen, Jacqueline Henry, Joel Hochman, Sally Huxley, Sandra Leong, Mary Medlin, Anthony Mohr, Hilary Orbach, Nicholas Samstag, Kristen Schwarz and Evelyn Weisfeld, as well as the late and much lamented Corinne Mond.

A shout-out as well to Angelo Verga, poet and curator of the reading series at the Cornelia Street Café, for his encouragement in trying out early drafts of this book in front of an audience.

And of course, my debt to my beloved partner, Jill, for her ideas, editorial suggestions, videography, support, patience—you name it!—is beyond measure.

READERS' GUIDE AND BOOK CLUB QUESTIONS

BECAUSE IMPORTANT PLOT points are revealed here, you may wish to explore these discussion topics only after you've finished reading *Problems of Translation*.

1. The book follows the story of Charles Abel Baker. What are your thoughts about Charlie? How would you describe him? Do you think of him as a simple or complex character? What do you believe really sent him off on his quest, and how did his character and history influence what happened to him?

2. Authors often choose names for their characters very deliberately. Do any of the characters' names in this book— Charles Abel Baker, Derek Wainscot, and so on—particularly resonate with you, and if so, how and why?

3. Which characters did you most enjoy reading about? Derek Wainscot? Jonathan Belknap? Svetlana Novgorodtseva? Marisol Lapinsky? Gennady Novgorodtsev? The Kano sisters, Creta and Malta? Lu Chi? Eduardo? Smilin' Jack? Pig? Sejal? (Woops! We mean Adela!) With which character or characters (Charlie included) would you most want to have lunch?

4. Charlie ultimately accomplishes the goal of his translation

project, but his voyage results in several important breakthroughs for him. How would you identify these? And do any other characters in the novel experience their own breakthroughs and life changes? Which character do you think is most transformed by Charlie's adventures?

5. Which of Charlie's adventures did you find most engaging, and why? The book's subtitle is "Charlie's Comic, Terrifying, Romantic, Loopy Round-the-World Journey in Search Of Linguistic Happiness." Which of Charlie's adventures did you find most comic? Most terrifying? Most romantic? And most loopy?

6. What do you feel about Charlie and Svetlana's romantic relationship? Were you at all mistrustful, at the beginning of their courtship, of Svetlana's interest in him? What did you think when you learned she'd accepted money to distract Charlie from his goal? Was there anything in her background that would explain this? Do you think Marisol was right to bring them back together?

7. If you were with Charlie on his adventures, at what point would you have suspected someone was trying to scuttle his project? What advice would you have given him?

8. Books are sometimes characterized as either plot-driven or character-driven. Would you say the action of this book is driven more by its plot or its characters—and why?

9. Is Derek Wainscot an awful man? Or just a person blinkered by his own ambitions and position of privilege?

10. Derek and Charlie come from very different family backgrounds as well as from opposite ends of the publishing spectrum, yet come together to collaborate at the end. Can you think of *any* ways in which they're similar?

11. The book's title, *Problems of Translation*, might refer both to the challenge that Charlie has undertaken—to see how

greatly successive translations can change a story—and the difficulties he encounters while trying to attain his objective. Are there other personal and interpersonal *mis*translations to which the title could refer?

12. *Problems of Translation* is about a man of advanced middle age who is overcome by a fantasy that he's driven to fulfill. Were you able to relate to this, and if so, how and why?

13. One theme of the book may be the interplay between perception and reality. For example, Charlie's experience in Stream of Wandering Spirits is later explained as a dream— or was it? And was there really a Wind-Up Bird? What about the "phone sex call" when Charlie was in Japan? Can you think of other examples?

14. The author claims in his acknowledgments that he has paid homage to other writers in this book, by borrowing a character, setting, plot device or style. Did you spot any of these? Did you find that this device enriched your reading, and if so, in what way?

15. The attendees at Charlie's party seemed to find the short story that had gone through all those translations rather amusing, though no actual sample of the translation back into English is actually revealed to the reader. How do you think such a translation experiment would have turned out?

ABOUT THE AUTHOR

JIM STORY IS a novelist, short-story writer and poet. He has published short stories, creative nonfiction, reviews and poetry in a variety of literary publications, has been nominated for a Pushcart Prize, won a Best New Writers Award from Poets & Writers, and held a residency at the Edward Albee Center in Montauk, Long Island. His writing has appeared in *Confrontation, The Same, Karamu, Folio, Pindeldyboz, Helicon, Aspen Anthology,* and many other publications. His blog, *Today's Story*, is to be found at jimcstory.com. He lives in New York City, where he is working on his next novel.

41496231R00238

Made in the USA
Charleston, SC
29 April 2015